WARRICK

ALSO BY:

Jenn LeBlanc

THE RAKE
AND THE RECLUSE
(BOOK ONE IN THE LORDS OF TIME SERIES)

THE DUKE
AND THE BARON
(BOOK TWO IN THE LORDS OF TIME SERIES)

THE TROUBLE
WITH GRACE
(BOOK FOUR IN THE LORDS OF TIME SERIES)

THE SPARE
AND THE HEIR
(BOOK FIVE IN THE LORDS OF TIME SERIES)

Jenn LeBlanc

THE DUKE AND THE DOMINA

BOOK THREE IN THE LORDS OF TIME SERIES

Dedication

FOR THOSE WHO SEARCH

my thanks :

JOYCE LAMB :
EDITING

MIA ASHLINN, ELISE ROME, YOU :
READING

TIFFANY REISZ :
EVERYTHING

KATI RODRIGUEZ :
EVERYTHING ELSE

LE MAÎTRE CHAT :
INSPIRATION

credits:

GRAYSON LOCKE DANFORTH

DUKE OF WARRICK

Mickael De Sinno

LULU

Shelly Das

PRODUCTION ASSISTANCE :

ASSISTANT — KATI RODRIGUEZ

PRODUCER : ELLEN HERBERT

MAKE UP / HAIR / PROSTHESIS :
KIMBERLY DISTEL

a note about the illustrations:

*These illustrations are meant to be
a work unto themselves.*

They aren't meant to depict the scenes with perfect accuracy in setting, costuming or design. They're meant to accompany the text and evoke the emotions of the scenes in the same way the words do.

More of a companion than a direct visual translation.

Certainly you will notice discrepancies between the scene and details in the images, but that's the nature of creation, some things don't work visually when they do work literally.

Thank you for understanding and I hope you enjoy this illustrated version of Warrick.

Hugs n' smooches,

Jenn

Epigraph:

HE'S POOR. SHE'S RICH.
HE'S A SUB. SHE'S A SWITCH.
IT'S NOT LOVE.

IT'S A MARRIAGE OF KINK-VENIENCE!

—Tiffany Reisz

PROLOGUE

In the practical art of war, the best thing of all is to take the enemy's country whole and intact, to shatter and destroy it is not so good.

—Sun Tzu

The Art of War

1885

The corset tightened, and Grayson let out his last breath of freedom, finally at ease. Corsets were popular with the men of Victorian society, but the reason he wore a corset was different from the rest. For them it was vanity, a softness of the waist, or a straighter posture. But for him? He had no need for help with posture or waistline. His structure was not at issue.

Grayson needed the binding and the constriction, the pain of the tension and the relief when it released.

Grayson breathed against the steel bones, letting them pinch as he watched the process in the cheval mirror. If he took a deep enough breath, if he held it long enough then shifted, he could bruise his skin where the boning crossed his ribs.

He put his hands against the front of the corset and breathed again, waiting for as long as he could before exhaling, then he used his muscles to prolong that feeling.

The pinch. The burn. The release.

Then he nodded to his valet in the mirror's reflection, and his shirt was brought to him. Then his waistcoat.

Grayson wasn't looking forward to today. It took everything in him to not run, leave Britain, and return to India—his home. It's where he felt safest. Here in England, a country he'd wished to never see again, he was constantly on edge. Terrified he would be discovered. There was too much scrutiny here, particularly for a man like him.

The fact that chance or fate or whatever machination would take his father and brothers without warning, without so much as an inkling, was beyond cruel. That today he was to meet the woman his father had contracted for his oldest brother, the woman he would marry, the woman who was now to become his duchess, was beyond him. Grayson couldn't fathom marriage to anyone, but to a society miss? The daughter of a duke? A highborn lady who would expect certain things from him? This was truly unfathomable.

This woman would be in his life and in his house. It would be impossible to escape her. The fact that he was an honorable man never rankled more than it did now. Honor was all he truly had, when the rest of him was... what he was, and he would be forced to hide who he was even in his own house, where he slept.

To live out his greatest fear in life, to be a man of society, a husband, a father, a proper gentleman—he choked suddenly and leaned over, his breath stolen from him. He rested his hands on his knees at the thought, attempting to catch his breath as the corset bit into his lower abdomen.

"Too tight, Your Grace?" Rakshan asked as he held Grayson's jacket.

Grayson lifted one hand and waved him off, unable to voice an answer. Breathing in through his nose, he stood tall again then pushed his arms back behind him. Rakshan slid his coat up his arms then yanked the tail, straightened the shoulders, walked in front of him, and buttoned him up. Then he pulled the brush from the dressing table and slid it across his chest, shoulders, and back.

Grayson closed his eyes and settled into the calm of the movements on him. He would need to take that calm with him today to meet the woman he would marry. The future Duchess of Warrick, his dead brother's fiancée, the woman who would prevent him from ever being himself.

He may not miss his family for the reasons people believed he should, but miss them he did, because they were all that had prevented him from becoming who he now had to be.

The Warrick.

2015

Lulu snapped the single tail just to the left of Oliver's shoulder, letting the sonic boom send shudders through his muscles. She loved the dance of muscle as it rippled across the back of a client, the skin undulating like a soft wave carried to shore. She snapped it again quickly, this time on the right before the first ripple had a chance to make its way fully across the broad expanse of his back—and Oliver did have the loveliest back.

With near-perfect symmetry and structure, he was simply beautiful with his arms stretched out to the bedposts above his head. The canvas of his physique, almost flawlessly balanced, could not have been more suited to her art. The thought of that alone could carry Lulu orgasm for days to come.

He pulled against the bindings on his wrists, his muscles tightening in the center and stiffening his spine. The tension straightened his back as the lats on both sides flexed. The action made his back even bigger and more impressive, exactly what she needed him to do, exactly as she had instructed, throughout his training. She was so proud of him and could not contain the grin and the rush of blood from her excitement.

Lulu waited for him to steady, then she struck him in earnest. First on the left just below his scapula, then on the right without pause.

Tonight she would give him the wings they'd worked so hard for.

She picked up the second bullwhip and tested the air with both bullwhips in tandem. This was her special trick and hers alone, and her clients paid thousands for the honor of it.

She followed the pattern of his muscles down his lats, not letting him breathe between the strikes because the tension played out in his back. The feathers of his wings, made by the welts of the whips, needed to follow his natural musculature in order to look perfect. It was a difficult and practiced dance. Each strike had to be exact, because she wasn't to draw blood, yet, and it was incredibly easy to draw blood with a single tail. Much too easy.

For her part, the muscle control required of her had taken years to perfect, the ability to strike in tandem with an exacting weight and placement was nearly impossible. She practiced daily and worked her shoulders and back twice weekly to train out all signs of dominance on her left side. She worked harder than anyone else had ever considered doing. That's why the clients paid, and they got exactly what they paid for.

Lulu painted his lats with the red feathers, different weights and lengths of strikes making different patterns until he looked as though his back would physically give birth to the wings she put there.

She set the bullwhips aside and picked up the Wartenberg wheel to add more subtle texture to the feathers. Then the evil stick for the center of the wings, for additional definition. The multiple tools completed her work, each of them leaving a different pattern much like a painter and their collection of brushes.

She wouldn't use the bullwhip where the bone was close to the surface, because the chance of drawing blood was much too high. Instead, she used the floggers to paint broad strokes, then the wheel and the stick to define. The final effect was well-defined crests with fluffier-looking feathers down to the tips, but it was the last feather that sold the piece. Lulu stood back and inspected her work, then took a steadying breath.

She picked up her whips again for the final strikes, the most painful of all. They would hit the soft hollows below his ribs, carefully avoiding his kidneys, and painting the final, long feathers that would go from his sides to just on either side of his spine. The feathers would bracket those beautiful dimples in a searing pain he would remember for the rest of his days. These would bleed, but only slightly, and only because he'd asked for them to.

Lulu squared herself behind Ollie and shook her arms out to release the tension that had gathered. She needed to be loose and nimble, there was no first strike, and there was no second chance. This was it. She lifted her arms to her sides for the tandem strike and filled her lungs with air, then she channeled her weight into muscle memory and let the bullwhips sing through the air.

Ollie yelled into it, a deep, throaty growl. They always did, if not during the process at least during the last strike. None of her subs could contain themselves through that final strike—blood or no.

Lulu dropped the bullwhips and moved closer to him inspecting his back. She held her hands just over his skin, letting the heat of him sink into her palms warming her body. Her hands moved down past his shoulders, then hovered over the last strikes. The small cuts at his lower back bled two small rills of blood which slid easily into the dimples at his spine, pooling there. Perfection.

"Don't move," she whispered reverently.

This moment, master and vassal, creator and subject, was the most powerful for her. She was one with her submissive and they weren't even touching. The heat his skin gave her was gratitude for the pain she bestowed him. She stretched these moments out for as long as she could, letting it warm her, fill her, trying to fulfill and complete her—but it never quite made it that far. That fullness of heart and spirit was like something she could taste but not savor—always just beyond her reach. She'd thought Ollie was perfection, she'd thought he would give her that peace…but the moment faded like a whisp of smoke in a sudden wind.

She straightened and leaned across his back, careful to avoid streaking the blood while brushing his newly formed wings with her corseted breasts, running her fingers down his sides, at the very edges of his feather welts. He was still her focus and she would still do everything within her power to make this the most satisfying moment she could for him.

"Don't move, don't breathe, we're almost there," she whispered over his shoulder into his ear. Her breath sent goose bumps across his skin, his welts, causing shivers of pain to rack his body once again. She loved the sound that came from the depth of his rib cage. She wrapped her hands around his waist, skimming her thumbs just at the edges of the last welts to the center of his spine.

"Thank you, Domina," he breathed, his voice tense and hard but gracious, and she was brought to life in that, standing tall and filling her lungs with air that carried the soft tang of blood and sweat. Because this wasn't about her and her disappointment this was about Ollie, it was entirely for him and she was inordinately proud of him and what he had accomplished today. Because when it came down to it, everything had gone perfectly and she found her satisfaction in that. Now it was time to finish the work.

She hit a switch on the wall, then walked to her camera. The lighting was already set, the stage created days ago, and now the work of art was ready. All Lulu had to do was check the focus and press the shutter, and they would both have a permanent reminder of why they were here.

She stared into the ground glass at the upside-down reversed image to check the framing. "Don't move, my darling," she said as she made the final adjustments to the focus. This was one of her best yet, and she had the beautiful man before her to thank for it.

She grinned and gave a little booty shake at her excitement, but when she stepped to the side to take up the shutter release, her heel caught on the tripod and her ankle rolled. Her hand flew out to grab anything to help steady herself, catching the leg of the tripod. As the camera tipped she went down hard, hitting her head on the floor, the camera crashing down with her.

The entire thing landed just in front of her as though she were composing an image, their legs tangled like lovers. Her head pounded, her temple beating against the cold floor. The back of the camera was just before her, the image out of focus, the tilted room projected on the shattered glass, the wings she'd only just created attempting to take flight as Oliver fought against his cuffs.

"Don't move…" she whispered softly as she fought the spin that took up residence.

She blinked, struggling to keep her eyes open, focusing intently on the back of her camera one more time to try to keep herself from passing out but the world around her whirled and there was nothing to hold on to. The warmth of blood pooled beneath her skull. She heard him yell her name, but she could do nothing but close her eyes and dream of wings.

ONE

...to fight and conquer in all your battles is not supreme excellence.

—Sun Tzu
The Art of War

1885

Grayson arrived at Exeter House at half past three as requested by His Grace, the Duke of Exeter, his future father-in-law. The man had been his father's best friend and therefore Grayson's enemy. He didn't trust the man, simply for that close relationship to his father.

Nearly half an hour after arriving, he was still pacing in the parlor—certainly a power play at the hands of Exeter. Grayson stopped at the front window, tugging his shirtsleeves to the cuffs of his coat as he waited. He didn't know how much Exeter knew of him, how much his father may have said, but he knew returning to claim the Warrick title under order of the queen would ruffle feathers, and every peer would be of a mind to put him in his place, especially this one.

It was one of the reasons he'd remained hidden, for the most part, since his return two years prior. Grayson wasn't thrilled to tie up the rein of his third-son-of-a-duke, worthless, spare-to-the-spare-of-the-heir position. He'd become comfortable with it. He pulled the tails of his coat and smoothed the placket of his shirt, retucking the front edge in his trousers behind his waistcoat to keep it tight.

It made him angry beyond bounds that he could not get out of the marriage contract. He would have preferred to simply walk away from all of his father's contacts, contracts, friends, and fellows, and that was why he'd waited until today to speak to his bride.

It seemed her father wanted the title for his daughter and would not relent, no matter how Grayson had attempted to break the contract. Grayson had no purse to buy him out, unfortunately, and he believed Exeter may actually be aware of that. A bead of sweat ran down his temple and Gray caught it with the sleeve of his coat, then started to pace anew. Standing still was beyond his ability at the moment.

Grayson knew avoiding his future wife had been crass, that he should have at least been sociable, but he was not a sociable man and had no sociable mien. He didn't want to be here in a fancy parlor in London. In London at all, for that matter, or in England, or even on this godforsaken continent. He didn't want—

The door swung wide, and a liveried footman in mint green stepped in. Grayson cringed. "The Lady Cecilia Lennox."

Resigned to his fate, Grayson straightened his shoulders and prepared to meet his bride. *A gentleman*, he said to himself. He was a gentleman. The footman stepped aside—and beauty walked in. Grayson's hands fell to his sides, and his jaw slackened—he knew it did. He tightened it and composed himself again as the footman introduced him.

"Lady Cecilia, His Grace, the Duke of Warrick." The footman turned swiftly and pulled the double doors closed behind him with a resounding click, and they were alone.

"Aren't you in need of a chaperone, or some such?" Grayson asked quietly.

"Am I?" she asked tersely.

He didn't have an answer for her, so he motioned to the settee and chairs. She took one of the chairs, and he relaxed only slightly and sat in the chair adjacent, so they wouldn't have to stare directly at each other.

Yet he did stare. She was vibrant, like a garden after a rainstorm, when the world is wet and the sun has just begun to re-emerge, the flowers open to the water and the warmth. The thought frustrated him because he didn't want to like her.

Her hair was a warm red, nearly brown, and her eyes were a heavy green threaded with mahogany. She was like a wood nymph from *Shakespeare's Midsummer Night's Dream*. Well, save the clothes. She was buttoned up rather close.

She looked to him, then away just as quickly. "This is fascinating," she said as she stood and walked to the fire in the grate, her words pinched and angry. "I simply cannot remember the last time I enjoyed such brilliant conversation."

She stared at the flames, and he felt instantly guilty. But the attraction he'd felt waned once she spoke. Her beauty couldn't make up for the way she spoke to him, the way she looked at him. Her demeanor seemed more akin to an empty vase, and truthfully, he didn't blame her. Perhaps they could come to some sort of honorable arrangement once others were no longer party to their contract. Once it was simply between the two of them.

He stood and approached her slowly. "Lady Cecilia, I beg your pardon for my abhorrent behavior. This is all yet a shock to me."

"A shock…to you? We've been betrothed for near on two years, and you haven't made a single attempt to meet with me for the entirety of that engagement. I've been betrothed since I was a mere child. And this is a shock…to you?" She turned on him, her skirts swinging toward the grate, sparks flying in all directions as her voice rose. "A shock. And what would you say it is for me?!" Her voice filled the room. Grayson watched in horrified silence as she moved toward him and her skirts caught up in flames.

"My lady!" He tackled her to the floor as she screamed and fought him. He heard an awful crack as her head hit something and she went silent but he had no time to check her pulse right now. He stood and stomped on her skirts as he yelled again, this time for help. His heart had never raced as it did now. Glancing at her face he could see she had been knocked out—he had knocked her out. He hoped that was all he'd done.

He pulled a pillow from the settee and knelt at her feet smothering the remaining flames in her skirts. Grayson heard the door open and looked up to see the footman. "Call for a physician!" he yelled, then turned and started separating the layers of skirts and petticoats to be sure the fire was out completely.

It was just as he reached her drawers, saw the gentle curve of her backside in the gap, that he heard a shriek from the doorway. He looked up to find Cecilia's parents, the Duke and Duchess of Exeter, standing in the doorway.

For fuck's sake, as if his life wasn't as difficult as possible at the moment. He looked down once more, to be sure the fire was out—it was—then looked up to attempt to explain. But the duchess had fainted, the duke narrowly catching her before she hit the floor across the room from him.

"What is the meaning of this? What are you doing to her?" the duke yelled.

"Your Grace, let me explain—" he started.

"What is there to explain?" The duke handed his wife unceremoniously to a waiting footman and approached Grayson. "Looks to me as though you attempted to murder my daughter."

"Sir, no, I—"

"I knew you were dishonorable. But I chose to hold to the contract your father and I signed, out of respect for his friendship."

"I'm attempting to be honorable, sir. This isn't—"

"Are you telling me you're currently behaving as a gentleman should?" he railed on.

Grayson shook his head and started to rebut him, but Lady Cecilia hadn't moved in quite some time and he needed to concentrate on her. He knelt at her side again and brushed his knuckles across her temple. "My lady?"

"I must insist you unhand her," the duke yelled.

"Your Grace, I beg you, just give me a moment. This is not at all what it seems." He felt Cecilia's head shift and turned back to her. He leaned closer, spoke softly, "Cecilia?" He skimmed the stray hair from her face, as her cheeks pinked a bit. "Cecilia, please," he said. She turned her face into his hand, and her eyelashes fluttered against his fingers.

"Holy shit, that hurt," she said. Her hand moved to her head, and she winced. "Oliver? What the fuck just happened? Who the hell is Cecilia?"

Grayson dropped his hand as the shock of her words washed through him, and every conversation he'd had with Roxleigh about the man's wife ran through his mind. Roxleigh's wife had behaved much the same when he'd met her. The complete change in demeanor, the language… Gray shook it off because there was no time to consider options at the moment. If this was what he assumed, he needed to handle the situation and protect the woman. Those were his marching orders.

Grayson looked up to her father, who stood agape as a footman rushed in, pulling a small man in a suit with him.

Thank God, a physician.

"Shh," he said, "try not to...try not to speak. You took a hard fall. The doctor's here. Just give him a minute to look you over."

She opened her eyes and looked up at him, their eyes truly meeting for the first time. She assessed him for a moment, then her eyes narrowed, and if he hadn't already been on his knees, that look would have sent him there. Every assessment he'd made of her when she first walked in—save how stunningly beautiful she was—vanished and was replaced in that look. "My lady."

Her eyes widened, and she started to look around the room. He felt her heartbeat pick up in the fingers he held on her wrist. She lifted her shoulders, and he tried to coax her back down. "Stay, try not to panic. I've got you."

Her irises flared. "Hands off," she ordered, and he carefully but quickly released her, immediately sinking back on his haunches. "Don't touch me." She didn't take her gaze from his.

Grayson pulled his hands back to his knees. Once she clearly decided he was no longer a threat, her hands began to move, touching her head as she winced and hissed a breath, then feeling down her corseted chest, waist, and reaching her skirts. One of her hands found her bared bottom, and she narrowed her gaze on him again as the doctor ordered the footman to help him lift her to the sofa. Grayson tried to tell them to wait, but they didn't heed his warning.

"Why is my ass hanging out?" she asked as she pushed the men away, and the doctor put his bag down and pulled out a syringe. Grayson saw exactly how this was to go long before anything happened. The doctor intended to drug her into submission.

Grayson didn't understand why this woman had such a foul disposition, but he was certain she was fairly lucid and didn't need drugging. She needed only a minute to gather herself. He stood, pushing the footmen away and putting himself between Lady Cecilia and the rest of them.

"You will not touch her," he said.

"Don't be ridiculous," the doctor responded. "She clearly needs to be sedated for treatment."

"No, she doesn't. What she needs is a minute of privacy. Get out. All of you."

The doctor gaped and turned to the Duke of Exeter, who said, "Excuse me, Warrick, but you have no right to give orders in my house."

"Where it concerns my fiancée, I certainly do. We have a contract. She belongs to me," Grayson said.

"I have a contract with your dead father and dead brother, not with you," Exeter spat.

Grayson looked directly at the duke as he started to backpedal. "You have a contract with the Duke of Warrick. That is me, and you pressed for it to be finalized. Now get out until I call for you to return." Grayson wondered if the man truly thought him a careless idiot but brushed that aside, since he didn't actually care and didn't have time to deal with the man's ranting.

Exeter and the doctor stared at each other momentarily, then he nodded and waved the footmen to the doorway. "This discussion is not finished," Exeter said as he pulled the doors shut behind him. Grayson had the distinct feeling they hovered just beyond the closed doors.

Grayson turned back to Lady Cecilia and once again sank to his knees at her side. One of her hands covered her eyes, and the other pushed against her waist. She was visibly shaking. "They've gone. Would you like me to help you to the settee?" he asked.

"And yet *you're* still here. I must be dreaming," she said under her breath, then she looked up to him. "Do as you will, because this isn't really happening anyway."

Lulu watched the man closely. He lifted his hands and showed them to her, and she nodded. He reached for her, and she allowed him to run his hands over her to check for injuries. Then she allowed him to pick her up as she tried to straighten her skirts and cover her backside.

She closed her eyes to concentrate. She had absolutely no idea what was happening. Last she remembered, she was with Oliver, painting his back with wings. He'd earned it. After months and months of submissive training, he'd finally been ready. Then…what happened next?

She felt her feet touch the floor but kept her eyes closed as she shifted her hands on the biceps of this man—Warrick? Wasn't that what he'd said? Yes—no—well, yes and no. He'd called himself the Duke of Warrick. Oh, she needed to stop reading historical romances.

The duke held her steady and didn't move. He was waiting for orders. She knew it like she knew what year it was. Like she knew where she lived. Like she knew who she was. It was second nature to her—this dance of submission—and apparently he'd been well-trained, which meant no matter where she was, she was safe. She trusted in this, trusted in the BDSM community she knew and loved and the universal truths it provided.

She shook her head. This was a dream. Of course she was safe. Lulu started to open her eyes again, but the light in the room was simply too bright, so she tucked her face against his shoulder and kept her eyes closed.

After a moment to gain her balance, she patted his biceps to let him know she was okay, and his hold on her relaxed. She tilted, and his hands returned. "Maybe I should sit," she said. *Oh man, that was loud.* She must have a concussion, but…*it's all a dream.* She felt him shift her to the couch. He released her as he sat next to her, but his hands stayed ready.

"Could you get the blinds?" she asked. "It's too damn bright."

"The—I can shut the curtains," he said.

Who cares what you have? Just close them.

She shifted as his weight left her side, and she put her hands on the couch to steady herself. The world behind her eyelids grew more dim, and she slowly started to open her eyes. Good Lord, she'd fallen into a BBC miniseries.

The man came back, and she looked up to him carefully when he sat next to her. He was…stunning, really. Dark, brooding, very well dressed, very well put together. Heathcliff maybe, or Rochester, some devious man for certain. She couldn't see much more than his hands and face because the rest of him was completely covered by his clothes. "*Downton Abbey* perhaps?"

"Pardon?" he said.

"Sorry, nothing, I just… What year is it supposed to be?" It was her dream, right? Wouldn't her actors answer her questions? As well as her dream man. *I mean, he is something.* She usually dreamed of famous people, but this man—she couldn't place him. He wasn't at all familiar, but by the look of him, he would be famous someday. He rested his elbows on his knees as if resigned to something, then he knotted his hands together.

"Eighteen hundred and eighty-five," he said simply.

"Ah, Victorian. Way before *Downton Abbey*. Cool. God, my head hurts. Can I get a cool rag or something?"

"I will ask for one. Are you ready to see the physician?" he asked. His voice was simply mesmerizing. She knew he tempered it to keep from hurting her head, but the depths of it resonated in her chest—as close as he was—and damn if he didn't smell amazing. She felt her nipples harden against the corset she wore. At least something was working properly.

This was one of the most vivid dreams she'd ever had. Her hands flexed against her legs, as if to hold on to it for a minute because she felt so incredibly lucid through the pounding in her head, and she simply didn't want to wake up yet. She'd have to hurry and get his ass naked and tied to her bed before she awoke.

"I beg your pardon?" His voice dropped so low it was feral, and for the second time, she looked into his eyes. His deep, black, heavy eyes.

"Sorry? Did I say something?" she said, and he nodded. "What did I say?" she asked, attempting to feign innocence.

"You… I fear repeating what I heard."

She laughed and instantly regretted it. "Yeah, probably something about you being naked and tied to my bed. Listen, can you send the doc away so we can get down to business? This dream needs to move along because I'm all kinds of horny right now."

He stared at her, a look of complete and total shock on his face. Holy crap, she didn't usually make her dream men so compliantly non-compliant.

"What do I need to do, make it old school? Fine! Fetch the physician, if you must. I would like to have a lie-down," she said putting on her best British accent. He flinched, so it probably sucked as usual. She flicked her fingers at him to shoo him off to the door.

His eyes narrowed on her before he spoke. "Cecilia, I'm going to ask a favor of you. I'm going to bring the doctor in here. Please do not make any references to time or place. Please simply convince him you are well so he will leave and we can continue our discussion."

Lulu smiled and wondered if she should ask him if he should be using someone's Christian name, just like the heroines always did in her favorite historicals. He stood before she managed the words and went out into the hallway. Well, all righty then. Looked like they'd get rid of the doc and get right down to it. *Fantastical.*

The door swung open again, and the doctor came over to her. He treated her as if she were a CPR dummy—with no senses—poked and prodded without so much as a by-her-leave. Then he asked her inane questions, to which she tried to respond in a decent fashion. It helped that the man she wanted to tie to her bed was standing behind him, shaking and nodding his head with the answers.

"She may need rest for a few days, but she should be just fine." The doctor looked to her once more. "We should check you for burns."

"Burns?"

"She had no burns." God, he was spare in his speech. She loved it. *Wait, burns?* She looked down at her dress and realized what the awful smell was. The skirts were in tatters, fringed with burn marks. She looked over to the fireplace. Huh, okay, apparently she caught fire and that's how she ended up on the floor.

Oh my God! She'd been a victim of the flaming crinolines. This was a seriously intricate dream. I had to be a dream, but the smell of burning chemicals hung in the air, bitter and sharp. Yuck.

She turned back and smiled at the doctor as if to say, *Time for you to go.* He watched her warily for a moment, and she tilted her chin up and narrowed her eyes on him. He stood.

"Your Grace, if you have need, call on me. I should return in a few days to check on her, make sure her head is clear."

Warrick nodded. "I will send for you, if necessary."

Lulu grinned at Warrick. "So," she said, "about that bed." Warrick's eyes looked like they might just pop right out of his skull, and everyone in the room stopped and looked at her.

"Too soon?" she asked.

Someone behind her whisked the curtains open, and the light assaulted her. She winced, stood, was immediately light-headed, and she felt Warrick's arms surround her and then…nothing.

Such bad timing. Damned dreams.

TWO

If you know yourself but not the enemy,
for every victory gained you will also suffer a defeat.
If you know neither your enemy nor yourself,
you will succumb in every battle.
If you know your enemy and know yourself,
you need not fear the result of a hundred battles.

—Sun Tzu
The Art of War

Grayson carried her up the stairs behind the lady's maid. Convincing her father and the doctor that she only needed some rest had been difficult. Well, that and his continued threats concerning the contract. Persuading her father to let Grayson accompany her to her room…that had taken more time than necessary in his estimation, but that he'd stood there holding her and refusing to release her had been part of what swayed their opinions.

They reached the second floor, and Grayson's lungs started to burn from lack of oxygen. The combination of his corset, his charge, and the stairs was beginning to wear on him, but he pressed on.

The door to her room was swept open, and he entered. Her bed was on the left, close to the windows. He walked over and laid her down, straightening her skirts. "Draw the curtains," he said, and the maid nodded and did as he ordered.

He turned back to Cecilia, and shifting his rib cage inside his own corset, he determined she needed to be out of hers. He turned back to the maid as she approached. "Send a footman for the Duchess of Roxleigh, at Roxleigh House on Grosvenor. I need her straightway. Tell him not to return without her."

The maid paused, most likely wondering if she should leave her mistress unattended with a man, but he just returned the look then motioned to the door.

She turned, finally, and Grayson followed her, shutting the door behind her before returning to the bed, tripping over the edge of the rug, and cursing. "Fuck." He caught his stride and made it to the bed.

"Thank God you're not *always* so formal," she deadpanned.

"You're awake."

"Oh yeah, and I'm in bed. So it's the best thing in the world right now. Skip the doctors and get your damned clothes off."

Grayson stopped. Everything about this woman reminded him of how Roxleigh's wife behaved. Completely brash, unapologetic—a bit crass at times.

Roxleigh had told him things, things he'd chosen not to believe but also not to dispute, for there was no point. He'd determined she was of no harm to herself or anyone else, and the alternative was committing her to Bedlam, so Grayson had decided to leave it alone.

"What year should it be?" he asked.

"Um…you said 1885, right?"

"Yes, but when you woke up this morning, or…when you are where you come from…when you—" He stopped. How in the hell was he supposed to ask this?

"Ah…will we play time traveler then? In real life, it's 2015," she said with a wink.

"Two thousand… That's over a century." He sat heavily on the bed next to her, unsure what to do. She could be insane, or the concussion could have affected her memory somehow. He pulled on the edge of his shirtsleeves again.

"I believe I told you to get your clothes off. I want to see this body naked." She sat up and reached for him, then immediately fell back to the pillows. "You'll have to do it yourself. My head still hurts."

"You have a concussion." He stood and reached for the pitcher of water next to her bed but his hands shook and the pitcher clinked against a glass. "Have you a towel or…" He looked around then put the pitcher back down and pulled up the hem of her skirts.

"Okay," she said, "now this is getting good."

"Right." He paused as his hands fisted the fabric, then he took a deep breath and separated out one of her petticoats and tore a thick strip from the bottom. He reached again for the pitcher, wetting the fabric then putting the cool rag to her forehead. She seemed to melt into the pillow with a heavy sigh.

"We need to get you out of these clothes." He tried to speak softly, and she looked at him like she was confused. He leaned over her. "The corset, the burned petticoats—we need to get rid of them because the smell of the fire is making *my* head hurt," he said. She nodded as she stared up at him.

"I'm going to touch you," he said. He twisted his hands together as he looked down on her deciding how to proceed before he carefully laid his hands on her shoulder and her waist and rolled her to her side. He started to undo the countless buttons, but looking down at the tattered skirt, he changed his mind and simply grabbed the loose edges, tearing the dress open all the way to her knees. He did his best to ignore the fact that there was a warm breathing woman beneath all of this fabric.

He repeated that on every layer coming closer and closer to her skin until he reached the corset, which he untied to loosen, then he rolled her to her back once again. The sleeves of her dress were fitted and covered in buttons as well, so he tore them open, buttons popping and flying around the room like popping corn.

"Muscles," she said quietly.

"They come in handy," he replied as he pulled the sleeves of the dress off, then eased the bundle of fabric from her, walked to the door, and tossed it into the hallway. He watched as the fabric fluttered to the floor, taking a moment to breathe. This woman made him nervous like nobody in his life ever had. He felt like asking her permission merely to look upon her.

He returned, and showing her his hands again first, he placed them on her rib cage, bringing the edges of the corset together and releasing the catches on the steel busk. She took a deep breath, and he felt instantly relieved that he was done with that as he tried not to stare at her hardened nipples through the thin fabric of her chemise.

She planted her feet and lifted her hips, and he slid the corset from beneath her, dragging his eyes away from the fold marks in the chemise the pressure had made. The fold marks that would also be pressed into her

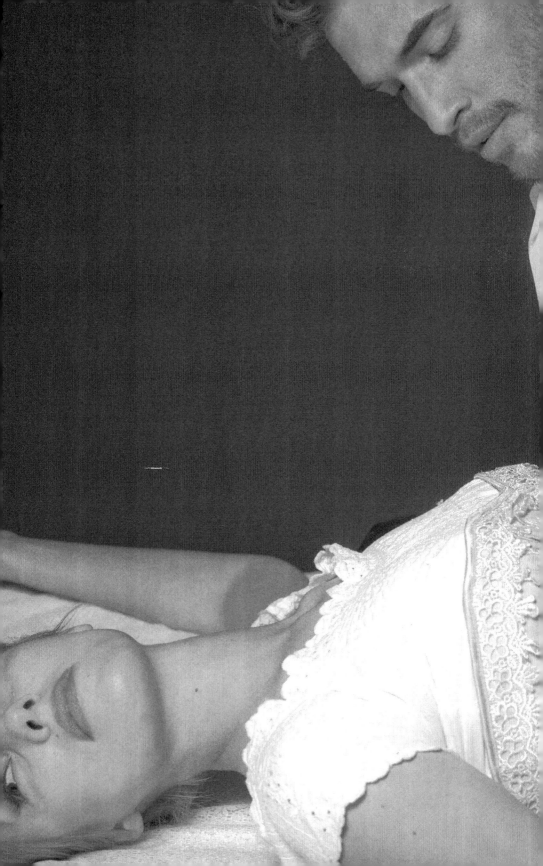

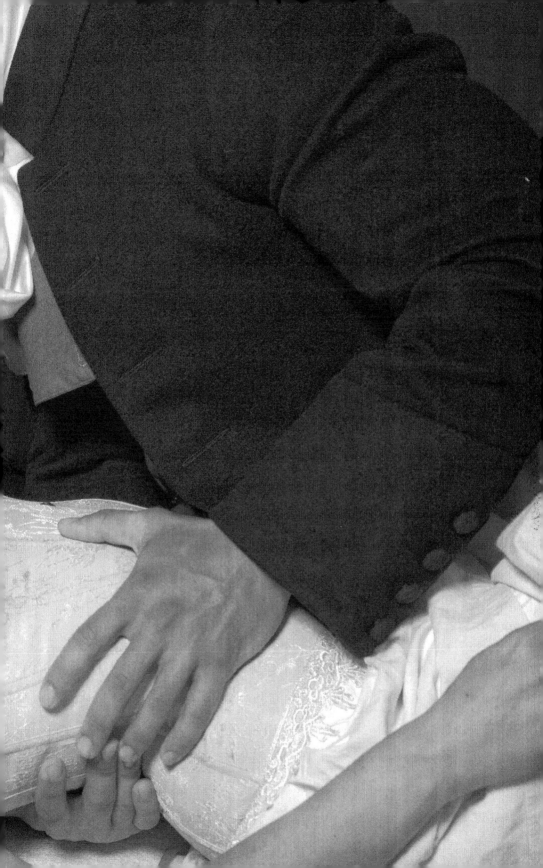

skin. Just the thought of it left him wanting. He wanted to drag her chemise from her and run his hands down those marks, only to see her skin quiver.

"God, thank you. Oxygen will surely help this headache."

Her words roused him from where his mind had run off to, and he tossed the corset toward what he assumed was her wardrobe, then looked back at her. She'd curled up on her side, the chemise still on. He could see it had been sheltered from the fire, not long enough that it caught up with her skirts, so he left it alone. But her stockings were singed a bit up the back, and he wanted to be sure her legs hadn't been burned.

He carefully untied the thigh garters, then rolled the stockings down her legs, lifting them only just enough to give him room. When he finished, he ran his hands carefully up her legs. *No burns. Thank god.*

He looked at the edges of her drawers, something he'd been avoiding entirely, but she seemed to be sleeping now, so he took this one liberty. The fabric was pure white linen against her pale skin. He wanted to run his finger down the edge of the drawers, across the soft roundness of her backside.

Instead, he carefully pulled the sheets back as she shifted to allow him access, then he pulled them up to her shoulder, hiding all of her from his

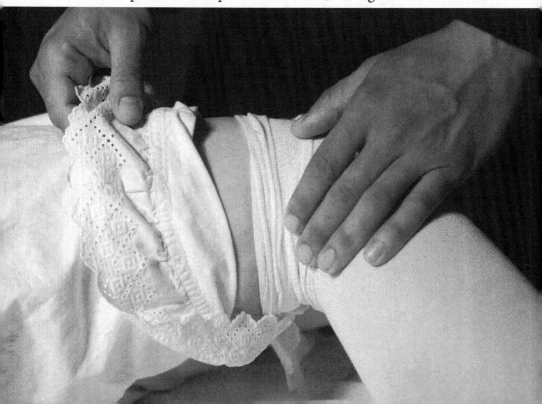

gaze. He shifted the scrap of wet fabric on her forehead and looked for a chair.

As he pulled the chair up to the side of the bed, the door to her room opened, and her maid entered. Her arms were full with the burned fabric from the hallway and Cecilia's mother was on her heels. He held his hands up.

"Please, Your Grace, she's only just fallen asleep."

Her mother stopped in her tracks. "Well, I…is she…how is she?" she asked.

He could tell she was uncomfortable. "Ma'am, she has a concussion. She should be watched carefully. I've seen injuries like this, the men recovered just fine. So should she," he said as quietly as he could.

She nodded. "This is so…" She waved her hand about.

"Yes, but she's to be my wife, so we will simply let it be." And he knew it to be true. He would have to marry her now. If she were like the Duchess of Roxleigh, she would need protection to keep her from being committed for insanity or immorality or some other catchall malady of the brain, like hysteria. And she was already his. He just hadn't known it.

Her mother nodded. "Will you be staying for supper, or…" She let the sentence hang in the air, allowing him to answer as he wished.

"I will stay for the time being." He turned to the maid. "Did you send for the duchess?" She nodded. "Please send her up as soon as she—"

"We can watch over her," her mother cut in.

"Certainly you're able to, but I wish to be sure. This is a serious injury, and I need her to recover properly…to protect my interests."

"Ah, yes, of course." Her mother nodded. Sometimes the only thing these people understood was asset protection. Chattel. Trade negotiations. Business. He closed his eyes for a moment and shook off the feeling of disgust.

"I'm going to watch her," he said, brooking no argument, then he turned to the maid. "Dispose of the burned garments somewhere else. The smell bothers her." The maid curtsied and disappeared, her mother behind her, and he turned back to Cecilia. He shifted the chair and sat down, then he put his feet up on the bed next to her, boots and all.

Meeting his wife had been exhausting.

Lulu shifted beneath the covers. Burrowed in a bit. She was so warm and comfortable. Her mind drifted to the day before, the scene with Ollie. His wings had been absolutely beautiful. She hoped the image came out. She didn't remember developing the plate, which was odd, because she usually went straight to the darkroom. It was her own personal aftercare.

She would develop it today. Hopefully, she hadn't slept too late. Didn't matter. She would stay up all night creating the Van Dyke prints of his angel wings for him. She loved this part of her work. The part where she spent hours in the quiet dark, the only sound the chemicals sloshing in the trays, the steady sluicing a comfort.

Lulu wasn't sure whether it was the creation of the wings themselves or the creation of the images that made her more happy. Both in equal measure, perhaps, because she loved every moment of it.

She rolled over to shift her pillow to a cool spot, then brought her hand to her pounding forehead. She wasn't generally one for headaches, but this was a doozy for sure. She adjusted the pillow to another cool spot and settled back in, hoping to get back to the dream with that duke.

"Are you feeling better?" The voice was deep and resonant and more… It was familiar.

Lulu froze. Time to assess. She felt a hand at her ankle, a gentle pressure, comforting, non-threatening. Still… "I did not give you permission to touch me," she said quickly, and the hand disappeared.

She took a deep breath and slowly opened her eyes. Too many pillows, soft white sheets, four-poster bed… She could be at the club. Something happened at the club. Her hackles rose. She closed her eyes and tried to remember.

"Francine, please?" The deep voice again. Someone else was here? She rolled over toward the voice and tried to sit up, then heard a woman's softer voice.

"Hold on a sec. Let me help." Lulu felt an arm under her shoulders then pillows being pushed behind her back. She leaned into them and looked up in the dimly lit room into a set of smiling blue eyes.

"Hi," the woman said. She sat on the edge of the bed next to her, then patted her hand. "My name is Francine." The woman was inordinately beautiful and oddly comforting. Her brown hair was piled on her head in some fluffy, curly, updo and she had freckles across her nose. Perhaps it was the freckles that put Lulu at ease. Freckles could sometimes do that. Nobody with freckles was dangerous.

"Lulu," she replied, then she heard a grunt from somewhere deep in the room. "Is that my hero, the duke?" she asked. "This is a great dream, but I think I just want to wake up now." She clenched her hands on the white comforter, but the room stayed as it was. Usually, if she tried to hold on to something with her hands while she was dreaming, the dream would fade and she would wake up, hands empty. "Fuck."

Francine giggled. "Yep, that's kinda how I felt. Look, I don't…I'm not sure how to go about this."

"Go about what?" Lulu asked. "If you have something to say just say it. Rip off the Band-Aid. Make it happen."

Francine smiled at her but still looked wary. "All right… Today is March 15th, 1885."

"Yeah, he mentioned that," she pointed off in the darkness then flipped her hand and pulled it back to her lap. "wherever he is. Warlock. No… Warrick. Warrick? Is that right?"

"Yes." She heard only the deeply gruff voice. He still didn't come into the light where she could see him. "I am Warrick."

"You don't sound too happy about that," Lulu said.

"He's not," Francine whispered.

"I'm—" He started to protest, but stopped. "No, I'm not."

"Look, I don't know if this is some kind of elaborate scene, but I don't remember talking limits or discussing any of this with anyone. I'm starting to be concerned, and I would like a phone. Or go get Byron."

"The poet?" Warrick asked.

"No, the owner of the club," Lulu whispered. Then she stopped staring into the darkness and looked around her again. Then back to Francine. "Who are you?" The woman took her hand, and she allowed it.

"My name was Francine Larrabee. I'm from Denver, but that's not where we are now."

"No, it doesn't seem so." Her eyes drifted around the room. It seemed a very well-planned set, good enough for any BBC production. But she was nowhere near the BBC London studios. She was…home. She had been home, and home was Denver, just like this woman.

"Lulu?" she asked, and Lulu turned back to her. "I imagine the next few days are going to be very difficult. I would like to help you as much as I can. Believe me when I say I know exactly how you feel right now. I'm happy to answer all of your questions, whenever you have questions. Right now I think we should arrange for you to come stay with me—"

The door to the room burst open, and Lulu heard shouting in the hallway. She could see a large man silhouetted in the doorway, his broad shoulders cutting off the encroaching light as he waited for whoever was in the hall with him to stop speaking. Then he spoke in a gruff baritone similar to Warrick's.

"Exeter, you've always been an ass. You're an ass in the House, you're an ass at the tables, you're an ass wherever you go. But you don't have to be an ass right fucking now." The door slammed, and the silhouetted man disappeared in the darkness.

"What's happening?" Lulu asked. Francine squeezed her hand.

"It's just my husband. He's a bit upset with…um…the Duke of Exeter." She smiled warmly, but Lulu could tell she was hiding something. "Do you think we could open the curtains for a moment? Is your headache better?" she asked.

Lulu nodded, and Francine turned to where the men were in the dark. Lulu heard heavy footsteps cross the room, then the curtains parted slowly, and she blinked, letting her eyes adjust on the man in the light, Warrick. She felt safer having seen him again, and something in her chest reached for him, though she kept her hands still.

"That's enough," Francine said. "Thank you." She turned back to Lulu. "Now, I'm going to go make some arrangements that I'm assuming haven't yet been made, by the sound of that conversation. I'm going to leave you here with these gentlemen. They'll keep you safe, I promise."

"Francine, a word?" Warrick said quickly.

"Okay," she said, then she turned back to Lulu. "I'm going to leave you with my husband. You can call him Rox. He'll see to you."

Francine stood and walked to the door, waiting for Warrick to follow, then they went out into the hallway where all Lulu could hear were hushed words. She looked at Rox. He looked back at her, seeming a bit uncomfortable. He was tall and broad, like Warrick, but he seemed much more refined and less angry, or tense, or something. She could see the green of his eyes even as far away as he was.

"Can I get you some water?" he asked suddenly, moving to the table near the bed with the pitcher. She'd probably made him uncomfortable with her assessment, she tended to do that at times.

"That would be nice," she said. He poured a glass and handed it to her, then took a step back. She didn't look away.

"You're frightened," he said, "but you can trust Francine. If you trust no one else, trust her."

"It seems odd, to me, that you wouldn't tell me to trust you," she replied.

"I'm a man." he said simply. She wasn't sure what that meant to him, but she understood. The voices in the hallway became harried, and Lulu swept the blankets aside, placed the glass on the table, and stood but was immediately repentant when the blood in her head seemed to knock against her temple as if to remind her of her injury.

Rox offered his hand. "I'm not sure you should be getting out of bed… right…um…" His eyes widened and then closed, and Lulu looked down. She had nothing on but a short, nearly see-through night shirt of some sort and a pair of—she wasn't even sure what they were considering they seemed to be only a pair of legs attached to each other by a ribbon at her waist. The point was that her nether bits were out to say hello to this stranger.

"Holy shit!" She turned and pulled the sheet from the bed, realizing he now had a view of her entire backside instead. What the fuck? "This would probably be pretty sexy under some circumstances… Is this someone's slave fantasy? Are you the client?" She looked at him as she pulled the sheet around herself, but his eyes were still closed. A client would want to watch and she couldn't remember arranging any of this. She didn't own costumes like this. She didn't understand where she was. Downton Abbey was a TV show.

"I'm not certain I understand your meaning, Lady Cecilia. Are you more decent?" he asked.

"You know what?" She paused, then decided to let him figure it out for himself. "Never mind, just…never mind." Who the fuck is Cecilia? She needed Warrick. She walked to the door in much less than a straight line, dragging the bedclothes behind her. Rox started to follow her, but she waved him off. She stopped at the edge of the doorway, then listened as Warrick spoke.

"I have a contract. I'll see it through, and she will be protected," he said.

Lulu shuddered, and something deep in her belly reacted to the depth of his voice and the determination of his speech. A contract. So he was the client.

"I understand that, but what about the future? What if she doesn't come to love you? She shouldn't be forced into marriage to a stranger, no matter her circumstance," Francine argued.

Lulu smiled. She kinda liked the woman—did she say marriage? She shivered at the thought but part of her, a very deep part of her that had never considered marriage considered looking at that man every day for the rest of her life and she knew what home would feel like.

"She hasn't much choice. If I don't marry her, the contract is void, and she's ruined—Cecilia is ruined—and her father has control. What happens then?"

Cecilia again. Was she supposed to be Cecilia? Seemed strange they would carry on the scene out of earshot, if she was supposed to be part of it.

Nope…this was a dream. She needed a quiet minute to sit down and think. She'd been at the club. With Ollie. His wings were…flying?

"I see your point, but I still can't force someone to marry without consent. It isn't right. The whole situation is bad enough as it is. Do you think marrying *you* is going to make it better?" Francine asked and Lulu could almost feel Warrick's disquiet at her tone through the wall.

"She'll be safe." Was all he said.

Those three simple words resonated through Lulu, and she knew he was all she needed at the moment. It was such a fascinating feeling, being drawn to someone. It was that pull that had always been missing from her relationships. She stepped closer to the door. What if this wasn't a dream? What if she truly was here? She could feel an almost tangible connection to this man.

"I know, I just…can we think about this for a while? The contract won't be void for some time, will it?" Francine asked and Lulu sensed Rox come up behind her, close but not touching her, as though she would fall at any moment. Warrick and Francine's voices rose.

"I don't want to discuss this. If I need to take this to Rox, I will—"

"You think to control me through Gideon? You might want to—"

Lulu stepped into the hallway. "I'll marry him." Yay, for snap decisions! They both turned to her. What did I just do? The fact was, if this was a dream it made sense to play along and if this wasn't a dream—she looked up at his shocked expression and the connection she felt to him tightened like a slipknot just before it let go—she was already his.

Francine rushed forward, but Lulu stepped to the side, into the lee of Warrick's form. "No, I understand you're protecting me, somehow, as much as I understand any of this. And I appreciate it, but I want him. He'll marry me. If that will keep me safe, then so be it."

"But you don't even understand what's happening. Please, let's just get you out of this house, and then we can talk—"

"No, whatever the plan was for marriage, we'll see it through." Lulu looked up to Warrick, who seemed to be assessing every movement she made, every word she spoke. "What—exactly—was the plan then?" she asked.

"We marry tomorrow."

Lulu felt her jaw slip open. "Oh, well, then that's settled. Can I have some clothes?" She turned and walked back into the room, leaving them all gaping after her. What have I done? She tipped, dizzy again, and big hands caught her, but she shrugged them off. Then Warrick had her and he kept her upright, her feet on the floor. His hands she did not shrug off.

"Find some clothes," he said.

"Warrick, you can't possibly mean to carry this out!" Francine's voice rose. "This is completely beyond the pale."

"You had no qualms with my marriage yesterday. You were helping to plan the damned thing," he said.

"That was different, Warrick. That was…that was different."

"How so?"

"You know how so!"

"Francine," Roxleigh said. "Come, let's get some of her things packed. You heard her. She wishes to marry Warrick."

"Stop addressing me as Warrick!" His voice boomed through the house, echoed through the hallways, and seemed to quiet the world.

The rustle of fabric as Lulu turned and placed one hand on his chest broke the silence. She curled her fingers around his waistcoat edge and held it in a fist.

Warrick inhaled deeply and suddenly, then tried to take a step back, but she didn't relent, and he stood tall, taking air into his lungs and broadening his chest as she straightened. "We haven't really been introduced," she said to him alone. "My name is Lulu. How would you like me to address you?"

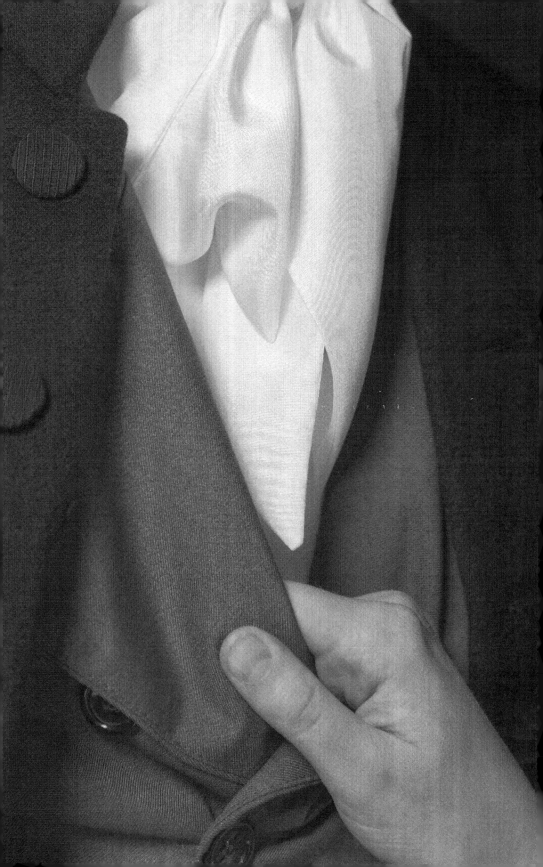

THREE

Ponder and deliberate before you make a move.

—Sun Tzu
The Art of War

G rayson breathed through the contact. Her fingers felt like fire with nothing but the thin linen of his shirt to protect him, and the tips of her fingers skimmed the corset he wore beneath his clothing as she held him in place. It would be easier if Francine and Rox weren't watching him—weren't watching *them*.

Her thumb moved, skimmed across his chest, and his skin reacted in a rush of sensation he very nearly couldn't contain. He felt it slide down the center of his chest, straight to his groin.

This was a bad idea. This woman was too forward. She would quickly discover him for who he was and be horrified by it—by him—and then what? He wasn't sure he could survive something like that again, and they would be bound together to live in misery, forever.

But damn him, his honor was getting the best of him. Though, if he was to be truly honest with himself, it wasn't merely honor but the way she looked at him—no, even more than that. She looked *into* him, as if she saw every deep, dark crevice of his soul and wouldn't shy. It was…something he didn't merely wish for, but yearned for with all that he was—as impossible as he knew it to be. He'd been fooled before, however, and he'd left his family because of it. He'd lived in solitude because of it and hadn't trusted anyone since.

He lifted his arm and placed one hand over hers, holding it to him as he kept it from straying any closer to his underthings. "You will call me Gray."

She nodded. "Gray. Okay, Mr. Gray."

"No, simply Gray. If you have need of an explanation, my name is Grayson Locke Danforth, Duke…of Warrick. *You* will never address me as Warrick. *You* will always address me as Gray."

"Danforth," she whispered. "Why is that familiar?"

"Gray." He corrected her.

She shook her head. "Unless I'm angry, then I might just call you a host of horrible things." She grinned up at him, and for the first time since returning to London, Grayson felt something stir deep inside. It told him the move wouldn't be as terrible as he'd thought. Grayson shook the feeling off as quickly as it came, because he couldn't chance letting his guard down, even for a moment.

"Agreed." He looked up to see Francine ordering Cecilia's lady's maid around. "Do you trust your maid?" he asked, then realized if what they thought about her was true, she wouldn't have an answer for him. The look she gave him only confirmed that. "Apologies, I… Francine, do you have someone who could serve for Lulu until we find someone we can trust?"

The young maid turned to him. She was a pixie of a thing, her dark hair stuffed under a white mobcap, her brown eyes big behind a pair of glasses. "Your Grace, I—" She looked around the room, then twisted her pale hands in her skirts and looked at the floor. "I apologize if I've offended somehow. Your Grace, I've served Lady Cecilia for a time and was expected to move with her. I understand if you'll not have me, but they'll have no use for me here, Your Grace." She stared at the floor.

Grayson understood he would be putting this girl out of a job. But the situation wasn't one in which he could take any chance of Lulu being discovered. Of course, Francine was much better than either he or Lulu… He looked down to see her watching his hand as his thumb stroked the back of hers. What was he thinking about? *Oh…the maid…* "Francine, would you find a position for her until we're able to determine she would be *appropriate* for my household?" he asked, then looked back at the maid, who, he could see from across the room, had begun to cry.

For fuck's sake.

Francine must have seen the look of horror on his face and turned to the maid, put her hand on her shoulder, and spoke. "Of course we will take you. Of course we will find you a position in our households. If you were meant to be with Lady Cecilia, then you will be with our family from here on out."

The maid nodded and brushed the tears from her face quickly and turned back to the wardrobe. She pulled out a dress and what looked like about a hundred pounds of fabric and stiff cages and laid it all out on the bed. She turned to him. "Your Grace, if it please you, I would ready my lady," she said, her voice quietly catching on the words.

He tensed every time she threw the honorific at him. She would need to stop that before she came anywhere near his household. He nodded and looked back to Lulu, who hadn't so much as moved, then he patted her hand to get her attention, and she looked up to him. Her eyes danced in late afternoon light from the window, the golden color bringing out the brown and green in striking contrast to her pale skin, and he felt that shift again, deep in his belly. He fought it. "Get dressed," he said finally.

She nodded and released his waistcoat slowly, then turned to the room. *The maid—what was her name? Did I even ask?* He would. *Later...* She took Lulu by the shoulders and steered her toward her dressing table as Rox and Francine walked toward him so they could give her some privacy.

They turned together for the door, and as he took the first step over the threshold, a scream the likes of which he'd never heard rent the air like a thunderclap.

He ducked from the shock of it, then turned back to the room. Lulu sat in front of the mirror at her dressing table, her eyes wide with horror, her mouth dropped open, her finger pointing to her reflection.

"Who the fuck is that?!" Her breath hitched, her skin drained of color, and her eyes rolled as she went limp, but he'd already made his way toward her and caught her body before she hit the floor.

He looked at the maid. "I trust you to keep this to yourself. Finish packing. I will take her as she is." He wrapped her up tightly in the sheet already around her then nodded toward the bed and waited as Francine brought another blanket to him. Between he and Roxleigh, they shifted her around enough to hide every bit of her.

Then, because she'd been very clear about how and when she was touched and handled, he spoke to her, even though she was unconscious. He looked down into the little opening for her face and whispered, only for her, "I've got you. I will protect you. Let's get you out of here."

"Your Grace?" He stopped, then turned back to the maid for a moment.

"Miss…"

"Amandine."

"Miss Amandine—" He paused, considering whether to tell her how to address him, then decided to save it for later. "I'll send carriages. Make ready."

She dipped into a curtsy. "Yes, Your Grace." He was pretty sure he'd snarled at her, but she'd already turned and started flinging fabric from the wardrobe into the open trunk at her feet. He blinked once, then turned again and walked out.

"My carriage is here. Did you ride?" Roxleigh asked.

"Hack."

"Still no men at your town home?"

"No. I only just gave up my rooms in preparation for the marriage tomorrow." They didn't need to know his father had nearly bankrupted the dukedom and the marriage settlements would be required for hiring a sufficient staff.

"We will take you home," Roxleigh said.

Grayson nodded and walked straight from the house without breaking stride, even as he heard doors opening and shutting, then voices calling after him for Lady Cecilia. He heard Francine's voice but couldn't be bothered to care what she was telling them. He needed to get Lulu out of here, and he needed to keep his promise to her. That was it. That was the extent of what he needed to do at this moment. Nothing more.

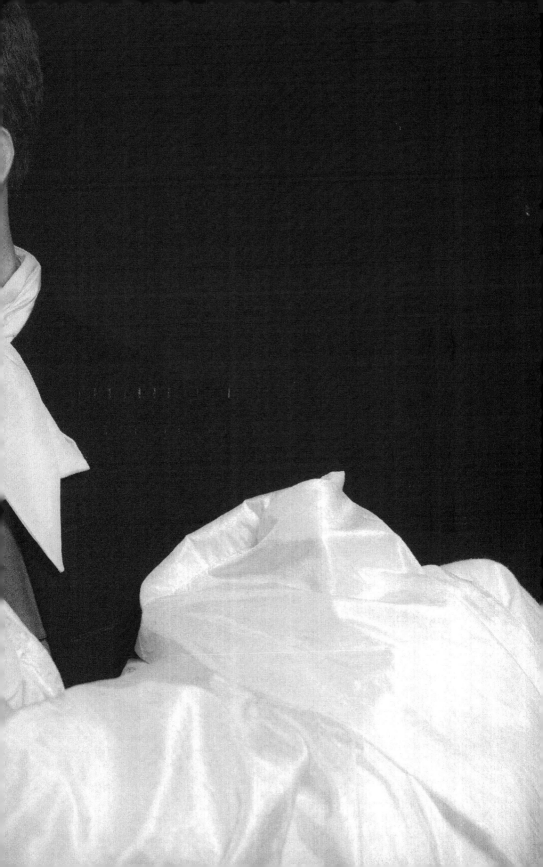

Lulu breathed slowly, coming around once again. What an interesting dream. She tried to stretch, but her blankets were too tight. She wiggled and started to open her eyes.

"Hello." She felt the reverberation of his words sink through the layers of blankets and into her chest, and she froze.

Good.

Right.

Perfect.

She tightened her hands on the blanket. Solid. Not a dream then. Still not a dream. She had to get out of the confinement. She hated being trapped, and she began to panic.

"Let me out." She started kicking and pushing and practically exploded from the blankets until she was back in the one loose sheet, sitting on the bench next to Gray. *Gray...* She looked over at him. He had his gaze the people across from them—Roxleigh and Francine—as if to say to her, *Mind your words in front of the company, dear.*

"What kind of name is Roxleigh?" she said without turning her head.

"My title," Rox answered plainly. These men were very spare with words. She appreciated that.

"So you're a peer as well?" she asked, still watching Grayson.

"I'm a duke. Warrick—"

"Grayson."

"Grayson and I are cousins." Rox and Gray batted words back and forth as if they'd been doing so forever, and she supposed as cousins perhaps they had.

"So, Francine, you're a duchess?" she asked. She still watched Gray, he still watched Francine and Roxleigh, they watched her. It was a perfect triangle of watching. No, wait... Rox shifted to look at Gray as well now, like Lulu, as Francine spoke.

"I am a duchess, yes. As will you be, tomorrow. Unless you wish to—"

"No," Grayson cut her off, his jaw tensing.

"I won't change my mind," Lulu said easily, to calm him. "But know that I appreciate your concern." Then she turned to Francine. "Thank you. Where are we going?"

"Roxleigh House, our London home. We prefer our estate up north to being in London, but of course we had to be here for the wedding. We'll be returning to Eildon soon, or…at least we'd planned on it," Francine said.

Roxleigh took Francine's hand without shifting his gaze, and Francine smiled. Lulu knew in that communication that Francine was saying they might not leave if Lulu needed them, and Roxleigh was agreeing to that. *Fucking adorable.* Lulu was suddenly grateful for her presence. She wanted to ask her a million questions but her mind could not seem to focus on one.

"So I'll be staying with you?" Lulu asked, it was a good a question as any for the time being.

"Yes. As will Grayson, since he's short-staffed." Roxleigh answered this time.

"That's easily remedied," Gray said.

"Not perhaps as expediently as you need, for the sort of staff you need," Rox said. Gray conceded with a nod, and Lulu knew it was because of her that staff would be more difficult to find.

"I'm sorry to have ruined your plans." They all deferred at once, and she smiled. "Well. So. 1885, huh?"

Grayson turned toward her then. "Yes. 1885 and, in case it hasn't become apparent, London, England. I assume you're from America?" he asked.

She nodded, then remembered the last thing she'd seen before she passed out for the five-bazillionth time. "My hair," she said and reached up to it.

Grayson's eyebrows came together in concern. "Yes, you…you were looking in the mirror when you screamed. Why was that?"

"My hair—it's big, and it's not red. My hair was red. Not like dark red, but like red, red. My hair was a bright, vivid red. I guess orange is a better description. It took a long time to get used to it, and now… I mean, this hair is pretty, but it isn't mine. I—"

"I was blond," Francine said.

Lulu looked up at the brunette, and Roxleigh and Gray looked at Francine, who looked back at Roxleigh. "Did I ever mention? I don't remember if I did, but yes, my hair was blond."

Then Roxleigh spoke. "Is that why? You mentioned Kansas wheat, and the thought of brown wheat was perfectly horrific to me. I didn't realize…"

"No—I mean, yes, that's why. I can't believe you remember that." Francine smiled at him and ran a finger down his cheek to his chin.

"I remember everything you've ever said," he replied.

Gray looked down at his hands on his knees, and Lulu was sure she groaned from the display, because Francine turned to her suddenly and spoke, breaking the moment. "I was a blonde. Once upon a time, as they say. You know…I hadn't really considered this, but I'm kind of excited that you're here. That's pretty selfish of me. But I am, I'll admit it." She turned to Rox. "I love you. I wouldn't change a thing, not for the world, believe me, but"—she turned back to Lulu—"I'm really excited to have someone who understands what I mean when I say iPod. Or Internet."

Lulu laughed when Roxleigh and Grayson shook their heads in tandem, then she stopped. "Oh, wait, you're serious. Oh no, ohhh no. My music." Everything she knew, everything she listened to—*this is just a dream.* Her hands flexed on the sheet again and her breath hitched.

"I'm sorry, I shouldn't have mentioned it so soon. This is not going to be easy for you."

"So that's what you meant when you said you understood. Because you're not from around here either."

Francine shook her head, and Lulu was tossed forward as the carriage came to a halt. Gray wrapped an arm around her and pulled her against him. "Sorry, I wasn't expecting that," she said. She wasn't sure whether she meant the carriage or the realization.

Grayson reached for all the blankets, and she assumed he meant to wrap her up once again. "I can't. Look, I'm claustrophobic. Please don't wrap those around me again." The door to the carriage opened, and Roxleigh nodded at Grayson and stepped down, pulling Francine along with him.

Grayson turned to her. "I think I understand the difficulty, but you're very nearly…you're…" He cleared his throat and nodded to her clothes, or lack thereof. She hadn't even considered it. One, this was a dream, so who cared? And two, she was naked most of the time anyway, or nearly so.

"I don't care. I'm perfectly comfortable with my body. What anyone thinks of me is their issue, not mine."

"Except that it's still light out, and even if this were our home, there are servants. Everywhere. They'll talk."

Lulu thought about it for a minute. She had an idea about how this worked, even if her manuals for behavior were twenty-first-century romance novels. This was so surreal, and she was sure the reason she wasn't screaming and yelling at the moment was that she still believed she would wake up. Because, really, time travel? Right. Maybe she was in a coma, maybe that's why her head hurt so very much. She took a deep breath. "Okay, okay, I trust you. But please, please take me somewhere where you can release me as quickly as possible."

Gray nodded and held the blankets up, blocking her from view as he backed out of the carriage. She stepped between his hands, into his arms, felt one wrap around her then the other.

He pulled her out with one arm still around her back and swept her up with the other arm under her knees. She closed her eyes and breathed slowly. In through her nose, out through her mouth. Repeat.

She felt him run, and she wiggled until she managed to get one arm out and wrap it around his neck. It was just an arm. He could deal with it.

They went up a set of stairs, then entered the house. He ran across the foyer, then up another set of stairs. "Rox!" he boomed, and it echoed through the entry—oh, this house was big.

"Over here, Grayson." Francine said.

Gray moved toward the voice, took her down a hall and through a doorway and immediately put her feet on the floor and released her. "Thank you," she said. "I...can I...I just need a moment." She suddenly felt completely overwhelmed. Francine came into the room and handed her a few dresses on hangers.

"These are all very simple dresses. No corsets, no petticoats, just slips and dresses. You should be able to figure them out. We'll leave you, and when you're ready, you can either ring the bell there"—she pointed to a large tapestry pull by the bed—"or you can simply come downstairs. We'll be in the study, and we'll leave the door open. My home is yours. Feel free to look around. Make yourself comfortable." Francine took a step closer, wrapped her arms around her, and hugged her. It was sweet. Then she turned and left.

Grayson contemplated Lulu for a minute as she stood there, holding the clothes, the sheet, and the bedclothes. She stared back at him and wondered how soon she was going to wake up.

"I'll go," he said stiffly. She nodded, and he turned, closing the door behind him. She dropped everything, the clothes, blankets, and sheets, and stepped away from them. She looked around the room and saw a tall mirror in the corner. She walked over to it.

The underwear was awful. It was like wearing chaps, but she generally had on lingerie, a thong at least. She could get used to it, though. It made her feel sexy, and she did appreciate the easy access. She was getting married tomorrow after all…if she didn't wake up. She fully expected to wake up.

She stopped in front of the mirror and swept the thin shirt—it must be the chemise they always talked about in the books—over her head and dropped it to the floor. She looked down at it, then picked it up and placed it carefully on the bed.

It was so beautifully made, it seemed to command respect. Laundry. Her laundry commanded respect. She untied the pointless underwear— drawers, they called them—and let them fall to the floor next, but she left them there.

She stood in front of the mirror, fully naked, and examined her body. It looked like hers but didn't really feel like hers. It felt like she'd gained weight and was trying to stuff herself into skinny jeans.

She held her arms out and flexed. The tone and definition she was familiar with were gone. Her abdominal muscles were not visible. Her legs were smooth and silky…not carved and strong. This body sat around and did nothing.

She screamed in frustration, then turned toward the door to see if someone came through. Nobody did. Part of her hoped Gray would, because she kind of wanted to do a few things to him at the moment. Stress relief. She thought he would be amenable. Her belly tightened as she thought of his tall, strong form, and she turned back to the mirror. At least some of her parts worked as expected.

Her hands started to shake as she reached up and pulled the pins and combs from her hair, then shook it out. It fell past her waist, the ends curling at her butt. It was a gorgeous head of hair, but her red hair—man, it had been a sight. She was known for that shock of red, and when she entered a room, fully decked out in black leather, everyone took note. *Everyone.*

She'd been powerful, and now she was just a girl. *Fuck.* She needed to wake up. She screamed again until her breath hitched. She considered breaking the mirror, but Francine had been so welcoming… This *had* to be a dream. But if it was her dream, it would be wicked. So why wasn't Gray walking in on her while she was stark naked and screaming?

She stared at the reflection of the door in the mirror. He wasn't coming. She dropped to the floor and brought her knees to her chin, wrapping her arms around them and holding herself together. *What in the hell am I going to do?* For the first time that day—for the first time in what seemed forever—Lulu cried.

FOUR

He will conquer who has learnt the artifice of deviation.
Such is the art of maneuvering.

—Sun Tzu
The Art of War

"Don't you dare move," Francine said.

Grayson looked up at her.

"Grayson." He turned when Rox said his name. "Don't even think about it."

"Think about what?" he asked.

"Moving," Rox replied.

Grayson leaned back in the chair and rubbed his temples with one hand stretched across his eyes. He was mentally exhausted but had no intention of leaving. A second scream reached down from overhead, taking his chest like a vise and squeezing it tighter than his corset ever could.

"Grayson, should we send someone for your valet?" Francine asked. He looked up suddenly, and her eyes widened. "I'm assuming that you'll be staying with us tonight. I assume that you will need your valet to ready for the wedding tomorrow."

"Why would you assume that?"

Francine laughed. "Oh, come on! I dealt with Gideon when he met me. I heard the stories of Perry and how possessive he was as well. I'm not stupid, Grayson. You're staying here, probably watching her sleep, if she'll allow it. Possibly even if she won't," she added quietly.

Grayson was fairly certain he growled.

"Yeah, go ahead and growl. You men don't scare me," she said with a laugh.

Grayson looked at Roxleigh, who only shrugged and walked over to the sideboard. "Brandy?"

"Really?" Grayson responded.

"Fine, whiskey then." Roxleigh flipped two crystal goblets and poured two fingers in each then looked back to Francine.

She shook her head. "No, thank you. One of us has to remain lucid."

"What happens next?" Grayson asked.

Francine turned to him. "Well, I imagine you get married and then you try to get to know your wife. It's not going to be easy, I guarantee, but I'll tell you this—however difficult it is for you, it will be ten times that for her. But she seems to have imprinted on you. She's lost everything, which will be difficult for you to understand…but—"

Grayson turned suddenly and looked directly at her, and she blushed. "Grayson, I'm so sorry. I didn't—"

He waved her off. "I understand what you're saying about the loss. I don't understand imprinting," he said.

"Sorry. What I meant was the way she looks at you. She seems to be drawn to you, and she'll need an anchor, something she can rely on. Trust."

"Will you help?"

"As much as I'm able, but she's chosen you. To be honest, Gideon was my savior and my landline when I ended up here. That he was patient and kind at what was the most terrifying time in my life was…well, it was everything I needed. I couldn't have asked for more, not even for someone who understood where I came from."

Grayson took the glass from Rox and leaned forward on his knees. "Thank you."

"Wives and sweethearts," Roxleigh said, clinking his glass against Grayson's as he looked up. "May they never meet," Rox said quietly with a wink.

"I wasn't in the Navy," Grayson said.

"But I was," Rox said.

"Gideon," Francine warned.

"Apologies, my lady," Rox said as he grinned over the edge of his glass and leaned against his desk.

Grayson downed the contents of his glass, placed it on a side table, and stood. "How long are we to wait?" he asked.

"She's a woman. We wait for as long as she makes us," Roxleigh said.

"Gideon," Francine admonished.

"Yes, my lady." He drank his whiskey and looked to Grayson. "We could go for a ride in the park, take your mind off of her. Supper won't be ready for another three-quarters of an hour. There's plenty of time."

Grayson nodded, and Roxleigh rang for the butler. "Sanders, have Harrison ready Samson and another mount." He paused. "Not Delilah."

"Yes, Your Grace," Sanders said, then turned and left.

"You don't trust Gray with my Delilah?" Francine asked. Roxleigh grinned.

Good god, Grayson needed to get away from these two. They were making him anxious. "I'm going to wait out front," he said, then walked from the room and nearly ran Lulu down because he wasn't paying attention to where he was going. "Damn. My lady—Lulu, I beg your pardon, I didn't…I wasn't watching. I was just—"

"Leaving?"

"Yes. No. Roxleigh and I are going for a ride. The horses are being readied. I just wanted to get away from…them."

She peered behind him at the open door to the study. "Too much cuteness, huh?"

"Cuteness?"

"Yeah, cuteness. I can see it on them. They're one of *those* couples. The cute ones that finish sentences for each other, can't stop touching each other. It's like they're dipped in love with a side of lust. Cuteness. They're genuine, so it's hard to hate them, but it's still a bit much when you feel so alone," she said.

"Would you like to ride?" he asked suddenly.

"I don't, well, I would, but I'm not really sure how I'm going to straddle a horse in this getup." She spread her legs as far as the sheath of fabric would allow to demonstrate, and he nearly lost his wits. She didn't seem to notice. "Plus, it's all white. I'll get filthy."

"Do you care?" he asked.

"No, but the dress isn't mine, and Francine has been so thoughtful—"

"I'll replace it." He looked back through the doorway to the study to see Gideon lean down over Francine to kiss her. "Come." He took Lulu by the hand and pulled her toward the front entry.

Outside, Roxleigh's steed bristled, and Grayson looked to the other horse, a dappled gray hunter nowhere near the size of Samson but broad enough that he could carry the both of them. Grayson walked down the steps as the sun began to descend. He hadn't realized it was getting so late.

"We can't be out long. The sun will set within a half hour," he said. "Raise the stirrups high," he said to the groom. He waited for Harrison to adjust the mount side, then lifted her easily as Harrison rounded the horse to adjust the other. Grayson placed her on the saddle seated sideways, facing him. He loved the feel of her between his hands and had a hard time letting go. His gaze followed her long legs, straight down to her pink toes.

"What?" He took one toe between his fingers and gave it a gentle squeeze.

"Nobody gave me shoes, so..."

"So you wander shoeless like some sort of nymph." Grayson shook the thought of those little pink toes from his head and grabbed the saddle next to her hip, put his foot in the stirrup, and lifted himself over the saddle, standing high up in the stirrups.

"What next?" she asked with a laugh, obviously avoiding looking at his crotch, which happened to be relatively close to her face. God, what a sight that was, this beautiful woman at his cock.

"Give me a second," he said. The groom held the horse steady, and he reached down with his right arm and wrapped it around her waist as he lowered to the saddle, pulling her to his lap. His knees rode higher than normal with the stirrups raised, giving her the perfect seat.

"He'll do fine by you, Your Grace," Harrison said. "He's a steady beast."

"Name?" he asked.

"Reliant, Your Grace," Harrison answered.

Grayson wrapped his arms around her, took the rein, and directed Reliant across the street. As they entered the gates to the park, he heard Roxleigh's laugh follow.

Lulu turned slightly and wrapped one arm over his shoulder and behind his back. She rested her head at the crook of his neck and seemed to relax. "Hi," she said.

"Hello," he replied.

"So…" she said.

"So…" he replied.

She batted at his cravat, then tugged on it. He reached up to stop her, but her breath across the underside of his chin as she hushed him made him stop.

"We're getting married tomorrow," she said as she smoothed the tails of his cravat down his chest.

"That we are," he replied.

"Maaawidge," she said with a giggle. He wasn't sure what to say. "Any regrets?" she asked. "Tell me now or forever hold your whatever."

"Hold my whatever?" he asked.

"Yeah, I'm not picky," she replied. He felt her smile against his neck and was immediately thankful he'd allowed her to loosen the cravat. "You didn't answer. Was that a purposeful deflection?"

This time, he smiled. He couldn't help it. His future wife was quite astute. "It is entirely possible that I was deflecting. Don't take offense. If I have any regrets, they are mine to hold."

"Yeah, me, too," she said. "You realize I still think I'm dreaming, don't you?"

"Well, if this is a dream, what do you want?" he asked.

"You. I want you," she said and skimmed her lips across the underside of his jaw. He jerked away, the contact of her mouth on the sensitive skin a bit of a shock.

"As of tomorrow—" He cleared his throat. "As of tomorrow, you'll have me," he said.

"It appears I have you now," she said. "Will we be going to the altar never having kissed? This is getting frustrating. All of my usual dreams are sex dreams, and we aren't having sex."

He had no response for that. He shifted in his seat, adjusting her. She was bold, and he liked it. A bit too much. He felt her hand on his chest, then it slid to his abdomen before he could stay her. She made a fist and

knocked on his belly, the hollow telltale thump of the boning echoing like a death knell in his head.

"Is that a corset?" she asked. "I mean, I knew men wore corsets in the Victorian era. I just…I guess that gets left out of romance novels because some people think it isn't very sexy on a man."

Grayson tensed. Everywhere. The horse stopped, and he took as deep a breath as he was able as he attempted to relax his muscles.

She lifted her head from his shoulder and looked at him. "I'm sorry, I—I didn't mean anything by it. I just thought it was common since you have one. I—"

"We need to return."

"Gray, I happen to be the type of girl who likes a corset on a man."

"What kind of woman likes a man who wears a corset?" he asked.

"Are *you* judging me now?"

He paused with nothing to say to that. What kind of woman would like a man in a corset? A woman who wants a man of a certain persuasion to take care of her, offer the protection of his name, and leave her be in all other areas. A woman who likes money and doesn't mind what the corset is hiding. Who else would like a man in a corset? Of course, she had no idea why he wore the corset, and she never would, but a woman would not like a man in a corset for the reasons he had for wearing it. That much was certain.

He turned the horse and headed back to the town house.

Lulu was instantly regretful. She should have known better. Known *what* better, exactly? That her dream man would be offended that she knew he wore a corset? Come on, if he wore it for vanity purposes, he would be offended, just as she would have been horrified if he'd seen her Spanx. But he quite obviously did not need this corset for vanity, and if this was her dream, seeing a man go all Dr. Frank-N-Furter would not offend, in fact— *whoa.* She needed to control herself. She clenched her thighs together and shut down the picture show in her head.

Shit. She should have known better. She looked at him, at his chest, at his arms. He didn't have any spare weight on him. He was strong and built well. He was all muscle, and she could tell even through his clothing that his form would be absolutely beautiful, which meant exactly what she'd first thought. He didn't *need* a corset. Which meant he had another purpose for wearing it.

She put her hand on his chest and spoke. "Stop."

He pulled the rein back, his hands meeting her hip, then turned his head and looked into her eyes. He really was incredibly handsome. His face was raw and edged, his beard just starting to show. He was all hard, straight lines and anger. She couldn't just see it. She could feel it, and he'd followed her order. This was getting interesting. "I'm sorry if I offended you. I've had a bit of a rough day, and I fear I may have lost some of my manners."

He didn't speak, only turned and faced forward, closing his eyes. She waited. He let out a breath. She waited some more. She had no idea what BDSM meant to anyone in the Victorian era, if anything at all. She knew some of the history and that there was no organization, per se. There were simply a few groups that got together underground. Very underground. Because BDSM, as she knew it, wasn't born until the latter half of the twentieth century.

If Grayson was a submissive, he might not even know it. If he did know, he might live in shame. If he liked to wear women's clothing, that would be different, but he had reacted to *her*, a *woman*, so even if he was a transvestite, he was straight. There was another possibility, though. If he used the corset as a binding, as a control…

Wow. She needed to wake up in her own bed. This was too much. She might be one of the preeminent and highest-paid Dommes in the twenty-first century, but that wasn't where she was now, dream or no dream.

"Can I ask a favor of you? A wedding gift, perhaps?" she said.

"Whatever you wish, if I can procure it, it's yours."

"I want a perfectly balanced, matched set of hand-braided, leather, single-tail bullwhips," she said.

His brows drew down over his eyes. "I will see to it."

"Thank you."

He continued on to the house and helped her slide to the ground when they stopped at the steps. She felt his eyes on her as she went up to the house, and her skin tightened everywhere. Oh…she was getting off on him tonight, whether he was present or not. She breathed slowly and concentrated so she wouldn't trip on the stairs.

When she reached the landing, she turned and watched as he removed his boots from the stirrups and loosened them, then let the waiting groom finish adjusting them. Gray's movements were stiff and precise. If she wasn't mistaken—and she very rarely was in this area—he would be getting off on her as well, unless… She considered him a moment more. Unless he couldn't without some domination. She wasn't sure what to think of him yet, but was fairly sure they'd moved backward and not forward.

When Francine opened the door, he nodded to them. "I'll return," he grumbled, then he turned the horse and kicked, and they tore across the park.

She turned to Francine. "Well, that was a smashing success!" She threw her hands in the air and pushed past Francine. When the smell of food hit her, she stopped short and pushed her hand into her stomach. "Oh my god, I need protein. Take me to the food." Francine took her hand, wrapped it around her arm, and led her to a massive dining room.

All remaining thoughts of her arousal—and the possibility of Gray's—left her brain when Roxleigh helped her get seated at the table. There was food. So much food. She wanted all of it. She waved her hands and then looked at her host and hostess, trying to keep from being too rude. *Fuck it.* This was her dream.

She pushed back from the table, reached toward the plate of meat, and speared a couple of pieces, dragging them onto her plate. Then she took a big helping of asparagus, a pile of mashed potatoes—she shouldn't have so many carbs—nope, screw it, she wanted it all. She ladled out a pile of spinach and sat back in her chair as she put the plate at her setting. She tried to scoot back in—to no avail—and Roxleigh stood and gave her a push.

"Thank you. Thank you. Oh man, I'm—" That was it. That's all she said. The next thing she knew, her plate was empty, and she was sprawled in her chair, as much as she could be, shoved up against the table as she was. "Oh yeah, I feel better now," she said.

Francine laughed, and she looked across the broad table at her with a grin. "Sorry," she said. "That must have been a sight. I was getting hangry. Couldn't be helped."

"Hangry?" Francine asked. "That must be a new one. I don't remember that term."

"Yeah, popularized by the clean-eating crowd. You know, physique competitors, lifters, body jocks? You eat clean, you eat often, and if you don't, you get hangry." She giggled. She patted her belly. "Thank you for dinner. It really was wonderful."

"I wanted it to be good. The first meal I had here was…well. Gideon blamed it on the chef being away."

"Which she was," Roxleigh said.

"We've since trained a sous-chef just to be sure it doesn't happen to any other unsuspecting guests."

"I see. Lovely. Truly, that was a fantastic steak, just the right temperature, just the right pink."

"Well, I took a guess. That's a Colorado thing. Grill them quickly and serve them hot and juicy."

"Oh yeah," Lulu agreed. "Good to know I'll be able to eat here. My romance novels always talk about the weird food. Sheep's eyeballs and the like."

"You should give them a chance," Roxleigh said. She winced, and Francine made a face.

"Just as soon as you try Rocky Mountain oysters," Lulu said, and Francine laughed. Lulu looked at Roxleigh in time to see his entire face light up at the sound of her. Damn if the two of them weren't mesmerizing, truly. She really hated cutesy couples, but these two were incredible together. "Well," she said, patting her full belly. "I should walk off some of this food baby I have gestating here. That was about twice the amount of food I usually eat, and apparently I have a wedding dress to squeeze into tomorrow," Lulu said.

"Would you like company?" Francine asked.

"No, that's okay. Just point me in the direction of the gardens. You have gardens, right?"

Francine smiled. "Of course. Out the door to the right, then follow the hall to the back of the house. That's the ballroom. It looks out over the gardens. Any of the doors will let you out."

Lulu stood, and they both followed. "Thank you. Really, this is the best I've felt all day."

"If you need anything, just yell," Francine said with a smile.

Lulu nodded and left them behind. After she traversed what must have been the biggest ballroom in a private residence in the history of the world, the gardens were a crisp, welcome feeling. It was a bit brisk outside, so she walked swiftly and warmed up soon enough. She caught sight of a path just off the terrace that bordered the line of French doors and headed toward it.

This had been...wow. She wasn't sure what to think of today. This morning—no, wait, that had been an evening session at the club. She had been painting Oliver with his wings. She flexed her arms and stretched. If she was stuck here, she would need to work to get her muscle tone back. She felt so weak. Maybe it was just the concussion, but no, she'd seen this body, and it wasn't hers. She knew her body. She knew what it could do.

She picked up her skirts and bolted down the lane as fast as she could, but after only a few yards, she was winded. She stopped and rested her hands on her knees, breathing hard.

"Fuck fucking fuckall!" she yelled. "This isn't me. This isn't my body, this isn't my life, this isn't happening!" she screamed. She shook her head, then stood and was immediately dizzy. "Shit."

She looked to one of the benches that lined the path and wobbled over to it, then stretched out on her back, her knees up and her hands on her belly. She stared at the starless sky and wept. "This can't be happening." She pressed her palms into her belly and breathed. In through her nose, out through her mouth. Repeat.

Her breathing slowed along with her thundering heart rate, and she relaxed slowly. Her side cramped. She shouldn't have run so soon after eating a huge meal anyway. Run—she wouldn't call that a run. She wouldn't even call that a sprint. She needed to work on her stamina, her recovery time, her everything. If she woke up here tomorrow, the first thing she would do is find some workout gear. She was going to hit it hard. Right after...right after she got married.

"Hello."

Speak of the devil.

She opened her eyes and sat up, her arm propped on the bench to steady herself. "They told me you were out here. I can go back inside if you don't want company." He stopped several feet from her, his strong legs brighter than the rest of him because of the lights bordering the path, his face in deep shadow.

"No, it's fine. I was just…testing my limits. They seem to have decreased a fair amount since I—oh, whatever." She dropped her head into her hands. "What the actual fuck?" she grumbled. She felt the heat of his body against her side as he sat next to her on the stone bench.

"You seem to like that word," he said.

She looked up at him. "Fuck? Yes. Fuck happens to be one of my favorite words. In all of its varied uses. Noun, verb, exclamation, adverb, all of it. Everything about it. Cock, too. Get used to that one as well. That's probably my second-favorite word. Cock is. Particularly since it's one of my favorite *things* as well."

"I assume you aren't referring to a chicken."

"Nope, not a chicken. Rooster, actually. You know exactly what I'm referring to."

"I do." They sat in a peaceable silence for a while as he seemed to wrestle with something in his head. Then he said, "I find your mouth fascinating."

"Do you? You should explore it some more. How hard is it to get a man to touch you around here anyway? I've been throwing myself at you since the moment I first saw you. I think." She rubbed her temple. The headache was back. She shouldn't have run like that, like an idiot. But she was still operating off the tenet that this was a dream, so…

"You have been. I recall something about…well, yes, I believe you have. Can I ask you something about that?" Gray looked away from her, off into the gardens.

"You can ask me anything. But, as they say, I reserve the right to *not* answer you."

He nodded. "What was your profession? Judging solely by your mouth…"

"Ah, yeah. I'm not a sailor or a hooker, if that's what you're getting at."

"A…hooker?"

"Yeah, prostitute? Working woman? Slut? Okay, maybe I was a bit of a slut, but I was a safe slut. Safe, sane, and consensual. Those are the standard rules—SSC. Or RACK, risk-aware consensual…*kink*." She looked at him from the corner of her eye as he stared at her. She'd thought maybe the word "kink" would get a response of some sort, but he didn't even flinch. She took a deep breath. "I'm not a prostitute, no," she said finally.

He nodded. "I hope someday you'll trust me enough to tell me of your life."

"Someday…it seems we have plenty of time for that. I reserve the right to wake up from this dream back in my little hovel tomorrow, though." She missed her hovel already. Most people laughed the first time they saw it, for while she referred to it as a hovel, it was pretty far from being an actual hovel.

She sighed and turned to him. "Please, would you kiss me? I'm just… not myself, and if there's one thing that could possibly bring me back—I just…I mean, we're getting married tomorrow, and we haven't even kissed." She was whining and hated the sound of it, but she didn't turn away, or take it back.

She waited.

He looked at her. This must be what it felt like to be a book, because she was pretty sure he was reading her. Flipping through her pages and trying to find all her hidden secrets, or possibly trying to edit out bits. All he actually had to do was ask. Well, no, he *had* actually asked, and she'd dodged the question, but *I beat the shit out of people for a living* seemed a bit too forward at the moment.

She looked away suddenly, but his hand caught her face and turned her back to him. She melted under his direct look. *Please, oh, please.* Did she just whimper? Oh my god, she had, hadn't she? His irises flared, and he leaned closer.

FIVE

There are not more than five primary colors
[blue, yellow, red, white, black]
yet in combination they produce more hues than can ever be seen.

—Sun Tzu
The Art of War

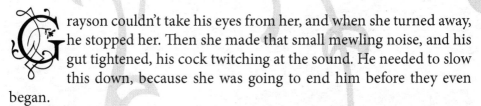rayson couldn't take his eyes from her, and when she turned away, he stopped her. Then she made that small mewling noise, and his gut tightened, his cock twitching at the sound. He needed to slow this down, because she was going to end him before they even began.

She closed her eyes as he leaned in, skimming his hand across her cheek and sinking it into the hair at the nape of her neck. Then he fisted it, held on to it, kept her exactly where he wanted her. He could not relinquish control to her, or he would lose his mind, because while his cock might twitch, that was all it was bound to do, and he couldn't let her discover that.

She lifted her hands. "Don't," he said simply. He brought her closer, and his tongue came out like a sentinel, testing, and he flicked her lips. She opened to him readily, and he covered her mouth with his, his tongue exploring, his lips teasing hers.

He felt her hands hovering around his shoulders, as though she were afraid to touch him, and he spoke against her mouth. "My shoulders. You may touch my shoulders." Then he sucked her lower lip into his mouth. She didn't hesitate, and she didn't merely touch him either. She fisted his coat in her hands and held on to him as hard as he was holding on to her. His other arm went around her waist, and he pulled her tight against his body before he could stop himself.

She was like no woman he'd ever met. She was forward, brazen, powerful...alive. The next thing he knew, she was straddling his lap, completely open to him, her hands still pulling, her tongue fighting his in the most intimate dance he'd ever had with a woman. She spoke against him, the words vibrating across his tongue. "God, yes, please. I need...I need to feel something I know to be real."

He needed to catch his breath. *He* needed...*he* needed to stop this.

"I'm so wet. Touch me. See how much I want this right now, how much I want you."

Every muscle from his fingers through his shoulders tensed, and he pulled her head away from him, looking into her eyes.

"Too much?" she asked timidly. "You just—"

"Hush." He cut her off gruffly, then considered her. Her face was flushed, her eyes bright, her breathing hard, her breasts full, and her nipples tight against the dress she wore. He released her waist, but not her hair. They were to be married tomorrow. It wasn't as if he would be stealing something not already his. Except that she wasn't his, had never been his. She was someone else entirely, and that much was patently obvious in the way she behaved.

No woman of his age would behave this way, not even a prostitute. She spoke of *her* needs, *her* wants, not *his*, not *him*. She was here for herself, and he wanted to be here for that same reason. He would simply... He reached between them and pressed one finger to her, and she was...

"Ohhh," he groaned. She was so wet for him. His head fell forward against her chest and he just breathed of her, then he looked back up.

She didn't move, only contemplated his face as he explored her slowly. His fingers gentle, his thumb on her clitoris, he slid through her wet folds, and oh, she felt good, so good, like coming home. His breath caught as the heady scent of her arousal built he did feel a modicum of interest from his penis, not nearly enough for what she had in mind, however.

Her hips tilted toward him ever so slightly, and her eyes went black. She was panting, her breath coming heavy and wanting, and he closed his eyes and concentrated on the slippery feel of her against his fingers. She didn't move, just allowed him to do whatever he wished. He wondered about her, that this body was Cecilia's, and if so... He skimmed her opening, then tested her gently with one finger. She cried out as she tensed.

She was yet a virgin.

He looked up to her, then released her entirely.

"I hurt you."

"Yeah, a bit. Were you checking? Did you know?" she asked quietly.

"I had a feeling."

Her face was tense and shocked. "Yeah, that hurt! What the fuck? What is it with virgins? Goddammit!" Her hands tensed on his shoulders then released him. "You're an ass. I just can't even." She dropped her head to his shoulder.

"Not what you expected?" he asked.

"Are you referring to yourself or to my virginity?" she asked as her head popped back up into his line of sight.

He looked away for a moment, sufficiently shamed. "I apologize. You invited, and it seemed the most expedient way to answer a question you had not yet asked."

"No, I hadn't. Why would I? I've been sexually active since I was sixteen. I was…I had been…I—" She grabbed his shoulders again, then reared up on her knees and screamed to the heavens as he wrapped his arms around her and held on.

"I'm sorry." It was all he could say, but he allowed her to scream, even as it did concern him for several reasons. But Roxleigh's property was secure, nobody outside the gates would know where the yelling came from, and if they did figure it out…well, he simply didn't give a damn. That piece of him, that separation in his belly, it shifted again as he thought of that small piece of membrane that, when he breached it, would make her his and his alone. Regardless of the experience she believed she had, this body had none, and he wanted her, even as he knew he couldn't complete the task.

She seemed to be finished, her chest heaving as she breathed, and he looked up, his chin on her belly. She was something, this strange woman. And she *was* his, and he would never let her go. Whatever she'd been in her past life, it didn't matter now. She was starting over.

With him.

It seemed, rather suddenly and terrifyingly, a great and awful responsibility. Unfair to her, at the very least. A woman this special should be trusted to a man who could give her whatever she wanted, however she wanted it. She should have life served to her on a platter, with many choices. He was…not available to her in all the ways he knew she would expect.

He ran his hands up her rib cage and held on as she sank back to his lap. He saw tears streaking her cheeks and he felt a despair he never had before. "I'm sorry," she whispered. "I'm sorry."

"Don't be. I understand, actually."

"Do you?" She lifted one hand and straightened his cravat, smoothed the fabric of his jacket across his shoulders. She seemed to need to keep moving. She started messing with his lapels, and he allowed it for the moment.

"I think I do. I may have more experience with loss than you know." He considered how much he could tell her. Nobody knew where he'd been, save the queen. Nobody knew what he'd done, period. "When they—" He stopped. That was too much. He couldn't tell her why. Perhaps someday, but not right now. She waited patiently. He'd already given too much control to her. Touched her in ways he should never have touched her.

He felt her small hands release his coat and skim up to his neck, wrapping around his throat as her thumbs skimmed his jaw. Her cool fingers calmed his blood. Quieted his mind. All he wanted was to share everything with her. She was so dangerous.

She held his gaze, something nobody did. Ever. She didn't threaten or hurry. She just waited for him, and it felt as though she would wait for as long as he needed, even if that went beyond tonight. So he spoke.

"When I left London, I lost my family. Everything I'd ever known. I lost the entire world as I knew it, and I never expected to return, never wanted to, in fact. I suppose that's where we differ, in that you do want to return home, wherever or whenever that is." That one thing saddened him suddenly.

She continued to examine him, her expression still open. "So you do understand. At least somewhat. Except for the whole part about it being a choice."

"Well, I later lost my family in earnest. There's a difference between not wanting to see them again and not being able to. I know that as well, keenly." But he would never admit to missing any of them. It was a feeling even he didn't understand, it was a desperate want for them to be alive so they could turn around, apologize, welcome him.

"You still have family," she said.

"I do. I lost my father, my brothers," he said.

"You never wanted this title. It's why you refuse the name."

Grayson didn't move, and she dropped her hands and looked away. Then she stood, and his lap was instantly chilled from the loss of her heat. "I'm so exhausted," she said.

"It has been a long day, and you do have an injury yet," he said as he stood. "Tomorrow will be…more so."

"Yeah." She started to sing. "Going to the chapel, and I'm…" She took a breath, and her voice fell. "Yeah." She turned toward the house, and he followed, her sorrow palpable. He reached out to her, turning her once more.

"You don't have to marry me. I know what we said, but I want you to know that I would protect you regardless."

She looked in his eyes, did the whole crawling around in his depths thing again, then said, "Nope, I'm marrying you. Done deal. I'm not a wuss. I can do this, if only to get rid of my virginity." She laughed. "Again. Why? What aren't you telling me?" She turned fully toward him and waited, her hands clasped in front of her.

"Nothing, I—well, there is something, actually. My title is destitute. The properties have outrun the coffers, the contract for your hand will replenish them, take care of the immediate distress and then some. Your dowry would. Your money."

"It's not truly my money, though, now is it? I know how this works. If I refuse you, it goes to the next man who offers and succeeds, so why should I care about it?"

He nodded. "I will ensure that you have control of how your money is used."

She took a deep breath and reached out to take his hand. For now, at least, this was her reality. "Thank you. I may hate numbers, but I'm actually really good with them, so I very much appreciate that. I happen to know that's not how things are done here. Neither one of us really wants this marriage for the right reasons, only the wrong ones. But I think…I think if we work together, we can make it work.

"Look, I'm not like the other girls. I hold no delusions of grandeur and one true love. I like friends. They're the most important thing in life, and I like sex and the pleasure it brings. I like a few other things. As long as we can come to some agreements, I think we'll be happy enough." She turned back for the house. "Yep, tomorrow I'll be a married woman, and I am getting laid." He tensed, and she looked back at him, stopping them both again. "I am getting laid, right?"

She looked concerned, and he could only surmise that she meant that he would take her maidenhead. He shifted, uncomfortably, and she grinned. "Oh yeah. I'm getting laid." She winked, then turned and pulled him along toward the house.

This was all… Perhaps he should stay at his own house tonight.

They entered the guest suite, and she started to undo her dress, so he stopped her, covering her hands with his.

"I don't think you should be alone tonight," he said gently.

"Is that an offer? Because I really don't think I could handle you backing off again. Please be sure what you mean. Because I don't actually want to be alone tonight." She tried to shrug off his hands, but he stopped her.

"You have a concussion. Someone needs to watch over you as you sleep," he said.

"Oh, yeah. *That*. I—will you watch over me?"

He thought about it for a moment, actually considered it, but he knew they both needed sleep, and if he were close to her, they wouldn't be doing that. "I will have someone stay with you."

"All right, then. I think we're in perfect agreement," she said, and her whole body deflated.

He took one hand and squeezed it. Then left. He found Gideon and Francine in the parlor, Francine's naked feet in his lap as they sat at opposite ends of a settee, sipping brandy. He cleared his throat to get their attention.

"Someone should watch over her."

Francine looked up. "You mean, you won't be keeping watch over her?" she asked.

He must have scowled, because Gideon took her hand and gave it a squeeze, moving her feet to the settee next to him as he stood.

"Give us a moment," he said.

Grayson followed him to his study. "I beg pardon, Warrick."

"Grayson."

"Grayson, Francine is still sometimes more forward than she ought to be."

"I understand, now, having spent time with Lulu. I—god, I don't know how to manage her."

"You can't manage her. You can only steer her in the right direction and hope. Apparently, the future is full of women like this."

Grayson shuddered, and Roxleigh laughed. "It's not so bad. I don't think you...well, I know I wasn't interested in some trained, simpering miss," he said. "Look, you've had a difficult year. I can't even imagine what you've been through. Five years, I guess. I mean...well. Then this? Perhaps the wedding should be delayed. Perhaps you need to take some time and think this through," Roxleigh said.

"I can't. I promised her, and I've given her ample chance to step aside. She wants this wedding, and so does the queen."

"I don't think she knows what she wants," Rox said.

"The queen?"

Roxleigh laughed. "Well, you may be correct there, but I was actually referring to Lulu."

"I think she knows exactly what she wants, but the circumstances are not what she's counting on. She's in for a rude awakening, and she'll need someone to trust even more when that happens."

"I suppose. But what if she changes her mind when she realizes she's here to stay?"

"I'll see to her." Grayson said and it wasn't merely a promise, but a vow. She was his, he would care for her no matter what happened. He shook his head. "How is anyone supposed to make any decisions about anything under these circumstances? It's maddening. Are women just going to continue to fall from the sky?"

"Well, she didn't exactly fall from the sky."

"No, she fell to the floor when I tackled her."

Roxleigh laughed again. "At least you didn't nearly trample her with a team of horses," he said.

Was this somehow their fault? But what was the alternative? "No, she was nearly burned to death. Those dresses are death traps. It's ridiculous," Grayson said.

"Agreed."

"You will have someone in the household watch over her?" Grayson asked. "Just for tonight?"

Roxleigh nodded. "Mrs. Weston traveled with us to London because she wanted to see her new grandbaby. She'll keep an eye on her. I would trust her with my life—I *have* trusted her with my life," Roxleigh said. "Are you returning to your own house, or…"

"I—have her things arrived? My valet?" he asked.

"Ah, yes, while you were out in the gardens. I suppose you didn't see the trunks in her rooms."

"I wasn't really looking," he said. "I'll stay. No need dragging Rakshan back to my house tonight."

"You're in the room next to hers. Don't give Mrs. Weston an apoplexy. I want her around for a good long while." Roxleigh stared at him.

"No, I'll be sure to…*not* do that." Grayson turned to leave.

"Grayson," Roxleigh said.

He turned back. "Yes?"

"This is the longest conversation we've had since you returned."

He dropped his hand from the door. Roxleigh looked both concerned and happy and Grayson appreciated that even as it made him nervous. "Yes."

Roxleigh nodded. "If you need anything."

"Thank you," he said, then left.

Lulu stared at her reflection as she listened to the maids fill the tub in the adjoining bath, then the door opened and a small, stout woman entered with a huge grin on her face. "Well, well, miss. I hear you're special in the way my Lady Francine is special. I'm here to see to you, and should you have any questions, please ask."

Lulu turned to her and smiled, and she couldn't help but be genuine. The woman was adorable. "Call me Lulu," she said.

"Miss Lulu. We've got a warm bath going. Doesn't that sound lovely? A warm bath will fix just about anything that ails you," she said. "I think Francine was in the water more than out of it when she first came to us." The woman smiled at her memories.

"And…what should I call you?" Lulu asked.

"Oh! Goodness me, I'm Mrs. Weston," she said as she stopped in front of her.

Lulu laughed. "Hi." She stood and started to pull the dress over her head, but Mrs. Weston shooed her hands away and turned her around to undo the buttons. She whisked it off, leaving the chemise, but Lulu pulled it off as well.

Mrs. Weston pushed her gently toward the washroom. "Goodness, you're not a shy one, are you?" she said. "Francine was terrible shy when she came to us."

"Was she? Yeah, I'm not. At all," Lulu replied. "I find no use for shyness."

"Francine hated when I dressed and undressed her. Nowadays, Gideon does it. He's such a possessive sort, and he's had practice."

Lulu laughed. "That sounds very sweet. I've actually learned how to get myself into and out of a corset without help. It's a talent that takes practice as well." She stretched her arms over her head as she sank into the warm water. "Though I'm not as flexible as I once was," she said before disappearing beneath the surface of the water. She stayed there, blinking up at the world from under the water, letting the air bubbles release slowly. Before she popped up again.

"You were nearly drowned," Mrs. Weston said with a curious gaze.

"Oh no, I can hold my breath for quite some time. That was actually short. It's just something else that takes practice and…well, it looks like I'm out of practice in this area as well." Lulu poked at a bubble on the surface of the water. "I don't really know what to think of all this, you know."

Mrs. Weston quit fussing with the stacks of towels and other things shelved in the room and turned to her. "I must say I wasn't sure what to think of Lady Francine when she first came to us, either."

"I still think I'm dreaming, you know." Lulu paused and thought of everything she'd said and done. "Oh god, if I'm not truly dreaming, Gray will think I'm…" She shook her head. "Yeah, wow, he has every reason to believe I'm no more than a street-walking prostitute." She scooted back in the tub, then put her arms across her knees and lowered her head. "I can't believe… I don't know what to believe. If I'm still here tomorrow, I'll be getting married. To a stranger."

"Well, that's not beyond the ordinary, here. As it happens."

"No, it may not be, but it is where I'm from. Living in sin is much more common than marrying strangers. I think I would prefer it. Actually, I wouldn't even want to do that. I would prefer what I have—my own home, my own space, a warm bedroom, an open living space and kitchen area, a good-sized darkroom for printing."

"You're a photographer, then?" Mrs. Weston asked.

"Yes, I…I'm an artist with many tools. Photography happens to be one of them."

"Grayson has a large house to fill. No doubt he could give you rooms to use for your photography," she said.

Lulu looked up to her. "Tell me about him?" she asked.

"He…was a lovely boy. Grayson and Gideon were close in age, and they were often together when young. Funny thing about being young, you can escape most of the troubles that happen around you. You just don't see it, and then you run off to play in the forest or…wherever. He and Gideon didn't stay close once Gideon began his training to take over the dukedom.

"Grayson's father, The Warrick, didn't have time for him because he had two older sons to train up, one of whom would be duke. He needed the most attention, of course."

Mrs. Weston sat on a small stool in the corner, then continued. "Grayson was distant from the rest. That's really all I can remember from when he visited Eildon last. We hardly saw him, really. He was off doing the things children did while the other boys were busy being trained up. Then he came of age, and he left," she finished.

"Where did he go?"

Mrs. Weston stood and pulled a bar of soap from a shelf, then got her hands wet in the tub and began to lather Lulu's hair. "He went to India, though none of us knew that at the time. The family was told he had taken employment outside of England. That was it. We didn't see him again until Her Royal Highness sent for him. His mother and Lady Poppy are the only immediate family he has left."

"What happened to his father and brothers?"

"Their carriage was attacked by highwaymen. There were rumors about the intent of the men, but Gideon quashed them to protect the family. The duke and his eldest sons were killed. Grayson was recalled to London. That was two years ago. Even still we rarely see him." That was a lot to take in, how horrible to lose so much family at once, even if they were estranged.

"He's solitary?"

"Yes, he doesn't come to the family gatherings, doesn't involve himself in society. He only just quit his bachelor rooms and reopened Warrick Place this week to have somewhere for his bride to live. For you to live."

"Only this week? Roxleigh mentioned he still needs servants."

"When he first returned, he pensioned as many as possible and closed Warrick Place. He's taken care of his mother and sister, keeping them from London mostly to protect them from the rumors surrounding his father's death."

Lulu didn't bother with rumors, in her life rumors were death if they took any precedent, so she ignored them all in favor of facts. "So he's an honorable man?"

"Absolutely, and he holds family above all else, even if he doesn't see them. When Perry needed help, he didn't hesitate. Perry said Grayson was absolutely necessary."

"Who is Perry?"

"Peregrine Trumbull, he is brother to Roxleigh and a viscount his own right."

Lulu nodded, "How was Grayson necessary?"

Mrs. Weston paused before continuing. "Perry said Grayson knew much more than any of them in certain areas."

"Areas?" Lulu asked.

"I…"

Lulu looked up, and Mrs. Weston shook her head a bit, then helped her rinse her hair in the water. "I shouldn't, but everything this family has been through… Please understand, I don't know the man well. All I know is, he is the same as Gideon. He's strong, brave, and honorable. You can trust him. He's more a Trumbull than a Danforth. Why he is the way he is and what that is exactly? I cannot tell you. I can only tell you I would trust him with my life should I ever have need to, even as he terrifies me."

It all sounded so nefarious. The disappearing cousin returns to save the family. So very…James Bond. "Did he leave for a job? Perhaps to spy for the crown?"

Mrs. Weston giggled. "Oh, miss, don't let your imaginings get the best of you. He was gone and missing, but I'm sure if he were that important to Her Majesty, we would have heard about something. Gideon would know at least, certainly."

Lulu shrugged and took the bar of soap when Mrs. Weston handed it to her. She washed herself, breathing deeply of the lavender and lemon scent of the soap.

"Now, Miss Lulu, feeling better?" Mrs. Weston asked.

"Yes. I suppose as good as to be expected for a time traveler with a concussion."

Mrs. Weston pulled a towel from the shelf and held it up for her. She rose and stepped into it, letting Mrs. Weston wrap it around her and dry her off. She trembled, remembering how Gray had wrapped her up in the blankets—so carefully. Mrs. Weston wrapped up all that long hair and piled it in another towel on her head, then led her back to her room.

"Would it be possible to speak with Gray tonight?" Lulu asked.

"I believe so, if he's not already abed. He's in the adjacent suite," Mrs. Weston said. "Let's get you dressed, and I'll have his valet let him know." Mrs. Weston put her at the dressing table and brushed out her hair, then braided it. Then Mrs. Weston pulled a long, white nightgown from the wardrobe.

It was simple and soft, covered in delicate pin tucks, with the fitted bodice and the long, flowing skirts at the back. The cotton was warm and comforting against her skin, and she sighed into it as Mrs. Weston adjusted it. "Fits well," she said with a smile. "I'll go find Rakshan, and I'll be back."

Lulu walked over to the cheval mirror in the corner and looked at herself. No makeup, no leather, no latex. No weapons. No toys. No buckles, no crops, no nothing.

Just a woman in a long cotton nightgown that covered her, neck to toe, her hair braided simply, her cheeks flushed—she looked innocent. She imagined she hadn't looked this innocent since she'd been a small child, and even then she usually had a mischievous grin.

Her pulse thrummed at her wrists as she was suddenly overwhelmed.

"Hello." His voice was so low it didn't even startle her.

"Hi." She smiled into the mirror. "I wasn't expecting you."

"You…I thought that…I mean, Mrs. Weston said—"

Lulu turned around, but didn't approach him. He still had on his pants and boots, but his shirt was loose, and his jacket and vest were gone. His hair was a mess, tossed around his ears, and she wanted to fist it and hold him still while she found out just how beautiful his body was. Her mouth went dry, and she cleared her throat.

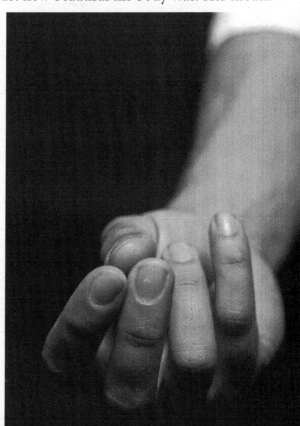

"I meant that I thought she would return, and then I would be taken to some neutral location wherein I would wait for your official arrival, perhaps with a cup of tea. Then a butler or some such would come and open the door and announce you formally, and then we'd be allowed to talk. With a chaperone, of course."

He smiled slightly, and it warmed her to her toes. "Well, it seems we've already surpassed the need for a chaperone," he said, then

he looked down, and the fingers of his right hand, the fingers that had explored her most intimate flesh, rubbed together as if to remember…and her breath stopped. She knew what those fingers remembered, and her nipples hardened easily in response to him, yet again. She felt naked.

She pinched the bridge of her nose and grinned to herself, then she felt his hand on her arm. "You did that on purpose," she said quietly.

"I did. I beg your pardon, I just…find your reactions to me fascinating. I was hoping, though, that something magnificently irreverent would come from your mouth."

"Well, fuck me," she said.

"If only," he replied.

"And why the hell not?"

He pulled her against him, wrapping the steel bands of his muscles around her waist as he kissed her, and she wrapped her arms up around his head and held on. He lifted, and she tangled her legs in the skirt of her nightgown, attempting to get them around his waist until she was laughing so hard he set her back on her feet and let go.

"Damn," she said. "If it's not one thing, it's another."

"Did you have a reason for asking for me again tonight?" he asked quietly.

"Your vocabulary has expanded somewhat. That was a full, polite sentence," she said.

"I figured you deserved as much from me as I could give."

"Speaking of that…"

"Yes?"

"Mrs. Weston said—"

"Mrs. Weston?"

"Yes, and before you get your tail feathers ruffled, she adores you and thinks I should trust you…with my life."

"Does she now?" He stared at the toe of his boot as he rearranged the nap of the Aubusson carpet they stood on.

"She does."

"So what did she say?"

"She said you have a large house and may have some rooms I can use for my photography."

"You're a photographer?"

"I was, yes, yesterday. It kills me that I can't remember what happened last. I know I'd finished Oliver's wings…but that's all I know. I—"

"Don't force it. Hopefully, it will come back to you." He took her hand and skimmed one thumb across the back. She wasn't familiar with being touched in such a manner, so sweetly, so reassuringly, so…endearingly.

"Thank you," she said finally.

"Are you a painter or sculptor as well?" he asked.

"Am I—why?" she asked.

"You mentioned finishing Oliver's wings. We'll skip over the fact there's a man's name there to make me jealous and on to the fact of the wings. Did you mold them? Carve them? Paint them?" he asked.

"Oh… I made them. I—I suppose I painted them, of a fashion. I'm a visual artist and work in many different mediums," she said.

"There's more to this."

"Yes. But I…hesitate to share it with you."

"Perhaps in future?"

"I desperately hope so. I feel as though I may be able to explain more but…just not right now." She wasn't bound to ruin what they had if it was to be gone at any moment, perhaps she would never have need to explain herself to this man. The thought was distressing, she wanted to know him long enough to have to explain.

"I understand," he said but she could see the disappointment in the shuffle of his feet. . "Was that all you needed from me, then?"

"I—" She paused. He was so incredibly good at evasion that even she didn't catch him most of the time. "Did you give me an answer?" she asked, and he laughed silently.

"My answer to you will always be yes, if I am able," he replied.

"It shouldn't be," she said. His eyes narrowed on her, and she turned away suddenly. "I only mean that we don't know each other that well."

"No, we don't, not yet, but we will. We have the balance of our lives to get to know each other. My answer for you will always be yes, regardless the question." His eyes caught hers in the mirror and held her there.

She shook her head. That was entirely too much of a gift from him. "I can't ask that of you." He seemed quite determined in the fact that she was here to stay.

"You never had to. Now, it's late, and we both need rest. Is there anything more I can do for you tonight?"

She turned to him with a wicked grin, and he smiled.

"You will be the end of me, my lady. I will see you on the morrow for our wedding. Until then, I hope you sleep well and dream of me." He sounded so hopeful that it tore at her heart.

"But I already am," she said as she attempted a smile and his faded. She suddenly realized that there was a part of her that hoped this was no dream. This man before her? He was worth losing everything for. She wasn't sure how she knew that…but deep inside she did.

He nodded and turned, leaving her standing there in the gaslight. Alone. It wasn't long before Mrs. Weston came back in and got her settled in bed. She didn't fight. She had none left for the moment, and sleep…or waking…or whatever happened when her head met this pillow seemed like a good place to try to start over.

Her heart ached for him, and she was afraid to go to sleep, just as much as she was afraid to stay awake. She turned on her side, away from Mrs. Weston, and let the tears soak her pillow as she drifted off.

SIX

Hold out baits to entice the enemy.
Feign disorder and crush him.
If he is secure at all points, be prepared for him.
If he is superior in strength, evade him.

—Sun Tzu
The Art of War

Grayson had gone into her room and teased her purposely, and it had been so easy, so inappropriate, and he had enjoyed it. He had actually taken pleasure in teasing her, and it was shocking to him how much and how naturally it had come. But he should never have done it, because there was no way he could follow through.

A tease was all he was.

Grayson turned and finished undressing. He'd dismissed his valet for the night when Mrs. Weston had come in search of him, so when he returned to his suite, he removed what remained of his clothing and tossed it across a chair.

He walked to the mirror in the corner and looked at the pressure marks that were already fading from his abdomen and sides. He had a few bruises over his ribs, and he knew they would be a stronger color the next day. As well, they would hurt beneath his corset—should he wear it.

While he actually welcomed that pain most days, he briefly considered not wearing the corset for his wedding, but he didn't know if that was a good idea. The pain kept him grounded, the binding kept him from fleeing. The reality of the corset was that it helped him be here, now, while his soul and his spirit wished to be somewhere else entirely.

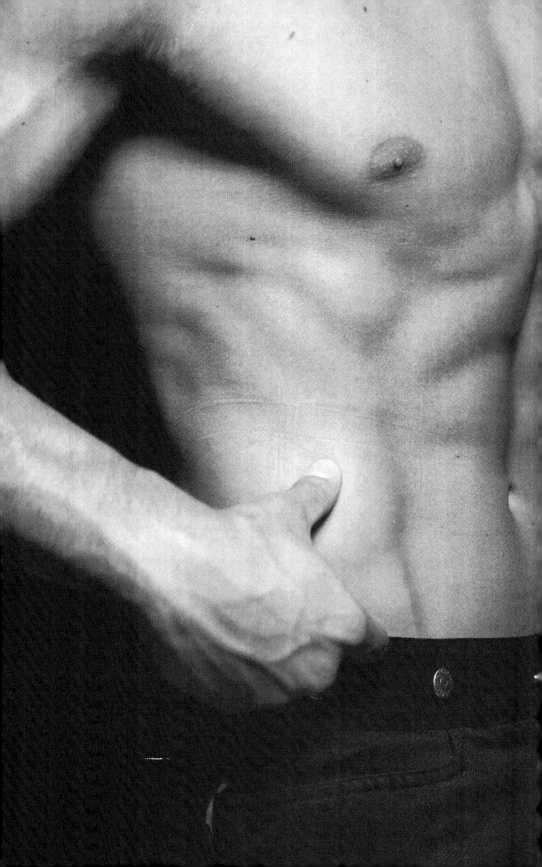

He would be seeing the entirety of his remaining family on the morrow, something that rarely happened. They all got together often, but he wasn't much for the gatherings. He could handle only so many of them at once, but for this, his wedding, he was certainly a requirement as much as his family would be.

And, oh, the fanfare they had planned for this. He scrubbed his hands across his face then through his hair as he turned. This woman, this day, this…was entirely beyond anything he'd ever wanted or expected.

Tomorrow he would be husband to a stranger, and from what he understood of Francine, Lulu would expect to be an intricate part of his life. She wasn't a trained wife. He wouldn't be able to put her in her place and leave her there, pulling her out only when necessary, like a trinket. Not that he'd intended to do so with Cecilia, only that with her proper training it was something that wouldn't have shocked her.

He was lying to himself if he believed that, that he had fully intended to put her in her place and leave her be. But that he had actually considered that to be a possibility before now shamed him. He sat on his bed and leaned on his knees.

He'd wanted to be an honorable husband as much as he could be. He'd thought the best way for him to do that would be to keep Lady Cecilia away from him, because he never expected Lady Cecilia to accept him for what he was, but *this* woman… There was something about the way she looked into him that demanded he strip bare and show her all of his scars, explain how they came about and why they were each one so important to him.

He didn't spend much time around his family, but he had spent some time with Perry and Gideon over the past couple of years. They didn't mind his brooding silence and accepted him however he was able to be there, which made his visits manageable at least, and that kept his family at bay. That at least he was making appearances somewhere was acceptable to them.

The men also never made excuses for him. If they were at a function and someone remarked on his silence on a topic, both Rox and Perry would simply stare at the offender as though they were the one at odds in the moment. For him, they were.

Primarily, though, they talked of their wives, of their impossible, unexpected love for their women. Grayson simply had no cause to hope, because he could see that at the very base of both of their marriages was an unerring trust, and trust like that wasn't something Grayson had to give. He hadn't trusted anyone in a very long time and wasn't sure he ever could again.

He rolled back, into his bed, and tangled himself in his sheets. As he closed his eyes, he thought of hers, so warm and demanding. So open and true. He'd never seen eyes like hers and could spend hours searching them, learning the pattern of each iris and casting it to his memory.

Grayson wanted to hit his knees every time she narrowed her eyes on him, and it felt like freedom. He'd never felt that under any gaze in his life, and it shocked him, even as he was sure she'd no idea what she did.

She was an artist, surely a pacifist, as most artists of his acquaintance. The violence he imagined, as usual, was all his own. He understood that to his core. She was so different from him. He was a man of function and physicality, not art and emotion. He imagined all the things her eyes had seen—all things he wanted to know.

He thought about their stolen time in the gardens, and his cock thickened. Something rare for him without a different sort of physical precursor. She'd followed his instruction and done only as requested, touched him only as he permitted, but what if he gave her leave? What would she do to him?

He adjusted himself against the sheets, and he hoped, oh, how he hoped, she could get him hard enough to complete the act. But that was only hope.

He rolled to his belly and breathed deeply. He wouldn't…couldn't manage himself, and he wasn't prepared to here and now. He wasn't home, and he would never be home again. He closed his eyes and breathed slower, trying to think of anything he could other than her. As his erection waned, he fell asleep.

Lulu walked to him, leaned across his back, careful to avoid streaking the blood while brushing his newly formed wings with her corseted breasts, running her fingers down his sides, at the very edge of his feather welts. She leaned over his shoulder.

"Don't move, don't breathe. We're almost there," she whispered into his ear as her breath sent goose bumps across his skin, his welts, causing shudders of pain to rack his body once again.

Wait, she thought. *This isn't…* "Déjà vu," she whispered across his back, then shook off the feeling. She wrapped her hands around his waist, skimming her thumbs just at the edge of the last welts close to the center of his spine.

"Thank you, Domina," he breathed, his voice tense and hard but thankful, and she was brought to life in that. She hit a switch on the wall, then paused before she walked to her camera as she looked around the room, but everything was exactly where it should be.

"Domina?" Oliver said.

"Yes, I'm fine. Just…I can't shake the feeling we've been here before," she said.

"But we have, Duchess. Many times," he replied. He took a heavy breath, his back expanding and releasing, giving life to his wings.

Did he say… Lulu stopped cold. "What did you just say?" she asked.

"That we have, Domina. We've done this many times."

She shook her head. "Of course we have. I meant this exact—never mind. We need to get this plate exposed." The lighting was set, the stage created. All she had to do was press the shutter, and they would both have a permanent reminder of why they were here today. For the first time. Ever.

Ollie had never had wings before. This was monumental, and she needed to shake off the feeling of déjà vu and get busy.

She rounded the camera, careful to avoid the legs of the tripod, and stared into the ground glass at the upside-down reversed image to check the framing, "Don't move my darling. Don't…move," she said.

Grayson…

The name pulsed once, a dark face coming from the back of her thoughts as a fleeting image of broken, ground glass and Oliver struggling in his binds flitted across her mind. She shook it off again, then made the final adjustments to the focus. Concentrated harder.

This was one of her best yet. With his excellent physique, the canvas could not have been more perfect for her art.

She grinned and gave a little booty shake at her excitement then stopped. *No, I've done all of this before,* she thought. *But…what happened next?*

Grayson…

Again with that name, again with the face.

She looked around the room. Oliver was compliant and quiet, patient, and she could not leave him hanging there—well, she could, but that wasn't what they were supposed—she'd fallen. *That's* what had happened next.

She looked at the floor, then closely at Oliver as she carefully walked around her camera and laid her hands on his shoulders. "Just one more moment, my darling. I'm only making sure everything is perfect." She ran her hands down his sides again, her fingers tingling across his skin, then she tightened her grasp on his obliques, and the world started to fade as her hands slipped through the reality of him.

"No," she begged. *Nononono…* She stared at her hands as she clenched them again on air and looked around before she turned back to the camera. She never pushed the button.

Lulu panicked. She had to expose the plate before it was too late. He'd worked so hard, endured so much.

She moved quickly for the camera, again. Checked the ground glass, again. And when she stepped around the tripod once more, her heel caught on one of the legs in her rush. She saw Oliver fight his bonds, the broken glass at his feet, and she screamed and jerked awake in the dark.

"Goddammit!" she yelled, then the room was sliced by light as the door opened and the light from the hall came in. Grayson. She concentrated in the dark, trying to gain her bearings. She clenched her hands and felt handfuls of linen. She was here. "Grayson?"

"I'm here," he said.

"I never pushed the button. He worked so hard, and I never pushed the button. I didn't push it, and because of me, he has nothing."

Grayson spoke. "Do you remember?"

She saw Mrs. Weston at the end of the bed, her hands skimming the blankets over her legs to calm her.

"Mrs. Weston."

"Yes, dear. You had a dream. A nasty one, I fear." She patted her ankle.

"Yes. I was…I was back. But I'm not, obviously. I'm here." She heard Grayson's footsteps and felt the edge of the bed dip when he sat next to her, and Mrs. Weston's hands disappeared. Lulu watched as the woman's silhouette left the room.

"You went back?" he asked when the door had closed them in the dark once again.

"No… I think I just dreamed of when I was last home…last there before I was here. Oh, seriously, this is impossible to talk about."

"Did you remember anything more?"

"Yes, I did. I remember that I failed him." Her hand went to her head, feeling for the blood she now remembered pooling behind her skull. Did she die? Was she dead? She felt a lump and winced from the gentle pressure of her fingers. Her breath caught, and she nearly choked, until he took her hands in both of his.

"Failed who? The man you spoke of?"

She nodded as tears coursed her cheeks. "I can't believe it. I failed so miserably. I only had to watch my footing. I'd done it a hundred times, walked around the base of my tripod during a scene."

"A…scene? You're also an actress?" he asked.

"I suppose you could say that," she whispered.

"Well, that makes you a photographer, an artist in many mediums, and an actress. You truly are one of the most creative people I've met."

She smiled. She hadn't really thought of it that way. She supposed it was true. "I'm also an athlete. Don't forget that, because I happen to be quite proud of it. Though this body doesn't seem to agree with that fact."

"We can remedy that. What kind of athlete? Fencing? Riding?"

"I lift weights."

"Weights. Like…a strong man?" He grimaced, and she laughed.

"Not quite." She started feeling drowsy again now that the adrenaline had faded from her system, and the feeling of despair took over. She'd failed Ollie and she may never have a chance to make that up to him, not in this world.

"So you're strong then?"

"Yes, I am. Or I was, and I would like to be again." Her eyelids started to droop, even as she fought it for another moment alone with him. Grayson.

"Strength suits you." He paused for a while. "It's hours yet before dawn."

His voice sounded far away, and she nodded. "Yes, dawn. Please—"

"Please?" he asked gently.

"Stay."

Lulu sank into her pillows as she felt him wrap his warm body around her back, and she disappeared.

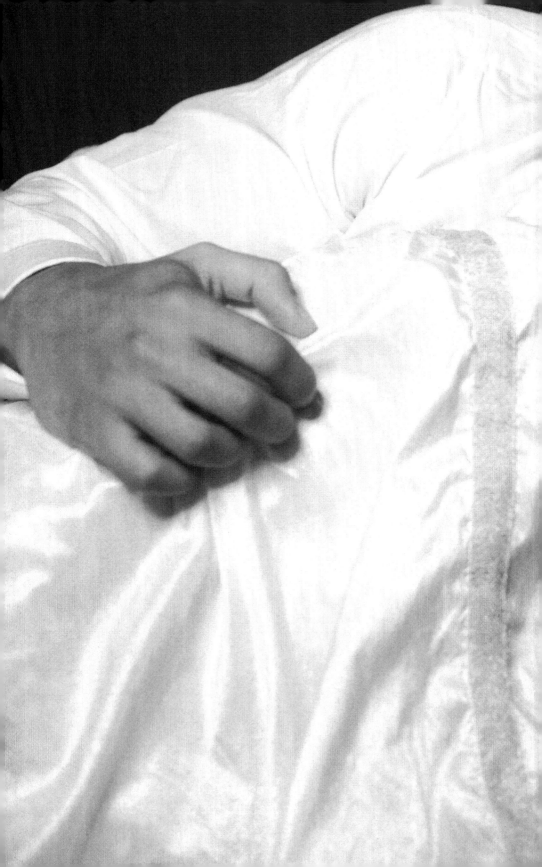

SEVEN

In war then, let your great object be victory, not lengthy campaigns.

—Sun Tzu
The Art of War

he next morning, Rakshan held Grayson's corset, the question obvious in his eyes. Last night, Grayson had been determined to wear it, but today… He didn't want to come to their wedding with anything between them.

He considered whether or not he could manage a day with his entire family and so much of society. He closed his eyes, ran his hands through his hair, then looked up to Rakshan and shook his head once. His valet set the corset aside and continued to dress him.

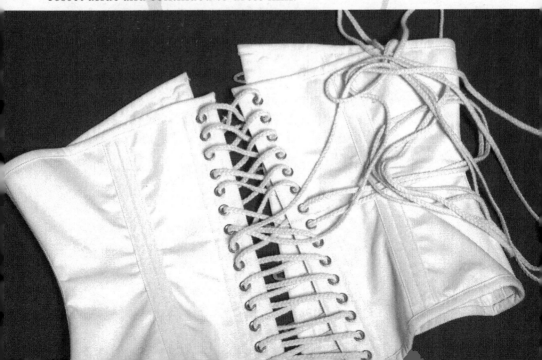

The suit had been made for this day. The shirt, the waistcoat, the jacket, and trousers. It had been sewn to his specifications, perfectly fitted, and it suddenly felt like a steel trap.

Rakshan tugged and pulled and straightened, then took up the brush and smoothed the wool across his shoulders, chest, and back, pressing the fabric against him until the suit felt like a second skin and Grayson could almost breathe.

"Thank you, Rakshan."

"Your Grace—"

"I'm still Grayson."

But Rakshan didn't miss a beat. "I will have your things returned to the town house this morning, along with any of Lady Cecilia's things you would like taken there. Everything will be ready for you by this afternoon."

"If you think we can manage without a staff," Grayson said.

"Your Grace—"

Grayson shook his head, but listened as his man just continued on. "I believe we can, unless she's somehow difficult. We have enough staff to manage two people, and your privacy would be more secure."

Grayson nodded. "Take everything," he said.

Rakshan, as his personal valet, knew more than anyone about Grayson's proclivities. If he was forced to name a man he trusted, it would be him. Of course, Rakshan wasn't of London. He was from India and had been Grayson's savior when he'd arrived there.

Part of Grayson had wanted to leave him behind when he returned to London, but Rakshan refused to be left behind. He said he owed him his life. Perhaps he had at one point. Grayson understood why the man would feel that way. But Grayson didn't believe in a life debt for anything, and Rakshan had already returned the favor many times over, whether he knew it or not.

Rakshan nodded to him, then started packing his things.

Grayson walked to the window, looking out over Grosvenor Square and the warmth of the sun that was only beginning to cast across the park. He was to be married today. The next time the sun rose on his body, he would be a husband. He would—for the first time in his life—be directly responsible for another human. He breathed deeply. Perhaps he did need

the corset. He looked back to Rakshan. Their eyes met for a moment, and Grayson shook his head again. No. They would meet on equal terms.

Well, not so, for she would have a corset. As it should be. He smiled, then immediately touched his lips, the feeling so foreign to him. Smirk, yes, sneer, certainly, but freely smiling? Not in all his recent years. He felt so free at the moment, and it wasn't just a change in temperament. He wasn't used to being able to physically take so much air so easily.

"How soon will the carriages be ready?" he asked.

"Any moment. Your Grace—"

"Rakshan."

"—the carriages for the men are to be here by seven. The ladies will follow at half past," he said, not even taking a breath when Grayson interrupted him. Eventually, Grayson would give up on correcting him, because he knew Rakshan was much more determined than he was.

Rakshan believed Grayson's life had been written for him long ago and that Grayson had always been meant for a position of power. Rakshan believed that it was his duty and privilege to ensure Grayson took that position. It was the only thing about Rakshan that made Grayson uncomfortable. Well, that and the fact that he refused to take charge of his own life and leave Grayson to himself.

Rakshan came to him with his sash, smoothing it across his shoulder then methodically affixing all the medals and pins that symbolized his service and his title. Grayson heard voices through the walls and knew his bride was being readied for him.

The day suddenly meant so much more to him than it had, and he wondered if he was to marry the same woman he'd met just the night before. He wondered if he was to marry the well-trained and submissive Lady Cecilia, or the domineering and unexpected Lulu. He smiled again. He knew exactly who he hoped would walk the aisle to him, and he was terrified that when she reached the end and he looked into her eyes, she wouldn't be there. His smile faded as a chill rushed his skin.

"Oh, my lady, this dress is beautiful. Your family spared no expense."

"It's not my family," Lulu mumbled. She rolled over, then sat up a bit too quickly. The blossom of pain in her head reminded her instantly of the previous day, and she leaned against the pillows, letting her eyes search the room. In the light of day, it was different. Warm and welcoming, less frightening and cave-like as it had been in the flickering of the gas lights. But she'd always preferred caves. She actually liked the flicker of firelight and the burn of candle wax that generally accompanied it—when it wasn't a necessary thing.

Mrs. Weston had several garments hung in the light of the morning sun, the curtains drawn wide, with the park beyond. "You have time for a bath if you'd like, Miss Lulu." She smiled as she approached her.

Lulu nodded. She was still here. She'd dreamed of home. Her heart stuttered. She had dreamed of home and it had felt how she expected this place to feel—untouchable. Her hands closed on the blankets surrounding her. This place was very much real beneath her hands. Her mind wandered but she had no time to consider before Mrs. Weston was bustling her into the bathroom and getting her ready. For now—*for now?*—she was here. She would be present. *You're in denial.* She shook her head. She didn't have time to care at the moment.

It felt like hours before she was dressed again, her hair curled and piled on her head, woven through with fresh flowers. She walked to the window and looked out to find several carriages readied out front. The procession was amazing, and it was a statement.

The lead carriage was black, heavily lacquered, with a shield emblazoned on the side, highly polished brass fittings, and a majestic team of four giant black horses in the lead, their harnesses heavy black leather with more brass than she thought she could lift.

She could train with those harnesses, she thought with a grin. She narrowed her eyes on the lead horse. She would put a man in one of those harnesses, she thought then, and an image of Gray in a leather harness with brass buckles flitted across her mind before she could shake it off. That life was gone now wasn't it? That life, whether it was gone or not was not the same as this one, and however she looked at it the two would never meet. Damn but that was depressing.

She saw a shadow and looked down to the front of the house as she waited for the people attached to come into view. She saw him, so perfectly dressed with a wide ribbon sash that went over one of his broad shoulders, then wrapped around his chest and attached at the opposite hip. It was covered with jewel-encrusted pins. She stopped breathing, and her forehead pressed against the glass of the window, cooling her hot skin.

This man is someone.

She closed her eyes, and her hand came up to steady her. Oh, god help her, this man is *someone*. This is no game. This is no dream. This man is important in his life, and he is to marry her, and she is…she is no one, and she certainly didn't belong here and shouldn't be married to him.

"Mistress?" Mrs. Weston said.

Her eyes flew open, and she avoided his gaze as he searched the window. She needed to see something from him, some recognition or some sort of connection, but he was stoic, not a hint of emotion on his stony face.

"Miss?" She felt Mrs. Weston pull her away from the window. "Come away before he sees you, Miss Lulu. We need to finish readying you. We've only half an hour before your carriage comes." The door opened, and Francine came in, and Lulu nearly cried out. Francine must have seen the terrified look on her face, because she rushed over and took her in her arms.

"Oh my god, this man is someone," Lulu whispered.

"You've seen him dressed, then?" Francine asked.

Lulu nodded.

"I remember when it hit me how important Gideon was. When I walked up the stairs at my wedding and saw him there with his riband on, his garter and shields, I was overwhelmed. To us, they're merely men, but to this country, they are quite a bit more."

"I'm not—god, it sounds so ridiculous to say this. But I'm not worthy. I am no one," she said.

"That's not true. It can't be, because you were brought here to him for a reason, as I believe I was to Gideon. We may not yet know why, and that you were brought here a mere day before your wedding…well, I don't know what to think of that. But here you are. I believe in fate. At least, I do now. And I believe you're exactly where you're meant to be."

"Now *you* sound ridiculous."

"I know this all sounds ridiculous, now, but it won't seem so ridiculous eventually. I'm sure of it."

Clearly, Francine had gotten into the punch and was happily drunk on it. She was truly in love with Gideon, and that quite obviously colored her world and her words. She was so damned happy, and Lulu wished she could resent that, even just a small bit. Instead, Lulu couldn't help but feel a slight bit better after talking with her.

Lulu had never believed in fate, or kismet, or whatever word it went by. She'd worked to find *her* place in *her* world. Not a second of where she was had been by happenstance or chance.

She'd found her people. She'd worked for her position. She was who she was and had what she had because she'd made it happen. Well, except for this whole…situation. She had no idea what to think of this, and the fact was, everything she'd worked for—her people, her world, her talent, her photography, her body even—was all gone.

Francine turned Lulu toward the mirror, then stepped back, and Lulu looked at herself for the first time that day. The dress was massive, the skirts endless and full. She could hardly manage the whole thing on her own, and she imagined that's what Francine was here to help her with.

Her skin flushed against the edges of lace, and she really took herself in. She looked like an honest-to-goodness bride—and a sweet and innocent, virginal bride at that. "This isn't who I am," she said breathlessly.

"I imagine not. This dress was made for who you were, or who you're supposed to be. It wasn't made for you. Today *you* will wear it, though."

"How big is this wedding?" she asked suddenly, the images of royal weddings, the trains that dragged behind the virgin brides for blocks, burned into her psyche as a young American girl.

"Big. Unless—"

Lulu turned. "Unless?"

Francine leaned in, conspiratorially. "I'll get you out of here. I have the money. I'll send you anywhere you wish to go. If you want to run, I'll help you hide." Francine rushed the words as if she didn't want anyone to catch her saying them.

Lulu heard Mrs. Weston hold her breath and squeak, and she turned and looked at the sweet woman. As their eyes met, Lulu remembered everything she'd said the night before, as well as everything Gray had said.

"No, I made a promise. I may want to run later...but I promised him I would meet him today at the altar, and I will."

Francine smiled and wrapped an arm around her waist. "Then let's go get you married," she said.

Lulu heard another carriage outside, the sound of many hooves prancing in time, then a whistle as the driver stopped them. She heard the calmer shuffling of those hooves on the cobblestones of the drive, the jingle of the horses' harnesses, the shouts of the men...and she nodded.

She looked in the mirror once more at an image she'd wished for only as a very young, very naïve girl, one who had seen too many princesses married and who'd had no idea what else the world could be for her. She embraced that tiny girl and turned for the door as Francine gathered up what seemed to be miles of fabric behind her.

"Mrs. Weston, do you have the veil?"

"Here, my lady!"

She heard Mrs. Weston running behind them and couldn't help but smile again at the thought of the sweet woman. They walked carefully down the grand staircase, and she had been right the night before. The foyer was... not merely a foyer. It was a Grand Entry, and she had another moment of simple, overwhelming shock.

Francine took the veil from Mrs. Weston and placed the combs in her hair, securing them behind her crown. Not the crown of her head, but an actual crown, she discovered, as she reached up to straighten it. Then Francine pulled the lace forward to hide her face and gave her a smile.

Two liveried men opened the double doors of the front entry, thank goodness, as she was far too wide for a single door, and she stepped out into the warming morning—to cheers. There was a crowd gathered across the street in the park.

"Breathe," Francine whispered behind her.

The carriage that was to take her to the church was...well, it was truly made for a princess. White, with highly polished brass fittings, the perfect counterpoint to the carriage Gray had been taken away in. The carriage was open so everyone would see her, the crowd gathering in the streets for that very purpose.

Francine leaned close to her. "You are important as well, you see?"

She shook her head. "Not me, this woman. Whoever *she* is, *she* is—or was—important."

Francine gave her a hug and kissed her cheeks.

Lulu looked at the team of six horses at the front of the carriage. They seemed to go on forever, even as she knew they didn't. They were white and so incredibly beautiful it nearly brought tears to her eyes. They had headdresses with feathers on their crowns and jewels on the leather.

"Who the fuck am I?" she whispered.

Francine laughed quietly. "I will tell you this is probably one of the most important marriages of the decade. Your father is Duke of Exeter. He's close to the queen. Not as close as Gideon and Gray, mind you, but that's why the fanfare. It's for the people. The queen was refused a grand London wedding for Roxleigh and I, and with all the coming celebrations, she was annoyed with him. So as much as Gray would have preferred something small, he was forced into this."

"So this is your fault," Lulu said dryly, and Francine nodded. "Remind me to thank you properly for that," Lulu said. She pulled her skirts up as several footmen helped her, and all of her skirts, into the carriage, and Francine closed the small door behind her. "Wait, what are you—"

"I'll be in the next carriage. You're to ride alone in this one," she said.

"Oh no, please don't leave me!" Lulu begged as she held on to the edge of the door.

"Don't worry, it's not far to Westminster Abbey."

"Westminster—Westminster Abbey? *The* Westminster Abbey?!" She practically screamed it as she stood and turned. The crowd stared at her in confusion. She heard the crack of a whip, and the carriage jerked forward, and she crumbled to the floor. She almost stayed there, hiding amongst the fabric, but felt a hand on hers as one of the men on the back of the carriage reached over the side and helped her up to the seat. She adjusted herself on the bench and held on.

Lulu closed her eyes and hoped beyond hope that she made it through today and this wedding. In *Westminster Fucking Abbey.*

What had she agreed to? This felt like the pebbles in the jar in that old Grimm fairy tale. Was it Grimm? The fox and the crane, or something, and the fox needed a drink so he filled the vase with stones until the water was high enough to drink. Her vase was about to overflow, just as her breasts did from this corset now.

She couldn't breathe. Her hand tightened on the side of the carriage. She swayed as it turned, and Lulu nearly hit the floor again to hide from the crowd that appeared before her. This was not happening…it was not.

She looked behind her to see another open carriage, with three women and Francine, who was smiling and waving. There were two men in full uniform on the rear of her carriage, then two more men in uniform on horseback flanking them. If she weren't so overwhelmed, she would probably entertain an Adam Ant fantasy.

Lulu wanted to crawl under the carriage seat. She turned back to the crowd, the people tossing white roses into her carriage. She caught one and held it up, then smelled it through her veil as the crowd roared. She concentrated on the sweet smell of the rose, the rocking of the carriage, the white noise of the crowd around her as it thickened, and she became the woman she knew Gray expected her to be today. She could play the part. She could be the woman the crowd wanted to see—because, God knew, when she was nervous she became just the opposite of that.

In that moment, for Grayson, Lulu became the princess she'd never truly wished to be. A princess he'd probably never wanted for, either.

EIGHT

Indirect tactics efficiently applied are inexhaustive as Heaven and Earth.
Unending as the flow of rivers and streams,
like the sun and the moon, they end but to begin anew.
Like the four seasons, they pass away to return once more.

—Sun Tzu
The Art of War

Grayson had never wanted to be elsewhere more in his life than right now, not even when his father and brothers had attacked him. He stared down at his polished shoes. Damn Roxleigh for refusing a London wedding. Damn Perry for doing the same. Damn his birth and his brothers' deaths for putting him in this position.

He waited out of sight from guests in Poets' Corner at Westminster Abbey. He hadn't been here since he was in short pants, forced to attend services.

He couldn't bring his head up to look at all the people he knew were filing into the nave, and he didn't want to go back to the sanctuary to be on display, so he would wait for the absolute last moment possible.

Most of these people were here to lay eyes on the errant duke, but the errant duke wasn't here to oblige.

He saw six pairs of polished shoes enter his field of vision and knew his cousins flanked him.

"Are we praying?" Perry whispered. Roxleigh laughed, and Grayson felt Rox nudge his shoulder, causing the circle to bump shoulders, the lot of them swaying and laughing suddenly.

"I'm not very happy with you at the moment, Rox. You may want to step back." The shoes to his right switched places with the pair of shoes right of them and everyone seemed to take a step back.

They should be joking and cajoling him—as he imagined normal men did on wedding days. He imagined they had done that for Roxleigh on his wedding day. Harassed him for coming to scratch…gave him pointers for his wedding night. All in jest, all in fun. But these men didn't do that with him, because he was who he was, and even though they were cousins and had grown up together, he knew they were frightened of him.

Grayson scrubbed his hands through his hair, then took a deep, steadying breath and looked up. "Is my mother here yet?"

"Yes. She, Poppy, and the rest of the ladies are front and center, which means your bride has been removed from the carriage and is waiting for you to take your position in the sanctuary," Calder said.

Grayson had spent more time with Calder since his return than with Rox and Perry, but Calder was a bachelor and more available than the others. Calder had his own secrets, as well, and left Grayson to his. Not that Rox or Perry pressed him for information, but he felt a kinship with Calder and his secrets, because they both understood what it was to have them. They both understood the danger should they come to light.

Grayson put his hands on his hips, closed his eyes, and nodded. "Well, then, let's not keep her waiting." He looked up at Perry, who was looking back at him like he was insane. "What?" Grayson grumbled.

Perry held his hands up, then stepped in front of Grayson and reached up to his hair, smoothing it back. "You just have a few…uh…there. That's better." Perry smiled, then smacked his shoulder and stepped back. Grayson grunted a thanks, then bumped through the circle of men as they turned and followed him.

When he stepped into the sanctuary, he looked to his left and nodded at his mother and sister as he passed them. He should spend more time with them. He would spend more time with them. He just couldn't force himself to spend more time with them. He was certain they missed his father and brothers. He was certain they would be disappointed in his handling of them, as well. He looked away before he felt their censure, keeping his eyes forward across the sanctuary.

The great organ began to play, and he saw the flash of sunlight as the doors were opened to allow the bride to enter the nave, then the light dimmed just as quickly. He was terrified to look down the aisle they'd created for the ceremony today. He heard Roxleigh clear his throat, and Grayson ignored him. He felt Rox nudge his shoulder. Then Roxleigh leaned toward him and whispered, "You really don't want to miss this, Gray."

Grayson shook his head. He really did want to miss this. In fact, all of this. He wanted to let the title die with him, let the entailments fall to the earth and be reclaimed. He was forcing a complete stranger to marry him in order to protect the very things he abhorred. He should, at least, look her in the eye while he did it.

Grayson looked down then turned his head slowly to his left and saw her for the first time that day. She stopped walking when he turned, and he quit breathing. Everyone in the nave was standing, watching her waiting there. His hand flattened against the buttons of his coat, pressing in. She fidgeted a bit, and he thought for certain she was going to turn and run from the Abbey. Then she took one uneasy step, and another, and he breathed anew.

He wished he could see her face, but the lace of that veil—he needed to see her face. He needed to know who he was marrying today. What he hadn't said to any of his cousins was that he feared the woman he'd met yesterday had gone, and he was left to marry a woman he'd yet to truly meet.

Why had she stopped moving when he turned to look down the aisle at her? Perhaps because she wasn't the same person, or perhaps because she was…and was having second thoughts.

God help him, he wanted to walk down the aisle and tear that veil from her head and ask her who the hell she was. Instead, he turned away, because he had to stop staring at her like she was the enemy.

He clasped his hands behind his back and listened as her footsteps grew nearer. He turned his back to her as she came up the stairs to stand next to him, and then they walked shoulder to shoulder toward the archbishop.

He heard her take a breath. "I thought for sure I was going to fall on my way up that aisle, so you should consider yourself lucky I made it here in one piece. You should have warned me this was going to be such a big damned wedding."

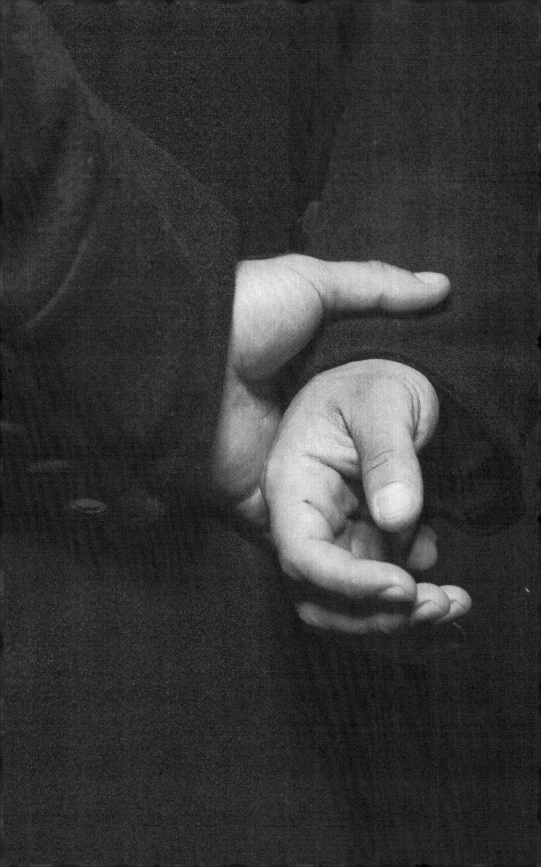

Grayson smiled. The officiant raised his brows. Then Grayson closed his eyes and said a prayer of thanks, possibly the first he'd ever uttered inside a house of worship.

When it came time to lift the veil and say her name, Grayson looked directly in her eyes and called her Lulu before placing the Duchess of Warrick's ten-carat emerald on her finger, then he turned it so the stone was against her palm and only the band would show.

He closed her hand on the ring and held it tight in his grip as he spoke his vows, because he wanted to be sure she knew he was marrying her and not the woman she was supposed to be—even though she wore the ring. He wanted Lulu to know that he wanted her—and it terrified him just how much.

Overwhelmed was an understatement.

Lulu was pretty sure she'd shocked that priest into…into what? He was already celibate. What was worse than that? Nothing in Lulu's estimation. Was that even possible? To shock someone into celibacy?

Now, now, she chided herself, *never insult another person's kink.* Maybe she'd merely reinforced his choices. *Well, you're welcome, Mr. Priest—or whatever,* she thought. *He has a fancy hat. Does that make him a bishop? You know what would be nice? If people were introduced before being a party to a major, life-changing ceremony. That would be nice.*

She turned and looked at the man in the carriage next to her as she fiddled with the inverted ring on her finger. Her husband. She would have to figure out religion at some point, since it was so ingrained in his culture. Grayson's. His culture, his family, his life. She was his.

She hoped he would be hers as well, but that really only happened in books, didn't it? In the Victorian era, she was property. What was the term? Cattle. No, not cattle—chattel. Same difference. She had more rights as a single woman of age than as a married woman. Perhaps she should have thought this through.

She looked down to the massive green stone that rested inside her hand. She had no idea why he'd done that, but he'd done it with purpose, that much was obvious. He'd placed it on her hand properly, then turned the stone to her palm. She ran her fingers over the large, flat surface. This ring could probably pay off the mortgage on her LoDo flat. Twice. Possibly three times.

The carriage took a turn, and she leaned into him, not that she was complaining. Considering she stayed pressed up against him—even as the horses straightened out in front of them—she really was just looking to get closer to him. To someone. To anyone—no, not anyone. She really just wanted to be closer to him.

"Are you well?" His deep voice juddered through her system, waking all of her nerves in one fell swoop as she looked up to him.

"Would it be too terribly forward of me to ask you to kiss me?"

His eyes narrowed slightly, then dropped to her mouth as she licked her lips. The world beyond the carriage was a cacophony of white noise as he leaned in and pressed his lips to hers. She wove her hand with his, the stone pressed between them.

It wasn't a sweet kiss, but it was one of the most chaste kisses she'd ever experienced. Even so, she felt all those enlivened nerves curl up their tips and sigh.

She smiled up at him, and the noise around them seemed to swell and press in. "Were they waiting for that?" she asked. He nodded. "Taking one for the team, eh?" She grinned. He shook his head but remained silent. She felt his fingers play with the ring on her finger, and she waited for a moment as he seemed to be considering something. "Why?" she asked.

"I want you to know that this life may own me, but it does not own you. This ring, this stone"—he turned her hand over and smoothed a thumb across it, skimming the surface of her skin and sending bolts of energy to her core—"is an outward sign of your fealty to me. Wear it however you wish to, but know that I don't expect that of you. At any moment, you may decide to leave, and you should know I'll not stop you. To that end, I will set up accounts for you as soon as I'm able."

So she wasn't to be his—not truly—and he would not be hers. Lulu couldn't breathe, and it had nothing to do with her corset. "I made a promise. I keep my promises," she said simply but the words—explaining herself to him cut a little.

Needing more of his solid warmth, she leaned against his shoulder as she considered his words, and he pulled his hands away. Distance, he already wanted distance. She could distance.

"Where are they taking us? To an empty house I hope, with many guards outside so we can..." He gazed down at her, and she stopped, sitting upright as she looked away.

Sex with him no longer seemed like something she could joke about. It all felt so awkward and real to her. Not that sex hadn't felt real before, but before, sex was simple. It was something she wanted, something she enjoyed, something she appreciated, something she did. It was a very big part of who she was.

Now, however, with him—her husband—it seemed to mean so very much more. She spun the emerald ring on her finger. "You guys don't require an audience to make sure we consummate our marriage anymore, do you?" she asked.

She felt his laugh, and she smiled. "Good. I've had an audience before. It can be fun if that's your kink, but I think I'd prefer it just be us...you know...for some reason."

She knew he was looking down on her, which is to say, he was taller than she was and he was sitting up straight, and she suddenly found herself sulking because she just could not manage all the things she was feeling between his mixed signals and her confusion. She straightened her spine and smiled at some little girls who ran alongside the carriage waving to her. She pulled a rose from the woven garland that adorned the edges and tossed it to them. They squealed.

"You've used that word before. What does it mean to you?" he asked.

Shit. Which word had she used? "What does it mean to you?" she hedged.

"Tied in a knot," he replied.

Ohhhh. "Kink?" she said with a grin. Yeah, knots could easily define kink. "Well...for me it means something you like to do for pleasure that perhaps others don't understand."

He nodded. Then he turned and waved to the crowd, a simple raise and tilt of his gloved hand. She should try out her light-bulb-changing pageant wave. She'd really never had need of it before now, except in snark.

Oh no… She was falling apart. She really needed to keep it together for a bit longer. She lifted her right hand and screwed in the light bulb, and the crowd went wild. She muttered, "Gonna be a big man someday…"

"What?" he asked.

She chanted, "Somebody better put you back into your place." She stomped her feet against the carriage boards beneath her skirts. Left, right, clap. Left, right, clap. "We will, we will—"

"You're rocking the carriage," he said quietly.

"Rock you?" she said sweetly. He simply stared at her, all that stoic Britishness of his on display. She smiled. "Sing it, yeah! We will, we will…" She let her voice fade under the confused scrutiny in his expression. She took a deep breath. "I just really thought you'd appreciate some Queen," she said.

"We'll be seeing Her Royal Highness shortly at Buckingham," he replied.

Her jaw dropped, and she knew if she didn't pick it back up, she was going to drool all over this ridiculous dress.

"The queen?"

"Is there another?"

She stopped to consider how to answer that, but her queens were certainly nothing like his. Buckingham Fucking Palace. He'd done it again, distracted her and evaded her question. Damn, he was good. She was better than he was at the mindfuck, though. She was just off her game at the moment, but he would find that out soon enough.

She rearranged her face into the best pageant smile she could and started to unscrew the light bulb.

NINE

There are not more than five musical notes,
yet the combination of these five give rise to more melodies than can ever
be heard.

—Sun Tzu
The Art of War

Grayson had been watching his new duchess all morning. When they arrived at Buckingham, they made an appearance on the East Balcony to quell the crowd, then they were rushed to the State Dining Room for the wedding breakfast, after which they retired to the Green Drawing Room. They all relaxed for a while with just family, higher peers, and Her Royal Highness.

He could see Lulu was trying her best to blend in. It was an admirable attempt, but every once in a while, something completely unexpected would come out of her mouth—and it thrilled him. He loved other people's reactions to her. They would stare at her, then turn to him, expecting him to correct his irreverent bride, but he didn't, and he wouldn't.

It seemed this marriage was going to be exactly what he needed, even as he hadn't known it. He imagined most men would be enraged by her behavior today, but he…he was enchanted, and it emboldened him to see her handle so many peers so masterfully.

She spoke her mind and refused to cow to others, and when she was paying attention and trying to be a proper duchess, she was absolutely stunning. He couldn't even fathom how she knew what she should be doing. It took him completely off guard how incredible it was to see her behave in this way.

He wasn't merely enthralled by her power but by her ability to quash that power for him, as she should do as a subservient duchess. That juxtaposition of subservience and power made him feel a bit wild.

He had to admit she'd let go her control a bit more today than he'd thought she should, but to be honest, today wasn't just any day. She'd just fulfilled another woman's contract to marry a complete and total stranger and, by god, he was so damned thankful for that.

He had fully expected his wife to hold her own at the palace, speak with the queen and her people, socialize with the powerful elite of London, but he'd honestly not expected Lulu to do the same, so when she did—and he knew she did it for his benefit, not her own—he'd been completely taken aback. A submissive woman he didn't want, and a submissive woman he didn't believe her to be in earnest, but she affected a persona that had every one of the peers here today fooled.

Lulu had even turned the stone of her ring outward as they arrived at the palace. He hadn't said anything. She'd simply done it. She was amazing, she was beautiful, and she was officially his. He had only to complete the task in the bedroom…somehow.

Her father walked to him slowly, a wry grin on his face. "Well, Warrick, it's done. The contract is complete. Welcome to the family," he said.

"We are not family, Exeter, and never will be. Your daughter belongs to me instead of you, plain and simple." Grayson wasn't going to give this man a toehold in his life or his affairs.

"You're mistaken. Our two great families have now become one, as has been planned for years. You are now indebted to me," Exeter said.

"You are the one mistaken, Your Grace. I'm indebted to no one save my queen. If there is confusion therein, take it up with Her. But leave us be."

"You can't tell me to stay away from my daughter."

"I can. She's my property. You know the law as well as I do. She belongs to me and no other. Nothing can keep her from me, but I can, in fact, keep her from you."

"Not against her wishes," Exeter said, his face going red with constipated anger.

"I would never keep her from anyone she would choose to see, but you're incorrect to believe that I cannot, or that I will not, if it goes against my wishes, which are paramount in my house." Grayson turned and leveled his gaze on the man, "Are we clear." It wasn't a question. "Stay away from my people," he said.

"People…not family?" Exeter said.

"Not simply people. My people. She is now one of my people."

Exeter made no reply. He simply turned and walked away.

"Making friends with your new family?" Perry asked as he walked up to Grayson. Grayson didn't reply, his gaze burning a hole in the back of his father-by-law as he left and walked toward Lulu. "Will we have a problem with him?"

"With him, possibly. With her, not at all," Grayson replied finally. "I have no doubt she will put him off, and if at some point she chooses to be close to Cecilia's family, that's her choice, even as it rankles."

Perry cast his gaze across the room, from Exeter to Lulu. "They're all under her spell," Perry said.

"She is masterful. You'll be amazed."

"So you're under her spell then as well," Perry said with a grin.

Grayson grunted. He knew Perry was attempting to lighten the mood, but Grayson said nothing, and Perry chuckled. "Alas, poor Warrick, I knew him well," he said as he glanced at his own wife, who sat quietly with the ladies and Her Royal Highness.

"Has she…how is she?" Grayson asked when he saw Perry's gaze shift. Grayson very rarely saw Lilly, as mostly when he went out with his cousins, it was to the back rooms at White's or a tap, not a respectable place for women.

"She's well. Thank you. And just as an aside, this feeling? It has never worn thin. It has only become…so much more."

Grayson nodded, hopeful for the first time in his godforsaken life. "I was expecting to need to be at her side, to make sure she didn't embarrass herself, or me. But just look at her. She's brilliant." He shook his head. "She's had the perfect balance of silence and charm. I don't think I could have done it had the situation been reversed."

"I have the crazy notion you could blend in anywhere you attempted to," Perry said, but then he moved on quickly. "Francine was the same way. Perhaps it's something about the women then, that they can be whoever they need to be for whatever situation they must handle. No doubt Francine has been helping your wife today."

Perry watched them for a minute, then shook his head. "Lilly is like that as well, though, in some ways. She's able to hold her own in this room, even as a year ago it would have terrified her to have eyes on her at all. I just believe women are smarter than we are. They figure men out relatively easily. The difficulty comes when we don't trust how intelligent they truly are."

Grayson looked down. Trust was definitely a difficulty for him, but he hoped he and Lulu would come to know each other, even as he knew he was terrified of her discovering his secrets. Lulu made him want to share all of his secrets and be absolved by her. She held the only opinion of importance to him. He'd known her for a single day, and already he knew that if he were to lose her, it would be the end of who he was.

Roxleigh joined them at the edge of the room. "Talking of wives, I assume?" he asked. Perry grinned but remained silent, and Rox nodded. "I imagine, Warrick—"

"Grayson."

"Grayson, even as this has all been planned for years now that it's a bit of a shock for you," Rox said as he put his hand on Grayson's shoulder and squeezed it. "Do you have need for any wedding-night tips? Shall Perry enlighten you as to the responsibility of the bridegroom on his wedding night?"

Grayson continued to stare at the floor, but he smiled for the second time that day. The ribbing he'd missed had arrived, and he knew it was because only Perry and Rox were party to the exchange. He was suddenly thankful to experience this small bit of normalcy on this day, for it was undeserved.

Perry clapped him on the shoulder and leaned in. "Listen, cousin, it isn't nearly as terrifying as you imagine," he said in a deep conspiratorial voice. "It's simple mechanics. She will enjoy it certainly, but you…well, men don't always. And"—Perry paused dramatically until Grayson returned his steady gaze—"there may be blood. So be ready for that and have some smelling salts nearby. You should show her how to use them. Should you swoon."

Grayson nearly laughed at that, completely forgetting all of his true concerns for the coming night.

Calder walked up, and they all turned to him. "Judging from the ridiculous grins you just hid, I suppose you were regaling our cousin with the horrors of wedded bliss?" he asked. Nobody spoke. "Ah...the actual wedding night, then. Terrifying, I'm told. Really. All the screaming and crying and whatnot." Calder cut his gaze to Grayson with a pronounced shudder. "I'm not entirely sure why women put up with that sort of carrying-on from men." Then he winked.

Rox, Perry, and Grayson all laughed in earnest at that, and every woman in the room turned to look, silencing him almost instantly. When Lulu's gaze locked on his, her eyes wide with surprise, his heart stalled in his chest. He had the sudden need to leave. He needed to thank his wife properly. He knew he'd been staring too long when his shoulder jerked, probably from Perry hitting it again.

"We should get on with it," Grayson said stiffly, and he walked to his wife, pulled her from the group, bowed to his queen, and led Lulu from the room without another word.

Leaving wasn't as easy as he thought it should be as the echo of laughter chased them through the halls. It was that never-ending train of fabric that weighed her down and pursued them through the house. He grabbed a footman and told him to carry it, and they started moving much easier.

When they hit the Grand Entrance, he pulled her toward the rear of the palace, to the secured entry away from any lingering crowd. He knew a separate, much less fanciful carriage was waiting there so they could return to Warrick Place unnoticed.

Grayson lifted her into the closed box, then shoved at the fabric until it was all inside the door and he could join her. He couldn't even see her over the pile of her skirts, but he could hear her laughter, and that was all he needed in the moment. As the carriage jerked into motion, he remembered her fear of being closed in and started shifting ruffles and bows and lace, looking for his wife.

His wife.

He stopped for a second to catch his breath, then continued on. He found a leg pointing in the opposite direction he thought it should be. He stared at it for a good long moment, his fingertips hovering as he debated whether or not to touch the soft pink skin at the top of her stocking. He decided against anything without her permission, so he shifted the skirts over it and searched on in the other direction, following her laughter.

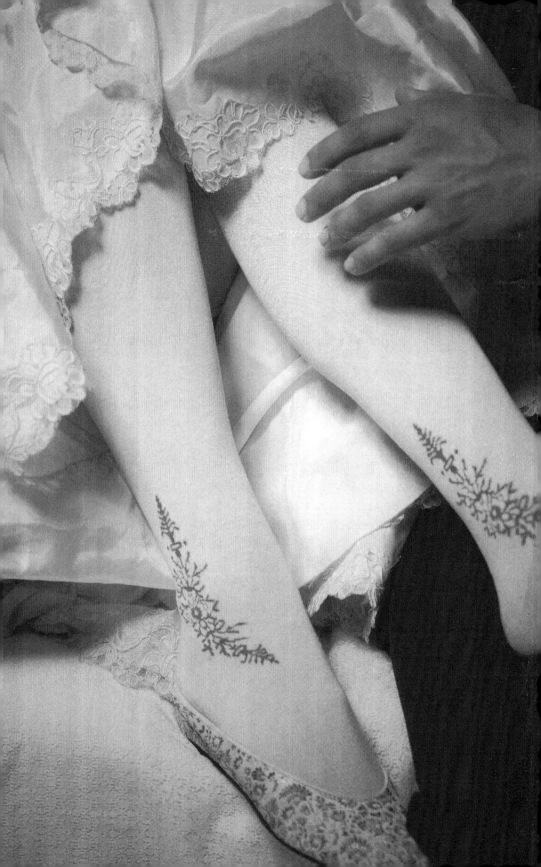

He finally found her, pushed all the way into the corner across from him. "There you are," he said.

"Here I am!" she replied with a bright smile as she lifted her hands and fluttered her fingers. She shifted, shoving fabric around until she seemed comfortable enough on the bench. "What on earth do we do with all of this fabric?" she asked. "I want to be rid of it, but it seems as though it would dress a hundred children."

He shrugged. "Then we will have it made into a hundred dresses and find some children to give them to."

"That would be nice. Please tell me we're headed home."

He paused and searched her face. It had never felt like home to him, but technically speaking, that's what it was. "I suppose so."

"Not your home?" she asked.

"Not the home I would choose," he replied.

"But it's where you and I are to live?" He nodded. "Then we will make it ours. We will vanquish whatever makes it a difficult place to be, or we will burn it to the ground and start from scratch," she said with a wicked grin.

"As much as that idea actually appeals to me, it's not something we can do. The house remains entailed." He thought about her humor and felt a cad for being so simple, so he added, "And I have neighbors." She laughed again, and he smiled because he had done that for her.

"I…I want to apologize for yesterday," she said. "I think I was quite out of line in the way I spoke. I would like to blame the head injury, but the truth is, I'm simply much more outspoken than this time period allows for."

"You will blame whatever you wish to, and I will find no issue with it. What you managed today in the queen's presence was astounding. They were all quite taken with you."

"I did my best. I simply pulled out all the my ladies, my lords, and Your Graces I could muster and had them believing I would do whatever they wished. It's actually rather easy to hide in plain sight with people who believe in their own power. They don't truly look at others unless they're challenged. I simply avoided challenge…for today. I'm trained to make people believe in whatever they want to believe in. I may choose not to do that in future, depending on how you wish for me to behave," she said.

"I would wish for you to be yourself. I don't want you to be anyone else on my behalf…and I would prefer you didn't use those particular skills on me," he added, suddenly nervous.

She looked away and nodded. "I understand how this world works. At least, I have a good idea about it. I have no problem with being submissive in public as long as I'm safe and I can be myself in my own home, wherever that happens to be."

"And I hope I can give you that home," he said. "As for your family, Cecilia's family—"

"I don't want to see them," she cut in.

"I will support any decisions you make where they're concerned, but there are things you should know about them before you do, should you change your mind."

"Like, their names?" she said with another giant grin.

"For starters," he replied with a smile, again. Good lord, on this track he would be smiling incessantly in no time. Like Rox and Perry. Abhorrent.

"Why did you pull me away from the reception?" she asked.

He sobered. "Because I wanted you to myself."

"That inspiring, was I?" she asked.

"Much more than inspiring." He ran a finger down her arm, and she fluttered her lashes. "Don't," he said stiffly as he pulled his hand back. "I told you I want you to be yourself."

"Yes, I—Grayson, there are many different facets to who I am, and each one of them is an important part of me. Sometimes I like to flutter my lashes at handsome men."

He nodded. He wasn't sure how to tell her that it was the moments wherein she made demands that were the most arousing to him. Her submissive side…he appreciated it for what it was, but it wasn't attractive to him, at all really.

"Grayson, touch me again," she said simply. He lifted his hand and ran it down her arm again, skimming his thumb over the stone that signified she was his duchess. "I have a feeling we may be able to get along better than you think," she said. "But you ask me not to use my skills with you, and I'm not sure I know how to manage that."

"How so?"

"I…have never been in a serious relationship…"

"There's more to it than that. You aren't the only one with secrets you're afraid to share."

"This, I believe," she said.

He dropped his gaze as he considered that statement. She certainly knew he wore a corset, because of the night before, but his purpose for that corset wouldn't be known to her. How could it? "How about we simply agree to not use your talents for nefarious purpose, and I will endeavor to be as honest as possible in all things? We will not lie outright, at any cost."

"That's a good start. I can agree to that," she replied.

The carriage pulled up in front of Gray's house with much less fanfare than the day had begun, and it pleased him immensely. Rakshan opened the door to the carriage and spoke softly. "Your Grace—"

"Grayson."

"Everyone has left." Rakshan held the door for Gray, and he descended the carriage and started pulling fabric through the door carefully, until one of Lulu's hands appeared, and he took it. He pulled until she fell into his arms from the carriage doorway with a squeal. Then he shifted her until he had her securely in his arms and turned to Rakshan, who looked at Lulu and bowed. "Your Grace, welcome home," he said.

Gray watched as she smiled. "Lulu, this is my valet, Rakshan. He is to be trusted."

"Hello, Rakshan," she said.

"I have prepared a meal in your rooms, as they are the only rooms currently suitable for occupancy," Rakshan said to Gray.

"I thought the duchess's rooms would be made up as well today," he said quietly.

"It wasn't possible," Rakshan responded. Grayson glared at him, not believing a word he spoke, but unsure if he should chastise his man in front of his new duchess. He felt Lulu watching, then her fingers tensed on his nape, drawing his attention.

"I imagine, as a duke, that your bed is big enough for us to share and never touch. I imagine you have space in your room for one little duke-ess in it," Lulu said as Rakshan moved behind them and pulled her train into his arms.

"It's duchess, not duke-ess," he said. She rolled her eyes at him, and he nodded as they started up the steps to the entry. When they reached the top, he stopped, and she waited for whatever he was considering.

"That wasn't what I meant," he said. Truth, he reminded himself. "I assumed you would want some private space to…take some time away from me." He said it so only she could hear him.

She shook her head. "I find you fascinating. I don't need to hide from you."

He paused to take that in. He felt the same about her. To a certain degree, he wanted her near him, but he didn't want to assume anything. They crossed the threshold and stopped in the dimly lit entry and waited.

"Your Grace—"

"Rakshan."

"—you will need to lead, as I have the train."

"Of course." He carried her up two flights of stairs, and when they finally entered the rooms that were now his, he carefully set her on her feet.

Lulu stood there by the entryway, unsure what to do next. She saw a cloud of white to her left as Rakshan tossed her skirts into the room beside her.

"A bath is ready for Your Grace," he said to her. "I will keep it warm should you choose to eat first." He motioned to the table covered in food set up before the fire. She hadn't realized she was so hungry, yet again. She hadn't eaten much at the wedding breakfast, considering she was still overwhelmed by the fact that she was having a wedding breakfast at Buckingham Palace while sitting within earshot of the Queen of England.

What was that Adam Ant song? Something about Tom of Finland— damn, she missed music. She lived her life with a constant soundtrack, and this world was so stunningly quiet.

"I'd like to eat," she said, "but this dress."

"As you wish, my lady." She felt hands come up to her dress, then Grayson spoke.

"Leave us." His voice was so powerful. She absolutely loved it, and her insides shifted and softened so easily at his command, just as they should. He was such a brilliant juxtaposition of power and submission.

She heard the door click shut softly, then she felt his hands on her shoulders, his fingers sweeping the edges of the bodice and coming together in the center of the back of her dress, loosening all the buttons.

Lulu tilted her head forward, and he brushed the few loosened curls from her neck as she shivered against his touch. His fingers paused, just at the soft skin near where her neck met her shoulder, his thumb skimming up and down that bit of spine as his breath warmed it.

"Please," she said.

"Please what?" he asked.

"Take this dress off." She couched the demand with a small voice, but she knew that he wanted orders. She could feel his need in her bones. She just wasn't sure he was ready to admit that yet, at least, not to her.

"Yes, My Duchess," he said as the buttons released quickly.

"Please call me Lulu. I—everything feels more real to me when you say my name." She had yet to take a full breath and waited patiently as he continued to loosen buttons.

"Lulu." Her name came on a breath against her spine, and she shuddered into it, every nerve in her body at full attention. She was more nervous than ever, she felt like…well, like a first time might, not her first first time, certainly as she was much too excited then to be nervous but now, with him, with everything being as it was…

He walked in front of her, pulled her hand into his, and released the buttons down one arm of her dress then the other. He stood before her for a moment as it began to slip, then she narrowed her eyes on him, and he fell to his knees, and her stomach dropped in his wake. That one small action was not so small in her world. Her hands started to shake.

He looked confused for a moment, then lifted the hem of her skirts and helped to remove her shoes. "Thank you," he said. "For today. For every day that will follow. I will endeavor to thank you each day as it happens, but should I forget"—he paused and looked up to her—"know that in this moment I am thanking you for every waking moment you have given me by simply agreeing to be my duchess."

Her hands came to her mouth to stifle a sob that she couldn't contain. This was…so much more than she'd ever expected from him. Not that she'd expected much, but he had made promises to her, stranger that she was, and she'd believed him. She wasn't entirely sure in this moment why he would feel this strongly. But she guessed he hadn't been treated fairly in the past.

It was something they could work on. But for now, this giant, powerful man was at her feet, and that fulfilled a wish in her she was afraid to hope too much for. He was hers. Of a fashion, anyway.

She reached out and touched his shoulder. "Please," she said.

"Anything," he replied.

"Rise."

He did, without taking his hands from her as he stood. He held her hips, held her gaze with his. Then he was standing over her, and she felt safer, in the lee of his size, than she ever had in her life, with the knowledge this man was her protector. She gave a little twitch and his hands moved away, then she wiggled until the entire dress fell to the floor and she was left in her underthings.

She reached out and ran her fingers over the jewel-encrusted pins and shields on his chest, then she smoothed her hand down the lapel of his coat, lifted it, and twisted the ring until the stone rested in her palm. Then she wrapped her fingers around the edge of his waistcoat as she gazed into his eyes.

"We are doing this together. Promise me, whatever comes next, we face it together," she said. "I see you, I know you are the protector, and in this day and age, it's your responsibility, but I want you to think of me as a partner, not a weaker link in need of protection. I'm asking this as a favor, because I can't live if I'm considered less."

He nodded. "I will do my best to include you and to ensure our life together is ours."

It felt like a renewal of, or perhaps an amendment to, their wedding vows. She clenched her fist on the edge of his waistcoat and tapped his chest twice with her knuckles. No corset, she thought. Then she knew he didn't want her to know about the corset, because what came next was sacrament to marriage, and it required nothing between them.

She spread her hands against his chest, letting the heat of him warm her fingertips. Her knuckles skimmed along the hard expanse of his abdomen as she undid some of the buttons of his waistcoat with one hand, her breath catching in her throat. Then she let go and reached up to her hair.

Lulu removed the combs and pins from her hair and let it fall around her shoulders. Then she reached behind her and loosened the knot of her corset as he moved his hands to her rib cage, pressing the edges together until the busk clicked and the catches released. He let it fall to the floor.

Such an intimate dance for two people who were only just on a first-name basis. Did he have a middle name? He did. He had, like, six names. But she couldn't think of any of them, save Grayson.

She paused, then reached up to that sash—riband, he'd called it a riband—and lifted it over his head. Someday she wanted to make love to him with his riband on. She wanted the impression of his jewels left on her skin, her blood on his diamonds.

He took the riband from her and placed it across the back of a chair, then returned to her. She undid the rest of the buttons of his waistcoat and then his shirt and unbuttoned his trousers. When she looked up to him, his eyes were black with passion, all color gone from the irises. He just waited as she implored him for permission.

"Touch me." He asked it more than said it, his command slipping.

She took a step back. Somehow, she'd slipped back into the whole this-is-a-dream functionality in her brain, and she suddenly realized she was breaking all of her rules. She put a hand on his chest. "Wait."

"Wait?"

"Wait. There are things I need to know, before we do this." They were already way too far beyond this conversation, but no way was she going to go back in time and marry a duke only to die with her favorite body parts falling off.

He stiffened and dropped his gaze to the floor, and she knew he would be nothing but honest with her.

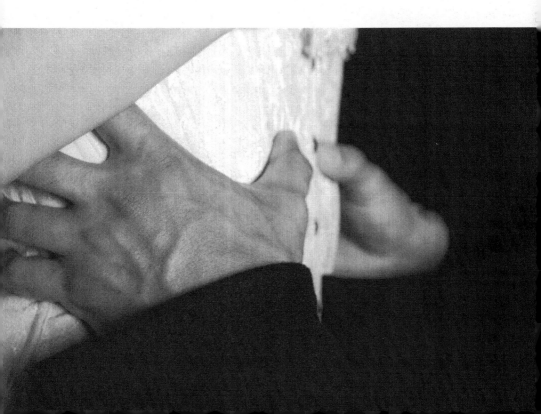

"Grayson. I need to know your basic sexual history, and whether or not...whether there's any chance you're carrying a sexually transmitted disease. I'm checked every six months. I'm not sure what the protocol is these days, but I'm pretty sure—"

"I'm a virgin," he said as he brought his gaze back to her.

"You're—" She stopped.

"I've never done this with a woman," he whispered.

"What about a man?" she asked, and it was so natural, she didn't even stop to consider her words before she said them. She probably should have, considering that sodomy was illegal in England, and he could be hanged for admitting something like that.

He looked up to her then, shocked. "No. Not—what do you think of me to consider—"

"I'm sorry, I didn't mean it like that. It's not a big deal in my circle, and I should have been more careful in my question. But I don't judge, I don't care, I only care that you're clean. Which...since you're a virgin, you should be," she said. "Nothing? Not even oral sex? I mean, I just find it difficult to—you're beautiful. You know that, right? I know I shouldn't judge you. I just—you're obviously quite virile and..."

He took a step back and adjusted his pants on his hips before they slid off. Damn, she'd gone too far and made him uncomfortable. She took his hand. "Why?" she asked as she pulled him to the edge of the bed and sat down next to him.

"I—" He stopped cold, and she knew she'd just come up against the secret he wouldn't be sharing with her. Her best guess was that he was a sexual submissive and had no way to perform without some sort of domination from his partner. "I simply have not found someone I trust enough to share that with."

"But you trust me?"

"I did."

"Did?" Her heart felt like it blew a hole in her chest, and she shivered against it.

"I do...I do. I only—I've never—I'm not sure how to continue," he said.

As he looked down, she realized that any progress they'd made toward him having an erection had come to a quick end. She was going to have to use some of her tricks on him tonight after all. Hopefully, he wouldn't mind too much. First, she needed to break the tension that currently lay across them like a heavy quilt. She smiled.

"Tab A, slot B. Pretty simple," she said with a smile. He looked up at her and shook his head in confusion. "Yeah. Well." She looked at the dinner laid out before the fire. "Do you want to eat first? Maybe talk a bit before we…" She spun her hand in a circle. "I mean, I did pretty much kill the mood there. We can get it back, no worries. It just may take a minute. Are you hungry?"

"Are you?" he asked. "I think you are."

"Are you just trying to please me? Because it's working. But I'm happy to get rid of this maidenhead—shit."

"What?"

"I'm a virgin, too," she said. "I don't want children. I'm assuming my birth control didn't come here with me. She reached up to her left arm and rubbed just below the shoulder. Pleaseohplease. "Nope!"

"You don't want children?" She could tell he was moderating his voice, it was something she'd noticed him do quite often, he was quite practiced at stifling hints of emotion.

"No, I've never wanted to do that. I—oh. Dukley-ness needs an heir," she said finally. "Double shit." She twisted her hands in her lap. She really wasn't prepared for this, but how was she supposed to argue it? It really, really wasn't her body, her will, or her choice at all. Not in this place. Not in this time.

"If you don't want children, we will do what we can to prevent them," he said as he reached over and wrapped his big hand around both of hers and it didn't seem that he was upset about it. "If you don't want children, we won't have them," he repeated.

Her breath stilled. "Okay," she said. "But what about—you're a virgin, and I assume you expected to impregnate someone tonight, so what now? I'm betting you have no birth control handy. I mean, we can do other things, but I would really love to ruin the both of us here."

He stood. "Just, give me a moment?" he asked as he buttoned the fall of his pants and straightened his shirt and jacket. He went to the door and called for Rakshan, then he stepped into the hall and spoke with him. When

he returned, he motioned to the trays of food, so she stood and walked over to him.

He pulled a chair out, and she sat, in her drawers, stockings, and chemise. Then he joined her, sitting in the chair next to her, in his shirt, open jacket, and waistcoat. She laughed, and they stood, and she helped him out of the jacket and waistcoat before they sat again. It was all very perfunctory.

The food was delicious. Finger foods, she noted. Nothing requiring utensils, very sensual. She approved of this. This, she could work with. "It looks amazing," she said, keeping her hands in her lap. She looked across the table to a tray she couldn't reach. "Are those pears?" He picked up a small slice of pear to hand her, but she kept her hands in her lap and licked her bottom lip, then dropped her mouth open and tilted her chin up to him.

He stared at her for a moment, his gaze catching on her eyes then resting on her mouth and she felt that look shiver it's way through her entire system. He placed the pear against her lip, and she sucked it in slowly.

When he fed her a second slice, his fingers remained against her lips, lightly caressing. She chewed, then swallowed, and darted her tongue out to lick the tip of his finger. He pushed it into her mouth, his gaze latched on to her tongue. She drew on him, giving him a sharp bite across his fingernail. His finger curled against her teeth, and he pulled her closer as she refused to release him. His breath came gently against her cheek, the soft pulses of air sending beats across her skin that expanded with each exhale. Every bit of her was waking up and taking note of his attention.

When she finally did release him, his finger remained there, curled against the air as though he awaited another command. The shape of it brought her back to the garden the night before, when that very finger had been curled, just so, inside her pussy and her want focused on that very spot, wetness sliding from her easily.

At the very least, he could rend her hymen with those strong fingers. She shivered, and her belly tightened at the thought of his fingers tearing her delicate flesh. Maybe she should rethink her strategy. His fingers tearing her flesh was all she could think of with every bite she took from then on out, and she wasn't sure she was going to survive dinner at this rate.

She knew they were waiting for Rakshan to do...what exactly, she wasn't sure. It wasn't like he could run down to the convenience store and buy some condoms, was it? But she was certain if they were putting this off for another night, Gray would have said something, and he wouldn't be caressing her breast as he licked the juice of that orange from her chin.

Oh man, she needed to pay attention, because this was getting good. There was a scratch at the door, and she thought for sure she would never take another breath. She put her forehead on the table and breathed slowly as he walked away.

Letting herself go to these feelings was a completely new experience for her, because she generally controlled everything when it came to sex, whether she was top or bottom. Both were about absolute self-control and she wielded her self control like an iron fist. She could not let him crawl so deep inside her that she lost that.

The door closed with a solid click, and she looked up to see Grayson approaching with a small leather box. "Now," he said as he took his chair, "where were we?"

"There was an orange involved," she said. She reached over to the tray of fruit and took one of the halves, then stood and pulled him with her toward the bed and pushed him to his back. He scooted up the bed until his legs weren't hanging off the end, and she crawled over him. She handed him

the orange, then undid his trousers, unbuttoned his drawers, and pulled his pants off, and oh, her mouth went dry at the sight of him, all of him, long and hard.

Well, most of him long and hard. Hopefully, they would get the rest of him that way soon enough. She rethought her idea of his fingers, as his cock would do the job quite nicely as impressive as it already was.

If she'd had to build herself a man to spend the rest of her life with, she very likely would have built something close to this man, except for the look of abject terror in his eyes. Her heart stuttered and she froze with guilt for whatever it was she may have done unwittingly. "What is it?" she asked.

He shook his head. "I'm not...I don't know what your intention is, and the box is over there, and I'm here—holding an orange—and you...you are magnificent," he finished on a breath.

She crawled up until she hovered over him. "We'll use that box soon enough," she said. She lowered herself over him, skimmed her hand down his jaw, and kissed him. It was chaste, again, unsure and curious. She knew he must have kissed before, because it wasn't at all awkward or unwieldy. But the fire she'd seen in his eyes earlier wasn't coming yet.

She scooted back a little. "Sit up," she said.

His shirt was open to his breastbone, so she fisted the edges and tore it open to the hem, then she pushed it off his shoulders and left it caught at his elbows.

She waited to see if he objected. He didn't. He pulled against the shirt but could only get his hands close to her hips, not much farther.

She pushed him back to the bed and followed him down, and he kissed her. He kissed her like he'd kissed her in the garden, like he was looking to find the key to his very existence. Like he wanted to taste every part of her.

"Better," she said as she lifted away from him and took up the orange. His eyes widened and went black again.

Lulu rested her core against his cock, then squeezed the orange across his chest and down the center of his belly, letting the juice pool in all of the nooks and crannies of his abdomen.

She then leaned over him and began to drink. She felt his muscles tense like a tidal wave rushing the shore, every single one becoming rock hard and staying that way as she put her mouth against his skin and sucked.

She shifted lower toward his abs and felt his hands, trapped as they were, come up to her knees and rest there. She licked her way to one side, inspecting the bruises across his ribs, knowing they were made by the bones of his corset.

She kissed each one, each side, then placed her palm over them and pushed gently, as though she just needed leverage to move. She felt his cock grow hard and hot against her skin. It was the pain and the submission. She shifted back toward the center of him.

When she sucked the juice from his belly button, his fingers tightened on her thighs, and she knew she would bruise. She smiled against him, then shimmied lower until she took him in her mouth, and his entire body lifted from the bed as he let out a guttural yell the likes of which she knew she would never, not ever, not in a million years or several lifetimes, ever forget.

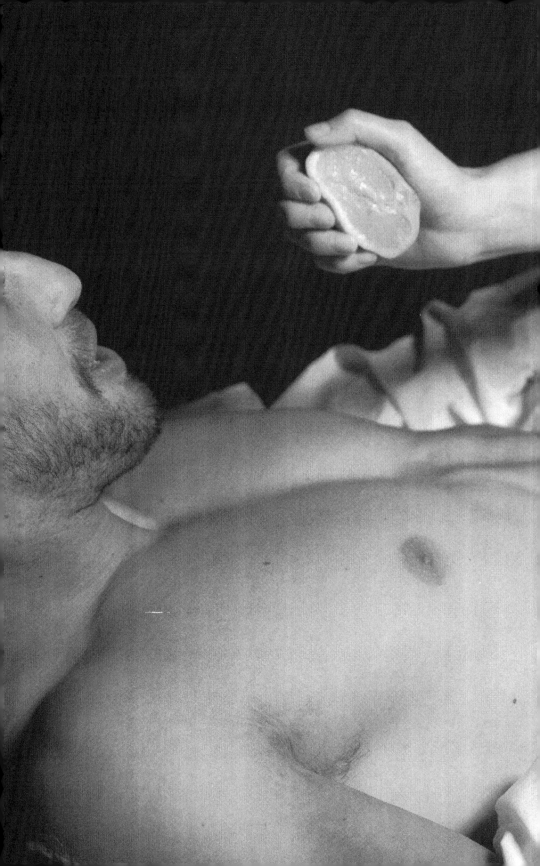

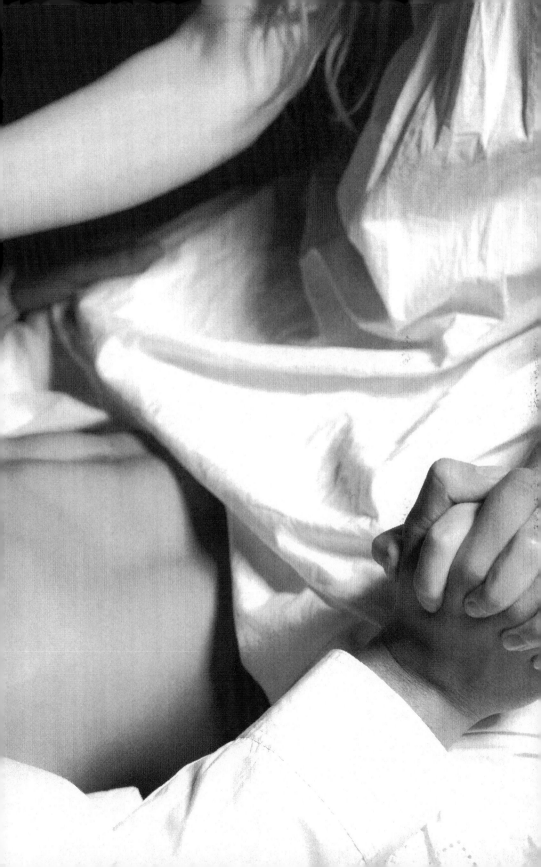

TEN

Appear at points which the enemy must hasten to defend;
march swiftly to places where you are not expected.

—Sun Tzu
The Art of War

Grayson wasn't sure that noise had come from him until he felt his stomach muscles clenched from the exhaustion of all of his air. She was…her mouth on him was—his brain was not working at all, and his shirt—he couldn't reach her. He couldn't reach anything or touch anything beyond her shoulders, and it was…there wasn't a word for how it made him feel.

Free. Just like his corset, being bound gave him the freedom to feel—and feel he did. He fell back to the bed and just let it all wash over him like warm water.

How her wet quim had slid across his cock, then her legs trapping his hips, the cold of the orange followed by the heat of her tongue lapping at his chest, her soft skin under his fingertips, then her mouth on him…it was too much.

He said a small prayer that he would stay hard enough, that she—in all the ways she was different, in all the ways she had stirred something in him that had never even attempted to shift before—could bring him off.

His arms bound the way they were was a start, and he struggled against the shirt, allowing the cuffs to bite the thinner skin of his wrists. His mind tried to panic and consider why she would do that, why she would bind his hands and not release them, because she'd obviously done it with purpose, but was it for her? Did she not want to be touched by him?

She drew on him hard, and his mind went blank as his back bowed until his hips left the bed and her hands reached up to steady herself. He'd never been so aroused in all his life.

If he could shut down his panic, if he could simply enjoy this…this gift. But his mind, his reflex action was to run, to buck her off like an angry stallion and keep her at a distance, because intimacy had been trained out of him. Slowly, surely.

He lifted his head to look down at her. Her small hands explored his chest, his ribs, searching him as though they needed to remember the details of his structure like a blind man with a bas-relief.

He felt one of her thumbs press into a groove between his ribs, and the sharp sting of pain from a bruise sent shocks through his system.

She moved on him, drew on him, tasted his flesh. "This?" she asked.

"Yes, that," he groaned, then one hand dipped below her chin and tucked between them to cup his bollocks, and all he could think was, *nobody has ever*, as he struggled against the binds to pull her away, but she moved her other hand to hold one of his as she simply kept on, refused to move or back down, refused to relent. She was drawing and holding and driving, and every muscle he had tensed as he came off, and she swallowed him whole.

He couldn't move. He concentrated as each of his muscles unlocked, and he felt like he melted into the bed.

She released him slowly, swiped her tongue once more the length of him, and kissed the wet tip of his cock, then sat back on his knees as she fidgeted with his sleeves until she found the cuff links, releasing them and pulling his hands from his shirt. His hands instantly went to her, wrapped around her, and pulled her down to his chest.

"I—" Nothing else came out of his mouth.

She wiggled and pulled the sheets over them.

"Shhh. Close your eyes and rest for now. We've plenty of time ahead of us."

Plenty of time.

Plenty of time, and he wanted to spend all of it doing just exactly that. When he'd told her he'd never been with a woman, or anyone for that matter, he was sure she would shy from him. For what kind of man of his years would not have had experience with a woman, with many women?

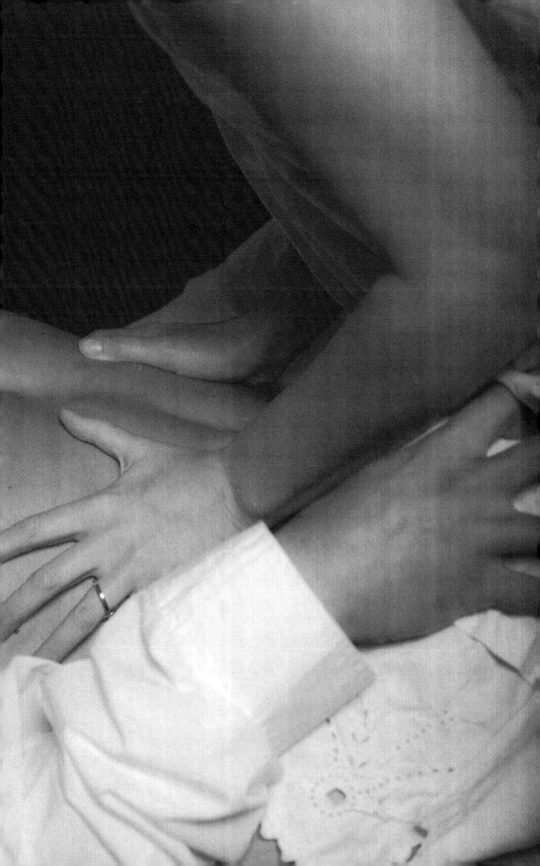

She didn't shy, however. What she did was— "Perfect," he said, and she stirred against him, and he pulled her in tighter. He had done nothing for her, and he wished to—oh, dear god, how he wished to worship her, to do whatever it was she wanted. To kneel at her feet and never leave if it made her happy. But this…this couldn't last. What she'd done to his hands, how she'd restrained him—surely she hadn't meant to do it. She just hadn't been able to get the cuffs loose fast enough. And he'd never been so hard in his life.

He felt her pat his chest. "Rest," she said quietly, and he closed his eyes and willed himself to sleep.

When Grayson woke, he felt her steady breathing against him. He'd never slept so soundly, and never with another person. He ran his hand down her naked back, wondering when she'd removed what remained of her clothing as she shifted against him. He knew when she came awake, because she tensed. He waited a moment, but she didn't move.

"It's me," he whispered, then he felt her hands tighten on him for a moment before relaxing.

"Oh, good. I just—well, I'm never quite sure lately," she replied.

He nodded. She'd said it was good. Did that mean—no. He wasn't going to overthink this, because it would surely drive him mad. He was in bed with a virgin who had just performed an act that should have shocked her to her toes at the mere mention of it. No. He would not overthink this. He would take this gift and hold it close and never let it go.

"Thank you," he said as she rose up and placed her hands on his chest, her chin resting there, and gazed at him.

"You're welcome, very much so. That was lovely, if I do say so myself," she whispered.

"Lovely?"

"Yes, quite lovely. You were…you were beautiful," she said.

"Beautiful." He simply didn't understand. She found this whole process beautiful? That was…an interesting idea, certainly not a common thought. "Why did you—" He stopped himself, because he wasn't going to overthink this.

"Bind your hands?" she whispered. "Suck you off?" she said next. He froze…*she knew what she was doing?* "Because it felt right. Because I wanted to." Did that mean it had been an accident? That what she'd done, she'd done for her pleasure and not his? She turned and put her cheek against his chest, and her tongue darted out to lick his nipple, then her hand started roving down his belly and all rational thoughts fled. Good god, did he love her mouth.

He stopped her hand before she touched his cock, then flipped her over to her back. "My turn," he growled, and he heard her sharp intake of breath as she shifted and steadied beneath him.

He kissed her mouth, then moved slowly, tasting every bit of her skin he could reach. She tasted of the orange she'd squeezed over him, and of salt. He moved lower, and she grabbed his hair with both hands. "Come here." And he did, oh, he did.

His lips met hers, and he sank in, savoring her. She pulled back. "I would like a bit more to eat, and I would like a warm bath to relax me," she said simply.

He paused to consider, but he didn't argue with her. He stood and lifted her from the bed to her feet. As he looked down at her, he realized that his life in the past two days had become a string of firsts. He stood here naked with a woman for the first time. His woman. He ran his hand down her arm, then back up again before he sank both of his hands into her hair and took her mouth with his again. He simply couldn't get enough of her.

She held his wrists and didn't fight, didn't attempt to break away, simply floated along with him, pressing herself to him, fitting her soft parts to his points and angles, and it was lovely.

When he broke the kiss, she gazed up at him with a smile. He looked around the room. "Do you want a robe? There should be some in the bathing room. Or just a blanket?"

She shook her head. "No, I'm warm. Just—can you stoke the fire a bit? I'll be fine." He walked to the fire, slightly uncomfortable being that close to an open fire with his nether bits hanging about. He tossed a shovelful of

coal into the fire and turned quickly to avoid any sparks as she laughed at him. He took up the poker and pushed it deeper into the grate, then turned and sat next to her. She'd pulled a sheet across the two chairs and was filling her plate with food.

"I'm going to need to start exercising to keep up with my appetite," she said as she started eating.

"I can arrange that. What do you need from me?" he asked.

"A large, open space?" she asked.

"Ballrooms have been known to be used for such things, and I happen to have one. It's yours. What else do you need?"

"Soft mats, or cushions? Weights or weighted balls as well, and something else…"

"Yes?" he said.

"A training partner."

He considered her for a moment, then nodded as he looked down to his food. He wasn't sure about training with a woman, but he could easily follow her lead. She seemed to finish eating, then turned toward him, pulling her feet up to the seat of her chair and wrapping her arms around her legs.

"Are you chilled?" he asked.

"No, just curious about you," she said quietly.

"I'm curious about you as well," he said by way of warning her to tread lightly because he knew she wasn't yet ready to share with him.

She nodded. "Where have you been? You only recently returned to England. I know you're not ready to talk about why you left. But where did you go?"

"India."

"And what did you do in India?"

Grayson paused and considered what he could tell her. He knew he wasn't able to tell her the truth, whether he was prepared for her answer or not, so dancing about it would be the best move. But he didn't want to break her trust either, so he would have to be cautious. "I worked in concert with others in service to the empress."

"The Empress of India?" He nodded. "Wow, that's quite a title. Who's the Empress of India?"

Grayson watched her carefully to determine whether she was jesting, but she didn't seem to be. The empress had considered the future of India carefully, and he was aware of the difficulties but…could it be that for her, the queen no longer held India? "The Queen of England is also the Empress of India," he said.

"Oh, seriously? That's interesting. So did England invade and take over? Or how did that come about?"

Grayson sat back in his chair, for the first time wary of her intent—what if this was some sort of elaborate trap? She reached out and took hold of his arm suddenly.

"I'm sorry. I only want to know about you, not about what you do unless it pertains to who you are. I don't mean to pry if you aren't comfortable. If what you were doing in India is…sensitive, then don't tell me. I want you to trust me above all else."

He nodded. "I'm simply not at liberty," he said and he started to relax again.

"Okay, then, don't go there. Tell me what you're able, or not able or…I don't know. I just thought we could try to start getting to know one another."

Lulu skimmed her hand up his arm, one cool finger dipping into the wide scar that stretched across his bicep and shoulder. His muscles flexed and he stopped breathing, so she turned and reached out to the small red leather box that Rakshan had brought. She opened it and poked at the contents. "Do you know how to use these things effectively?"

Grayson shook his head. "I haven't had the need." She closed the box and looked over to him. Grayson ran his hands down his thighs, suddenly feeling quite vulnerable in his nakedness.

Lulu stood, shoved her chair up against his, then sat back down and draped her legs over his lap, pulling the sheet from behind her and covering them.

"How is it," he said, "that you seem to know what I'm thinking?"

"Practice. I'm a student of human nature. The human condition. Action and reaction."

Grayson considered her. He wasn't sure he should ask about what she did considering he had just refused her the same. "You're an artist. Did you have work in museums or did you work for commissions?" he asked.

She thought about it before answering. "I'm afraid…what I actually do, what I am, is so very closely related to who I am that if you were to reject me, I don't think we could continue on. As it is, I don't think there's anyone in this time period I could equate with what I do, so to explain it might paint myself in a negative light. I would prefer to show you. As soon as I'm able."

Grayson breathed. He wasn't sure if her words had been helpful, or if it was worse than simply not knowing. Of course, his mind worked and raced and attempted to figure out which of all the negative positions she could hold was the one she referred to. But then she'd said it wasn't that. It was just related closely with that. What did that even mean? He shook his head and put his hands across her legs, pulling her closer.

"I don't know how either one of us has much choice other than to trust at the moment. I have asked you to trust me to take care of you, and I will. I will take care of you. I will also trust that you will continue to share with me as you're able to," he said finally.

She scooted closer to him and ran her hand down his chest, her smooth fingers tensing muscles in other parts of his body as they went. She stirred something in him that no one had ever managed to touch before. Perhaps it was the intrigue of not knowing her, of not being able to figure her out at all. Perhaps that's what he was built for. He had always been good at figuring out mysteries and working to fix problems. Of course, he'd usually worked on things without anyone's knowledge of him. He was never recognized for his work, and he'd come to like it that way. She touched his mouth, and he turned his head toward her and kissed her.

He shifted on the seat of the chair, turning to her, and she wrapped her arms around him. He pulled her closer, then stood with her in his arms and walked for the bathing room with the sheet trailing behind them.

They'd been distracted long enough. He'd had a taste of what passion could be with her, and he wanted more. He wanted inside her as a husband takes a wife. He wanted to rid them both of their virginity, sink into her body, and claim her maidenhead for himself. He felt that he could after what she'd already managed. Even if he had to do some things he wasn't keen to do. For her, he would do them.

There were candles lit throughout the room, the oversized bathtub brimming with steaming water. Rakshan must have heard them moving about and warmed the water. He set her on her feet and pointed to a row of glass bottles filled with herbs and oils that Rakshan had collected.

She walked over and started to smell them, picking a couple dried herbs, crushing and sprinkling them across the water, then a couple different oils, dripping them sparingly. The bathing room bloomed with a wild and sensual fragrance.

Grayson reached into the tub and swirled the water, then took her hand and helped her into the bath.

Lulu stepped in, her entire body sighing as she did so. She melted to the bottom, then tugged his fingers until he slipped into the tub behind her. "You weren't expecting to be invited?" she asked.

"No, I thought you would prefer to bathe alone," he replied.

"Never. Well, occasionally. If I have a good book to read, I'll take a bath and expect my privacy, because I'll be reading. Never disturb a woman who is reading," she whispered reverently.

She felt his smile against her shoulder. "I will do my utmost to remember that request," he said. "What do you read?"

"Everything. Anything. I grew up with Stephen King but we broke up after the one with the crab and the playing card. I read some Clive Barker but it wasn't the same. Classics were a bit hard for me. I liked Dan Brown once, but only once, and Umberto Eco, oh man his books were powerful in a way I couldn't even begin to explain."

"Is that all?"

"No, Kushiel's Dart changed my life, so did the The Vintner's Luck—what beautiful non-traditional sort of love stories they were."

"You like to read love stories?"

"Well, I wouldn't characterize those as love stories exactly, but I do read romances. I like to cut the heavy stuff with a bit of fluff, but mostly historicals."

"Historicals?"

"Yes! Oh you'll like this, America is obsessed with Great Britain, there's an entire genre of books about romance and the UK. Georgian, Regency, Victorian…yeah. Love stories."

"That makes no sense to me. What is there to romanticize?"

"Oh they find things, dukes and barons and viscounts, oh my!"

"I'm no romance," he said quietly.

"Perhaps not a traditional one, but then you already know I'm a fan of the non-traditional."

He fell quiet and Lulu wondered what he was thinking about, but the movement of his hands on her arms, over her scalp, across her shoulders lulled her into a peace she couldn't escape."

She settled against him. He did make for a lovely pillow. She considered how easy it had been to be familiar with him, but that was part of who she was. That's how she had to be. Her clients expected that familiarity whether they'd met in person or not. Something about him though…it was as though she'd known him all along, but they'd had yet to meet.

Her biggest concern at the moment was sex, because she wanted it, oh, how she wanted him inside her. She knew it would be lovely. But she wasn't interested in the items in the box Rakshan had brought—what looked like a small sea sponge, a syringe with who-knew-what inside of it, and a condom that looked to be ill-fitting and awkward. She cringed as she considered what to do next.

"What is it?" he said behind her, the ripples of his deep-seated baritone moving through her slowly. He had that kind of voice that was more vibration than sound—almost a full bass instead of baritone—and when he whispered, she had to concentrate to hear what he said.

"I…really wanted to…not be a virgin after my wedding night," she said.

"You don't approve of the items Rakshan brought," Grayson asked.

"Now who's reading who?" she replied with a laugh. She shook her head. "I'm not entirely familiar. I don't believe you are either, and the items all look a bit disconcerting. I'd like to speak with Francine, if I could? Before we…before? Would that be okay with you?" she asked quietly. She suddenly felt shy asking this of him.

His penis pressed lightly against her hip with the slightest hint of erection, and she wanted it inside her so very, very much. To lose herself in an orgasm seemed like the perfect thing to do right about now, to let that pleasure wash over her and loosen all of her nerves. That would be great.

"You are my wife, and I will bed you. But I'll not force you. We will not have relations until you are ready. I simply can't do that. I don't care what the tradition is. I've waited—"

"Here's the thing," she said, stopping him before he got the wrong idea. "I really like sex. I really do. I understand that the hymen I seem to be in possession of speaks for itself in the sex department, but to be perfectly honest, I think we both know it isn't mine." She felt his chest hitch with a laugh, then continued. "I'm sorry if this disappoints you. I just—"

"I'm not sure disappointed is the correct word. I've actively practiced abstinence for many years."

"How do you actively practice abstinence?" she asked, but when he didn't speak, she went on. "I'm sorry, I shouldn't harass you. I find your willpower quite enthralling." In fact, she saw it as a talent and something that pointed to his wish to serve. That kind of patience, the ability to pause a want so desperate…not many could manage it and the very thought of it made her thighs ache from pressing together.

"I see. Lulu, please make no mistake that I—I've looked forward to, and dreaded, this particular night for one single reason, and it seems that's not to happen. To say I'm not disappointed in that fact would be incorrect, particularly since you have already done something for me in that vein. However, I will not rush you to a decision either. I've already done that once, and once is enough. The facts have greatly changed since I began to consider the one possible positive outcome of marriage."

"Thank you. That was…more than you've ever said, and I very much appreciate your thoughts and your consideration." She rolled in the tub and put her hands on the edge, bracketing his head as she slid her breasts across his chest. "I do, however, wish for you to ruin me tonight…if you're willing."

Gray rubbed one hand across his mouth and jaw, nearly hiding another smile. "One thing I'm beginning to understand, Lulu, is that for some reason, with you, I seem to be ever willing. But I don't—all that being said—I don't understand how," he said.

She skated her belly across his cock, teasing him even though it didn't respond to her as eagerly as she would like. She flexed her arms, pulling herself tight against him, then whispered directly into the shell of his ear. "Use your hands."

She felt his breath catch, his chest vibrating with the tension. "Your fingers, Gray. Those strong fingers that tested me last night. Those fingers that are already familiar with me." The tension moved and rippled through the muscles against her as he shifted his hold on her. She slid back a bit and breathed in between his open lips as though to remind him, tempting him with a kiss, taking his breath as her own.

"You want me to claim your maidenhead with my hands." He groaned against her open mouth, then he licked his lower lip, his tongue brushing her mouth as he did so, sending shudders through her. He had no idea the power he held.

"Yes, please. Would you?" She really wanted to be rid of that bit of flesh. It had never meant anything to her in her former life, and it meant even less now. However, she knew it would mean something to him, and if they were to abstain from intercourse until she could figure out the whole birth control issue, she feared breaking her hymen in other ways, even as thick as it seemed to be.

She'd met a sub once who had torn her hymen horseback riding, and another who had torn it doing gymnastics. Lulu was no simpering miss. She was going to be active. She'd felt this hymen, and she knew it was going to hurt just by the small pressure he'd placed on it the night before. But she wanted very much for him to claim her on their wedding night. She wanted to gift him with that, and this was how it could be done.

As for the ruination of her husband, that would happen soon enough. She could use her mouth on him every night to alleviate any qualms he may have for patience, and she could get creative if he had problems getting an erection without submitting somehow.

He spread his hands and skimmed her sides, then cupped her backside before he smoothed those big hands down her thighs. Lulu held her breath as she spread for him beneath the water, her knees bracketing his hips.

He scooted down a bit more in the water and pulled her to him, his cock resting just where she wanted it, between her labia. She heard his groan and looked up to see his eyes clenched tightly.

She wanted him to know how he felt to her. She knew he'd never had this from someone, and she wanted to give him as much as she was able, so she decided she would talk him through all of it, make sure he understood.

"You feel so good there," she said, "just there, like you belong." She rubbed against him as she watched his face. He was only barely hard, a start that wouldn't get them far. He must have an idea about that…or perhaps not.

She reached down and pinched one of his nipples, testing him. His eyes flared, and his cock twitched against her. She let out a sharp breath and pushed against his chest.

"Hold me, tight," she ordered, and she felt his fingertips bite into her hips. "Oh god, yeah, just like that," she said on an exhale as she began a rhythm against his penis, slow and steady. "You feel so good, so right. Your hands on me…I feel safe, Gray. It feels so perfect."

"You're wet," he whispered. "Wetter than water, a simple impossibility, but still true."

"I am wet, for you, because of you. Gray, I need you to do something for me," she said, and he nodded against her forehead. "Do not come. You can't come in this water. Do you understand?" She didn't think he would be able to regardless, but she wanted to be certain.

Gray's eyes were the clouded dark that she was beginning to love seeing. He nodded stiffly, then said, "I won't. I won't come off unless you tell me to." Then he let out a breath that sounded like relief before he moved his forehead to her cheek. He breathed heavily against her neck as Lulu nodded and rode the ridge of him until she quickened, but it wasn't enough.

"Touch me, please," she said. "With your hands, your fingers. Touch me, Grayson."

His right hand skimmed around her hip as he leaned toward her in the bath, his other arm pulling her tight against him as his hand slipped between them and found her. Their bodies were so close that without the slip of the water, his arm never would have fit between them.

"Yes, Grayson, yes," she said as she wrapped her arms around his neck. She felt one of his legs come up to steady them in the bath as his finger slipped between her folds. She felt the twinge as he tested her again.

"Wait," she said. "Just give me a moment." She loved pain, took it onto and into her body like a prayer from her lovers, but this pain…it felt like so much more was happening by the simple rending of her flesh with his fingers. "I'm scared," she whispered.

"Don't…" His hand slipped away, and she relaxed a bit. "We can wait. We don't have to—"

"No, please, I want this, I want you." She cut off his words, then took his wrist and pushed his hand back between her legs. "Please, please help me feel you," she whispered against him.

She let her head fall back as she rode his cock and his finger, allowing it to slip past the taut barrier of this body's virginity, then she felt him hook that finger and press into her just behind her pelvic bone, and she groaned and sank down as his thumb found her clitoris.

"Oh god, you're amazing. Don't stop…don't stop, just there." She leaned hard against him, her breath echoing in the shell of his ear as she played with the soft bit of flesh with her tongue, and he panted against her.

"Grayson, oh god, Grayson." She pushed back and held his black gaze. "Now. Do it now." She breathed it, and his eyes darkened as he tensed and hooked two fingers inside her and pushed back against the tender membrane.

"Harder," she said as she took his mouth with hers, her hands skimming around his neck. "Harder." Her breathing took over, the spinning sensation overwhelming her system as he worked her from inside and out and she bit his lip.

Gray groaned and pulled out, then pushed his thumb in, smoothing it side to side along the tight flesh as he tested her. "Now, Gray, please. It's yours. I'm yours, Grayson. Make me yours," she begged.

"You're mine, Lulu," he said as he pushed against that flesh, and she felt it give way. The shock of it tensed every muscle in her body, and her fingernails sank into the skin at the back of his neck, pulling him toward her.

She looked into the deep black of his eyes and saw a possession so powerful she felt it seep into her bones and lock into place like shiny brass tumblers. He groaned against her, his arm tensing on her like a band of steel. His fingers replaced his thumb, thrusting as he teased her clitoris, and she came with a scream.

It crashed down on her and she trembled against him, the water slapping against the tub as it overflowed the sides and hit the floor, and she cried out and held on in a moment that was deeper than she'd ever expected it to be. She fell against him, boneless, as he wrapped her up against himself.

He caressed her gently, then released her and pulled his hand from the water to caress her neck. He rested his hand, streaked with blood, on the side of the tub as she held on, and he stared at his hand as she saw it register for him what he'd just done.

He rubbed his fingers together, those same two fingers and thumb of his right hand, then rinsed them in the tub, rinsed her neck, and held her closer.

"God, Lulu," he whispered against her.

"Thank you." She put one hand against his chest, and his came up and covered it as he tucked her head into his shoulder.

"No... Thank you," he replied.

"You were amazing, the way you moved your fingers. You haven't done this before? You've never touched a woman like this?"

"No—" He paused, and she realized she needed to stop second-guessing him. "Never. I just...you felt so good against me. I only want more."

"You will have it all. I will give it to you," she said. She felt his smile against her.

"We should get you to bed. I don't know the protocol. Will you bleed for long?" he asked as he smoothed the hair from her face.

She looked down and realized they were going to need some fresh water. "I don't know. That was a tricky bit, more difficult than the first—the last—the other time."

She lifted away from him, and he complained, but she stood, and he released the water and ran the tap. He pulled a washcloth from the pile and let the water run over it, then squeezed it over her body, starting at her neck, letting the water sluice down her figure. He followed each rinse with wet kisses against her clean skin, and the goose bumps followed him.

He went to his knees as he worked, rinsing and kissing her mons, then, after looking up to her for permission, carefully washing between her legs. Lulu reached a hand out to the wall to steady herself.

She'd never been touched in such reverent and intimate ways. Thinking about that surprised her. She'd experienced aftercare at the hands of some of the best Dominants, but this...it felt like so much more.

He stood and quickly washed himself before she could clear her mind enough to take over—and, oh, how she would have loved to take over that act. He stepped from the tub and took her hand, guiding her out safely and into the heat of a warmed towel. She dried herself, checking to see how sore she was. She hissed a breath and he cringed.

"Why does it seem more drastic that you used your hands on me?" she asked.

"I have no basis for comparison, I can't—"

She laughed, "Yes, sorry. I'm just...thinking out loud, I suppose. I think I'm going to be sore for a day or two." She wrapped the towel around herself and walked toward him. "But every moment of it will remind me of your hands on me, tearing my flesh and claiming me as yours. Every twinge will bring my mind directly back to the feel of those hands touching me, your fingers inside me," she said as she pressed against him.

He was frozen in place, and she knew he had no idea what to think of her, then his hands came up to frame her face. He ran his thumbs across her eyebrows and kissed her.

"Now you're mine," he said against her as he deepened the kiss. "Mine."

Oh, it was an inappropriately possessive exclamation, but damned if it didn't feel good to be claimed for once. She floated along on the words, because that orgasm had done one very definitive thing. It had anchored her. She belonged here, with this man, and that knowledge was exactly what she needed at the moment.

ELEVEN

A hasty temper, which can be provoked by insults,
is one of five faults which may affect a general.

—Sun Tzu
The Art of War

Grayson lifted her and walked to the bedroom, closing the door to the bathing room with his foot so Rakshan could take care of the mess they'd made. He laid her out on the bed and pulled the linens and quilts up to her chin. He turned, intending to stand at the fire for a while and think about the last day, but her hand snaked out and caught his wrist.

"Warm me," she said.

Warm me. How could two simple words affect him so? They stopped him in his tracks. How could a woman trust him so readily, so sweetly? She'd come from…somewhere, had never met him, had never known of him or his life or intentions for her, and she seemed to so easily place her future in his hands. To allow him his secrets without qualm, to open to him without fear or complaint. He didn't deserve her, and she deserved so much more than him. She released him, and he walked around to the far side of the bed, crawling in behind her, fitting himself to her.

His chest heaved on a breath, and he tensed, the power of his thoughts overtaking the reality of his body. He wrapped one arm around her waist carefully, trying to keep from crushing her to him.

He would make every effort to be the man she deserved, and if he couldn't be that man for her, he would allow her to walk away in order to find that man. He pushed his face into her wet hair and inhaled the herbs she'd prepared in the bath, savory and soothing.

He kissed her hair, breathed in and out slowly, and eventually drifted off to sleep.

∂

Grayson became conscious at the smooth touch of fingers exploring his face and neck. Tracing his bones and night beard, scruffing against his cheeks and twirling along his ear. He remained as still as he could, relaxing so he could see the smallest sliver of her in the dawn light from beneath his lashes. She traced his nose, then over his eyebrows, and leaned her cheek against his and burned her delicate skin with his whiskers.

He smiled. He couldn't help it.

"Finally," she whispered. She continued to trace him, and he held as still as possible, allowing her attentions. It was incredible and a bit shocking— after so many years of, not simply celibacy, but no true human contact— to have a woman in his arms and her hands all over him. Last night was beyond compare, and as he woke he could only pray she was not a dream.

He groaned and wished—*wished*—he could want her enough. He thought he did want her enough, but *wanting* wasn't the problem before. He wanted women, this one in particular. He didn't understand his body, and why it reacted the way it did…or didn't, and it had never frustrated him so much as it did now.

He wondered how she fared with all of this, considering she shouldn't even be here. Perhaps he could take her to get some things today such as… things. He didn't know what, just whatever she might want. He needed to run some errands today and Rakshan could manage the tasks in the house without him.

Her hand made its way under the covers to smooth down the edge of his back and round his arse, and he pushed toward her. He concentrated, closing his eyes. Without warning, she pinched the muscle of his backside— hard—and he opened his eyes and looked down at her.

Before he could consider her actions, she gave him that look, that one look, the look he would die upon if he had a choice, the one that buckled his knees without permission, and his cock strained to meet her.

He paused to examine why she would do such a thing, but she shimmied down his body and pushed him to his back, taking him in her mouth in a quick, smooth maneuver he didn't have time to evaluate, and then all considerations fled, and he was simply lost in her mouth.

He reached for her, but she intercepted his hands, twisting their fingers and pushing his arms to the bed. She held him so tight, her fingers were strips of white and red. Her hair blanketed them, hid her movements from him as he strained to see, and he did strain, because he wanted desperately to see that mouth. She ran the edges of her teeth up his cock, and his breath stilled.

When he looked down again, she flipped her hair back over her shoulder, resting his cock between her breasts. "I want you to come," she said.

Jesus, he thought. He groaned and nodded, keeping his eyes on her as she shifted, his cock peeping out from between her breasts. She slid back down and took him gently, sliding the foreskin against the crown of his penis, back and forth, as her tongue darted out to tease the tip at a slow, maddening pace. Her hands twisted against his, and he felt a quick shock of pain, and his cock grew harder.

"Oh god, Lulu," he groaned, and her lips slid around him until he disappeared into her mouth. She released his hands to take his bucking hips, and he tangled his hands in her hair as he came against the back of her throat.

He lay there for a moment as she licked and kissed him. Then he smoothed the hair from her face, wrapped his hands around her jaw, and pulled her to him as he sat up. He took her mouth, tasting her, and himself, and he relished the moment. For he may still be a virgin, but the gifts she bestowed upon him would keep him happily for a long time.

She laughed against his kiss, and he fell back to the pillows, pulling her up against him. "If I had known marriage…but no, I don't believe marriage in general would be like this," he finished. He looked at her. "Are you content? Is there anything I can do for you?"

"Beyond what's already been promised? No, I think I'm about as content as one can be after being removed wholly from my time and place, my people and my life."

Grayson moved her away from himself and sat up, throwing his legs over the edge of the bed. He felt her shift on the bed behind him, but he didn't turn. There wasn't much to be done about her situation. He felt utterly helpless in that. But even more now, he also felt this absolute terror that at any moment she would leave him, either for her own time or her own life here, as he had offered her.

Perhaps it would be better that way. Perhaps she needed to leave before she realized he was getting hard only because of the accidental bursts of pain she provided him. Perhaps he needed to be left to his secrets. But he didn't want to be.

"I can't apologize for that," he said quietly but stiffly.

"I didn't ask for—"

"No, no, I realize, but I think someone should be at your feet apologizing for what has been done to you, and it would be me except," he paused, unsure whether to forge on or cut bait and run from the conversation. "except that I won't, because I'm not sorry you're here." His hands shook and his stomach tightened but he'd said it, and now he would make her understand. His voice rose as he continued. "I'm no longer sorry you were taken from your life and given to me. Because it feels like a gift, and if there's anything I should apologize for, it's that I am completely unapologetic."

He stood and started to pace. What was wrong with him? Only moments ago he'd taken pleasure in her. She'd given it freely to him, and now…now he raged, like a maniac who couldn't stop himself.

He sat down and tried to temper his feelings, tried to rein them back in. Instead, he went on. "So, I will not apologize, and I will not allow you to leave." He knew he said the words much more adamantly than he should have. If he'd couched them in a sympathetic voice, it would have been better, but he hadn't. He'd been harsh.

Lulu was quiet at his back. Maybe he shouldn't have said anything, but that was how he felt at the moment, and they had promised… He felt the bed shift as she got up from the other edge, and he shrank inside his skin.

But, damn it all, he would not apologize, not for any of it, not for the night before, and not for the streaks of blood on her pale skin. His thumb skated across those two fingers once again in remembrance. He definitely would not apologize for the feeling of her flesh rending against his fingers and the overwhelming sense of possession it brought—coupled with something else he had no name for.

He rubbed his thumb against his fingers as if to feel her again there, as if to remember the moment in some tangible way. He wanted her, he wanted her here, and he would do whatever was necessary to make her happy so she would stay here. His head fell to his hands, and he sank his fingers in his hair, fisting it to feel the burn of the tension.

Lulu stepped away from the bed to the trays of food by the fire. That was what had woken her. She rarely slept through a sunrise, much less a tray-wielding man trying to be as quiet as a mouse as he shuffled around the room. When Grayson seemed to be finished speaking for the moment, she walked to the bathroom and shut the door. She needed a minute.

He had just gone all caveman on her, and it was entirely her fault, and she knew it. What had she expected to happen after she allowed him to take her virginity with his fingers? She might as well toss him her ponytail and lie down on the floor.

The problem was, as a sub, he shouldn't have gone caveman like that. Or maybe he should have. She didn't know him at all, even if it felt like she did. This man was trained to control, but wanted to submit. He wasn't a switch, but he wasn't a textbook sub either, whatever that meant.

She felt like she'd known him forever. From the first moment she'd seen him, she felt a delicate thread of trust between them that would be so easy for her to break, but she knew if she pulled it gently, he would follow to prevent that.

She needed to give him some space to assimilate as well, because this situation hadn't just happened to her, even if it did feel like she was the only one making concessions. Like marriage to a stranger. Well, no, from what he'd said, for him, marriage itself was also a concession.

Her brain was too tired to sort through the mess she was in, which was exactly when she would have gone to the peace and quiet of the complete darkness required for developing plates. Even printing—the amber light that removing all hint of color. Or the bulb she used for exposing contact prints. She closed her eyes and remembered the slosh of the chemicals in the trays, the tang of the stop and the fix, the first hint of tone as an image came to life in the chemical soup. It was everything to her and now it was nothing.

She missed it like she would miss a piece of her body. She wanted to fry her nose hairs off in that first whiff of acetic acid just to feel alive.

But she had no darkroom.

She threw a towel on the floor and slid down the wall to sit on it, resting her elbows on her knees. What in the hell was she supposed to do? Even if she was now an heiress, she'd lost everything, and all the money in the world wasn't going to bring it back. Music, photography, her body, her talent. It was all gone. She agreed with Gray in that he also felt like a gift to her, but she wasn't in the mood to tell him that.

My god, it was amazing that they'd gotten as far as they did, really. He was terrified of her in the beginning, then he relaxed only enough to be closed off until she controlled him. But, oh, how he blossomed when she took over and showed him her world. Of course, he wasn't aware she'd manipulated him, and she had no idea how he'd feel if she told him the truth.

Even so, she would never paint another human with wings. The sudden thought broke her somewhere, and she cried. She became a full-out sobbing, wretched mess. She lay down on the cool tile of the bathroom floor and let herself have it. She fell into the despair like she never had, and she let it flow from her unrestrained.

TWELVE

On the field of battle the spoken word may not carry far enough.

—Sun Tzu
The Art of War

rayson had to concentrate at first to verify her crying, but after a moment the sound of her sobbing carried throughout the house like nothing he'd ever heard. She seemed to wail uncontrollably, and he panicked.

He stood and dressed as quickly as possible. He didn't know what else to do, so he left the room and searched out Rakshan. He found him in the library, cleaning shelves.

"I'm leaving."

"Yes, Your Grace."

"Call me Grayson, damn it, Rakshan!" he yelled. Then he yelled in earnest, filling the halls with his mighty roar, and damned if it didn't feel good to let that out.

Rakshan turned to him, and his eyebrows shot up. "Do you need to be dressed?" he asked simply.

Grayson looked up as though he could see through the ceiling. All of his things were upstairs in the room with Lulu. He did not want to go back up there. He shook his head. "Ensure she's cared for. If she has need of anything, send someone for it immediately. I don't care what it is, get it. Just—do not let her leave." He rolled his head, popping the bones in his neck to try to relieve the tension.

"Is she a prisoner?" Rakshan asked.

"No, Rakshan, no, I just—I want to protect her and…" he pressed the heels of his hands to his eyes then dropped them, pleading with him to let him be, to understand, "just see to it. Can you do that?" He stared at him, challenged him to argue but Rakshan simply cocked one eyebrow and waited patiently and Grayson wanted to shake him. He turned and stormed through the entry to the door. As he pulled it open, Rakshan's response chased him from the house.

"As you see fit, Your Grace."

Grayson slammed the door behind him. He stopped when he reached the street, wondering where the hell he was going. Rox wasn't far, so he took off running. It felt good to stretch his legs, even if he was wearing…

What the hell am I wearing? He looked down. He had on his suit from the wedding, complete with torn shirt and badly wrinkled jacket and trousers. Yeah, he couldn't be seen anywhere like this.

He finally ran up the entry stairs to Roxleigh House and hit the door. The butler opened it, and Grayson walked in without a word. He smelled bacon. "Breakfast room?" he asked.

"Yes, Your Grace," the man responded.

Grayson stopped short, wanting desperately to turn around and throttle the man, but he continued on. The next person to throw his title at him was going to be incredibly sorry.

He pushed through the door to the breakfast room and nearly hit a footman in the process, sending him scurrying backward. Roxleigh looked up from the end of the table. "Well, good morning, Grayson. I wasn't expecting to see you so soon and—" Rox's gaze ran over him, and he stood too quickly, his chair toppling to the floor behind him as he rushed forward. "What the hell, Warrick? Is she all right?" he demanded.

Grayson stiffened at the title, then breathed through the anger. He looked down, straightening himself as best he could, tucking in the tattered edge of his shirt and buttoning the jacket. Francine came up next to Rox with a concerned look in her eyes. Roxleigh threw an arm out to keep her back, as though to protect her—from him.

For fuck's sake.

Grayson shook his head stoutly and tamped down his temper as he turned to Rox. "She's…at the house. She is well, but she is not," he said, his words stilted and awkward.

Rox turned to Francine and whispered in her ear, then bussed her cheek and steered Grayson from the room. They crossed the front entry to his study. Rox closed the door behind him, then walked to the tantalus on the sideboard and pointed at the whiskey decanter as he looked back at Grayson.

Grayson shook his head. "No, I—god, I haven't even—I just left."

"Well, that much is obvious," Rox said as he motioned to the chairs at his desk, and Grayson followed him. They both sat silently.

"Grayson. I won't pretend to know what you've done in your life, but you're my family, and beyond that, you've proven yourself a good man. I would like you to know that you could tell me anything, and I would not judge you."

Grayson tensed. He couldn't even begin to imagine what everyone thought of him. He kept to himself. He didn't discuss anything personal. He knew what it was like between men who were friends. He knew because he watched. He was the silent man in the corner just outside the circle, always watching, learning, paying attention, trying to figure out why in the hell he was so damned different from everyone else. Though it did serve other purposes—those dedicated to queen and country—he didn't fit in anywhere. He didn't belong with anyone.

Even though Rox and Calder and Perry had brought him back into the fold and accepted him regardless of his behavior, he knew he didn't belong with them because he simply didn't understand them at all. He didn't understand the need to rule, to control, to dominate. He'd learned it, honed it, forced it into his subconscious, but it was more like a splinter in his brain than something to be assimilated. He leaned forward on his knees and lost his face to his hands. This wasn't who he was, and the pressure was more than he wished to manage.

He had to say something. Some thing, any damned thing. He came here with what seemed like purpose. He needed to make use of it even as he felt like simply standing, leaving without a word, and running back to her—to Lulu. To the only person he'd ever considered opening his mind to.

Oh god, what have I done? "She's—" He didn't know what to say next. He saw Rox freeze from the corner of his eye, as if he didn't want to startle him.

"For fuck's sake!" Grayson stood and walked to the window, looking out over the expanse of green gardens. He fisted one hand but refrained from punching something. The breaking of glass just seemed like it would sound so satisfying right now, not to mention the grounding feel of pain from the cuts. He flexed his hand. "I don't—I can't—I just— goddammit!"

"Can I get a vowel please?" Roxleigh said lightly.

Grayson turned and looked at him. "What?"

"Sorry, something Francine says. Thought it was cute. I don't entirely understand it." Roxleigh stood and approached slowly. "I'm glad you came here. This cannot be easy for you, or for her. It wasn't for Francine and I… and the fact is that her status as a person from another time wasn't even known to me until we were deeply in love. So to know this at the outset"— Roxleigh seemed to shudder—"I cannot even imagine, actually."

"Did you send Francine to see to her?"

Roxleigh straightened and put his hands in his pockets, rocking back on his heels. "Yes."

"Because you thought I'd done something. To Lulu." He didn't pose it as a question.

"No."

Grayson turned on him.

"All right, it crossed my mind—albeit very fleetingly. But look at yourself. What happened to your shirt? Did you sleep on the floor?"

Roxleigh's easy demeanor was slowly bringing Grayson's mood down from the fever pitch it had reached. Grayson looked down. "I am a bloody mess. She happened to my shirt, and no, I didn't sleep on the floor. My clothes did, and I left in a bit of a hurry when—" He shook his head and turned back for the window. He wasn't sure why he couldn't get this out. "I think I hurt her—" He could feel the tension in the room spike, and he rushed on. "Not like…not…I said things that—I said some things."

"Nearly complete sentences, well done." Rox grinned, and Grayson tensed. "Look, how about we get you changed? You can wear something of mine. We can get Calder and Perry, go to White's—"

Grayson rubbed his eyes. He would feel better if he were properly dressed. He pressed a hand to his belly. He would feel even better if he were properly dressed for him. He nodded, and Rox walked from the room, letting him follow.

"I'll take you up, to be sure Francine has gone." Once Roxleigh determined that his suite was empty, he came back and waved Grayson in. "I left some trousers, a shirt, and the rest on the bed. I'll be in the breakfast room. I'll have them warm something for you. No one will disturb you. Ferry is gone for the morning."

"Ferry?"

"My valet. He's the only person, save Francine, who would enter here without warning. So there's nobody currently here to bother you. Take your time."

Grayson nodded, and Rox left, shutting the door with a heavy click behind him. Grayson took a deep breath and walked over to the bed as he pulled his jacket off and let it fall to the floor, then removed his torn shirt.

He held the shirt in his hands reverently, looking at the two crumple marks where her hands had crushed the fabric as she tore the shirt open. He wanted to keep this shirt…exactly as it was. He laid it carefully on the bed, then removed his trousers. He didn't even have drawers on, but he sure as hell wasn't wearing Roxleigh's.

As he bent to put the clean trousers on, he caught a glimpse of himself in the cheval mirror across the room and stopped. He dropped the pants and walked over to it, turning. He had the beginning of a bruise, ringed in red, about the size of a plum on his arse. His memory flashed to that morning when she'd grabbed him and pinched. It still stung a bit and was only just starting to purple. He ran a finger over the bruise, and his cock twitched.

"Bloody fucking hell!" He went back to the bed and pulled the trousers on, then sat. He breathed through it, forcing his desire to slow. He thought he'd worked that out of his system—the arousal with the pain. He thought he could manage pain without becoming aroused now, but she seemed to be bringing them back together unwittingly.

He shook his head. He'd worked for years at controlling it. It was extremely difficult for him to get aroused without pain, but the rest of the damned world did it, so why the fuck couldn't he?

He dropped his head to his hands again, the wet from his tears pooling in his palms. He couldn't let this happen again. He simply couldn't let anyone find out about this, because the last people who did, nearly beat him to death before driving him from London, and his country.

What would Lulu think of him… He stopped and thought about everything she'd done, restricting his movement, burning his skin, pinching and poking and bruising him—no, it wasn't possible that she knew. How could she?

But then, how could she not? That could not all have been happenstance, could it?

He scrubbed at his face. He needed a shave. He palmed his eyes, then stood and put the undershirt and the shirt on, tucked them in, and buttoned the trousers. Then he caught his reflection again. What he wouldn't give for a corset. His gaze went to the wardrobe in the corner. He couldn't…

He looked away and slowed his breathing, but it wasn't slowing his racing heart. He turned and walked to the wardrobe, opening drawers. He didn't even register the frilly underthings until his sight caught the steel busk of a corset, and he stopped. He ran a finger over the cold metal. He would take one from the bottom, and swore he would return it…somehow.

This was wrong, so wrong. He looked around, even as he knew he was alone. Grayson pulled the shirt loose and flung the corset around his torso. He fastened the busk, then walked to the cheval. Just as Rakshan had taught him, he took the two loose loops at the center back of the corset and pulled until his chest compressed and his ribs complained. He shifted to settle the laces more evenly, but they wouldn't shift much since there was such a large gap. He definitely didn't have Francine's measurements. He pulled the two loops to the front and tied them off, then pulled the shirt back down.

He grabbed the waistcoat and jacket and buttoned both of them up, making sure the corset and the knot weren't visible.

He could finally breathe.

He was going to need to distance himself from his wife if he was going to survive this marriage, because she'd unlocked something in him he'd thought was well hidden. Something he wished to remain hidden. Something that could not, under any circumstance, come out again.

Lulu spread herself out as wide as she could. She tried to reach all four corners of the massive bed as she stretched. She thought about the last couple of days. At least she'd survived the day, the wedding, and the queen.

Wow. She'd met Queen Victoria. She'd seemed like a very sad and somewhat angry woman. That, juxtaposed with her want for such an extreme wedding for Gray, was truly bizarre to her. Lulu thought she understood the anger the woman held at the loss of Albert. She'd seen the movie with Emily What's-Her-Face a hundred times because the cinematography was stunning. She sighed remembering how beautifully it was shot. She couldn't wait to have a darkroom again, to get her hands on a camera, chemicals, and some plates of glass. To create her own images.

She turned to her side and looked out the window to the grand manicured park, wondering where Gray was. He had to be out there somewhere. She knew he'd left, because she heard the yell and the slamming door. This house was big, but not too big for that.

It was a beautiful house, barren, but lovely. She felt like she was describing an older woman. She's barren, but lovely. Hey, that was exactly what some men wanted. Not every man wanted children. This one did… or—actually she hadn't asked him. She'd only informed him that she wasn't amenable to children, and he'd conceded.

She pinched the bridge of her nose and stood, walking to the windows. She placed her hands on the glass, still cool from the night, as she watched the sun rise further. Well, only the light, really. The sun was behind the house and couched in layers of smog.

She realized she had asked very little about him. Sure, she knew what he did and where he lived, and those sorts of things. But she hadn't asked about his wants or needs, and being who she was, she really should have. What she had done was assess him. Very cold and distancing of her. Well done, she thought.

The door behind her opened and closed, but she didn't turn, because she knew who it had to be. Well, particularly since there were only about four people in this giant house, and none of them would have permission to enter his bedchambers—save one.

"Grayson," she said.

"No—"

Lulu whirled. "Oh my god, Francine." She ran to her and hugged her. "I don't know how the fuck you manage this, because I'm pretty sure I'm about five seconds from a complete and total breakdown."

"Are you okay?" she asked as she looked her top to toe.

"Yes, I—oh shit, is he okay? You look terrified."

"Well, we were worried, but we're never sure what to think where Grayson is concerned. When he's angry… I would never have thought—but the look on his face when he busted into the breakfast room this morning with his clothing a complete wreck… Yes, we were worried."

"He was a jackass, that's all, a warranted jackass, but a jackass nonetheless. I locked myself in the bathroom for a bit, after he said some horrible things, and was having a cry when he took off. I probably scared the shit out of him."

Francine laughed. "Yeah, I bet you did. I've never known him to have a woman around. He looks at us with terror at any hint of emotion, so…" She shrugged, then pulled Lulu to the settee before the fire. "I'd actually considered that he might be gay, only because of that."

"No, definitely not. You've never mentioned that to anyone, have you?"

"Never. Punishment for sodomy is death. There's no way I would say anything about that. Trust me when I say that this family protects its own. He's not in any danger from anyone's assumptions."

Lulu nodded. "What a day. A night, a…two days. It's been two days now, right? It already feels like a lifetime."

"I imagine. I was so lost. But Gideon was always there."

"Gideon? Oh, Roxleigh, yeah, sorry. Just…so many names. Everyone has ten names here." She breathed and twisted her fingers together. "It was wonderful. I don't want to give you the wrong idea. He was amazing all night. Then this morning—I don't know. The light of day must have brought us from the cocoon of whatever, and he realized he just—wasn't interested."

Lulu thought about what she could ask Francine, and what she could say. She would not betray him to anyone, even if his family did close ranks, but asking her about things… She wasn't even sure what kind of person Francine was yet.

There was still a great deal of prejudice concerning BDSM in the twenty-first century, so she would need to tread lightly either way. "Can we just…talk about something else? God, could we get smashing drunk? I would love a hard cider. Or some shots. Oh, a Kamikaze."

Francine laughed at her. "Yeah, I think we can scrounge something up around here. There has to be something, wine at least. Do you want to get dressed first?"

"You know, I would? But I looked in that closet, and I'm not sure how to...the order of things is just... I have no idea." Lulu generally wore her corsets on the outside.

"If we aren't leaving the house, it isn't imperative anyway," Francine said.

"Well, in that case, I'm keeping the nightgown, and we're getting drunker sooner. Let's do this thing."

Francine smiled and walked for the door, and Lulu followed. Liquor sounded like a good idea at the moment. She honestly didn't drink often, but when she did, it was in the safety of her own home, with other women. She was never much for co-ed drinking, which...she hadn't really considered until now.

Gray could probably use a good stiff drink as well, or ten, or maybe none, how was she to know what he needed? She shook her head. Yeah, she didn't know him at all. How could she?

Francine opened and closed a few doors in the entry before Rakshan came out of nowhere.

"Your Grace." He bowed to her, then looked at Francine. "Your Grace. How may I be of service to you?"

"Rakshan, we need alcohol. What have you got?" Francine asked.

"Nothing, Your Grace."

Lulu groaned and headed back for the stairs as Francine kept chatting with him, then she heard shoes clicking on the stairs as Francine followed her up. She walked into Gray's room and sat on the bed, then fell to her back and stared at the giant canopy overhead.

"Come on, now we do have to get you dressed, because if liquor is out, the next best thing is retail therapy."

Lulu sat up. "Shopping?" she said.

"Shopping."

"I don't have money, do I? Do I have money?" Lulu asked.

"Of course you do, or will. They'll bill it to Warrick, and if he hasn't yet set up accounts, I still owe you a wedding present, so we'll be fine," Francine said with a grin.

"Okay, this could work," Lulu said.

An hour later they were bundled into that familiar black carriage, but this time there was a top on it, and the horses weren't nearly so dressed. It was stunning nonetheless. "How long?" Lulu said as she looked out the window.

"Nearly five years," Francine replied.

"Wow. You don't miss it?" she asked.

"No, but I didn't have a family. I was completely independent. There was nobody left behind, some friends, but none that were very close to me."

"I have friends. I'm pretty estranged from any family I had. By choice," Lulu said.

Francine nodded. "Roxleigh's mother was the same. From what I can tell from her diary, she came here from the mid-1900s… She didn't manage well."

Lulu was intrigued, but Francine turned toward the opposite window, so she wasn't going to push her. How was this all possible? Three women, thrown back in time. How many more could there be?

"I'm sorry," Lulu said.

"Oh, I never knew her. But it's a sad story, and I fear for others who come back in time and can't manage. I feel like I'm always looking at women to see if they look like they're about to snap."

"Yeah, it's got to be that wild-eyed stare that we get when too much shit hits the fan. I feel like it's been plastered on my face for two days."

"No. Well, at times, yes, but you've done remarkably well."

Lulu laughed at that. "Oh, good, I'm glad I can hide the crazy. I wouldn't want to end up in an asylum in the Victorian era."

"No." Francine paused, then went on quietly when she turned to Lulu.

"That's what happened to Melisande, Gideon's mom."

Lulu let her head fall against the side of the carriage. How horrible. She was no history major. In fact most of what she'd learned from history had been from reading novels. She was a fan of historical fiction, because it was based on fact, but what was actual fact versus fiction was a bit of a dilemma at the moment.

However, the fact was, Bedlam was infamous, and it was a real place, and it was still referred to as a place nobody wanted to go. Or—it would be.

Francine took her hand. "Hey, I'm sorry. We have tons of time to talk about all the stuff. Let's talk about something else. What did you do?" Francine asked.

"I was a photographer," she said quietly.

"Oh, that's incredible. Digital or…?"

"Oh no, never digital. I mean, yes, with my iPhone, but no, my art was done on a one-hundred-and-fifty-year-old eight-by-ten camera I found online. It took a month to get, because it had to be shipped from England," she said. It seemed everything they spoke of was bound to make her sad at the moment.

"You realize that means you can still do that, right?" Francine said.

Lulu smiled, finally. Most of this was so depressing, except for that man, and she suddenly wanted him next to her again. When were they going to get to the stores? As if on cue, the carriage pulled to the side and jerked to a halt. The door opened, and Francine stepped out, and she followed.

"Grover, you stay with the carriage. Gentry will accompany us since you hate this place," Francine said.

The man nodded and closed the door before mounting the front and putting one boot on the brake handle and leaning back. She felt Francine tug at her hand, and she turned. Every once in a while, it just hit her that she wasn't in some sort of BBC production.

Oh god. She'd thought that in earnest yesterday, hadn't she? Or… no, the day before, she'd thought… She closed her eyes. She was starting to remember some of the things she'd said and was happy that Francine had come to this world before her. She looked at her. "You being here has probably saved my life."

Francine's smile faded, and she reached out and wrapped her up and hugged her tight. "Never mention it. I'm glad I did."

Lulu nodded and tapped out on the hug before she started crying again. Then Francine linked their arms and turned her for the store, which looked like a massive conglomerate of buildings overtaking several blocks of real estate. She looked at the giant, fancy doorway. Oh man, this was retail therapy of the highest order. Harrods.

THIRTEEN

Simulated disorder postulates perfect discipline, simulated fear postulates courage,
simulated weakness postulates strength.

—Sun Tzu
The Art of War

rayson felt better after breakfast, and Roxleigh let Calder and Perry know where they'd be later. They headed to Southwark. Rox had promised him the best shave of his life, and Grayson was looking forward to it.

The barber's shop was small and dark, but very well designed and appointed. The man himself was small, bent over, and half-blind with thick glass in front of his eyes.

Grayson stopped at the entry. "You mean to have me killed. I told you Lulu was well, Roxleigh. Murder isn't necessary," Grayson said.

"Do you jest? This really is a whole new side of you," Roxleigh said.

Grayson just shook his head and followed as the man waved him over to the chair to sit down.

"Mr. Greene, this is…"

Grayson tensed as Roxleigh paused.

"Lord Danforth," Rox finished, and Grayson relaxed.

It had been entirely too long since someone had called him Danforth, and he hadn't realized how much he'd missed it. It was a good name, and even though it belonged to his father, it had been lost to the title, so his father was rarely, if ever, referred to by it, because he was *The Warrick*.

"Lord Danforth, you need a shave." They were the only words Grayson heard from the man the entire time he was in the shop. It was lovely.

As they walked out nearly an hour later, Grayson ran his finger along his chin, appreciating the close shave. It felt good. Rakshan was good, but this…this was a masterpiece. He saw Roxleigh smiling at him and turned to him as they walked down the street. "What?"

"He's good. I had to find someone new after Ferry nearly removed my neck once. Feel better already, don't you?"

"God, yes. Thank you."

"He'll take you on. He doesn't add to his list without a recommend, but he'll add you now."

"I can see as how he would be entirely too busy if he did."

Roxleigh's hand reached out and took Grayson's arm, stopping him and pulling him back behind a hack at the curb. Grayson looked to where he pointed, then Roxleigh spoke. "God help us, they've gone shopping."

Grayson looked at the carriage pulled up at the main entry to Harrods, the Roxleigh crest shining on the door.

"This is bad?"

"This is…" The look on Roxleigh's face was nearly comical. "Well, I suppose it depends on how you look at it. A woman who is upset and goes shopping is a woman who either has some revenge to get in the way of a dent in your credit, or needs time to think of a plan for future revenge. Either is terrifying."

"I—see," Grayson said. He actually thought it could be a good thing. She needed to get out into London and see some things, perhaps get to know her new home. "I meant to set up accounts for her, well, for Lady Cecilia, but I hadn't yet."

Roxleigh remained completely silent, and Grayson looked at him. "What?"

"That won't stop Francine. You're going to owe me quite a bit of money," he said.

Grayson nodded stiffly, he didn't want to tell Roxleigh no, but he also didn't want to promise money that wasn't his. All of the money was Lulu's. He would have some cash once his rooms let. He could just put him off until then.

"We could join them," Roxleigh said. "If you're brave—"

"I'm not." Grayson shuddered at the thought. He'd considered shopping with Lulu, but not Francine. She was lovely, but tended to look at you in a way that made you vulnerable. It wasn't for him. But then he remembered. "I do actually need to get some things. I need some custom tackle. Do you have a man? Of course you have a man. Is he close?" Grayson asked.

Roxleigh smiled.

Much later—only because there had been so many decisions to be made at the tackle shop that Grayson had never considered—they made their way to the Iron Duke to meet Perry and Calder.

"I don't understand what you need those for," Roxleigh said as they entered the pub.

"A wall display. That's why they have to be perfectly identical."

"But in balance as well? I think you terrified my saddler, to be honest."

"I'm particular about my weapons," Grayson said, hopeful to drop the subject.

Roxleigh paused but Grayson pushed ahead through the doors and found Calder and Perry at the back of the pub. The men stood and greeted them as Roxleigh caught up.

"Weapons?" Rox said.

Grayson just turned to him and nodded. "Should we be getting back? I don't want to—"

"You just walked in," Perry said as he reached to shake his hand.

"No, they won't return until nearly supper. I guarantee that much," Roxleigh said.

"Lost your wife already?" Calder asked.

"She's off at Harrods with Francine," Roxleigh answered.

"Bollocks!" Perry said as he waved to their favorite buxom blonde barmaid. She sauntered over with a glare to both Perry and Rox, then assessed Grayson and Calder. "Now, Lucy, don't be angry," Perry said as they sat.

"Well, ye've all gone an' got hitched, an' I'm not even allowed a perch when I bring yer ale or take yer blunt. T'isna fair." She pouted.

"True, Rox and I are married, and I'm assuming you know this is Warrick, so he also hasn't a knee for you. But this here," Perry said with a strong slap to the back of Calder's shoulder, "is Calder. He's still amenable."

Calder grumbled, "Amenable is a stretch."

"I imagine so," Perry replied.

Calder's eyes widened as Lucy approached him. Perry shoved Calder's chair from the table with his boot, and Lucy took his knee. She gathered her bosom between her arms and grinned at Calder, who assessed her, then wrapped an arm around her back, his hand a fist.

"Lucy, is it?" he asked. She bounced. "Sweet Lucy, would it be too much trouble to bring my cousins and myself each a pint?" He grinned and squeezed her, and she leaned in and whispered in his ear. As Grayson watched, Calder intuitively pulled back, then forced himself to still as he allowed her to share a secret. He seemed to be staring in terror straight into her bosom.

Lucy's hand strayed down Calder's chest as she spoke to him, but his caught it and held it before it went too far. Grayson looked away for a moment, thinking of how that exact maneuver on him had sparked his nerves last night. He shifted in his seat. Abruptly, Calder stood, taking Lucy with him, then she dragged him from the taproom through a door at the back. Gray imagined this was all for show.

"I don't think we'll be getting our ale soon if we wait. Perry, keep your mouth shut," Roxleigh said, then he stood and walked to the bar himself.

Perry grinned and turned on Grayson. "So. Shopping. What did you do to her?" he asked.

Grayson rubbed his temple. He'd only just begun to calm from the entire morning, and here was Perry...doing what Perry did best.

"Please," he said.

"Gray, I jest. Don't mind me. If she's with Francine, she's in good hands. Not to worry. You may be destitute when she returns, but she'll return. You'll still have a wife," he finished with a wink.

Grayson breathed as Roxleigh came back over with two pints in each hand. He put them on the table and glanced at Grayson. "Bloody hell, I should have told Perry to keep his mouth shut. Oh, wait, I seem to remember that I did." Rox shoved his brother when he grabbed his ale, and Perry nearly spilled it down his front.

"Damn, Rox! Not the ale, never the ale," Perry said.

Grayson shook his head and downed half his ale in one draft, then slammed it back to the table. "It's not—it's fine."

"Jesus, Perry, you've already regressed him to two-word non-sentences. All my hard work over the past hours was for naught. Do you know," Roxleigh started, "that I had him actually explaining things to me today? It was marvelous. He's actually quite brilliant." Rox smiled at him, and Grayson nodded a concession. He actually preferred the banter when it centered on someone else, but he was becoming more amenable.

"Well if that's true what was he off to India for then?" Perry said with a smile. Grayson and Rox both just turned to stare at him, and Perry lifted his ale again.

Calder stumbled back to the table and wrapped his hand around the final tankard as he sat. Grayson cocked an eyebrow at him as he brushed some chicken feathers from his jacket. Grayson, Rox, and Perry all turned to find Lucy smoothing her hair and shaking feathers from her skirts as she returned to the bar, and the yelling tender, who had several orders stacked up.

They all turned to Calder, who lifted his ale and shrugged. "Send me to play the sacrificial lamb, and I'll not shirk my duty," he said, then downed the ale and yelled for Lucy. She bounced over and took the empty tankards with a wink.

"Someone has to keep the ale coming." He reached out and tapped Grayson's forearm. "This is a fine jacket. Who's the maker?"

"Not mine," Grayson said. "Roxleigh's."

"I thought it looked a bit tight." Calder winked at Rox.

"Are you saying I'm getting soft?" Roxleigh asked.

"I said no such thing," Calder replied, then looked back to Grayson and shot one eyebrow up. "Did she scare you out of your own house?"

Grayson paused for a moment, then gave in to the ribbing. "Yes, in fact, she did."

When the laughter settled, Calder spoke again. "I have to be going. Gray, you look like you could use a walk. Your house is my direction."

Grayson nodded and stood, saying farewell to Rox and Perry, then followed Calder from the tap.

When they got outside, Calder spoke to his driver, and his carriage pulled away. "What are you doing?" Grayson asked.

"Walking, just as I said," Calder answered. "Look, I know you better than most. You don't have to say anything, but if you have need, we have several blocks and two parks between us and your stoop."

Grayson nodded. Roxleigh was good company, but Grayson still didn't trust him enough to tell him anything of importance. Calder, though, Calder had those secrets—and a man with secrets worse than his was someone he knew he could trust. It was devious and calculated, but it was true.

They crossed the street and rounded a corner, heading for Grosvenor.

"I want to trust her. Everything in me is telling me to trust her, and it's terrifying because I've never felt that in my life since…well, since it was proven to be a bad idea to trust those close to you," Grayson said.

"You could have her thrown in an asylum inside a day. You haven't thought to use that?"

"No."

"And why not? Aren't you currently wielding your knowledge over me? Don't pretend you aren't."

Grayson wouldn't even argue that point, but Lulu? "I…we made a promise I intend to keep. Or attempt to keep. I'm not yet at the point where I want to break that," he said.

"I see. So you do trust her, somewhat."

"Not with anything of import."

"What would be important at this point? I mean, really, Grayson, you've got nothing nefarious to hide beyond what you've been doing in India." Grayson shot him a look, and Calder shrugged. "If I hadn't seen you there, I wouldn't have any idea. You know it."

Grayson thought for a moment. The night he stumbled on Calder at that haveli changed both of their lives in a permanent and terrifying way but also, eventually, found him purpose. He wouldn't know for a few years what sort of purpose it was but now he was hopeful that what he'd been searching for then would help them cease the despicable practice that ended up bringing Roxleigh's bride to him.

"What I did in India is irrelevant now that it's tied to the machinations of certain members of the peerage here in London."

"Not entirely irrelevant considering how disturbing it was. So what has changed between us?" Calder asked.

Grayson stopped him and looked directly at him. "Not a damn thing where you're concerned. I can still use it against you," he said stiffly.

"As can I," Calder said.

"The quiet purposes of the Crown are not something to be bargained with," Grayson said.

"To save my life?" Calder asked.

Grayson put his hands on his hips and stared at the ground.

"You both have secrets," Calder said. "You may need to use them against each other in the beginning, but in the end, well, I trust you with my life, quite obviously," he finished.

It was the truth. Grayson would never truly use his knowledge against his cousin, because if someone discovered he preferred fucking men instead of women and he crossed the wrong person Calder could be imprisoned for life. Grayson thought that sentence worse than the hanging sentence it was only 20 some odd years earlier.

Grayson nodded and looked up to him. "You know I would never—"

"I do. Now," Calder replied, then turned and started walking again. Grayson followed. "I lived in fear of your return to London—and to say I lived is speaking gently. I lived like a man about to die because I believed at any moment a simple missive from you would do me in. Then when your father and both brothers were killed… I was in true hell waiting for you to be found. I never helped them, you know. I lied, as promised."

Grayson nodded. He'd known Calder hadn't betrayed his location. His work for the Crown had.

"But there was a time after you did return that I lived in terror," Calder said. "The only thing that kept me from jumping from my skin was the sense that if it ended, well, it was done then, wasn't it? But you came to see me. I knew you sought me out first specifically to allay my fear, and over the past two years, that fear has subsided."

It must have been devastating. "I knew you hadn't broken your promise. So neither would I, and even as you have nothing tangible to hold over me now, I still will not." Calder had been the first of his family he sought out because he knew. Well, not so—he didn't actually seek out any of his family.

So Calder had been the only one. His family had slowly drifted toward him when they felt it was safe enough to approach. It had been wrong of him, but he didn't much care.

"I appreciate that. So you understand the way you have learned to trust may be of use to you in this situation?"

"I still hesitate to do it. I simply—I can't force myself to want to lie to her."

"Then don't. Tell her very clearly what's being done to her. Explain that you have issues with trust and then explain what that difficulty forces you to wish to do. Then explain the problem at hand. Don't threaten her. You're a clever man. You completed how many…tasks, for Her Majesty? You found ways to get them all done. You can manage this task as well. Merely because it has breasts and a mouth shouldn't scare you off."

"You must be speaking for yourself, for she isn't a task to be managed. But as far as the breasts, they don't scare me one bit. I found great use for them last night."

"Please don't regale me."

"I won't. She's not a conquest, not like that. She's something more."

"I have one more bit of advice."

"Yes?" Grayson asked.

"Gifts."

"But she's been off shopping all day."

"Those didn't come from you. The ring, even, didn't come from you. You need to give her something—from you."

"I'm actually working on that."

"Well, then, you're figuring this out well enough."

"Attempting to. This morning I was determined to keep her, against her will if need be. Then I was determined to shut her out entirely because…" He shook his head.

"I know there's more to you than what I know. I'm fairly certain that whatever your proclivity is, it won't get you murdered, so keep that in mind. Grayson, whether you like it or not, you're now The Warrick. You can do just about anything you want, and nobody will say a thing. Being a duke brings certain benefits, one of which is eccentricities being ignored."

He didn't like hearing it, and he certainly didn't like it thrown in his face but Calder was correct. The eccentricities of the peers of the realm were largely ignored...until they weren't. That's the thing, Grayson had no intention of walking silently through his service in order to protect himself. He had an agenda which included destroying several of Victoria's peers and on top of it all Grayson refused to accept that he was The Warrick. "I'm not—"

"Oh, but you are, and you need to embrace that, sooner than later."

Grayson felt every one of his muscles tense to the point he had to stop walking to breathe. "I wish to walk away," he said.

"Then renounce," Calder said easily. "You say you don't want it, yet here you are, Grayson. At any moment you could have renounced and returned to India. But you didn't."

"I have honor." Grayson didn't want to leave the title to a distant cousin unprepared for dealings with these impossible men.

"Unlike your father, apparently. Believe me, I know more about him than you might think. You may want to keep distance from your new family as well."

Grayson looked at him then. It seemed that the more information they uncovered about the men they sought the bigger the net became. Maybe Calder did know his father wasn't the man everyone else expected him to be, and he was already aware Exeter wasn't an honorable man.

What was it with being honorable? Perry was prepared to walk from his title to protect Lilly, because his dedication had shifted—not entirely— just enough to allow for a new paradigm, one in which Lilly was of the utmost importance. Perry had rebuilt his entire world around that, and managed to retain his title.

He thought of Lulu. If he concentrated on her, ensured she was safe and protected, then perhaps he could fall into whatever role was necessary to that. Because, right now, above all else was the need to keep her safe. He had promised her that. Above all else, he would see to it.

Grayson realized he'd felt perfectly useless since his return. Except for the shenanigans with Perry and Calder, he'd had no purpose since becoming a duke. When he'd been in India, his life had been full of purpose. It kept him busy. It kept his mind clear and centered.

A strange calm came down over him like a blanket, shrouding his entire being. He'd never felt anything like it, and it came from this specific decision.

"Warrick?"

"Yes?" he said when he realized Calder had been calling him for some time.

"Warrick," Calder said again. Grayson merely watched him. "You didn't attempt to kill me—Warrick," he said with a grin.

Grayson thought for a moment. "Perhaps it's no longer necessary," he said.

Francine took Lulu's arm and led her down the block, Gentry close behind. "I thought maybe a bookstore? I know you'll need something to read." They'd already shopped Harrod's where Francine helped her buy some clothes and a few other things she would need, kind of a life hack Victorian style shopping trip which included a package of condoms. They were relatively expensive, but Lulu figured it was worth it.

Lulu grinned. "Yes, please." It was the second best idea so far that day. Shopping, as it was wont to do, gave her much needed distance and perspective. She could see the situation from Gray's point of view, because though she didn't feel quite as strongly, she did feel similarly. She wanted to be close to him. She felt an undeniable connection to him. She wanted to explore that even more, but she also wanted some books.

Francine stopped in front of the store and turned to Gentry. She placed a hand on his arm and smiled up at him as he narrowed his eyes and put his back to the door like a sentry. Francine took Lulu and led her into the shop. "What was that about?" Lulu asked as the bell over the door rang then swung closed behind them.

"Oh, I was kidnapped outside this store, and as much as Gentry would like me to shop somewhere else, I've become fond of Mr. Bandyworth."

That stopped Lulu cold, but she didn't have a chance to say anything as a small man in tweed came out of the stacks. His white hair circled his crown, and his round spectacles made his blue eyes huge.

"Oh, Lady Francine!" he said. "So good to see you today. Who do we have here?" he asked, turning to Lulu.

"This is Her Grace, the Duchess of Warrick." Lulu froze. She knew—of course she knew—but it was the first time someone had said her full title in deference to her, and it was unsettling. She realized the man had said something else to her, so she nodded in reply and tried to smile.

"If you'll just give us a moment. Perhaps the sheets? And do open an account for Warrick, please," Francine said.

"Straight away, Your Grace. Lovely coverage of the wedding in Miss Witwick's," he said as he hurried around them to the front window. Lulu felt Francine take her hand and pull her into the stacks.

"Sorry, I just…sorry," Lulu said.

"Don't worry. I should have known better. I had so much time to get used to this whole mess, and you've been here all of, what, forty-eight hours?" Lulu nodded. "Do you want to go home? We can come back another day," Francine said.

"No, I really would like a book. Alice, I want Alice. Oh god, is there Alice?" Her heart raced, she'd already lost so much of her world, what if this one thing that she'd loved since childhood didn't exist yet either? "What year was Alice?"

Francine wrapped her hands around Lulu's cheeks and smiled. "Not to worry. We have Alice."

"Thank god," she said, taking a deep breath. "I've lost everything else. I don't know what I would do if I lost Alice as well, and I must admit…I do feel a bit down the rabbit hole at the moment. I need something crazier than this to balance it out."

"Yes! That's exactly how I felt. I thought…well. Let's get that and then whatever else you'd like. Mr. Bandyworth will extend credit for you and send the items to your house. Simple."

"I'm not sure I should spend…"

"We've already been through this," Francine said. "These men are ridiculously wealthy, the lot of them. You need a few things, and he won't mind. I haven't been around Warrick much, but from what I've seen, he is like the other men of his family, strong, sure, dedicated…and wealthy. Not that that makes a difference in personality, but it does mean you can get a few simple comforts, and he won't mind. He will expect you to."

Lulu considered what Grayson had told her about his finances, and that the money—that was hers, and then his—would be hers. She couldn't figure why she didn't actually feel that way, though, probably because it, in fact, wasn't actually hers.

Her money was separated from her by two century marks. All of her money. Well, if she wasn't sad before, she certainly was now. If she hadn't been strapped into this steel boned corset she would probably have slumped over from exhaustion. She'd worked hard for that nest egg. She sighed as she considered. She could always return things if there was a problem.

She nodded then reached out to lean against one of the book shelves. She really needed to get some of her stamina back. She wanted to run and jump and feel the stretch and burn of her muscles, but she was tied in knots. Literally and figuratively. Or...tied up in knots she supposed, she really wanted out of this corset. "Home, please. I'd just like to go home," she said. "Thank you, though, for everything. I did have a lovely day today. I just... need some time alone, and I would like to be there when he returns. I... I miss him."

They pulled up in front of Warrick House, and Lulu stared out the window at the front door. She wanted to paint it red. A nice, bright, vivid, shiny, lead-based red that was so saturated it would need repainting every week—red.

She wasn't sure what she was doing, sitting here contemplating his front door, Francine patiently waiting, the outriders standing by. What else could she do besides go inside? Nothing. She could go in and wander about the place at least. It was massive. She wondered if Gray had returned. She missed driveways with cars that signaled who was home.

She turned to Francine. "I'll call you?" she said.

Francine bit her lip. "I don't think Warrick Place is on the exchange yet, but you can send me a note by messenger at any time. If you want me to come over, just say so and I'll be here. And if you want to come to my house, just do so at any time. Okay?"

No phone. Right. No phones. At least they had toilets. She should be thankful for that. She closed her eyes and breathed. "Okay."

"Are you going to be all right? Do you want me to stay with you?"

"No, I just… I think I need a nap, and then I just want to wander around this place and figure it out. I'll send you a note later, though," Lulu said.

Francine took her hand. "If you need anything at all, please just let me know."

She nodded. "I will."

The carriage door opened, and Lulu heard the clank of the steps, and she took Gentry's hand and stepped out. As she walked up the steps to the front door, it opened, and Gray was there. She couldn't read his expression. He seemed to be doing everything he could to not show any emotion whatsoever, so she stopped as she looked up at him, unsure.

He waved absentmindedly toward the carriage and she listened as it pulled away. The shaking of her hands mirrored the sound of the wheels on the cobbles. Lulu started to turn, but she couldn't manage to take her eyes from him, so she stopped.

She once again felt like crying, but this time…it was from relief. She'd needed to see him. She'd needed to talk to him, to apologize or explain, or try to find out what happened, or…just talk. About anything, she didn't even care anymore. No—she did care. She wanted to know more about him. She needed to give him that much. She felt so drawn-out and exhausted emotionally and knew she was going to be dragged down if she didn't find something to buoy her.

"Lulu."

She blinked and realized that neither of them had moved an inch. They'd merely been standing there staring at each other. Then he lifted his hand to her, and she walked up the stairs and took it.

As they stood toe to toe on the threshold, he leaned toward her and kissed her sweetly. "Welcome home."

She squeezed his big hand and smiled. "Thank you. Would it sound strange for me to say I missed you?" she asked.

"Perhaps, but I'm not much for etiquette or formality. I much prefer it when you say whatever you like."

They stood there, each holding one hand, looking at each other for a while, and it calmed her heart, which felt like it had been racing for days now. She took a deep breath and reached up with her loose hand, letting it hover between them. She'd wanted to put her hand on his abdomen, but didn't want to bring tension where there was none, so she dropped her hand and looked away, breaking the moment.

She felt him tug, and she followed him into the house and up the stairs to the bedroom.

"I believe you've figured out I don't know what I'm doing, but it's more than just not knowing how to be a husband." He turned and sat on the bed, and from his posture, she knew he wore a corset, so she looked away carefully. "I've never had people who were close to me as an adult. You might say I'm not adept at interpersonal communication. I tend to stay on the outside and watch."

Lulu wanted to ask a million questions, but that he was talking to her... She wouldn't interrupt him. She'd wait until he stopped.

"That's what makes me good at what I did. I can figure people out rather easily just from watching them. But you—" He shook his head. "I can't seem to figure you out."

She waited, but he just looked at her, and she knew he expected something from her. "Well, I—" she started, then she took a deep breath and moved toward the wardrobe, laying her hat and shawl on a small dresser as she passed it.

She opened the doors and looked through the things in the wardrobe, hoping she would find something different, more comfortable to put on. She would really love a warm pair of sweats or yoga pants right now, so she could curl up at his feet and listen to him talk.

It was odd to her that she both wanted to dominate and submit to him. She usually wanted only one, very clearly. She turned toward him. "I don't seem to be myself lately. That may have something to do with that," she said.

He almost grinned, but not quite, and he didn't look up to her. "Nor I," he said finally. "I haven't been myself since I left India."

"What's different?" she asked. "I mean, beyond the place and the title here. I know that's all different, but how is your daily life different? Can we change that?" She started taking her clothes off, and his eyes narrowed on her, concentrating on every move she made.

Just his eyes on her like that made the blood thicken in her veins to a slow honey. She let the corset drop and stepped from the skirts. Leaving the chemise and drawers on, she walked to him and sat at his feet, crossing her ankles and tucking her knees under her chin.

"My daily life in India?" His voice was rough-edged and deeper than usual. "Peace and quiet. Reflection. Meditation. Training. Reading… Masala chai," he said.

"That sounds lovely. I love chai tea," she said.

"That's a bit repetitive, don't you think?"

"Why?" she asked.

"Chai means tea. You effectively said tea-tea, and I don't understand why," he responded.

She laughed. "I see, how lovely. America has this tendency to acquire and bastardize. That's my only defense."

He nodded, but didn't comment. "What was your daily life like?" He shifted as though he were going to stand, but then pressed his hand to his stomach and settled instead. What she wouldn't give to see this man in his corset.

She abandoned that thought to consider her daily life. It didn't seem that much different from his. "Training, reading, shopping—I suppose that could be considered my reflection time. Meditation…that could be my bath time, that or the steam room after I worked out."

"Worked out?"

"Yes, trained. We call it working out, um…training as well, but working out seems to denote getting rid of stressors, and that's what it was to me. When I think of training, I think of very specific things."

"Like?" he said.

"Like…" She paused. "Practicing certain maneuvers. Honing movement and strengthening specific muscles for performance. What do you mean by training?"

"Working with weapons," he said.

"Oh. Well, then, I suppose it is similar," she said.

"You work with weapons?" She was struck by the sudden gleam in his eye.

"Yes, I do. I'm a Colorado girl, through and through, so I own and use weapons," she said with a wink.

"What kind?" he asked.

"My favorite is—was—a Colt Python revolver. Very smooth action, simply lovely to shoot."

"Colt is the American gunsmith. Rather infamous," he said. She nodded. "The bullwhips?" he asked, and she paused, considering what she should say to that. They were, technically speaking, a weapon—because she was no horse trainer.

"Yes," she said.

"Blades?" he asked without pause.

"Not many. I think swordplay is beautiful, and I admire people who are able, but it wasn't ever something I pursued. I prefer to keep people at a distance." The moment she said it, she realized just how true it had been. She had no close people in her life, nobody who truly knew her. "Wow," she said. "That was deeper than I intended."

"Would you be interested in learning?" he asked without missing a beat.

Her hands dropped to the floor, and she straightened, wondering just exactly which part of that he was referring to, but the idea of learning sword play, or training in hand-to-hand combat, with him— "Yes. Yes, I would." The idea of facing him with a sword was…fantastic.

"We should start easily. You already said this body of yours is not familiar with work." He gestured to her, his hand moving the length of her several times, but his eyes caught in various places and rested.

"No, it isn't." She felt suddenly shy and moved the subject along. "I need to do something about that. I wonder, though, how much muscle memory is in the muscle, and how much is in the brain. I suppose a fair bit of both. Physically speaking. these muscles have no memory. but I can still feel the maneuvers with my mind… I bought some clothing, and Francine said she was going to take me to her tailor, who could make a few things that I'd like."

Gray nodded again. "Good. I'm glad you're getting the things you need."

"About that," she said. "The money thing. I don't know how it works. I don't know what I have—what we have. I feel very uncomfortable spending on credit. I hate credit. I was a cash-only kind of girl," she said.

"We do need to discuss that—and not because I want to control you. You should be taught the basics of money. I assume it's completely different. What's the rate of increase in value over a century anyway?" he asked.

Lulu laughed. "Inflation, you mean?" she said.

"I—of a balloon?"

She loved his confused expression more than anything. Well, not so, she loved when his eyes went black with passion more than anything.

She was starting to feel better, but she still wasn't of a mood to do much. "I'm exhausted," she said then.

Gray stood and took her hand, pulling her from the floor. "Perhaps some rest?" he asked. She could tell he was actively keeping his eyes above her neck. She nodded. "Would you like company?"

She nodded again, then looked away. She couldn't seem to hold his gaze at the moment. It seemed he had his duke hat on, all power and control, and she naturally deferred to him. She glanced up and found him staring out the window as though he considered something, then he took her hands and placed them on his chest.

"Undress me," he whispered.

Her breath stopped. He'd changed his mind, or something else had changed. Some part of him was trusting her with this secret, where only two days ago her knowledge of his corset had angered him.

"Are you..." He knew what she was asking without her saying it. He knew because he nodded.

"I'm sure," he said.

It was silly, being that they both already knew she knew he wore a corset, but it wasn't silly at all because she knew this was a huge step, so she would treat his decision with due reverence.

She'd worked with many clients, helping them to discover and accept who they were, not merely sexually but also in life. It was one of her favorite parts of her work as a switch, and she was very good at what she did.

She reached up first and explored his hair with her fingers, smoothing it back to relieve his tension. She ran her hands over his eyebrows, around and across the crests of his cheekbones, down his jaw and across his lips savoring the heat of his breath across the tips of her fingers. It sent sparks through her and she lifted herself on her toes and kissed him. He tasted of bitter hops. His hands came to her hips, but they didn't hold her, they just hovered there, barely touching her and it sent shivers up her spine and a groan from her lips. His eyes darkened.

She wasn't going to rush this, as much for herself as for him. He may not understand how she felt at the moment, but seeing him like this, seeing him so vulnerable… it not only made her want to reach out and hold him but it also made her heart race, her blood forced through her veins to all the right places because he was giving in to her.

She took a deep breath against his mouth, smelled the soap from his shave, the sharp undertone of sweat, the starch of his linen. When she pulled back from the kiss she held his gaze and her hands drifted down his neck and pulled the end of the silk tie and slid it off, laying it on the bed. Her hands shook as she unbuttoned the waistcoat and helped him from it and his jacket together.

When she brought her hands back to him she could feel his tension and she smoothed her hands down his shoulders, his biceps, willing him to relax for her. She waited patiently until his breath steadied and he looked up. She caught his gaze and held it, refused to let him look away. She kept him on her level, kept them equal partners in the moment as she unbuttoned his shirt, and pulled it from his trousers. He lifted his arms, and she pulled it over his head.

Then, slowly, without taking her gaze from his, she lifted her hands and placed them on the corset. She could feel him shaking through the tension in his muscles. His chest vibrated as he looked up to the ceiling and she placed a kiss in the hollow of his jaw, under his chin. She ran her thumbs along the edges of the corset, feeling his warm skin just at the upper edge of it, the dusting of chest hair, his wide nipples. He looked back down to her and his breath stilled, and his hands wrapped around her wrists as though to say, *There, you've reached my limit. You need to stop now.*

She nodded, and he looked away, so she looked down to the corset—it was beautiful and not at all what she expected—and untied the knot at the front, then loosened the corset and released the busk. It fell away, and she ran her fingertips down his rib cage, giving him that shudder-release that she loved so much.

He took her in his arms and lifted her to the bed, crawling in behind her, pants, shoes, and all. He pressed all along her back, held her waist tight against him, and just like, that they fell asleep.

FOURTEEN

There are not more than five cardinal tastes,
[sour, acrid, sweet, salt, bitter]
yet combinations of them yield more flavors than can ever be tasted.

—Sun Tzu
The Art of War

hen Grayson awoke, Lulu was watching the sunset from the bedroom window. Her hands were splayed against the glass as she gazed out across the park. He rose quietly and walked to her, let his hands hover above her shoulders tentatively. She closed her eyes, so he let his hands drift down and rest.

"I feel like I should apologize for this morning. I was so overwhelmed, and I just don't really react well to that. I'm not much for surprises."

"It's...not your fault, really. I believe the fault to be mine, particularly after yesterday. You made what would have been a long, dry, difficult day much more entertaining. I believe the Archbishop of Canterbury was in need of new prayer subjects at any rate."

"The Archbishop of Canterbury... The guy with the hat?" Grayson nodded. "Well. I'm happy to oblige the once, but after that he needs to find another reason for prayer," she said.

Grayson ran his hands from her shoulders up her arms to her hands on the glass. He placed his larger hands over hers, then spread them against the glass next to hers.

He leaned his head down, resting his forehead on her shoulder, and she turned and stuck her nose in his hair and sniffed.

What?

"I'm trying to get used to how you smell," she said by way of explanation when he crooked an eyebrow at her. "Most of the men I've been with simply smell of soap and cologne. They don't really have a scent of their own. Don't get me wrong, guys smell great, just…they all smell about the same. But you… I can smell different spices on you, and I can tell that some of that is just you. It's really awesome actually." She wanted to familiarize herself with his scent.

"I'm not sure if that's a compliment, or if you're trying to tell me that I need a shower."

"Shower… Shower! You have a shower?"

He tilted his head and grinned at her. "Yes, I have a shower."

"Could we please?" she asked. He gazed at her. "Nothing sexual, just a nice warm shower. I'll wash your back."

"I don't know," he replied. "I think—maybe not." He needed to slow her down a bit. He wanted the pleasure, he did, but what he also wanted was much more of her, and he was afraid of what she could do to him. Of what she could learn of his secrets if they continued on so quickly.

She pouted and turned to look back out the window.

"Lulu."

"Yes?" she said.

"I want you to know that I am sorry for your situation, and I will endeavor to be the best possible husband for you. I know this can't be easy for you. I—please understand, if I felt I had a choice…"

"Well, if we had choices, I don't think either of us would be here. But at least we're both going to attempt to make the best of it. Right? I mean, we still are, aren't we?" she asked. He nodded. "Good, so at least that part is out of the way," she said.

"About this morning."

"No, please, I think we can just sweep that under the rug. I heard you, I did. I'm sorry if I frightened you."

"Frightened?" Grayson straightened and turned her in his arms, her window-chilled hands coming to his ribs and sending shivers through him as he gasped. He pulled her close and pressed against her, his hands moving to hold her hips, his mouth quieting hers gently. Then he smiled and shook his head. "I really like your mouth."

"And I like your mouth, on me, anywhere, pick a spot," she said with deep rolling words.

He inched back. He wanted this intimacy with her, but he was determined to slow down, to try to figure out…everything. He had so much to learn about her.

"Tell me more about your past. I want to know who you are."

"There's plenty of time for talking when we get old. How about right now we put these young, virile bodies to the test and see how long they'll last us in the sack?" she said.

"The sack?"

"Slang… Slang? Is that a word yet?" she asked. He nodded. "Oh, good. So that's slang for bed."

"I already forgot what you said."

"Figures." She ran her hands down his chest. She went slowly. He knew why, but he held himself steady. Then she reached his trousers. He narrowed his eyes on her, and his hands covered hers. "Look, isn't it the guy who's usually trying to get into the girl's pants?" she asked.

"Pants?" he said.

"Oh, come on! Pants isn't a word?"

He shrugged. He wasn't sure what to say to her sometimes. "Do you mean pantaloons? They aren't very fashionable."

She yanked on his waistband. "What are these?" she asked.

"Trousers."

"Fine, isn't it the guy who is supposed to be getting into the girl's trousers?"

"I suppose I understand your meaning, but women don't really wear trousers, and I want... I just feel like there should be something more here. I can't help but feel that we should—I don't know."

"I can't believe a virgin male is putting me off. This world is completely backward," she said flippantly.

"I thought the ruination was on hold until you could obtain some appropriate...accessories," he said.

"Yes, I asked to speak with Francine and...I did so. Today."

He dropped his hands and turned toward the windows, crossing his arms over his chest. There was a very specific reason he was still a virgin. Even though they'd managed so far, he wasn't ready to share that truth just yet.

He wanted more. From her, for her, with her. He wanted it all, including the sex. God, yes, he wanted sex. But something told him he needed to get through to her without it, because sex was easy for her, and it wasn't easy for him. What an upside-down and backward relationship this was turning out to be. She was right about that.

Grayson heard a scratch at the door. "Enter."

The door opened, and Grayson watched in the reflection of the glass as Rakshan walked in with armloads of boxes and bags. He froze. He was going to have to sell his house to pay Rox back for this trip. Then he saw the perfect, naked, round globes of Lulu's backside reflected in the window. He turned swiftly, moving in front of her. He felt her hand on his shoulder and looked down at her, then shook his head and tried to not look panicked.

"Sorry?" she said. He paused, confused. She pointed at the pile of things.

Oh, right, that—not that she was naked. Why would he ever think she would apologize for being naked in front his man?

He shook his head again. "Don't be, you need things. I wanted to get you things. You now have some things. It is as it should be," he said. She shifted to walk around him, but he blocked her. She looked up at him, and he leaned toward her ear. "You're naked," he said gruffly.

"Oh," she replied. "Well, not completely, but close enough." She didn't even blush.

"Dinner is prepared. I can bring a tray, if you prefer?" Rakshan looked at Grayson with his eyebrows raised.

"No, we'll be down shortly, thank you."

"Yes, Your Grace," he said.

Grayson stiffened, but didn't say anything in response. Calder was right about the title. It only had the power over him that he gave it. If he was smart, he would wield the power with an iron fist in his own favor. He turned back to Lulu.

"You should put some clothes on. Rakshan may not mind your dishabille, but I have a problem with other men seeing what is for me alone."

She looked down, then smiled up at him. "Honestly, I'm so comfortable with being naked, I don't usually pay attention. But I'll try to do better and be more modest since others come into our private rooms. However… you're the one who told him to come in."

"Point taken. We both have things to learn, we will learn." What kind of woman was that comfortable with being naked around strangers? It made him uncomfortable, but he shook off the thought and turned to his wardrobe and pulled out a fresh shirt and put it on. Then he thought about the one he'd forgotten at Roxleigh's house. He wanted it.

Lulu dug through the packages until she found a shirt much like his and threw it over her head. Then she pulled on a pair of soft riding trousers.

She looked at him and raised her brows. "We're not expecting company, are we?" she asked.

He shook his head, but couldn't manage a word at the sight of her nipples grazing the inside of that shirt.

"Pants," she said and turned, smacked her own arse, and headed out the door.

What was he going to do with this woman? He grumbled, then chased her, taking her hand and leading her down the hall.

When they got downstairs, he turned down the hall to the dining room, but it wasn't lit, so he pulled her back into the hall and followed the soft glow of lights coming from the atrium at the side of the house.

Inside the atrium, Rakshan had laid out a lovely picnic on the moss expanse under the fruit trees.

Charming, and a complete setup. He hadn't wanted dinner in their room because he was hoping a less casual meal would mean a more formal meal, making it easier to keep their distance.

He couldn't seem to do anything to pry them apart. Once in the same vicinity, it was as though they were magnets constantly bending one to the other. He took a deep breath and put his hands on his hips.

"Not what you expected?" she asked.

"Not particularly," he replied.

"This is lovely. I need to explore more. I had no idea you had a massive greenhouse attached here," she said as she wandered down the path.

"You should explore the house. It's yours," he said. She turned and looked at him, that mouth dropped open on a question. "I told you," he said. "What's mine is yours. I will find a way to make it so—well, this house is currently entailed because my father was such a stalwart, but there are ways of breaking those entailments moving forward," he said. "And you are legally only an extension of me, so you can't own anything. I do...I...but I will find a way." He suddenly thought the marriage laws incredibly unfair simply by looking in her eyes as he spoke those words.

Lulu walked back to him. "Thank you."

Goddamn, the way she trusted him. If she had landed at the hands of his brother... A shiver coursed his skin and stopped the thoughts from progressing. He would be honorable if only because she believed he was.

She walked over to the pile of cushions surrounding the low trays and took a seat, leaning over the tray and inhaling the scent. "Oh, this is lovely. Curry? It smells like Indian food. I always heard that Great Britain has the very best Indian food," she said.

He joined her, stretching his legs out before tucking himself under the tray. "Why would that be?" he asked.

"Because of the high population of Indian people in London, I believe," she said.

"There have been some people moving here, but I wouldn't consider the population to be very large. And if you tried to sell Indian food to the majority of the population of London, they would probably be horrified."

Lulu stared blankly for a second, then nodded. "Okay, okay, so when did Victoria become empress?" she asked as she started piling the bright saffron rice on her plate.

"Her Royal Highness," he emphasized, "became empress in 1877. Benjamin Disraeli was paramount to that happening, even though we have controlled India since the mid-fifties," he said. "Do you refer to President Arthur as Chester?" he asked.

"President Arthur? Oh. Wow."

"You've gone pale. Are you—"

"Yes, I—I suppose being in England adds another level of separation from reality. President Obama, not Arthur, where I'm from, and no, I would never call him Barack. Point taken."

"I thought you had to be born in America to be president," he said.

"Oh, he was. His father was from Kenya, his mother American. He is actually our first African-American president."

"You now refer to people by their parentage?"

Lulu laughed at that, and his gut tightened against it as though it raised a shield.

"I never thought of that with respect to him, actually. But no, African American is the new politically correct term for men and women with black skin."

"What if they aren't from Africa?" he asked.

She smiled. "There are still problems in America with respect to people of color." She looked sad, so he tried to steer her away from the topic.

"I'm starving," he said simply.

She hummed a reply as she started to eat. "Oh, this is lovely, this is... Yes, this is very good."

Grayson took a plate and filled it, then joined her in praising Rakshan and his talent, while simultaneously wondering why he'd been hiding it all this time. He hadn't once cooked for Grayson.

"I think Rakshan likes you," Grayson said between bites.

"Is that so? Well, it's good to know someone likes me," she replied.

Grayson considered her for a moment. He knew the comment was offhand, probably in jest, but it still struck him. "I like you," he said.

"Oh, yes, you've mentioned how very much you like my mouth," she replied.

"Yes, I have, but I like you as well, Lulu," he said.

She looked up at that, a piece of curried chicken hanging from her mouth as she paused. Her tongue darted out and swept it inside. She smiled.

"Of course you like me. I gave you a blow job. What's not to like about that?" She grinned and continued eating.

Oh, that mouth, he thought. Why was she deflecting? "No, Lulu." He stopped and took her wrist. "Listen to me. It's more than that. I like you," he said gruffly.

Lulu stopped eating and pulled her wrist from his grip, then twisted her hands in her lap. She *had* heard him and had tried to be playful, but he just wasn't allowing her.

"Lulu, look at me."

She didn't move, just shifted her eyes to him.

"I like you, you understand? I like you as a person. I think you're funny and, yes, quite arousing, but I like your opinions and your... Look, I like you. It isn't just your mouth and how you use it. It's what comes out of it as well. You're brilliant," he said.

She nodded, not entirely sure how to respond to him since he wasn't allowing her snark. "Thank you," she said finally. She saw him nod once and continue eating.

"Just so we're clear," he said. "You can still use your mouth however you'd like to."

Lulu smiled then. "You know...I, um, I like you, too," she said. How weird was this conversation? They'd already been intimate, beyond intimate. The man rent her flesh with his fingers, for god's sake. And here they were exchanging...pleasantries.

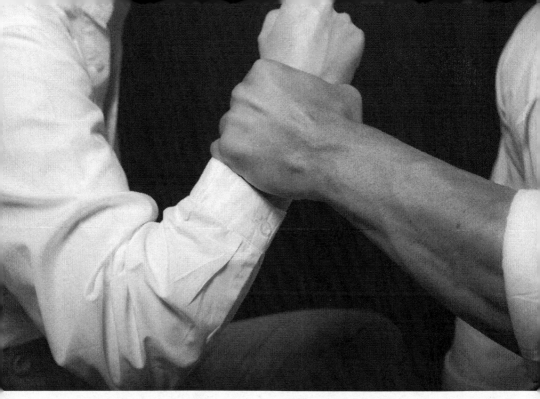

He nodded at her admission. "I know this has been an interesting few days. I would like for you to have some time to settle into your new home. I have some things to attend to tomorrow. I have contracts to finalize, that sort of thing. So tomorrow you should explore the house. Perhaps we can have a formal supper tomorrow night?" he said.

"Are you asking me out on a date?" she asked.

"A…date?"

"Yeah, uh…are you courting me? Because, sir, I must tell you I'm a happily married woman—"

"Happily?"

She winked at him. "Yes, happily, and my husband doesn't take kindly to men who get the wrong idea about me." He just looked at her, and for a moment she thought she'd gone too far.

"I will…ask your husband's permission, but I have a feeling he won't mind my taking you on a *date*," he said, emphasizing the last words.

Lulu laughed. Getting to know her husband would be fun, she thought, as long as he didn't completely cut her off. She knew he needed time to adjust to their new arrangement, but hopefully they wouldn't backpedal in the intimacy category, because she desperately wanted to fuck this man.

She heard the door to the atrium open, and Rakshan and another man walked in to take the large trays of food away. She curled up on the cushions and gazed at Gray.

"Rakshan," he said. "Have you been withholding your cooking skills? Somehow I don't believe my English cook prepared this."

"No, Your Grace. My sister did."

"She's come to London?"

"Yes, Your Grace," he replied.

"Anything she needs, Rakshan, you know this."

"At the moment she only needs a kitchen to work through her frustration, and I already offered yours."

"Good. Anything else, please let me know. And please thank her for the food. It was magnificent," Gray said.

"Please add my thanks as well, Rakshan," Lulu said. She liked him, but still wasn't completely comfortable around him, considering how close he could get to her without her knowledge. Rakshan and the footman finished clearing the trays and left the atrium, and she turned back to Gray, stretching out on the pillows.

"So tell me a story. It's nearly bedtime. Tell me a bedtime story," she said.

Gray looked at her, expressionless, for several minutes, and she had to force herself to keep from squirming under his gaze. Finally, he cleared his throat. "Once upon a time…"

"Oooh, all the best stories start that way."

"Hush," he admonished, narrowing his eyes on her. Her skin prickled, and she couldn't help but grin as she settled further into the cushions.

He started again. "Once upon a time"—he glared at her. She didn't say a word, so he smiled—"there was a young girl. She went by the name of Lulu."

Lulu felt her heart expand in her chest as he said her name, and she sat up, too restless to lie still.

"Lulu was magic. She came from a faraway land to tame the wild beast known as—"

"Warrick!" she yelled.

"*Who* is telling this story?" he asked.

"You are, sir," she said sweetly.

His eyes flared, and she knotted her hands in her lap.

"Good. Lulu came from far, far away to tame a beast known as…The Warrick." He ground the name out between clenched teeth, and her nipples tightened against the loose fabric of her shirt. His voice was deep and cutting, and she loved the way it sounded when he said the name.

He cleared his throat. "Warrick," he said again, and he looked off into the darkness of the atrium, seemingly lost.

"Your father wasn't a nice man," she said carefully.

He shook his head, then stopped and turned to her. "Why would you say that?"

"You're the one who called me brilliant," she replied.

Gray looked down. "Were you referring to him when you spoke of the monster?" he asked. She hadn't been, but she didn't want to say anything, now, that might stop him from talking, because the story was suddenly getting to be much more interesting. "I suppose a young boy once thought that of him," he said finally. "Though at one point that young boy also thought him the bravest of knights as well, so it's all perspective, isn't it?" he said.

She nodded, but he didn't say anything more. "I'm sorry," she whispered finally.

He looked up to her and held her gaze. "No, don't be. He made me who I am. If he hadn't done what he'd done, I likely would have continued to worship him and been someone else…or quite possibly be dead. Then I never would have met you.

"Never apologize for a past you have no control of. It will do you no good now, and it certainly won't change our future," he said.

Lulu nodded and reached out, skimming a hand down his arm, then squeezing his hand.

"I've forgotten the story," he said then, as he pulled away from her touch.

"That's okay, I think I would rather we write our own," Lulu replied.

He considered her for a moment. "Once upon a time, there was a woman named Lulu…" He paused as he searched her gaze. "She was all he'd never known he would ever need. The end."

Lulu launched herself at him, pushing him back to the ground and kissing him as his hands flew around her waist and held on.

Damn, her husband was going to wreck her. He was just that good.

FIFTEEN

By discovering the enemies dispositions and remaining invisible ourselves
we can keep our forces concentrated while the enemy's must be divided.

—Sun Tzu
The Art of War

The next morning, Warrick went to his study and attempted to get
some work done. He did. He gave it a good, honest effort. But
leaving Lulu upstairs in bed had been one of the most difficult
things he'd ever done. That and keeping her in her clothes the night before.
That may have been slightly more difficult, particularly after dinner in the
atrium. She was quite intuitive, figuring out his father wasn't necessarily the
ideal, but nice wasn't necessarily a requirement of being a parent.

They'd kissed and pawed at each other in the atrium until Rakshan
had returned with pastries, and then they'd pretended to be civilized. He
realized much of his life with this woman would be spent pretending to be
civilized, because she was anything but, and he never had been.

He shifted the papers around, looking for the one he wanted. He
thought he'd just organized them all, but apparently all he'd done was move
things around, forcing them into more disorganized piles. He sighed and
shuffled through one of the piles until he found what he needed.

He looked at the settlement agreements from Lulu's—no—Cecilia's
father. Cecilia, the woman who should be his wife, who should have been
his brother's wife. He wondered what came of her when Lulu took over.
Perhaps she got swept forward somehow. He didn't want to think of her as
simply ceasing to exist. That seemed quite morbid and terribly sad. Roxleigh

had said Francine had some theories, perhaps one day soon they could all sit down and discuss it. When Lulu was more comfortable.

He made some notes about the accounts so Rakshan could see to household needs and teach Lulu whatever she needed to know about money. Then he let the paper fall back to the desk and leaned back in his chair. He would also need to start making arrangements for his successor, since Lulu didn't want children. He hadn't ever considered having children until he took the title and it was a bit of a relief to him that he wouldn't have to now. The successor would need to come to London, and he would need to learn of the money as well.

Money. Something he hadn't had much of, for a very long time. Certainly he had his pension from the Crown, but it wasn't much compared with the amount of money his cousins maintained. Of course, the Roxleigh title had also been ruined before Gideon had taken over the title from his father. He'd had to completely rebuild the coffers, and had done so brilliantly, so it shouldn't seem so outlandish to Grayson that his own father had also mishandled funds to the point of bankruptcy. Yet Grayson still couldn't bring himself to discuss it with others.

Someone scratched at the entry, and Grayson sat forward in his chair. "Enter."

"Your Grace, most of the deliveries you requested have come, though there will be more arriving in the next week as many things had to be ordered."

"Thank you, Rakshan. Where?"

"I had them put everything in the ballroom. It can be moved at any time," he said.

"Thank you. Has Lulu taken her breakfast yet?"

"Yes, Your Grace. I believe she went to explore the upper floors. She said something about being an archaeologist today."

Grayson smiled. "Lovely," he said.

"Will that be all, Your Grace?"

Grayson paused. "Rakshan, do you remain part of my household of your own accord?"

"For the moment, Your Grace."

"That is all. Thank you, Rakshan."

Rakshan bowed and turned to leave the room, but he paused and looked over his shoulder. Grayson knew he was waiting to be admonished for using his honorrific.

"Thank you, Rakshan," Grayson said again.

Rakshan's eyebrows rose, and Grayson thought he saw the glimmer of a smile before he closed the door behind him.

Grayson wondered if he should disturb Lulu or let her be an archaeologist for a time. If she was exploring and having fun at it, he should probably leave her be, but he really didn't want to.

Perhaps he could persuade her to go exploring with him this afternoon before supper.

No. He needed to let her explore alone.

He kept insisting to himself that they needed to slow this down, to get to know one another better. He stood and walked toward the main entry, then vaulted his way to the third floor. When he got there, he paused at the top of the stairs, listening for his little mouse.

He heard shifting of furniture and quiet curses coming from the south wing, so he quietly walked down the hall as he wished, momentarily, for the back halls and hidden passages that were so prevalent at Roxleigh's Eildon Hill Manor. This house was all open and inviting, not devious and deceptive as he preferred. He heard a loud crash followed by a curse.

"Shit!"

He peered around a corner to see Lulu fanning one hand through a cloud of dust, her face tucked into her elbow, while a large box of who knows what settled on the floor at her feet. He kept himself from running into the room, since he could see she was well. She sneezed, and it was the sweetest sound he'd ever heard. Then she let out a string of curses the best of the Royal Navy would be hard-pressed to match.

He swung away from the door, pushing his back up against the wall next to the doorframe. He heard another sneeze, and something light and bubbly bloomed in his chest and made him want to laugh.

He stayed there, listening to her sneeze and cuss for the next five minutes, until he thought she might discover his eavesdropping when he could no longer hold his laughter. He moved back down the hallway toward the stairs.

"You stop right there."

He froze. Far be it from him to disobey a direct order. He turned and looked at her. She wore the…*pants* she'd bought the other day and another shirt, without a corset. No wonder Rox liked to keep at home up at Eildon, if this was what wandered around his house. She was adorable, really, and he needed to get away from her, because he could feel that faint pull already, drawing him in like a fish on a delicate line.

"Are you spying on me?" She cocked one hip and put a fist on it.

"Apparently not. If I were truly spying, you would never have known it," he replied easily, because it was true.

"I see. Now you'll have me constantly looking over my shoulder."

"No—I didn't mean—"

"I'm only harassing you," she replied with a wink.

He was beginning to love that wink, the half-cocked grin that accompanied it, and the flash of white teeth. It was beyond lovely.

"I suppose I should get back to work," he said, moving to turn away.

"No—wait. Please?"

He stopped. "Do you need something?"

"At the moment? No, I just… Do you come here often?" She winced when she said it, and he crossed his arms over his chest to hold back his laughter. This side of her was fun. She was…cute.

"I…no, I do not come up here often. I did come up here when I was young, my brothers and I. We would play hide-and-seek in these rooms. We managed to break all sorts of things."

"The potential for a studio up here…if you'll allow me. The light, it's—"

"Lulu, you may do whatever you wish here. If you need men to help clear it out, only tell Rakshan what you need, and he will ensure it happens. If there seems to be something of value, just…find a room to put it all in, and the rest—toss it out."

She nodded. "Thank you."

"No, thank you," he replied.

She smiled. "Well, I suppose I should…" She pointed at the room she'd come from. "Are you sure you have no interest in the things—"

"They are merely things, Lulu. I have no need of…things. I only have need of—" He shook his head. He didn't know what to say. "Do what you will. I will have no complaints."

Lulu watched him through the dust motes in the light drifting down the hallways. *Things*, he'd said. He had no use for *things*. She understood that, even if she did have use for certain *things*, like her tools and her camera gear. Without these *things*, she continued to feel a bit lost.

To think that this man could pick up from wherever he was and simply walk away from everything with just the clothes on his back, start again wherever he found himself…no trappings, no anchor. It was sad, yet oddly attracting.

"I was attached to certain things back home. I miss them dearly," she whispered.

He nodded. "I will do whatever it takes to make you comfortable here. Just because I have no affinity for fodder doesn't mean I don't understand the need for it. After all, we can't eat dinner from a floor, now can we?"

"I believe we did last night," she replied with a grin. He was so incredibly giving. She walked toward him, and he jerked as though to step away, so she slowed her pace. "Grayson, don't you have family that needs these…or would want these…things?" she asked.

He looked away suddenly. "I do—I do have family, but they abandoned this house as I did. If they had wanted to retrieve anything from here, I would think they would have done so by now."

"Your family wasn't at the breakfast."

"They were there, they just…they give me space. If they didn't make themselves known to you, it wasn't out of disrespect. Quite the opposite, really. I've kept myself from them. I assume they're waiting for an invitation," he said.

"And will you extend one?"

"Eventually, I'm sure. Right now, I need…" He shook his head, and she froze a mere two steps away from him.

"You need?"

"I need to become familiar with my wife."

"So I don't embarrass you," she said. She was disappointed, but she understood.

"Not at all. Not at all. I think I've already told you I wish you to be whomever you wish to be, that I do not want you to behave in a manner you're not comfortable with. If I felt differently, I would have said differently. If someone doesn't appreciate who you are, well, they can simply fuck off."

His eyes flared in a cut of sun across the hallway, and Lulu felt the words sink into her. He really did mean what he said when he spoke, and this man of few words was finding them more easily lately.

"I appreciate that, but you must have some sort of relationship with your family. I mean, your close family."

He shifted, putting his hands in his pockets as she reached for him, so she pulled back, clasping her hands at her waist to show she wouldn't touch him while he was clearly sending the sign he wished to remain untouched.

"I haven't had a relationship with anyone in my family since…since I left for India. That was more than ten years ago. I have seen them briefly since I returned. But nothing more. I'm afraid I'm no good for women with delicate sensibilities, and I prefer to keep my distance. I don't want them to… I don't want—"

"You're protecting them? From yourself?"

He didn't move, not a nod, not a tick, nothing. He looked away. "I should get back to work," he said.

"Grayson?" He turned back to her, and his face was softer. He pulled his hands from his pockets, and she reached out and took one, smoothing her thumb over the broad back of his right hand. "I'll see you this afternoon? For our date?" She smiled up at him, the sweetest, most open smile she could muster.

He squeezed her hand. "About that," he said, and she was instantly disappointed, thinking he was going to cancel on her. "Would you like to see some of London, before?"

"I would very much appreciate that," she said, unable to curtail her excitement.

"This afternoon, then." He pulled his hand from hers and walked away.

She watched him until his back disappeared around a corner in a swirl of sunshine and dust.

She sneezed again, then stopped to listen when she thought she heard the distant rumble of laughter, before she turned back to the room. She'd been moving boxes and furniture around in an attempt to get to the wall of ceiling-high windows that stretched across the front of the house. She'd seen the windows from outside, but had no idea they extended the length of such a large room, full of possibility. She stopped and looked around the room, assessing. She would need help from Rakshan, because she needed somewhere to put all the things that needed moving.

She pushed aside a large desk, shifted a few more boxes, and finally made a path to the windows to look outside. She could see across the park and out over the tops of the other houses in the area. She saw some small boys running across the roof of another house—chimney sweeps. Surely not as adorable as the little dancing sweeps she'd grown up singing with.

She started humming songs from *Mary Poppins* as she cleaned. The room was perfect. It would make for an incredible studio. It was large, the walls were solid, the light was divine. Something inside her unfurled at the idea of having a studio once again, and she smiled and hugged herself. It was something. It wasn't everything, but it was something.

SIXTEEN

When the position is such that neither side will gain by making the first
move,
it is called temporizing ground.

—Sun Tzu
The Art of War

Grayson had never felt so much distance between two people in such close confines. The carriage jolted and tossed them against each other as it was steered across the muddy ruts and cobblestones that made up the streets. It was as if the draw they'd felt over the past few days had reversed completely, and they now had nothing to say to each other.

He'd wanted to slow this down, not kill it completely. Even her usual demeanor seemed to have been quelled, that smart mouth and randy behavior. Perhaps his talk of family had frightened her.

He shifted on the bench in the carriage, waiting for something, anything, but she just looked out the window, smiling and asking simple questions. She didn't push him, she didn't prod him, she made no demands of him.

And he hated it.

He wasn't sure how to rectify that, however. She'd accepted his admission of the corset, even though he was fully aware she didn't know why he wore it. For him, it had been a confession, the opening of a door he wasn't sure he would walk through or slam shut. He wondered, though, how much she assumed, and where that brilliant mind would take her.

She had hurt him, bruised him, and it seemed like it had been on purpose, even if at the time he had excused her behavior as accidental. It could still be that, or she could be the kind of person who liked to tie people up and strip them down, and not necessarily in that order.

She wasn't a prostitute, though, and he didn't believe her to be a birch mistress either. She'd made it clear that she didn't sell herself. He had no interest in that, and if he had, he simply would have sought one out. He was certain the infamous *London Whipping Society* would happily make arrangements for him.

He shifted his seat, feeling the sensitive knot where she'd bruised his arse, and a spark of something lit inside him. It was still there, this connection he'd felt to her. It hadn't been killed, only dampened by his maundering, no doubt. He shifted to the corner and put his feet up on the seat across from them and did nothing but look at her.

He could see her discomfort form in his inspection. He knew she wasn't sure what she should say right now, and he had been rather abrupt with her today. Pushing her away.

She reached out suddenly and took his hand. He didn't move.

"That's the Tower," she said. "I recognize it because it was in the news last year. They filled the moat with red poppies in remembrance of the hundredth anniversary of the first World War, one poppy for each British life. It was an incredibly moving display. So much red. So many lives, nearly a million, I think. They spilled from the windows and filled the moat. I desperately wanted to see it in person, to be a witness."

He looked out the window at the Tower looming in the afternoon light that filtered through the smog. A world war? He wasn't sure how he felt knowing this. Sad didn't cover it. It was so much more than mere sadness. It was something he didn't have a word for. The knowledge that so many men would die protecting his country, and he didn't know what he could do to stop it. "What year was that?" he asked.

"2014, so 1914," she said as they drove on.

A mere thirty-one years from now, and he would still be alive, god willing. In thirty-one years, hundreds of thousands of men would die. Would he send them to die? Would he remain part of the parliament that chose the lives sent to battle?

She shifted, and he looked at her, realizing he was squeezing her hand much too tightly, and he released it. "I'm sorry, I—that's terrifying," he said.

She leaned back in the seat. "I don't like knowing these things. What's worse is not knowing enough about them to do anything differently. I didn't study history that closely. I was too determined to get out of high school and start my life. I passed the tests and promptly forgot. But I remember those poppies. Thousands upon thousands of them. Overall, the world lost millions of people to that war."

Hopelessness. That's what this feeling was, hopelessness. His chest froze, and he pulled his feet to the floor. "How can I know this and do nothing?" he said.

"And what would you do?" she asked. "I wouldn't even know where to begin. I don't even remember enough history to know how the war began. I'm so sorry, I shouldn't have said anything." She looked away and twisted her fingers together in her lap.

Grayson shook his head. "No. Don't—remember, no apologizing for the past. The war is not on your shoulders, only the burden of knowledge. There's nothing…there's nothing." He leaned back again and looked out the opposite window. "I will always shoulder that burden with you."

The Tower had always symbolized certain things for him, and for his country. It wasn't necessarily a cheerful and happy place at any time, but he wasn't sure he could see it now and not be saddened by what he knew was to come. "Lulu, don't ever feel like you shouldn't tell me something because it will hurt me, or because I will feel powerless against it. Can you promise me that? If there's something in our future that you wish to make me aware of, please do so. Please don't hold back because you're afraid of what I might think," he said.

He saw her nod in the periphery of his vision, then he closed his eyes to the afternoon. It was incredibly difficult to know millions of lives would be lost, nearly one million of those British. What of the lifetime of other knowledge she carried with her? He couldn't imagine knowing what was to come and being powerless to help any of it. But this was her new life. She had all these experiences that she must now somehow reconcile in order to survive here and not go mad.

He suddenly felt that her being here was much more difficult for her than he had yet considered. There was an entire world he knew nothing about, and it went beyond simply that she wouldn't tell him who she was. It was terrifying to consider that his entire world was gone wherever she came from. In a mere one hundred and thirty years, everyone he knew would be a ghost, including Lulu.

And then something even more terrible occurred to him. She had said the *first* world war. Oh, dear God in Heaven… She had said the first world war, which meant, at the very least, that there had been a second.

The loss of life had been more for Great Britain than one-sixth the current population of London. One in every six men on the street, dead.

Grayson felt a weight settle in his chest.

The tour of London had been terrifying. She'd only just realized the powerlessness that came with the knowledge she had, and she suddenly wished she could give it all up. She shouldn't have said anything to Gray. She should have kept it to herself, but she hadn't even considered… What of the other things she could remember? What of Jack the Ripper? What of assassinations of presidents and world leaders? What of the future of the world?

What was she doing here? Was she sent here to change the world or to change one life? She looked at Gray in the reflection of their bedroom window.

He indulged her interest in so many things, even though her thoughts about the Tower must have terrified him, as they did her. They'd also made another pass at Buckingham, though she refused his offer to call on the queen. Her wedding day had been so incredibly surreal, she wasn't prepared to face the reality of it yet, not that closely. She wanted to remain a tourist in this life. She *wished* she could remain a tourist in this life.

The entire afternoon in the carriage she'd felt a distance and a weight come down over them, wedge between them. The minute they got home, she shed her clothes to change because she wanted to be rid of the formal clothes. She wanted comfort and to be comforted. They had no control of the future—all they truly had was each other.

She felt a hand at her shoulder, his warmth skimming down her arm, taking the chemise with it, and she turned. "I want to know more of you," she said as she looked up to him. His thumb stroked the inside of her arm, above her elbow, and she shuddered into him, her forehead coming to rest on his chest as her other hand came up to steady herself, and she felt the corset through his waistcoat.

He shifted away, and she steadied herself from the loss of his support. "Grayson."

"No."

His voice was stiff and abrupt and it cut a little. She nodded and turned away so he wouldn't see her hurt. She put her pants and a shirt on over her chemise and drawers, a simple barrier. She was finding it more difficult to be naked around him without purpose. The reality of him was demanding she pay attention to her behavior, and regardless that he asked her to be true to herself, she was finding it much more difficult to know what that meant. It had always come easy to her to be out there, naked, passionate, loud, brash, singular. She was only now realizing that all those things kept her safe.

In all honesty, it was who she was. She was simply that loud and that brash, and she had always loved it. But letting someone in so close to her had her putting up walls to keep him out. Even if the walls were constructed of thin pieces of linen and silk. She'd thought it was just him who needed work. She'd been very wrong.

She considered him as he stared into the fire. There always seemed to be a fire to chase the chill. These houses were all so old that their bones needed constant warming to protect them. Like a city of frail old ladies. No wonder London was so badly polluted. The coal fires burned with a constancy she couldn't believe, something else she couldn't speak on without sounding like a lunatic—global warming. What she wouldn't give for some pine or ponderosa. At least it would smell good as it destroyed the ozone.

"Will dinner be ready soon?" she asked. It had to be the most inane question she'd ever asked him.

"Supper, you mean? Yes, in perhaps an hour," he said distractedly.

Dinner, supper. Pants, trousers. Chai, tea. For speaking the same language, they really were a world apart. She walked over to the fire and stood behind him, leaning against his arm and wrapping one hand around his biceps. "What are you thinking of?" she asked.

He paused, and she knew he was considering whether to tell the truth or put her off somehow, so she waited patiently.

"Death and family," he said. "Talking about them this morning… It was easier to ignore their existence before you came here with your questions and your insinuating your way into my life. Everything was easier before you came here." He paused, and she waited.

"I had assumed my wife would be easy to keep. She would be away from me—separate rooms, separate lives. I would be able to go on as I had before. Give her rein of her life, and she would leave me be. But family…I've been considering it now." He turned and looked at her. "Not for us, I know. I'm aware you don't want children. That's not at all what I'm considering. But I have a sister and a mother. They've gone without my intervention or my protection for a long time now."

"Do you want children?"

"I actually have no idea. I'd never even considered it, and now I won't."

Lulu nodded. She wasn't sure where he was going with this, whether he was trying to ask something, or simply trying to work through something, but she allowed him his head to do what he needed.

His hands came up, and he ran his fingertips down her arms so gently she wanted to weep. "I'm not sure what—in less than a sennight, you've changed the entire trajectory of my life, Lulu." He paused. "I—can we leave this for now? I have something for you."

She nodded, and Gray took her hand and pulled her behind him from their room. He went down the back way through the kitchens, startling the cook, who was preparing dinner. Supper. Food.

When they passed the kitchens, she was out of breath, and he stopped and raised his eyebrows as if to offer help, but she shook her head. He nodded once stiffly, then led her through some halls until they emerged in what must be the ballroom.

By the time they got there, she was winded and frustrated. It stretched the length of the back of the house, similar to Francine's house. But the floor wasn't as polished, and the walls were in need of fresh paper. The chandeliers were wrapped in a gauzy fabric, no doubt to protect them while unused, which lent a creepy air to the room.

"I apologize," he said quietly.

"Don't be. Cardio is important to stamina. I need more. Don't be shocked to find me running the stars of this massive place."

"Running the—" He stopped when she gasped and shoved past him.

"What have you done?" she said as she grabbed the front of his shirt in her fist, her other hand came to her mouth as she chewed her lip and stifled a whimper. Lulu knew she was going to cry. She knew she was going to fall to the floor in a sobbing heap and scare the crap out of her husband. *Again.*

Most of what she could see was in boxes shoved up in a corner, but the words on the boxes said everything. Glass plates, collodion, dry gelatin, sodium thiosulfate, silver iodide, bromine, chloride, silver nitrate, potassium iodide, potassium ferricyanide, ferric ammonium citrate, ferrous sulfate. She turned back to him.

"I told Rakshan to acquire everything a photographer could possibly need. Some of what you need is on order and will be delivered soon. The rest is here. He will help you to assemble whatever else you may need. I was thinking of the attics, but he mentioned a cooler environment for the chemicals and such. So perhaps one of the empty wine cellars. They are entirely lightproof. All in all, I believe this to be a good start." He rambled, and then he fell silent and his eyes were wide as he shifted his stance and tried to find something to do with his hands. He finally put one on his hip, the other running through his hair.

She almost fell to the floor when her knees buckled. Her hands shook, so she wrapped her arms around her waist to calm her nerves. There was enough chemistry for making negatives and prints. Van Dykes, salt prints, calotypes, tintypes, cyanotypes, daguerreotypes.

She started doing a mental inventory as she dropped her arms and marched to the stacks. "First off, you can't keep Van Dyke chemistry in the same area as cyanotype chemistry, because an accident would create cyanide gas and kill us all." She grabbed a few boxes and rearranged them. "Second, I can't believe you did this. When did you do this? I can't believe you did this." She toed one of the heavier boxes on the floor and pointed across the room.

Gray lifted it and moved it away from the stacks in the corner. "You mentioned this the first day. I told Rakshan that night. He took care of it."

"Third, I'll need some sort of ventilation, so perhaps a wine cellar isn't the best—" She opened an unmarked box and stared at the contents. Gray walked over and stood beside her, then he reached in and pulled out the most beautiful camera she'd ever seen. No—that wasn't correct. She had seen this camera before. She used a similar camera in her studio. One that had taken months to receive because it had come from an estate sale in London. She had liked the family name. This one was much newer, of course...or older, or...whatever. "I can't...oh, Grayson, I—" She ran her finger down one edge. "What was your full name again?"

"Grayson Locke Danforth," he said.

"Danforth," she echoed—that was the name. Was this her camera? If this was the same camera, could she somehow warn herself? Would she even want to?

He held the wood box for her, and she saw the panic in his eyes.

"It's not right. I'll find whatever is right. I can help with that. If you need technical lessons? No doubt the technical aspects have changed some. We can arrange that. I will do whatever—"

"No…no, you don't understand. This is perfect. This is everything. This is…too much. It's much too much." She felt her muscles vibrating, and she wrapped her arms around her middle again as he held her camera. **Her camera.** She'd never been so overwhelmed by gratitude. Not for a single person.

She had always taken care of herself. If she needed something, she got it. If she wanted something, she bought it. She never asked for anything from anyone and now…placed here, basically at a stranger's mercy… this man was doing everything she would have done for herself. He had provided her with her heart's desire.

He took a cautious step toward her, and she wrapped her arms around his neck, then bussed his cheek. He wrapped one arm around her, and she felt the wood of the camera press into her side as he shifted it and held her tight against his frame.

She would have a darkroom.

She felt like she could breathe.

"There's more," he whispered into her ear.

She shivered as wisps of loose hair brushed against her cheek as he spoke. "I need for nothing else. Nothing."

He squeezed her and released her slowly.

"Well, maybe a room…" she said then.

He brushed her hair back and tucked it behind her ear with one finger, and the simple sweetness of the act had her melting. "I have rooms. You found them this morning."

Lulu took the camera from him and held it to her chest, her arms wrapped around its giant frame protectively. Then she looked in the box to find three different lenses. She pulled out what looked to be a mid-range lens and smiled at him. She pointed to the tall tripod that leaned against the wall. He grabbed it for her, but he didn't attempt to take the camera from her. He was a smart man—she wouldn't have tried to pry it from her arms either.

Gray set the tripod up next to her, and she adjusted the head, then carefully placed the camera on top of it, tightening the bolts to make sure it was steady. She then loosened the catches on the box and rolled it open, running her fingers over the bellows with a smile as she installed the lens. She opened the shutter, pointed the lens at the row of French doors, and motioned him to come around to the back side of the camera.

She had to shade the glass for him as he bent to look, because there was too much ambient light in the room to see well. The windows projected on the ground glass, upside down and backward in perfect focus.

"That's…well. That is interesting. I've never bothered to look at one before," he said.

"It's perfect," she whispered as he straightened and turned to her. "Absolutely, beautifully, perfect."

"Yes, beautifully perfect," he said, but he wasn't looking at the camera like she was.

She looked up to him, and he leaned down, and she kissed him. She took as much of him and gave everything she was in that kiss, a thank-you. Her fingers slipped from the shutter release, and the glass went dark as he wrapped his arms around her.

"You're stunning when you're excited," he whispered against her. "I don't believe I've ever seen anything so beautiful as you touching that camera."

She felt the heat of an honest-to-goodness blush rush her skin from the tips of her breasts all the way up to the edge of her hair. This was more than she'd ever considered when thinking about her future here. Granted, she hadn't had much time to consider, but this… She couldn't really ask for more. She ran a finger down his chin.

"Thank you."

"I would do it a thousand times over to see that face again."

"Oh, you'll be seeing that face plenty, believe me. I'm probably the happiest Victorian lady in all the world at the moment."

"A man could ask for no more," he said. "However…" He paused and looked like he was considering something. He took up the hem of her shirt, rubbing it between his thumb and forefinger, and she knew something big was coming. "There is more."

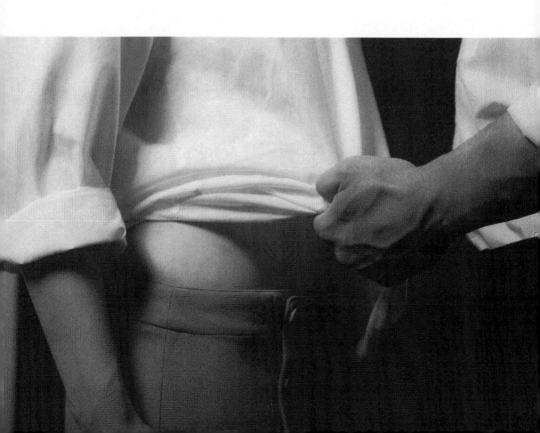

SEVENTEEN

Peace proposals unaccompanied by a sworn covenant indicate a plot.

—Sun Tzu
The Art of War

Grayson couldn't believe her reaction to the photography equipment. It was as if she'd come to life, and he'd only just seen her for the first time. Now he had more to show her and wasn't sure of the reception. As excited as she was for the equipment, he wasn't sure he wanted her excited about more things. What he wanted was for her to look at *him* the way she'd looked at those musty boxes of chemicals.

He was absolutely astounded by her intelligence, as well as thankful, considering what she'd mentioned as far as danger. He didn't know some of the chemicals, but was familiar with others and knew them to be quite toxic. It was encouraging to know she was aware of the dangers associated with them. He hadn't really considered how dangerous until she'd mentioned it, which meant he really hadn't been paying attention the way he usually did.

His attention to detail was generally impeccable. He should have been wary of the chemicals before they were brought anywhere near his house. Her presence must be clouding his judgment. He fought the urge to push her away again, because he wanted her to touch him with the reverence she showed that camera.

"You wanted a place to train, so Rakshan has obtained mats, and he's going to tape out a sparring lane for sword training and fencing."

She turned and looked around the room as though she only just realized where she was, then she released him and clapped her hands. "It's perfect. It's perfect!" She spun in a circle, then ran back to him. "Could we install a barre on one wall? About waist height? For stretching? And then another bar, higher up, for doing pull-ups?"

He shrugged. He didn't see why not. This room wasn't going to ever see another ball if he could help it. "Talk to Rakshan. You can do whatever you wish to."

"I'm overwhelmed," she said then. "I am. Thank you."

He felt suddenly awkward with her, as though she were a different person. As though now that he'd given her all she asked for, perhaps she wouldn't need him anymore.

She reached out and took his hand, then turned for the gardens. "The sun will be gone soon. Can we go for a walk?"

"Certainly," he said.

She pulled one of the French doors open, and they stepped out to the balcony that overlooked the small garden. Nothing as grand as Roxleigh's town house, but his own father had to sell off some of the back gardens with the mews when he'd started having problems with money. Someday Grayson would reclaim that land. He wasn't sure why he would want to since the house itself was entailed—perhaps to prove a point to his dead father. He didn't know.

"What are you thinking?" she asked.

"I'm—just maundering," he said. He wasn't sure he could separate all the different thoughts he was having at the moment. From the Tower earlier, to his family, to the camera, and her hand…her hand sliding across that wood like a sigh.

"Grayson."

He stopped, and she pulled him over to a bench to sit down. Then she turned toward him. "You've done so much for me. I can't believe how much. I would like to repay you somehow. If I can."

"There's nothing. I expect nothing. I did this for you as an apology, or…" He thought for a moment. An apology. *I'm sorry you had to marry me. I'm sorry you were placed in this life. I'm sorry you're stuck here.*

"There isn't anything for you to apologize for. You didn't bring me here. Remember what you keep saying about apologies? Same goes for you, Gray," she said.

"Perhaps, but I do feel terribly that you're here and not where you wish to be. I told you I would see to you, and I will. Anything you have need of."

"And what do you have need of?" she asked.

A few things popped into his head, but they weren't things he could share with her. He wanted her to bind him again. He wanted her to hurt him again. He wanted her mouth on him again. He was a beast. He shook his head and turned away to hide the thoughts that were probably quite blatant in his expression.

"I hope that someday you'll be able to trust me," she said and he turned back to her.

He wanted the same thing. He took her hand and traced the lines of her palm. "I—" He choked, and she waited patiently. *I wear a corset because it controls me. Because without it, I feel like I will fall apart. Because with it, I can face the world. Because without it, I feel like I don't deserve what I have. I need pain in order to have sex.*

He froze suddenly and considered her. Did she know? He thought again about the bruise on his arse. He hadn't been truly hard until that moment… He shook his head to drive the thoughts away again and felt her cool fingers wrap around his jaw, her thumbs skimming the crests of his cheeks.

"Grayson, we have all the time in the world. I'm not going anywhere from what we can tell. If you're not ready…I'll wait. I'm here." She ran her hands down his neck, then tapped his chest. "I'm here. I'm not going anywhere." He nodded. "I bought some things while I was out with Francine," she said. "I think you may appreciate them." She smiled, and he thought he knew to what she alluded.

Her hand skimmed across his chest as she leaned into him and whispered in his ear, "Would you like to lose that virginity of yours?"

Yes, he did know to what she alluded, but why was she doing this now? Why, after today, was she pushing him away with sex again? He didn't want that. What they'd shared intimately had changed his life, and he didn't want it made into something tawdry and cheap, but it felt like that's what she was doing.

He turned and looked into those forest eyes that were so close he felt like he could walk into them. "Why are you pushing me away?"

"What?" she asked.

"You…today was difficult, I think for both of us. We only just—I think we had only just begun to be comfortable again, and the minute we did, you twisted it into something else. Something cheap."

The words felt like a slap, and Lulu turned away. He was right. Today had been difficult, and ugly, and terrifying, and then…incredible beyond words. So why did she ruin it by coming on to him like that? "I'm sorry, I—shit." She stood and walked a few paces away from him. He stayed on the bench.

She wasn't sure what to say to him, because she was only just realizing herself how much she used sex and nakedness and pure unabashedness as a shield against anyone who dared come close to her.

When she had considered him somewhat of a client, it was easier for her, but he'd become more and more real with every beat of her heart and… She turned back to look at him.

"I do need to apologize for this, because I should never have done that. I'm sorry," she said. He motioned for her to come back to the bench, and she did. She sat beside him but didn't touch him.

"Why do you try to put empty space between us? I thought…I realize there are still things we're both keeping…one from the other, but I thought we were learning to trust and to be…better with each other," he said.

She nodded, sufficiently admonished. "Wow, once you relax enough around a person, you get downright chatty, don't you?"

"Lulu."

She shook herself. "Yes…better with each other. I don't know how to do this, Gray, to be perfectly honest. I've never had much of a family. I've never had very close friends. I had my clients and my work, and that was my life. My closest friend was my darkroom. People and I, we just don't really get along very well." She wrapped her arms around her middle and held on.

"I understand. You were treating me not like someone you wanted to know. You were treating me like a client for whatever business it is you conduct."

"No, Gray, no. That's not—I have never felt so close to another person in all my life. I don't…" She stopped to consider before just running off another excuse, perhaps a lie. "I suppose I did fall back on my training somewhat because it's all I know. I don't know how to do this. But I do want to learn." She whispered that last bit, terrified of what might come next from him.

"I see."

They sat for a moment, side by side in the waning light. Lulu shuddered against the growing chill, and Gray removed his jacket, placing it on her shoulders. She snaked her arms up into the sleeves and let his heat envelop her, then she breathed deeply of his scent, which lingered in the heavy fabric, hoping that they would get through this difficulty quickly, because she wanted his body to surround her and comfort her like his jacket was now. She wasn't fond of Come to Jesus discussions.

Gray took a deep breath and turned to her. "Let's remember what we promised, shall we? To be truthful in all things with each other? Can we add genuine to that?"

She watched him, castigated, as he attempted to explain, this man of action, of extreme action. She nodded. "Genuine. So if I just want to get laid?" she asked sincerely.

Gray shook his head. "Then say so. But don't throw sex out there because you're uncomfortable with our discussion."

She nodded. "All right, I think I can manage that." She was beginning to feel better already, back to her snarky self. "Gray, you know up until that point, I believe I've always been genuine with you when it comes to sex," she said.

He seemed to consider that, then he spoke. "Perhaps you have, and I would like it to stay that way. I may be a virgin, but that doesn't mean I need to rut like a beast just to be done with it. It's not what you did for me, and don't pretend your words the other night were anything but true. I realize you wanted to be rid of your maidenhead, but your true purpose in my ruining you with my hand was a gift. Don't take that back now. Don't take my ability to gift you with this away from me in some callous fashion."

Lulu couldn't breathe. She held on to the lapels of his coat and hid her face in the neck. She couldn't bring herself to look at him. He was right. It had been a gift to him. He was absolutely correct. He felt that way because that was exactly what she had intended him to feel. She'd wanted to gift him with her maidenhead. She'd couched it all with her bravado, but she could have waited to be done with it. That act was entirely for him, and that he realized it was a very intense sort of feeling.

She'd thought he was nothing more than brute strength and hidden passion, but he was hiding quite the cunning intellect as well.

"If we don't change the subject soon, I am going to be groveling at your feet for the rest of the night," she mumbled from inside the jacket. She popped her eyes open and looked at him. He seemed to be doing the internal poke and prod during which he tried to find the darkest recesses of her mind and turned on the lights.

She hoped that, whatever he found there, whatever decision came with it, it wouldn't change his mind about her.

EIGHTEEN

Do not pursue an enemy who simulates flight.
Do not attack soldiers whose temper is keen.

—Sun Tzu
The Art of War

"Today at the Tower, it occurred to me just how difficult this life will be for us," he said. "I say 'us' because I refuse to allow you to keep secrets from me. I refuse to allow you to manage the things you know on your own."

"I'm afraid," she said quietly.

"I imagine you are, but I believe we've both faced some of our fears recently. What are a few more? Lulu, the past is done. The future as well, as far as we're concerned. The only truth we have…is us."

Lulu nodded, and he caught that green gaze again, wanting to go exploring in the forest of her mind, to take refuge in the clearings where the sun would shine brightly and she would be waiting, warm and wicked, for him to come. He took a deep breath and steeled himself.

"I wear a corset—because I'm afraid of how I feel when I don't."

She held his gaze and refused to release him. Then she shifted and seemed to come back out of his jacket and regain that strength that he was so enamored of.

"I understand that, and there are things I can do for you," she said.

His breathing was suddenly stilted, and he wasn't sure what to say. Admitting what he had…it had come as a shock to him, but when he looked into her eyes, it had simply come out. She did know. She did. He knew in that moment that everything she had done to him had been done with purpose. What was she?

"What can you do for me?" he asked carefully.

"I can tell you about my life and hope that you understand."

His eyes narrowed on her, and Lulu froze. "Where I'm from, a man in a corset for things other than vanity is not a rare thing," she said. "You are simply a man before your time."

He considered that for a moment, his forehead wrinkling. "That would make us a matched set, since you are, quite literally, before your time," he said.

Lulu nodded. "Yes, it would, wouldn't it?"

"You're not offended?" he asked.

"By a corset? God, no. It takes a lot more than that to offend me, Grayson. In fact, a man in a corset fulfills certain fantasies I've had since I was a kid sneaking out of my parents' house to see midnight movies on Colfax." His face turned up to hers with a hopeful, albeit confused, expression. "I believe I know how you feel about your corset. Because I work with people who did similar things. In my day…" She took a deep breath, then blew it out. She had to start trusting him, because he had already given so much. "I'm a switch. I'm going to give you some terms to see if any of them are familiar. Okay?"

He nodded.

"BDSM?"

He shook his head.

"Bondage, discipline, domination, submission, sadism, or masochism?" She said each word slowly and scrutinized his features for any sign of recognition.

"I understand the terms, somewhat, but I'm fairly certain that the way I understand them and the way you do are not the same," he said. "Or, at the very least, I hope they're not."

She nodded. Considering they weren't currently far removed from the Marquis de Sade, she understood that. Sadism was primarily a descriptor

in her time, as was masochism, yet they had only recently been removed as mental deficiency diagnoses from the DSM-V, so in his time…they would definitely be a derogatory labels.

"Submission?" she asked. He didn't move an inch, and that lack of shifting was a dead giveaway that she'd touched some sort of chord.

"Sexual submission?" she continued. He tensed, and his eyes blazed. She nodded and took his hands in hers. "Please listen to me. There is nothing wrong with submission."

"There is everything wrong with submission. I'm a man. More than that, I'm a titled man and meant to dominate, not submit."

She waited. "What about masochism? In my day, a masochist is someone who…*needs* pain."

His eyes narrowed on her. "I believe this discussion is over." He took his hands from her and stood, walking away. *Oh god*, she'd gone too far. She had to rein it in somehow.

"What you do in public is not necessarily what you do in private. The two are not mutually exclusive," she said, but he was moving. She stood. "Warrick, stop." He did, but she saw the tension run through him. She walked up to him carefully. His breath came in short bursts, his shoulders heaving against his lungs. She walked in front of him and placed one hand on his chest. "You want to be dominated, and there's nothing wrong with that."

"I do not want to be dominated," he said.

"I mean, that some part of you, even as you fight this need, something inside of you needs domination."

"This is some sort of elaborate scheme," he replied.

"With who?"

"My father."

"Your father is dead, but it sounds like he did a number on you already. If he did something to you because of the way you are, then I'm glad he's dead, because you want to submit. It's part of who you are. Whether you like it or not, you stopped when I commanded it. Your body reacts to my dominance without your permission, whether you're yet aware of it or not," she said.

His eyes flashed black, and she straightened. "What we do is between us and nobody else. Not ever. I will never judge you for what you need in order to experience pleasure. I will never tell another soul… I will happily bind you. I will happily hurt you—"

"What?" he yelled, and she knew…she knew she should have stopped sooner. She wasn't handling this well at all, and it was because she was too close to him.

He pushed her hand away and walked off, but she didn't follow. Never follow a dragon to its cave. That's what she'd always been taught, and right now he was most definitely a dragon. She could only hope that he'd listened to, and heard, what she'd said.

Lulu wasn't sure how his father had treated him, but she was getting a fairly good idea of it. Obviously, his father knew about his need to feel pain. She wished he could talk about it with her. He'd trusted her with the corset. Perhaps he would trust her with the rest.

Or perhaps she'd gone too far, and he would have her taken away.

She could do nothing but track him as he stalked toward the ballroom, his body a silhouette against the lights inside. How could she prove to him that he could trust her with this? She hadn't wanted to approach him as a client, but she'd been doing exactly that, or some version of it.

She followed behind him slowly.

When she reached the ballroom, she found him swinging a long, wooden staff. He'd pulled his shirt from his pants and tossed it aside with his waistcoat and cravat. Barefoot, he faced a wall of mirrors at the end of the room. He held the bō staff between his hands, then bowed.

What followed next was some of the most beautifully choreographed movement she'd ever seen. It could have easily been performed as a ballet at the Met, and she would have paid happily.

She slid to the floor in silence as he moved with the staff in perfect form. His muscles bunching and stretching, his entire body engaged and nimble. She wanted that grace used on her. She wanted that talent and muscle control for herself.

She stood and removed his jacket, tossed it aside, then began to mimic his movements as he concentrated. She was soon covered head to toe in a sheen of sweat from the controlled work of her muscles—as was he.

She feigned the weight of a staff in her hands, but made every move along with him. It was a beautiful dance, and one she hoped he would allow again. Once she learned the movements he repeated, she closed her eyes and concentrated, feeling the pull of her own muscles.

She swept her leg out and made the final turn, coming up against a hard wall that hadn't been there before. She opened her eyes and looked up to him. "Hello," she panted.

"If you close your eyes, you leave yourself open to attack," he replied.

"Do you mean to hurt me?" she asked breathlessly. He didn't answer, only looked down at her. "Will you—will you teach me?" she asked after it was clear he wasn't going to respond to the first question. He handed her the staff, and the weight of it brought one end to the wood of the ballroom floor immediately.

She lifted it, carefully, then handed it back to him. "Perhaps one not so heavy, is it a bō staff?" she asked, even more impressed by the grace of his movements now that she knew the heft of his staff.

"Rokushakubō. This one is weighted, for training."

Lulu fiddled with her fingers, avoiding his gaze. "I want to apologize," she said.

"I don't want your apology. I can't trust you." His voice was sharp and it cut to the quick.

"You could have me sent to Bedlam at any moment, for any reason, and you don't trust me? What exactly could I do to you?" she said.

"You could use this against me," he said.

"And who would listen?" He was closing himself off from her and she didn't know how to stop him. She rubbed her hands down her thighs when her palms got sweaty, her nerves taking over the functions of her body as she panicked.

He turned and leaned the bō staff against the wall, then he shook his head.

"We seem to be constantly on the edge of an argument," she said. "I don't want to argue with you. I simply want to know you, and give you everything you could wish for…within my means." He turned to look at her. "You are still compartmentalizing me, even if you think you aren't. I will do whatever you wish. I will never judge you. If I was brought here for a reason, it was because we are the same. I know you don't want to trust me. I understand that whatever happened with your father is most likely the basis for this, but I'm going to hope that someday you will. I'm going to trust that what we've said will not come between us and that you won't do anything to hurt me. I am going to trust."

"I'm sending you away." The words were so calm they sent a chill down her spine. He stood before her, his arms crossed over his chest, his stance level and strong. His voice steady and his face void of emotion. Lulu shook her head, she couldn't fathom—

"Sending me away?" Lulu couldn't breathe. "Please," she begged suddenly.

"I have a country estate. We will never have need to cross paths again."

"But I don't want that. I want to be with you. I want our paths to cross. Why would you do this after… Why?"

"Because what you speak of will destroy me. Whether you believe it or not. Because what you speak of is absolutely unconscionable." His voice gained power as he continued, and she shied from him, because he didn't sound at all like the man she'd been getting to know.

"Because I am not that person. I am not weak. I am not twisted and…I am not. I am The Warrick, and it's about goddamn time I started acting like it! Pack your things." He turned and walked away from her.

Lulu panicked and shouted after him as he retreated. "No! Gray, please!"

But he didn't listen, and when the ballroom door slammed like a death knell, she knew it was done.

NINETEEN

When you have the enemy's strongholds on your rear,
the narrow pass in front of it is hemmed in ground.

—Sun Tzu
The Art of War

rayson stormed to his room without pause. When he reached it, he gathered a few things, then left so he wouldn't have to see her again, because if he did… "Rakshan!"

"Yes, Your Grace?"

Grayson turned as he moved quickly toward the hallway. "Get her out of this house," he said. Rakshan stared at him. "What?" Grayson said.

Rakshan shook his head. "I expected more of you."

"You—what do you mean?"

"This is not how a man of honor treats an innocent," Rakshan replied. "And you know this."

"Innocent? She could destroy me," Grayson said and the very thought made him tense. He rolled his head on his shoulders letting the bones of his neck pop and release.

"What has she done to make you believe she would?"

"She knows."

"I know, and I have not destroyed you, nor would I ever. Therefore, that is not enough. It is what she has done that should be your guide, not what she hasn't."

Grayson looked at him, but couldn't bring himself to believe what he'd said. "You have no idea how London works," he said.

"Neither does she, but you're determined to show her the worst of it now, aren't you?"

Bloody Fucking hell. What did he say to that? "Her ignorance of London will do no good if she ruins us both in the process."

"Then you should be her guide. She is born new unto this world and should be treated as one in need of guidance, not as one who has gone before."

"I need—"

"You need? What you need has been given to you, and you refuse to see it. You refuse her, and she has nowhere to go. You expect to shame her by sending her back to her family? To people who are complete strangers to her? Or perhaps to shame her by sending her to the country for society to judge why she was sent away. It is not her shame that should be considered in your next move, but your own." Rakshan turned and disappeared into the bedroom, and Grayson stomped off with his clothes.

He heard shuffling on the stairs and ducked into a room before she came too close. What was he doing? He was a coward in the worst sort of way. He had just declared his intention of becoming The Warrick, and now he was hiding in…he didn't even know what room this was. He was a jackass, and he knew it, and Rakshan had been right about his shame.

What she said… He thought about their wedding night. Had that all been on purpose? Had she bound his arms because she knew he wanted it somehow? Had she bruised his arse for the same reason? He had to quit making excuses and trying to deny the fact that she had.

Rakshan had called her an innocent, but he needed to stop thinking this way. Certainly he had considered her one even as she had spoken of her former life. She was no innocent to certain things. He dropped his clothes and put his hands against the door, leaning into his arms until his muscles started to vibrate. She was a danger to him, no matter how he looked at it. She already knew too much about him.

He was trained to be invisible. How could he possibly let this happen—and in such a short period of time? He had quite obviously lost his senses. Now he had to control whatever damage came of this.

He would have to be sure that society knew she was unstable. He would have to be sure that nobody believed a word she said. He knew how to start rumors—

I made a promise.

He needed to stop and consider everything. He had already acted too quickly out of panic, and he needed to stop. He needed to heed his years of training and approach her as though she were a target, which meant he needed her to stay close, not in the country. He couldn't keep track of her if she were in the country. She could go to Roxleigh's house. But what if she talked to them... No, Roxleigh would come to him first and they would quash any rumors she might attempt, wouldn't they? Just to put a point on it, like she had said, who would she tell? She didn't know anyone.

His mind raced. He could chance it. Roxleigh could control the ton, and he would do so to protect the family. Grayson knew that much about him. He needed her close enough to watch, but far enough away he could think. This massive house was the perfect place. He just needed to keep her busy and away from him somehow. He listened for her footsteps in the hallway.

As of right now, everyone was the enemy.

But not Rakshan. He trusted Rakshan, and he was right. If she did know, if she'd done those things to him on purpose, she had known all along and hadn't betrayed him to anyone.

Grayson slammed a hand into the door. His mind was racing much too fast. He wanted to be in India. Earlier, she had asked what his life was like there and if they could do that here. Why not?

It seemed a brilliant idea in reality. And now he was taking the advice of the one he had only just named as a target… Sun Tzu counseled to hold your enemies close… So he couldn't send her away—but then what if some dark part of him was only attempting to keep her here for another purpose?

He roughed his palms across his face. He needed sleep. He reached down and gathered his clothes to open the door, then looked up and down the hallway. He caught Rakshan leaving his bedroom and walked over to him.

"You haven't come to your senses if you think spending time in an old room full of broken furniture will bring you the answers to your questions," Rakshan said.

Grayson turned and looked at the door. He thought it might have once been a nursery, but he didn't remember, and it didn't actually matter. "Rakshan, she can have my room. Please move my things to another suite— the abandoned dowager suites in the north wing. I can return to my rooms on the square for the time being if necessary."

Rakshan looked at him for a moment, his gaze free of all judgment, and Grayson realized this was one reason he'd always trusted him. Rakshan made it easy.

So why was it so difficult with Lulu? She never looked at him in judgment. She did look at him like she could see everything there was about him, however, and that was uncomfortable for a man with secrets.

"Send for me at my rooms, once the suite is ready. Please let Lulu know she…" Let her know what, exactly?

"You should not make me a messenger of this sort," Rakshan said.

Grayson froze. He was right. He had declared himself and then promptly hidden from confrontation in a closet.

"Is she dressed?" he asked. Rakshan nodded and stepped aside so he could pass. Grayson stood before the door to his suite, then tossed his clothes to the floor beside him. He put one hand on the door and closed his eyes, trying to pull strength from somewhere, anywhere. Then he reached out and turned the knob, pushing the door open with a calm he didn't have a strong hold on.

When the door to the suite opened and Gray walked in, Lulu steeled herself for the worst.

"I owe you an apology," he said. "You will remain here, if it is your wish to. Though I understand should you wish to leave. Please understand, I—" He stopped, and she waited, unsure what to do. She wanted to let him think on everything she'd said. She didn't want to push him further at the moment.

"If you need anything at all, please ask Rakshan. I have things to attend to that the wedding festivities have delayed. I will have my things removed so you might have your privacy. It's late. I'll leave you."

"Your Grace," she said then. He'd brought up a wall, and she didn't feel like it was within her rights to breech it. She felt cold, and very alone.

"I gave you leave… Actually, I informed you that you would address me as Gray. That hasn't changed. Should it be necessary, I will inform you. I'm sorry if I—" He shook his head, and it was obvious he had one heck of an internal struggle happening at the moment. "I need some time to consider."

"Thank you, Gray. If you need anything, even just to…talk. Or anything. Someone to sit in a room and make it less empty. Anything at all. I will be here."

"You're not a prisoner. Please take care if you choose to leave the house and do not go alone. Go with Francine or have Rakshan attend you. But… you are not a prisoner."

"Thank you. Gray."

He nodded, then left.

Lulu collapsed to the bed, unsure what she should do next. She was emotionally exhausted from this day but had no idea if she could even sleep. She looked at Rakshan. "Where is he going?" she asked.

"Nowhere if I can help it," Rakshan said. "But I do fear he may wish to leave." She nodded and expected Rakshan to leave, but he remained standing there. She'd gone too far. Why couldn't she help him?

She felt goose bumps rise on her arms as it occurred to her that this whole time she had been merely concerned with him and how he was opening up to her, putting off any notice of herself. Putting aside his comments about her shutting him out or avoiding honesty in their conversations.

She'd demanded he open up to her. She wanted him to realize who he was so she could be herself, but she was refusing to give him the same thing.

She heard the shuffle of feet as if to remind her of his presence and wished it was Gray, but she knew it was Rakshan.

"You dress him," she asked.

"I do. You and I have knowledge of him that will intersect without doubt, but you and I will never discuss or confirm these things with each other," he said.

She knew it was his way of warning her, but she didn't need the warning. She just wanted that bit of confirmation from him, perhaps to feel not so alone. "I'm frightened," she said, speaking only of herself and not of anything to do with Rakshan.

"It's understandable. A new life, a new world, a new husband. Any one of these things would bring an average person to their knees, yet here you are. Resilient."

"I don't feel resilient," she said.

"You must give yourself time. You must not be so harsh. You expect much of him, and yet yourself you berate as though this should be simple, while it certainly is not."

It was true, and it hurt. She was forcing herself into the role of dominant to a client where she'd promised to be only herself. She had done nothing but lie to herself about her actions.

"Any relationship is give and take, Your Grace. It is not a tug-of-war. It is an exchange of gifts. What have you given?" he asked.

What had she given? Plenty of physical manifestations of action, but what of herself? She'd told him only superficial things. Well, not so. Her photography was very much a part of her, but he didn't understand to what level. She hadn't told him anything about what it meant to create.

She'd tried to explain herself in the garden, but only in terms of what she could do for him, not what it did for her. What did it do for her? It was who she was, not merely what she did. She lived to serve and be served.

"I have to tell him," she said as she stood.

"Shall I fetch your husband then, Your Grace?" he said.

"Yes, Rakshan. If you please."

TWENTY

When you penetrate deeply into a country it is serious ground.
When you penetrate but a little way it is facile ground.

—Sun Tzu
The Art of War

Grayson heard the scratch at his study and turned but remained silent. The door opened, and Rakshan entered.

"Do you know what my name means, Your Grace?" he asked without pause.

"No."

"It means protector," Rakshan said simply.

"That's fitting, considering what you have meant to me," Grayson said.

"And what you have meant to me, Your Grace. Without your intervention, I would not be alive today," Rakshan said.

"I did what any man would do."

"As it was men who attempted to kill me, I disagree," Rakshan said.

"While I can't argue that, I don't believe those men could be considered people of honor, so perhaps I should say it's what any gentleman would do."

"And how do you define a gentleman?" Rakshan asked.

"I don't...a man of honor."

"And yet many people here refer to your father and brothers as gentlemen. Do you believe they had honor?"

Grayson was silent once again. He wasn't sure where Rakshan was headed with this, but he knew where it would lead in the end—to a wall which Grayson could not climb to escape Rakshan's reason. Grayson wasn't

of a mood to be cornered into understanding at the moment, however. "Rakshan," he said.

"Your Grace," Rakshan replied.

Grayson narrowed his eyes on him but didn't say anything.

"We can call an ant an ant, and it may well be an ant, but there is also the possibility that the ant is an elephant," Rakshan said.

Grayson shook his head. He was much too tired to reason this out without being led.

"Your father is neither an ant, nor an elephant. But you are absolutely a gentleman."

Grayson pinched the bridge of his nose. He didn't feel much like a gentleman at the moment.

"It is what you are at your soul, Your Grace. It is how you would behave toward others under the best and the worst of circumstances. What happens in the interim is a gray area, but without a doubt, at your best *and* at your worst, you have always been, and remain to be, a gentleman."

"So this is not the worst of circumstances then?" Grayson asked.

"Far from it, Your Grace, because the moment has not yet passed," Rakshan said.

"I don't understand most of what you just said," Grayson said.

"Someday you might. For now, we should gather your things." Rakshan turned and walked from the room.

"Rakshan." He didn't stop, and Grayson followed. "Rakshan!"

Rakshan turned then and looked at him, "Your Grace, she's in the bath. It's perfectly safe to return and gather some things," he said.

Grayson nodded and walked into his room as Rakshan held the door. He looked up to find her standing there, staring directly at him.

Grayson turned back to his man.

"It seems I lied." Rakshan shrugged. "Who will you trust now?" he said, and he pulled the door closed behind him.

Lulu had heard them in the hallway and knew that Rakshan meant to trick Gray. He knew she wasn't in the bath. He had just left her here moments ago.

Gray stared at the closed door, then placed his hands on the frame and leaned against it, his head dropped. Lulu had no idea what to say, so she backed up, sat on the bed, and waited patiently.

She looked away and considered what she should do next. She needed to explain who she was to him. She needed to get past the fear of his judgement and lay everything out before him. Perhaps she should just show him what she meant when she spoke of training. She stood.

"Turn around and face me," she said.

"No. I don't want to play any games," he replied.

"You act like this is a game, but it isn't. This is who I am, and by coming here, by being forced into someone else's body and life and marriage, I have given up everything about myself. So you're The Warrick? Fine, you be The Warrick. Just remember that I am now your duchess. But allow me to show you who I was. Call me by my title."

"Duchess," he said.

"Whose duchess am I?"

"You are my duchess."

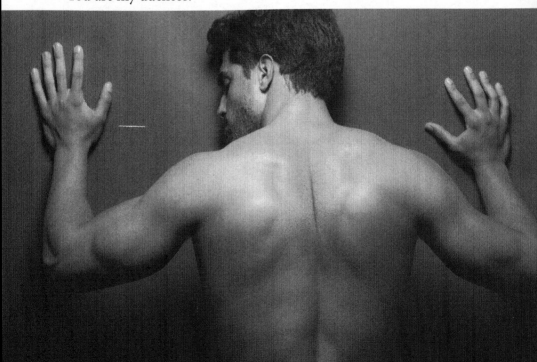

"Then turn around and face me." He straightened, the muscles across his back rippling in a sensual dance as he steadied himself. She wanted wings across that back, and the thought of it made her shudder.

He turned and caught her gaze, certainly a bit lascivious. She raised an eyebrow. "The way I see it, you have two choices. First choice, you can send me away and continue on in your miserable life, not understanding who you are and what you were meant to be and the power that it holds. Or second, you can train with me, and I can show you a world you obviously never imagined. One where you can be yourself, one that will not make you weaker, but stronger."

He said nothing in response, but he watched her carefully. She waited. She wasn't going to push this, because it had to be his decision.

"What if I can't—" He stopped and shook his head.

"What if you can't?" she repeated.

"What if you're wrong?" he asked.

"Then I'm wrong, and we'll know, and we can move on to find something else." She walked toward him, and he stiffened. She reached out and coasted her thumb across the bruise on his backside she knew was there, relishing the hiss between his teeth. Then she reached out and palmed his hardening cock with her other hand. "But I'm not wrong, and you want to know," she whispered in his ear.

He moved away from her quickly, walking across the room to the windows.

If she were being paid…if this were a scene, she would follow and give him orders, but they would also have limits already negotiated. But this wasn't a scene. He wasn't a player, and he didn't know anything about any of this. She needed a new set of rules, a new paradigm.

The fact that he was such a complete and total virgin was what stalled her, because she didn't want to harm him. At least in her own day, people knew of the practice of BDSM, but here, apparently, he had no basis for knowledge. It was probably very much underground. Certainly it existed in some form. He simply hadn't sought to find it because he'd managed himself in other ways. An ungodly patience, lots of meditation, and tea.

Gray stood across the room, staring out the windows, and she took a deep breath to steel herself. "Gray, what I would really like to do is tell you about my life, about who I am and how I help people like you. Like myself.

Because then you would know better what you want, and you could express to me how you feel about certain things, and you could trust me because we would have very specific limits set. But if this were the twenty-first century and you were my client? I wouldn't be so gentle with you right now. I would command you. Your limits would be learned by trial and the use of a safe word, and you would learn what I am, because I would show you."

She came up behind him as he gazed out at the park across from his house, and then, because she could, because she felt like she'd put all her cards on the table and there wasn't any point now in pulling punches, she skimmed her palm down the round of his ass again and pushed into the bruise.

His muscles bunched and shifted, and he groaned loudly—more like some sort of primal growl than a human sound. "What am I?" he asked.

"Beautiful," she breathed the word over his shoulder.

He turned to her, dropped his hands to his sides, and spoke. "Show me."

Lulu had never in her life been more turned on than she was from those two words. If she could have, she would have had them tattooed on her skin so she could touch them whenever she wanted to remember.

"You said very clearly that you do not trust me. We can't do this without a certain level of trust. Do you understand?"

He nodded.

"You need a word, any word. That word, when spoken, will bring an immediate stop to anything and everything I'm doing. No questions asked. If you're not comfortable with something, you only need say the word and we're done. It's that simple. Do you understand?"

He nodded.

"It needs to be something that will be easy to remember, something you can't forget, but something you wouldn't say normally. Do you have a word?" she asked.

He looked around the room as he thought, then his gaze stopped on her wardrobe. "Armoire," he said quietly.

"Armoire?" she repeated. He nodded. She shrugged. She supposed it was as good as any other safe word since it wasn't something typically shouted out in the heat of the moment.

"Gray, I would like to ask you some questions about limits, because we're just learning each other. If you want me to proceed without the questions—"

"No questions," he said, then he looked in her eyes. "Duchess."

The way his eyes bore into her almost had her on her knees, and she reminded herself that she was topping him, not the other way around.

"Armoire," she whispered again. "Don't forget it."

TWENTY-ONE

There are five dangerous faults which may affect a general:
a delicacy of honor which is sensitive to shame is one.

—Sun Tzu
The Art of War

Grayson had no idea what was about to happen to him, but a sudden weight lifted from his shoulders as his knees hit the floor at her feet, and he gave himself over to her keeping.

Absolute worst-case scenario? He could do this with her tonight, then disappear in the morning. Nobody would ever know, and if she spoke of it, he would send her away as he'd first said. On the other hand…he could use this to force her to open up to him, to better explain who she was and why she was intent on doing this to him…with him.

He ran his hands up her legs and pulled her close, wrapping his arms around her and holding her tight. She pushed her hand through his hair, his head tilting back as she did so. Then she grabbed a fistful of his hair and pushed his head back farther until he looked into her eyes. Her voice seemed timid when she spoke.

"I've done this for years. Trained, practiced, studied human nature. But with you, it all feels so different. I keep straying from the rules. I'm desperate for you to understand me. To know me. I've never felt this before," she whispered.

"I've been trying to slow you down since the moment you got here. But you're like a train off the rails, and I can't seem to find the brakes." He felt as though she was already attempting to pull back from him, to shut him out.

"I want you inside me so bad I can't think straight. Never have I been drawn to anyone like this, Gray. I want to both serve you and dominate you.

I want so many things, but patience… It's not one of my virtues. I want it all, and I want it now." She seemed to consider him as the tension on his hair lessened and she released him, then she sank to the floor in front of him, crossing her legs.

"I want the same things," he said, "but what I have, that you don't, is patience in abundance. I realize I haven't behaved that way since meeting you, and I can only blame myself for it."

He sat back and considered her. This day had gone from one extreme to the other and back again so rapidly it felt to him as though they'd just lived many years together. They weren't like magnets at all. They were elastics, forcefully pulling away and slamming back into each other. Yet she already knew more of him in four days than his entire family had learned in the two years since his return.

"You like pain," she said.

"No." That wasn't true. Nobody liked pain, did they?

"Then…you *need* pain for certain things," she said.

He considered her. Perhaps if he never admitted to it, if he never agreed outright to anything… Then he thought of Calder. In all of his maundering, the decisions with Calder were the most calm and lucid. He shook his head and looked away as he prepared for his truth. "Yes."

"Grayson, I don't need pain like that, but I do like it, and I like to submit, to follow orders. We could start there. I could prove to you how powerful it is. I know you don't wish to be dominant. I understand that, but I can be either dominant or submissive." She leaned forward, and her voice dropped an octave. "Put your duke hat on and order me around. You'll see how fast you can make me come, how wet you'll make me with just your words. You'll see and perhaps come to understand just a bit." She said these words—again—as if she were simply conversing about the weather.

"I don't want—I can't hurt you," he said.

"That's the difference between you and I. I don't need pain in order to get off, Gray. I just need your dominance."

He considered this for a moment. He could be a duke here, what he was trained for. To be powerful, to control. That was drilled into him. He knew it easily. So what did he want?

"I want you naked and on the bed," he said, and she stood instantly. "No, wait," he said, and she stopped, her eyes cast down. He didn't feel right, ordering her around like this. "I don't know if I can... You had me choose a word. Do you have one? A word?"

"White," she answered.

"White?" he repeated. "And you have to do anything I say, whatever I say?"

"No. I don't have to do anything you say. But I want very much to serve you, so I will."

Grayson stood and walked to the bed, sitting down. He suddenly wasn't so sure about this. He didn't want her to behave. He didn't want her to follow his orders. He very much liked it when she didn't. He looked up to find her still staring at the floor, facing the window, and he wanted her to come sit with him. He took a deep breath. "Come sit down," he said. But his voice shook.

She turned and knelt on the floor at his knee. She'd done that before, though last night she'd sat and crossed her knees under her chin, and now he knew that specific position at his feet had been purposeful. Had she been testing him all along? He shook it off, because he'd been testing her as well, of a fashion.

She would do anything he asked of her, and it seemed such a powerful position with a great deal of responsibility. Keeping her safe, keeping her trust, giving her what she wanted... But what did he want?

"You like to give pain?" he asked.

"Yes, sir," she answered.

"Stand," he said, and she unfolded, rising gracefully. He put his hands on her hips, then undid the buttons of her trousers and stood before her. He pushed the trousers off her hips and let them fall to her ankles. He considered her a moment, then reached up to the neck of her shirt, his thumb coasting over the silk of her skin at the indent of her collarbone before he fisted the placket of her shirt and tore it straight down the front, the few buttons popping and flying first before the rest of the fabric was torn asunder. He smiled, his breath heavy in his chest.

Put on your duke hat, she'd said. "Take it off," he said with a dismissive wave of his hand. As if the fabric itself offended him by keeping him from seeing her.

She shrugged from the shirt and let it fall, then cocked an eyebrow at him.

"All of it. Take it off," he said again.

Lulu pulled her chemise over her head and let it flutter to the floor behind her, then kicked free of the trousers.

When she reached for the tie of her drawers, he stopped her and pushed her hands away. "No, not this. I want to do this." He let his gaze fall on her, travel up and down her smooth, pale skin. The flutter of her heartbeat at her neck, the rise and fall of her chest from her breathing, the shift of her ribs as she moved slightly.

He skimmed one hand down the center of her chest, down her belly, then let his fingers stop just above her mons, barely touching, just feeling the heat of her sinking into his fingertips like an oath. His breath caught in his chest and his toes seemed to go numb.

She whimpered, the sweetest, softest sound his ears had ever known, and he pressed his hand against her, slid between her legs to feel how wet she was for him. "Dear god," he said as he closed his eyes and rested his forehead against hers. "This is…"

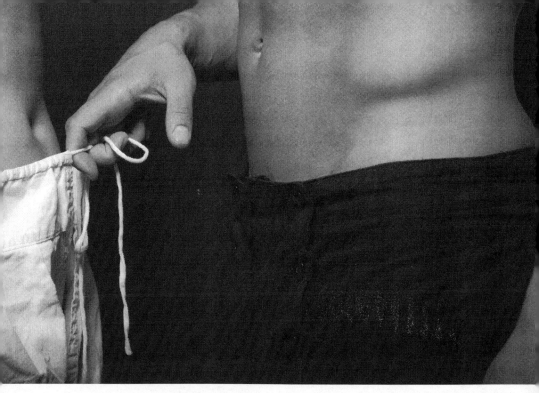

"For you, Your Grace," she said.

He slipped one finger into the folds of her quim, just feeling the wet warmth of her, and she trembled against him.

Grayson used two fingers from his other hand and pulled one of the ties of her drawers slowly as he watched the flutter at her neck increase. He saw her mouth drop open and her eyelids lower to her cheeks. He pulled slower, and her breath caught up, then started over again faster. When the tie came loose, he let go of it and stuck one finger behind the knot at her belly.

She was so soft, and he wanted all of that softness underneath him, moving against his weight, soothing his skin. He itched everywhere to touch her.

He pressed against her opening gently, and she hissed in a breath, bringing him immediately back to the present from the moment she'd wrapped him up inside, and he pulled both of his hands free slowly.

"You're still sore?" he asked.

She looked up to him and nodded. "But it's a burn I want for, because it's from you," she told him.

He shook his head slowly, "I don't want to cause you any more pain. I can't—" He took a step back from her.

"It's okay. Every time you touch me, it eases somewhat, so don't stop."

"You don't understand. I really can't," he said quietly. Her eyes seemed to lock on his, and she considered something, then she nodded.

"You're a true submissive," she said. "That's a rare and beautiful thing. I can't image what your life has been like fighting with that part of you in order to function in your world, in order to do the things you've done. It cannot have been easy."

"No, but I learned. Just like you said—you trained, you learned things, you managed."

"I manage very well, but I've been lucky enough to be true to myself," she replied, then she lifted one hand, ran her thumb across his lips and held his face. "I'm sorry that you've had to manage, in order to survive."

"I've..." He shook his head. There was no other word for it. He had managed, and he had survived against everything. Why was she making him feel these things? He didn't want this...this warmth that bloomed inside him.

"Would you like to *live*?" she asked.

"I am alive," he said.

"I mean...what you're doing now is simply managing to survive. Would you like to actually live? To enjoy life, to truly live?"

He thought about that. He didn't understand her because he had no idea what she'd meant. He hadn't truly lived since he was a young, ignorant child with no knowledge of how the world truly worked—before he learned that *family* meant only the people who would look after you so long as you served their purpose. So to *live*? To be his own man and to feel something akin to happiness?

Yes, he absolutely wanted to live, but he had no idea how. "I would...I would like to know what it means to *live*," he said.

Lulu picked up his hand and placed it back on the knot at her waist. "I can show you what it means. Tell me what you want. Tell me what to do," she said.

His finger slipped behind the knot again and pulled it loose. Her drawers hit the floor, and she kicked them aside. His hands shook as he fidgeted, looking for something to do as he considered what he wanted from her the most.

"Hurt me," he whispered.

The slap came from his left with no warning, the sound ringing in his ear, his jaw hanging agape as his fists hung in the air and he stayed himself. All of his training called for him to fight back, but his instinct—the purest part of his soul—kept him from moving.

He hadn't been expecting that at all. He looked at her, but she simply stood there as if nothing at all had actually happened. Her hands relaxed, her eyes down, no hint of her fervor.

"What do you want of me?" she said, prodding him, reminding him that he was in control.

What did he want? He wanted to be inside her, however he could manage that. Her mouth had been a revelation, but to sink deep inside a woman? That was something he'd yearned for, for entirely too long—and his cock began to rise again from that slap.

He adjusted his cock in his trousers as he looked at her hands.

"Again," he said.

Her right hand twitched, but her left hand met his cheek, and as she connected, he took her right hand and pressed it to the hard ridge in his trousers. "I want to be inside you," he growled.

Her breath caught as her hand grasped his length, and he couldn't believe how easy it had been. "You bought condoms," he said. "Get them."

Lulu turned and walked over to the boxes and bags that were still covering the settee by the fire. She could feel his gaze on her like a hand caressing her skin, heavy and insistent.

She dug through the bags until she found what she needed, then returned to the bed and opened the small black box and pulled out several smaller packages. "Though I would prefer some true birth control, this will do. I'm not going to deal with the witchery of sponges and syringes."

She pulled out a condom, then handed it to him and dropped her arms, casting her gaze to the floor. "I can't wait to have you inside me. Do you want to be inside me?" she asked softly.

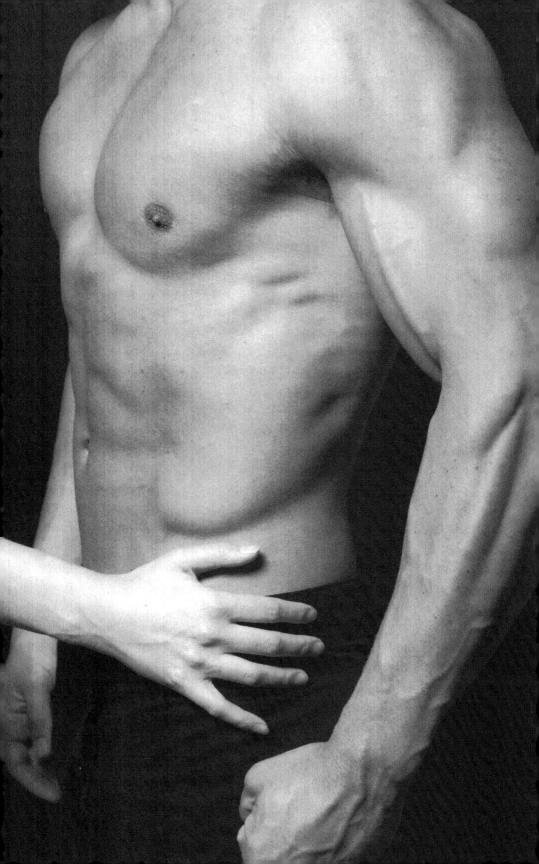

Her voice had been so gentle she almost thought she hadn't spoken aloud, but his mouth dropped open as though to say something, and he nodded.

"What do you want?" she asked when he didn't move or speak. This was such a precarious dance, the pull and sway of control. She could feel to her marrow how much he truly didn't want it. He was quite obviously having a difficult time topping her.

"Pain."

The word was like a breath, and Lulu froze while it crept along her skin, rousing the goose bumps as a flush sneaked up her chest to warm her neck. What a beautiful word it was.

"Do you understand how control works? Do you understand who holds the power?" she asked.

"Yes," he replied, and she pulled away far enough that he looked into her eyes. "Yes, Duchess."

She loved how his voice bottomed out on the vowels as he dragged them from his mouth and gave them to her. She leaned toward him, lifting herself on the balls of her feet as she whispered in his ear, "Tell me what you want me to do."

He took her left hand in his, caressing it, then, with his thumb, he slid her ring until the stone rested against her palm. "I want you to show me your world," he said.

Lulu shivered, then balled her hand in a fist around the stone. She reached out with her right hand and wrapped her palm around the crest of his hipbone, just below that gorgeous slab of muscle on his side, and coasted her thumb across the junction where his hip met his abdomen.

Deep in that crease was a bundle of nerves attached to ligaments that, when pressed, would send a soul-keening pain through his system. She let her thumb dance gently across his skin, knowing what was to come and how much he was going to love it, how in the future when she played with his skin here, he would also know what came next, but for now, for this first time, he had no idea what she intended by touching him here so sweetly.

That was the charm of virgins, that pure, unadulterated response. She wanted to bathe in the beauty of it, to take it into her soul and keep it forever.

"What is your word?" she asked as she undid his pants with her other hand, pushing them from his hips.

"Armoire," he breathed it.

She pushed him to the bed, then crawled after him, and when he lay back on the pillows, she continued to caress that spot, rising over him. She leaned down to kiss him, then pressed into his hip, letting her thumb slide into the perfect position on that bundle of nerves.

The shock of it nearly doubled him, his face tucking into her neck. She listened carefully, her mouth at his ear. "Do you remember your word?" she asked, her other hand around his throat, her thumb at the pulse in his neck.

"I remember," he replied gruffly.

"You didn't say it."

"I didn't want to."

"I won't ask you again. Do you understand?"

"Yes." It was a single word but had all of his strength behind it.

She pushed him back into the bed and licked her way down his chest before she took his cock in her mouth and pressed into him again, beginning a rhythm of pleasure and pain that had him writhing beneath her.

His hands tangled in her hair, not restraining but simply holding on. She skimmed her other hand up his chest and tweaked his nipple and was given a heady, gut-deep growl in response. She crawled up his torso, sucking his skin into her mouth and leaving marks in his flesh along the way, then she took the condom from his hand and pulled it from the envelope.

He shook and shuddered beneath her, his muscles unable to contain the tension as it was released and spilled forth in a vibration from his very core. It was a visceral response and could not be controlled, because it was who he was. Eventually he would learn that.

Lulu knew she would miss this reaction as well once he became familiar enough with it that he could minimize it. It was a reaction she was quite familiar with, in truth. The level of tension so extreme from the wanting to control—not her, but his own body.

Gray would be sore for days after tonight. Lulu leaned over him, sudden concern rushing her when he didn't relent. "Grayson, look at me." His eyes snapped to hers.

"I see you," he whispered. "I see you." He nodded, and she reached down and sheathed his penis without taking her gaze from his, then she shifted, adjusting over him.

"How do you want me? Grayson, this is for you. This is all for you," she said.

His gaze searched her, slid over every part of her face, from her mouth to her ears and her nose. He seemed to be inspecting every bit of her. Then he lifted his hands and put them on her breasts, bringing them each to his mouth as he kissed and suckled them until she panted against him.

"God, you're beautiful," he said.

"What you do to me." She wanted to collapse against him in a heap of spent muscle and bone, and he had yet to penetrate her. His hands slid around her, grasped her backside as he pulled her to him, and she rocked there against his hardness until his hands moved away. He caught her gaze once again, pleading.

She took his wrists in her hands, wrapped her fingers around them tightly, and twisted swiftly to burn the sensitive flesh of his wrist. He hissed, and she felt his cock thicken further.

She pushed his hands into the bed over his head and shifted her hips until his cock lifted and was poised perfectly at her entrance. She stayed there, at the cusp, keeping him from pushing forward, but not letting his length fall back to his belly either. She teased him with her muscles, watching his face as she waited for him to beg.

TWENTY-TWO

The onrush of a conquering force is like the bursting of pent-up waters
into a chasm a thousand fathoms deep.

—Sun Tzu
The Art of War

"Please," Grayson said. His entire left leg burned, his wrists stung, the bruises on his chest throbbed, and his cock was so hard it pulsed in near agony—something he'd never known possible.

Lulu released one wrist and slid her hand down his arm to his shoulder, then pressed a thumb into the soft space just behind his chest muscle. The pain shot through his chest and spread up his arm until his fingers went numb. He tensed and screamed, and she sank onto him with a hiss.

The warmth…the warmth was not merely indescribable. It was simply otherworldly. In all his life, he'd never imagined how soft, how slick, how warm and welcoming a woman's body would feel when it encompassed only that one part of him.

He couldn't breathe against the tension running his muscles, and he gasped into her mouth as she licked his lips, ran the tip of her nose along the crest of his cheeks, and teased him mercilessly.

Then she did something he hadn't even known to be humanly possible. She clenched her muscles around his cock, her face transforming to that of a warrior as she looked on him. He couldn't even move, as slick and wet as she was, she held him so tight and solid inside her body. Then she relaxed slowly as she rose off his cock and let the tip, just the tip, kiss her entrance before she slid back down on him fully once again.

Powerful. Majestic. Graceful.

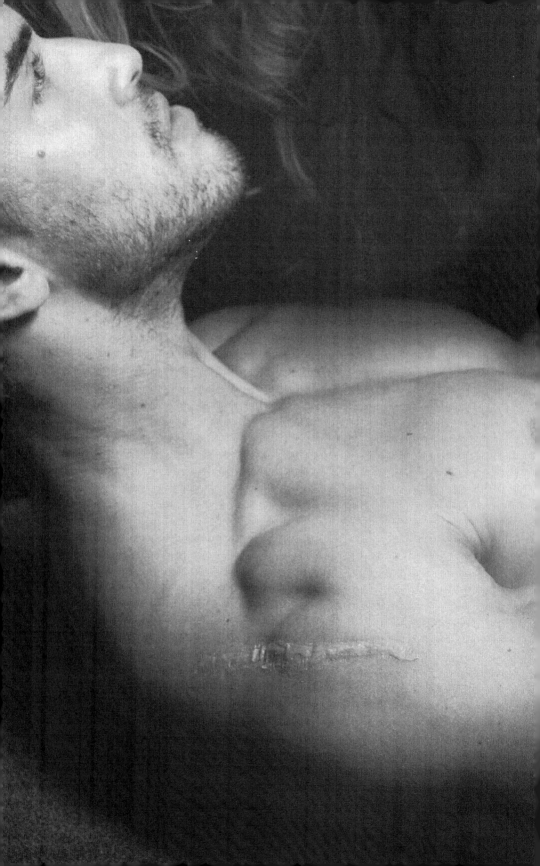

She owned him. He would do anything. He no longer cared. How had it come to this? That he didn't merely feel as if he belonged with her—but to her? He shifted his hips, and new sensations shot through him, resting in the tips of his fingers as they tingled.

He felt her thumb press again under his arm into the space behind his pectoral, and the pain bloomed across his chest like blood spilled from a glass. It warmed and thickened and pulsed as it spread, infesting every nerve it touched.

"Lulu, I—Lulu." He wanted to close his eyes and feel, just feel, just soak in all the physical sensation that rushed him, but it was so overwhelming he thought he might disappear, to give up that much control…to let himself go that far into what was happening.

So he watched her, memorizing the look in her eyes, the pure joy on her face as she crawled and moved over his body, playing his pain like an instrument. It was…more than he had ever dreamed possible.

His breath rushed. His movements became more erratic as his muscles jerked. He was going to come off, and it had taken only moments of time with her. Mere moments, like breaths. He wanted to slow time, but he was at her mercy.

He felt her hand stray from his chest down his abdomen, achingly slow, and he knew what she intended, but he had no intention of stopping her. He wanted that pain, that first intense burst of pain that had doubled him and stolen his breath. He felt his breathing pick up with the knowledge, and her other hand came to the center of his chest, and she flattened it, pressing the stone of her ring into his skin as she leaned into him.

She sank as far as she could go on his cock, her pelvic bone grinding against him as she pressed into his hip all at the same beautiful moment, and he came off, his hands coming to her hips to hold her there, his breath rushing from him in an oath, his eyes locked on the flush of her face, his soul reaching out from the depths of where it had hidden for all of his life and latching on to hers, holding it tight.

The moment was everything he'd ever been afraid to hope it would be. As the pain receded, as his seed warmed the tip of his own cock inside her, as her body trembled around him, he felt claimed by her as well.

He moved his hands to her face, wiping the tears away as he pulled her down to him and kissed her. It was an oath and a declaration. It was wet and open and full and lovely. It was powerful, and it was permanent. It melded them together.

There were no words for how he felt. There was no way for him to explain these things, so he showed her. Worshipped her mouth, that mouth, the mouth that had fascinated him since the moment she first opened it and let loose a string of words no proper woman ever should.

"Grayson," she whispered against him.

"My duchess," he said, holding her there as he went soft and slipped from her. He rolled her, coming over her and pressing her body into the mattress with his own. He wanted contact. He wanted her skin against his. He was so overwhelmed by the force of…everything. When he shifted his left leg, the pain shot back, and he froze, falling back to the bed.

She came up on her side next to him. "Lie back and let me care for you," she said. He nodded, the pain echoing in his head like a bell sounding too close. She stood and went to the bathing room, returning with a towel, the basin for water, and a bottle of oil.

"What we did—you need to recover." She smiled gently at him then looked away as she placed the basin on a table next to the bed. "You were amazing. I've never seen anything so beautiful, Gray. I've just—" Lulu shook her head, there were no words. She warmed the small towel in the basin. She removed his condom and tossed it to the floor before he could stop her, because when he moved, the pain came, and he fell back to the bed again.

She pulled the towel from the basin and washed him carefully. In the same breath, it felt amazing and demeaning, but he allowed it. He took the whole experience in. To lie there and be worshipped by her in such a way, so delicately. He couldn't feel anything more. It had already been so much, and when she poured oil in her hands and began to massage the feeling back into his leg and his arm, he felt so warm and relaxed that he simply drifted away.

He woke again in the dead of night, that amazing mouth on his cock. "Oh god, Lulu."

Her warm, soft body slid up next to his, and he pulled her close, buried his face in her hair and just breathed of her. "Lulu." He ran his hands over her body, warming her skin as he breathed and rolled to his back, pulling

her across his chest as he did so. He fell back asleep with only her name on his mind and her body in his hands.

As the sun began to warm the window across the room, Lulu thought about the night before and this man beneath her cheek. Truth be told, she was terrified. What she'd done to him was much more than she'd ever done with someone so unfamiliar with her people, her lifestyle.

That sort of pain was something many of her clients were averse to because it was a bone-deep pain, much different from anything you achieved with an implement. This pain started on the inside and saturated the nerves as it worked its way out of the body, as opposed to beginning on the surface and spreading from the strike point. It wasn't as sharp. It was full and heavy and exhausting.

She'd known, however, that she would need to employ some creativity with him, that using some sort of tool on him this first time was going to be out of the question, even if he knew of people who did such things. Probably even more so if he knew of people who did such things. He was so averse to someone giving him pain, to being thought of in that manner, it simply wasn't conducive to a healthy future living with a masochistic and sexually submissive personality.

She had to give him that pain in a much more intimate and direct way. And it had been what she'd wanted anyway, at least that's what she'd thought. For her hands to be the cause of his greatest pleasure, his awakening? It had been absolutely the most wondrous thing in the world, he had been beautiful, and she was wrecked by it.

He had done so incredibly well but this sort of true intimacy terrified her. She'd never experienced such intimacy with anyone, not a client, not a boyfriend, nobody. She hadn't realized how frightened she was until now because of how hard she'd been fighting *for* him. Because, without this piece of her life, there could be no future with him. But bringing all these pieces together? It was a mistake and she had only just admitted that to herself. What's more, she also admitted to herself that a future with him was possible but how could it be when being this close to him was so frightening for her...she closed her eyes and tried to sort out her feelings. She didn't know how to be this open to another person, she'd spent the entirely of her life guarded, fractured, defensible—safe.

He was much too much for her in all his muchliness.

"Something funny?" The words came through his chest against her ear, like those spoken at the back of a cavern instead of right next to her.

"No, I—I was just thinking about all of this," she said. She patted his chest. "Back to sleep, rest. You'll be sore today." She felt his body tense beneath her then a sharp intake of breath on the realization of just how sore he would be.

"Maybe another minute," he said. She felt his muscles shift slowly as he turned his head into his pillow, away from the light of the window.

She traced the bruises on his chest from her bites until his hand came up and stilled her, and she smiled. "Sorry," she whispered. She pulled the sheet up higher to block any temptation. And it was such a great temptation, to play with his bruises, to remind herself of last night, possibly to take him again.

That was the other thing she wanted to teach him, how powerful the marks on his person could be for him. For days he would be able to see them and orgasm just looking at them and masturbating. She knew she would.

His hand took her wrist gently, and she realized she'd been circling one of the bruises, once again, beneath the sheet. This time she didn't stop. His thumb smoothed up and down the side of her wrist slowly, until he wrapped his fingers around her wrist more solidly and pushed her hand down to his cock.

His very aroused cock. She smiled, he was a quick learner. She scooted down in the bed.

"No, I want..."

"Shhh...you're sore. Let your muscles wake up with pleasure instead of discomfort. Just let me," she said, then she disappeared beneath the sheet.

TWENTY-THREE

When there is no place of refuge at all, it is desperate ground.

—Sun Tzu
The Art of War

rayson sank into the feather tick and allowed her to play. He hadn't imagined this part of it all, the day after, like the ripples in a pond, how they carried on after that first impact, more peaceful but still powerful, shaping the very shore.

He shifted slowly, determinedly, as she wrapped her warm mouth around him and began to play his body again like a piano, his bruises the keys. Like any true maestro, she didn't even have to look to find them. She knew them like she knew her own body, exactly where they were, just how hard to press or skim, to call forth the perfect shudder or shock from him.

She leaned up then, long strokes of her tongue on him, and he reached for her, but she shook her head, and today that was enough to stay him. She pulled another packet from the table and wrapped his length, then sank down on him, and her face…oh, her face was like sunrise and sunset. It was like every nerve in his body was lit by the expression of surprise and sensuality and pure, carnal lust that shone there.

He reached up slowly, took her breasts in his palms, and her nipples tensed to hard peaks, then goose bumps spread outward, like the rest of her skin was jealous of that sensation, like…the whole of her was involved in this act, not merely his cock and her cunt.

He felt his heart pick up a beat, his cock reached farther into her, the pulse of his blood concentrated and strong in the bruises on his chest. She put her palms down on two of the bruises and leaned into them, grinding her pelvis against him as she came, and the flutter of her internal muscles shocked him. He froze, simply relishing the experience and attempting to sway his own orgasm for long enough to know the extent of hers.

"Lulu," he groaned and took her hips, pressing hard into her.

"Come for me," she said, and her eyes met his. "Come for me, Grayson."

And he did. He pushed up into her, the tip of his penis meeting the deep inside her. His breath stuttered from his lungs as he fought for purchase with his feet against the sheets, trying so hard to be farther inside her, closer to her soul. He wanted to fill her up. He came off, the warmth of his seed flooding the condom as she tightened herself around his cock and he jerked against her, and she held on, her eyes wide and searching.

They stared at each other, unmoving for what felt to him a lifetime as he saw her expression change, some sort of realization dawning like the light outside. Something had happened and he had no idea what it was and he didn't want to push her. She seemed impossibly fragile. Their eyes held, like a hunter and doe in the clearing, and he knew he had to be careful to not spook her.

He let his features soften and relax, and his fingers on her hips followed. He smoothed his thumbs over the red marks on her delicate skin but kept his gaze on hers.

Her body jerked, as though it had attempted to move without permission, and she stayed herself. He skimmed his hands slowly the length of her back, pulling her down against him. Once he had her tucked into the crook of his arm, he swept the condom off and dropped it from the side of the bed, then he stroked her skin until her eyelids grew heavy, and they both slept again.

Lulu's eyes opened the same as they had before, watching the sun on the window in his bedroom. But this time her entire body felt heavy, sated, and immovable.

She'd thought she could manage him, teach him, bring him to her world, and then…what? Glory in the triumph of his training? Live happily ever after in the castle? But everyone knew Grimm's fairy tales always ended with body parts missing and lovers dead.

The night before she'd believed he would accept her truth, and then… what then?

She thought he'd be able to manage one pressure point, but he'd taken three strikes, and not at all lightly either. She'd gone deep and full on the pressure. She had not let him off easily.

It had been the single most fulfilling moment of her entire life, even more so than painting wings… she wanted to give him wings. She shook the thought off, because her training alone had taken years.

Even if he agreed to it at some point…she wasn't sure if this body was even capable. She had to let it go, which seemed much easier today than it had been before. She shifted to look up at him and caught his gaze, intent on her. She froze, but her heart kicked against her ribs.

So far they hadn't survived a morning-after moment, the earlier coming together notwithstanding. Sex was easy for her, but calling what passed between them last night and this morning nothing but sex would be an outright lie.

She held her breath and waited for him, because she knew he was registering, documenting, categorizing, and scrutinizing every single little thing that had happened between them, not just today and last night, but quite possibly every single word she'd ever said and action she'd ever made since arriving in his life.

She wasn't sure if she should leave and give him some space, or if she should stay.

Generally, her clients worked through their feelings about being hurt before they were actually physically hurt, so the mental recovery from it was much easier, but with him… She just had no idea how he felt at this moment because he was still fighting her, and she was afraid to ask, to break the bubble of happiness she'd felt was created the night before.

"I am well," he said.

She closed her eyes so she could think. That wasn't exactly an answer either way. It was a calculated statement that was meant to ease her, certainly, and she was sure she'd looked concerned—something that might ruffle his feathers in and of itself—but that statement was neither here nor there.

In truth, it meant nothing.

She slid her hand up his torso, then flipped the ring around with her thumb to prevent scratching him, and smoothed across the skin of his chest

to his shoulder, this time avoiding all of his bruises. She just needed some sort of true contact with him, even as she lay across his chest, close enough for his heartbeat to sink into her skin.

His fingers started to play with the small of her back, and his other hand came up and held her wrist, but he didn't stop her. She breathed again. That was better. He was okay, this was difficult, it was intense, but he would be okay.

"Lulu, we have much to discuss," he said as he shifted, then moved up in the bed, leaning against the headboard. She moved with him, sat up facing him.

"Yes, I—Gray, I feel like I need to apologize for the way I've been treating you. You spoke of being managed, and I now realize I was no better than the rest in my behavior, even though I believed I was. I wasn't. I hid behind my want to show you my world. To make this connection. To prove something to you."

"Are you…do you feel you have proven something to me now?"

She watched him closely. She felt like he was laying a trap for her, but she sincerely hoped he wasn't. "That's up to you to decide, Gray. You enjoyed last night, as did I, but you have yet to tell me how you feel."

"Enjoyed doesn't quite cover it. I feel…free. I feel lost. I feel confused. I feel like I've been found, rescued. I don't understand what happened, not really."

Lulu nodded. "All perfectly reasonable responses to your first time. Is this…" She stopped.

"You're still afraid to ask me questions," he said. "A perfectly reasonable response." He winked.

Winked.

Lulu took a breath. "Is this why you were a virgin? Because you could not complete the act without some pain?"

"Ah, I see why you hesitated to ask."

"Do you?"

"Only yesterday a question like that would have had me angry with you and running away."

"And today?" she asked.

"What about you? Are you ready to tell me of yourself now?" he said suddenly.

Lulu wrapped the sheet around herself, leaving the tail to cover his lap. "What more is there to say?" she asked. She was still frightened of his response, but…he had put everything he was at her feet, and now he waited for her to work through it on her own, saying nothing.

She took a deep breath. "I told you I'm a switch. I told you what that means, but it does go beyond that. I worked as a Dominant in a professional capacity and I hired Dominants as a submissive client. My clients paid me for my expertise, for my talent, and I did the same."

"You were paid to have sex with people, and this is different from prostitution…how?" he asked.

She could feel his muscles tighten and knew he struggled to keep any condescending tone from his words, it hurt, but she'd known it would. It's why she avoided this to begin with. If he couldn't understand this, accept her… "I didn't have sex with them. I dominated them. I often brought them to orgasm, but there was no intercourse involved. I was never engaged with them in that way. With a client, it's all about the client and what they need."

"I don't understand. What we did was quite clearly—"

Lulu shifted, uncomfortable. "What we did last night was very different from what I did in a professional capacity. What we did was so very much more," she said. "I honestly can't even categorize what happened between us. It's not something I'm familiar with." He had…opened a door to something she'd been leaning on, trying to shut, without even realizing it.

"Lulu," he said, and the sound of his voice sliced through her armor and settled in her gut. She shook her head. "Tell me. Explain this to me."

"I—" She took a deep breath. "I don't know how to," she said.

"Try."

She nodded, and her stomach twisted in revolt. He had given her so much, so much, it was only right that she give something in return, but this hurt. Thinking about it hurt. "I think you were right, last night. I use sex as a weapon to keep people away from me. I've used it to keep everyone away from me, I've never allowed for the sort of intimacy that we've shared. I've used it…to keep you away from me."

Then the words rushed from her like the levy had broken. "You frighten me with your honesty. What you've done is strip my defenses then destroy them. You've taken all these pieces of me and turned them into something different. You've forced me to combine everything I was into a single being. The domination, the submission, the sex, the passion. Never before have I ever felt so much. I told you I wasn't a virgin. I told you I loved sex. I never had sex with clients, but I dated. I had assignations. It was completely separate from that part of me.

"My world was compartmentalized, which helped me maintain my defenses. It helped me keep everyone out. No one person ever truly knew me. My boyfriends knew a nice girl who had vanilla sex. My clients knew a Dominatrix who would beat the shit out of them and give them the most powerful experience of their lives. Those I submitted to were professionals,

and they probably knew me better than most because I did come to orgasm through pain and submission. But you…you've brought that all together and what's more you've made it mean something."

"How do you separate domination and submission from passion?" he asked, and she realized he was making the connections any submissive or masochist or Dominant would just understand—that they were linked, hand in hand. Something that, for him and by him, was previously forbidden. He had separated them, probably forcefully, which is why he was still a virgin.

"That's the thing, you don't separate passion, passion is part of the submission and domination. But if you're a professional, or you see a professional, you separate the domination and the submission…from intimacy." Her voice dropped so low on the word that he leaned forward to hear better. "My body is—was—just a body. I could walk down the street naked and not care, but the way you look at me, like I am so much more than skin…"

Lulu took a deep breath. She was having a hard time explaining, and every bit of her wanted to run from him and hide because this was so much more than just her job, this was who she was, it was not that simple. She had never felt this, she had no experience with it, she hadn't even fully considered it for herself yet and he expected her to explain it. She had never experienced intimacy with submission and domination. She didn't understand how to explain the difference. How could she tell him something she simply didn't know? He reached out, and one finger met the skin at the side of her forearm, and just that touch stayed her like no shackles ever could.

She needed to keep trying. She owed him that—that and so much more. She forced herself to stay. As if she were chained to the bed, she submitted to this verbal flaying.

"The way you touch me…so reverently." Her breath left her in a rush just thinking about this hands on her in a more tangible way and she looked down at that finger on her arm. "Gray, you strip me bare and put me back together," she looked back up to him. "My clients, those I dominated, they paid a great sum to train with me. I was something of an aberration, even in my time. I was talented with—"

"Bullwhips," he interjected. "I wish to see this."

Her gaze snapped to his and her skin tightened at the thought of him watching her. She groaned. "I can't…this body can't do what I used to."

"You trained before. You'll train again." He paused then pushed. "Tell me about Oliver," he said, like they were discussing a stranger, and for Gray he was, but for her…Ollie was her masterpiece. How could she explain her passion for another man?

"Oliver…" she shook her head and looked down, unable to find the words. What if she told him and he refused to allow her to do this? "I— Gray I—"

"You could do this again," he said, cutting her off. Once he said it, she felt him tense as though it had come out before he truly considered it and her momentary hope was lost. "I would see you do this again if it is that important to you."

"I don't know," she replied because he didn't seem very sure of his decision, he also didn't know what that decision entailed. Had he misunderstood her? It wasn't the bullwhips and the wings and Ollie, they had nothing to do with this feeling. It was him. She looked up to find his eyes on her, and he relaxed. His lazy posture against the headboard was inviting and soothing, and like nothing she'd ever witnessed in him because his usual demeanor was always so very buttoned up. Literally and figuratively. "I don't think you understand, it isn't about the bullwhips, though..." she

shook her head. "It isn't about the bullwhips with you, it's just this between us, whatever this is, it's so overpowering to me, I can't control it."

"I want—"

"What…what do you want," she asked.

"I want to see how you react to me, perhaps you could show me what you mean, like you did last night. If you don't have the words to explain then show me." She swallowed against a sudden tightness in her throat, this wasn't exactly where she thought the conversation would go. "I want to see more of your body. You say I stripped you bare, let me see how bare you are for me, let me see how truly close we can be. Let me do as I wish with you."

She almost shook her head. Why would this be any different from the sex they'd already had? He wanted to explore her. He wanted the control, something he hadn't wanted before, he wanted her to submit to him. Something she hadn't ever done with a lover. He had tasted what it meant to let go and now he wanted it all and she simply wasn't prepared for that. Did he even realize what he was asking?

"Show me the difference between passion and intimacy," he said and his voice scraped the bottom of his chest as he spoke and her skin pebbled everywhere with the sound of it.

He held one hand up and waited for her to refuse, but she was frozen. He reached out and cupped one of her breasts, his fingers skimming the delicate underside through the cotton sheet as his eyes darkened and Lulu held very still. Her breasts moved with her breath, against his hands. She wanted this exploration for him. She wanted him to feel her. She had yet to truly allow it, because she'd been so much in control of what they did and yet—wasn't that of paramount importance when learning about sex? Figuring out what made a body do…what it did?

He'd never had his opportunity to be an explorer of the flesh, so she tried to relax, tried to allow for his exploration, but it felt like so much more than sex. Because it was so much more than sex. It would be exactly what he was looking for, what he wanted to see, it was intimate. It was their two souls colliding, her skin a mere vessel.

He shoved the sheet down, moved her arm away, then took her breast in his hand again and watched as her skin flushed and thickened. He watched as her nipples tightened and her breasts became heavier with blood. He watched every action and reaction. And she watched him and it was overwhelmingly pure, divine.

Her breath came in small pants and she couldn't seem to catch it. She felt like she chased it but it stayed just beyond her reach rising and falling with his movements. Lulu knew what this dance looked like, so she closed her eyes and concentrated on the well-worn feel of his fingers so very different from most of the men she'd known—professionals, businessmen, not the least bit tactile and possessive.

But him, he skimmed her nipple with the back of his hand, then cupped her and weighed her, testing her in his palm before pinching her nipple gently and she drew in a surprised breath.

She hadn't noticed before that it felt differently, perhaps in her excitement all the erogenous zones simply blended together, but now with him being so very specific in his movements she felt the intensity of this one soft touch and how it flowed in her blood so powerful at the apex, like a heartbeat carried throughout her body all the way to her toes.

When she opened her eyes, he was watching her face, her every expression as it played out with his perusal. It was a very personal sort of inspection, and one she hadn't expected, though she should have with his obsession with military precision. He would watch her body, then repeat an action while he examined her face. Methodically.

Physical reaction. Emotional reaction. Repeat. Watch.

She'd done this sort of thing in high school, but back then it was playful and not so very intense. It was more childish and impersonal. Since then this sort of intense perusal wasn't really necessary, though people had their own preferences and quirks, bodies generally worked int he same fashion. Once you found a G-spot, you knew how to find the next one.

Gray had said he'd never touched a woman like this. He should be allowed to touch a woman like this so she would submit to his inspection. She turned and lay next to him, and he stretched out beside her on his side as his hand swept the length of her, unceremoniously pushing the sheet away from her figure.

His hand moved back up her leg, then her side. He held her rib cage for a mere moment as his thumb skated along one rib before lightly skimming over her other nipple as it tightened to a hard peak of sensation and her body bowed off the bed. Her mouth dropped open on an inhale, and she looked at him beneath her lowered lashes, as if that was enough of a barrier to protect herself.

His gaze was immediately drawn to the movement of her mouth, and his hand followed, tracing her lips, then the length of her tongue as she drew on his finger. She lifted one hand, but he pushed it away, then he traced her once again, his finger following the pulse in her neck to the center of her chest, where the beat of her heart resonated through her skin and into his palm.

He lifted his hand, just barely off her skin, and she could feel that shock of electricity between them, so subtle only the hairs on her arms responded.

This was nothing like anything she'd ever done. She felt more naked than she ever had, and she closed her eyes, attempting to control her racing heartbeat as he watched her reactions to his touch.

One finger came back to her skin and traced down the center of her, skipping her mons. Then his hand shoved her leg over, opening her body up for him as he inspected the warm folds of her pussy. She opened her eyes, and his gaze snapped back to hers. One finger entered her, and he studied the changes in her expressions.

He slid that finger slowly, pressing in all directions, until she cried out and he saw something cross her face that he liked. He stayed in that spot, pushing up toward her pubic bone as he slid, achingly slowly, in and out and back in again. The tension in his expression tightened, and she arched against his hand as her body quickened, but she didn't move to touch him. Not yet.

"Has anyone ever touched you this way?" he asked in that guttural drawl.

"No...not—never," she said. She didn't even recognize her own voice, so thick and heavy. Never in her life had she felt so bare to a man.

"Is this intimacy? The knowing?"

"I don't know," she said as she closed her eyes against the sting.

Gray pulled his hand away and shifted over her, but this time he used his mouth, his tongue, lips, and teeth, where before he had used his hands. "I want to taste you," he said as he started with her breasts, moved to her mouth, then down her neck, never once taking his gaze from her face. "You taste like"—his brow crinkled as he considered—"flowers," he said finally. "And spice."

Never had she ever let anyone go down on her. It was entirely too intimate an act for her. She realized that thought was perhaps a bit backward, but for her…there was nothing more intimate between two people. It was a nerve-racking act for her to receive such a thing, one she'd never been able to accept and this was too much. She could no longer keep still, and she started to push him away, but he stilled her, holding her wrists to the bed at her hips and continuing on, heedless.

"What are you—"

"Shhh…" He drew the word out into her name… "Lulu. So beautiful, so…alive. So tempting." His voice bored through her, shattering bones as it dug in and held on.

He shifted his big body as he went lower, down the center of her. When Gray reached the base of her sternum, her body started to shake. When he reached the soft of her belly, Lulu looked away. When his tongue dipped into her belly button she covered her face with one arm, trying to hide from him, but he reached up and pulled it away, holding it again at her side under his hand.

His thumb caressed the inside of the wrist he held, then his head dipped again as he shifted lower. Lulu clenched her eyes and tried to move away from him. There was something about his mouth on her like this that she simply could not reconcile. She realized, rather suddenly, that she'd never had a man go down on her. Or a woman for that matter. There was something about his shoulders holding her legs wide for him, his face so close to her pussy, his eyes hungry and wanting and watching.

She attempted to draw her legs together, but his broad shoulders prevented it. He paused and studied her. She knew he did. "Don't," he said. He didn't move, and his breath skated up her abdomen from where he lay sprawled between her legs, watching her.

His face between her legs, his eyes staring at the most private part of her, it was one thing to touch and pleasure and see, it was something else altogether to have someone so close and so intimate. She couldn't take anymore. As one tear coursed her cheek, she panicked and then she was done. "No, please, stop. Please." She shook her head and his weight shifted higher, over her, until his warm breath was on her neck. "Please," she whispered.

"Why won't you allow this?" he asked. "I want to see how I can pleasure you in the same ways you've done for me. I want to taste you."

She shook her head again. "I just…I can't. I can't do this. Please." He let go of her and sat back on his haunches, her legs still spread around his, her body still open to him. She covered her breasts and her open body as best she could with her arms. She twisted her face further into the pillow beneath her head.

"Lulu, I want to know your body as you now know mine. I want to do all the things I've only ever heard of."

"Gray, I'm scared, I just…I don't know how—"

"Why is this so different from the rest of what we've done?"

Why was it? That was a good question. He had already touched her everywhere, why was this so very intimate to her. She looked up to his face and saw the concern and fear there. She shook her head. She didn't understand. She whispered, "White." And she closed her eyes and turned back into the pillow.

She heard his swift intake of breath, then the entire bed shifted, and his weight was gone.

Lulu rolled away from the windows and tucked herself in a ball, attempting to dissipate the feel of his fingers rousing her nerves, hoping he would forgive her. She felt his hand skate down her spine then the sheet float down over her body. She hoped he wouldn't hate her for stopping him. All she heard was the door to the bathing room close behind him as he left her alone in their bed.

TWENTY-FOUR

On dispersive ground, therefore, fight not. On facile ground, halt not.
On contentious ground, attack not.

—Sun Tzu
The Art of War

rayson pulled the washroom door closed behind him quietly, then turned on the water in the attached shower closet and started rearranging things, making sure there were towels warming for her.

He thought about how antsy she'd been while he explored her body. It hadn't seemed at all fair that he'd allowed her to do to him as she wished, but she still held back. And then there was Oliver. She flat-out refused to talk about the other man. It felt a betrayal of sorts, even with one hundred and thirty unbreachable years between them.

Perhaps it was just another way for her to keep distance between them, even after everything they'd done last night. He turned and rested on the edge of the tub, his entire body sore. Just like the soreness he felt after he trained hard for a day. It was the recognition of great accomplishment to him. It wasn't something he was prepared for today, but the remembrance of the night before was welcome nonetheless.

He reached across his chest and slid his hand behind his pectoral, then down to the crease of his thigh. There wasn't any pain there, and he didn't get an erection doing it, but the nerves were alive, as though they'd been brought to the surface and the slightest touch would bring them up again.

There were techniques in hand-to-hand combat wherein you could disable an enemy using bundles of nerves…but using them for something like this had never occurred to him.

He looked down his chest as he waited for the shower to heat and ran his hands over the bruises, pressing lightly. Here, there was fresh pain, and his cock responded to the prodding, but he was much too exhausted for any further action, so he dropped his hands to his thighs.

She had opened up to him, explained herself some, and he had told her he wanted to see her do this. But to think of his wife touching another man in this fashion…he imagined this was what a normal man felt of his wife cuckolding him, but he hadn't meant to make her so nervous with his tone. He should have thought it through first, but he couldn't seem to hold his tongue anymore.

Her pain should be for him and him alone. He would not allow her to do that to someone else ever again. Not only would it feel like something beyond intimacy to him, but finding someone willing who would keep their mouth shut about his duchess…it wasn't going to happen.

At the time he hadn't realized when he'd told her she could use her whips again, that it would need to be on him, that she would train with him. He shuddered at the thought—it was too much.

Just yesterday, he was shutting her out of his life, then pulling her back in again. Of course she had difficulty trusting him—he wasn't sure of himself. He wasn't sure he could manage a relationship like this.

He knew she could feel the hesitation in him, and it was why she held back. But what if he gave everything to her? What if he told her everything and allowed her to do whatever she wished to his body? What then? Would she trust him then? And what did that make him? To give her his body like that was to give her his soul. To tell her his secrets would be to lay himself at her feet.

He scrubbed his face with his hands, then saw the steam rising from the shower. He stood and turned back for the room. Time to give her something more than empty promises. She'd said her life was fractured—passion, dominance, submission—and that he had brought all of those together. He needed to keep it that way.

He found Lulu exactly as he'd left her, curled up in the middle of his giant bed. Less than a week, and already this space wasn't his alone, and he would never be able to think of it that way again. Grayson had to crawl up on both knees to reach her, to pull her into his arms and take her to the bathing room.

He looked at her face as he carried her, but she refused to open her eyes, tucking into his chest.

"I'm sorry," she said, and the movement of her lips against his skin sent a shudder through him.

He took a deep breath, but didn't respond. He needed to stop giving her things to apologize for. He got to the door for the shower, the steam rolling heavy around them, and set her on her feet, pulling her up against his body as he let the sheet fall away.

He tried to shift her, but she felt anchored to the spot. "Lulu, I have warmed my shower for you, but it won't last long," he said. She nodded against his chest, and he led her into the steam.

The steam rose and shifted, allowing Lulu glimpses of the metal cage, like ribs, that made up the shower. The warmth that enveloped her smoothed the wrinkles from her muscles. It felt like the heat came from everywhere at once, and he gently eased her to the confluence of the spray, then his hands disappeared.

She couldn't believe how much she'd missed a good shower in a mere few days. Baths were nice—they served a purpose—but showers had a very tactile feel, and this one was lovely.

She took a deep breath, then she opened her eyes. The room itself was fully tiled, the floor sloping in an arc to a center drain, where she stood wrapped up in the silver cage.

Lulu reached out and held on to one of the bars that wrapped around the shower, and she just let the water beat against her skin. Her hands ran the hard length of the metal around her, and she had visions of images she wanted to make. Hard, gritty, and raw. Not Grayson, but Warrick.

She smoothed her hair back and opened her eyes to look at him over her shoulder. He was leaning one shoulder against a standing pipe as he

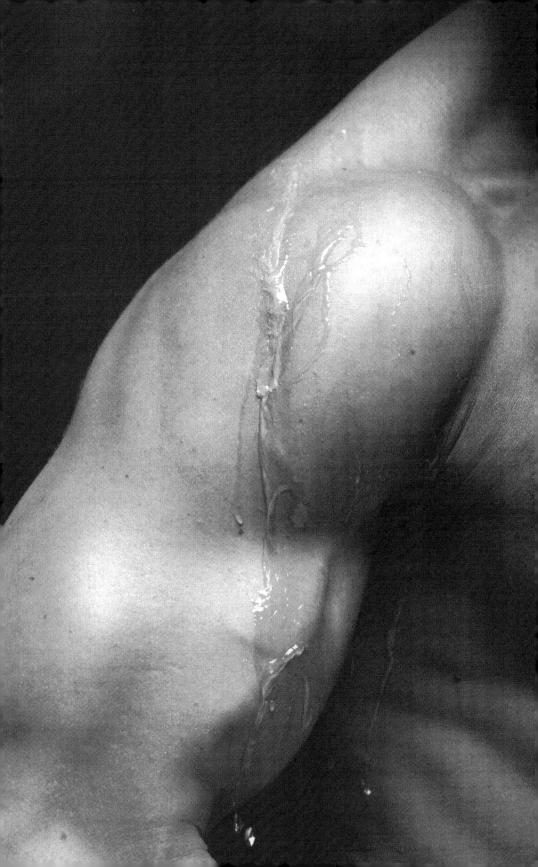

watched her. The water ran the length of his arm, skimming that silver scar across his shoulder and biceps like a river through a gully. It was fantastic. She would shoot him in here someday, and those images would grace the walls of their bedroom.

She turned her face back up into the overhead stream again and let the water sluice over her, taking her worries away as it coasted the length of her body. She turned and reached for him, and he stepped into the spray with her, his hands up to catch the heat and help spread it across his shoulders.

Lulu wiggled to the side to allow him some extra space, his giant body taking up much more than she had on her own. She leaned back against the pipes to watch. He really was strikingly beautiful. She could see the slightest hint of a waist created by wearing that corset, something nobody else would pay much notice to but she was familiar with.

She reached out and traced his ribs, his arms coming down quickly when she tickled him. Then he pulled her in against him, lifted her chin to him, and kissed her. His mouth on her, the water rushing over their faces, the only breath she got was from him, and in no time she was panting from lack of air.

"Oh god, Grayson," she said.

He pushed her back toward the cage, lifting her body and wrapping her legs around his waist as he rested her backside on one of the ribs behind her.

She tilted her head back against another rib, then stretched her hands above her and held on as she let him do as he wanted. She loved the feeling of the bars against her back. But why was this easier? This passionate, shoved-against-a-wall, standing, wet sex… She inspected all of his wet skin, then let her fingers trace his neck, his shoulders, and then the scar.

He froze as he looked at her, looked into her, as he considered her. She dropped her mouth open to say something, but instead, she pushed lightly against his shoulders, and he stepped away. He placed her back on her feet and turned back into the spray of the shower.

He knew, somehow he knew, she wasn't ready for more right now, but neither was he. When he turned back, he held a bar of soap between his hands. He washed his hair and body swiftly, then turned her and started soaping up her long curls.

As she rinsed the soap from her hair, he moved down, washing her body in a perfunctory manner, then he handed her the soap, and he turned his back without a word.

She finished washing then reached out and touched his broad back. He pulled her out and shut off the shower.

He led her to the room with the bathtub and wrapped her up in a warmed towel, then took one for himself and walked out to the bedroom. She just watched him go. Silently. The whole thing had been perfectly, blessedly, nerve-rackingly silent—until he turned to her and spoke.

"I have some things that need attending. I shouldn't be too long." He turned and pulled the bell for his valet, then nodded to the tray of food that now lingered next to the fire.

Lulu was still disconcerted by how attentive Rakshan was. He was like a stalker, knowing when they were in the shower so he could bring in food. She turned to the wardrobe to see Gray's clothing for the day hanging on one of the doors, hers on the other.

Just because she could, she removed the dress, put it back in the wardrobe, and pulled out a different one. Then she heard him chuckle.

"I'm not a child—"

"No one said you were, or that you behaved as such," he said stiffly.

"No, of course not, but I'm capable of choosing what I wish to wear today." She watched the heartbeat in his neck, a rill of water as it trailed down from his hair, around his neck, and down the center of his chest. Then she saw the marks she'd left on him. The push of her ring into the center of his chest had cut his skin, and she hadn't even noticed.

He interrupted her perusal. "The suggestion is merely that, a suggestion. A valet—or lady's maid—in general would know your schedule, any appointments you have, where you need to go, what the weather out of doors is like…and his—or her—job is to make your life easier. So you can concentrate on what you need to concentrate on." He pulled on his drawers and trousers, shirt and waistcoat, socks and shoes.

"Is that all he is to you? A valet who runs the mundane parts of your life?"

"Not at all, what Rakshan is to me is indefinable, " he said as she pulled a robe on and let the towel fall from beneath it, realizing as she looked at it pooled around her feet that she had kept her naked body from his view as she'd done so. She tied the sash and went to the table to sit.

The door opened, and Rakshan walked in and helped Gray finish dressing, fitting his jacket to his shoulders and arranging his hair.

She'd always just thought of valets and ladies' maids as being eccentricities reserved for the extremely wealthy, a status symbol of sorts. She hadn't considered that they had a greater function in their service.

He came and sat next to her. She knew he was watching her and wondered how soon the eggshells would crack and one or the other of them would rage and run away, or collapse and disappear.

"How are you feeling?" she asked.

He dropped his fork and leaned back in the chair, his broad shoulders hiding the back of it completely. "I'm not your client," he said.

"I realize I—" She wasn't sure what to say. She didn't know how to do any of this. Was it that she still expected to wake up in Denver? He appeared to be completely resigned to his fate with her. He had never wavered in that. How could he do that? How could he be so sure that she was here, with him, forever? She stared into those deep eyes, unable to look away.

"You don't think I'll ever leave here, do you?"

"Here, London in this time, or here, my household?" he asked.

"London, this time."

"No, this is where you belong." The simple surety she saw in his eyes terrified her.

"And your household?" she asked then, because her breath was suddenly coming up short.

He considered her for a moment. "My answer stands."

Her breath hitched, and her ribs tightened on her lungs. Her skin stretched tight around her chest. This was no game, this wasn't a scene, this wasn't a dream or a vacation or anything else. This was her life.

It fell over her like a net, pinching in all the wrong places, holding her down. It was quiet and peaceful, this takeover of her mind. She had always imagined such a massive shift in perspective would be loud and raucous, like fireworks. But no…this one crept up and simply bloomed there silently, like an iris before dawn.

"Lulu."

Her heartbeat picked up as if to fight the tightening of her chest, and her hands went clammy and cold. She tightened them on the edge of the table, but the table didn't dissipate. Of course it didn't dissipate. It never dissipated. She was here.

"Lulu?" He shifted his chair away from the table and stood.

She wasn't focused on him anymore. She wasn't focused on anything.

"Lulu." She turned her head to the voice as it came up next to her. His hands peeled hers away from the table, wrapped them up in the warmth of both of his, as he turned her chair and knelt at her knees.

"I—" She shook her head, the world she knew flashing in her head as she stared off in the distance. Her whips, her photographs, her camera, her hovel, her collection of vintage negatives, her shoes, that can opener for her pickles with the man-chest on it.

She looked at the bright light of the window, as this slide show of loss careened its way across her consciousness, and he spoke. But she didn't hear his words. She just saw her room at the dungeon, her leather, the wall of implements, the chains, the bindings, the hooks on the bed, the bars underneath, the framed cyanotypes on the wall.

The window fluttered as though she were drowning, and she blinked, a stream of tears cutting hot streaks to her chin.

"Say something, Lulu."

"I should never have married you. I thought...I never thought..." She shook her head. "I shouldn't have done this. I didn't know." She looked up at him, "This was all supposed to be a dream," she said.

TWENTY-FIVE

If you know the enemy and know yourself, your victory will not stand in
doubt:
if you know heaven and know earth,
you may make your victory complete.

—Sun Tzu
The Art of War

Grayson froze, tried to control his sudden need to remind her of her place as his duchess, her place in his life, in this world…the agreements they'd made and promises they'd yet to keep, but he held himself. He refrained from reminding her that she'd made her choice, and there was no going back now. This was it. But she was frightening him in earnest. She looked away from him, but not at anything, her eyes unfocused as she mumbled words he knew were English but he didn't recognize.

He couldn't imagine being her. She had been taken from the only home she'd ever known and placed in a completely foreign land with no hope of return.

Or could he? His father and brothers had nearly beat him to death, and he'd lost his entire life because of it. He smoothed his thumbs over her hands, trying to work the blood back into them.

"When I was sixteen…" He took a deep breath, then released her hands and steadied himself, placing his hands on her thighs, bowing his head.

"Young boys tease and cajole each other. Their fathers do the same to some extent. I knew there was something wrong with me when my body didn't respond in the same way my brothers' bodies did. It wasn't like it was a test or… But as children we bathed together, we were naked together, we had beautiful maids…

"I knew something was different about me for years, but I watched and was able to hide that part of myself from the men of my family, the other boys. They didn't suspect anything. Boys...who like women, we...well, I knew how to handle myself, and it included hurting myself. I thought I hid it well. "

Grayson breathed through the tightness in his chest, willed the words to come, words he'd never spoken aloud. He sank back on his knees, holding her hands as she stared out the window.

"Perhaps not well enough, though. I always assumed my father didn't approve of me simply because I wasn't slated to be important. No title, no lands, no purpose to him. But maybe it was more than that...

"My father wanted us to learn to fence. It's a gentlemen's sport. It teaches you to plan, to anticipate and forestall your opponent." He knew she was listening because her hands twitched.

"So when I was sixteen...I was only sparring with my brother, and we had tipped foils, but he advanced on me rather violently. I held him off, but at the last, my blade slid against his, and I faltered. I fell, and as I went down, his blade sliced my arm."

He looked down to her hands as she pulled one free of his grasp, then her hand wrapped around his biceps where the scar was safely hidden beneath the layers of fabric.

"He was older, the oldest, my father grooming him to be The Warrick, and he was using me as bait to that end. It took me a minute to get up then, just from the shock of my brother's anger. The shirtsleeve over my right arm turned red with blood. As I saw it spread, I concentrated on the pain of the cut, the sting of the skin, as well as the deeper hum of my blood rushing through my veins in the gash.

"My brothers laughed and shook hands, my father goading, but they ignored me there. Nobody helped me up. He'd done well, forced my hand, backed me up, then taken the win. He was victor.

"I pulled myself up to lean against the wall and put my hand over the cut, but it slipped and pain flared from the wound. So I pressed my hand steady against it, but not to stanch the flow of blood this time. This time, I pushed the edges together, then separated them again to bring back that sting. I did it over and over again until the world around me fell away. I might as well have been alone in the room. I simply couldn't stop myself."

Grayson clenched his eyes shut tight. Lulu's hand skimmed up his shoulder and rested on the back of his neck just above his cravat, dipping into the hair at his nape, cooling his hot skin. He knew she was watching him now.

"I realized then my blood was rising in other places, and without thinking about it, I reached down to adjust myself in my breeches as it became—uncomfortable. The next thing I knew, my father was yelling." He swallowed and leaned forward again, resting his head against her knees.

Her hand smoothed the hair at his nape, calming him. He took a deep breath, not knowing if he could continue. "I was an aberration, the devil's child, not of his flesh…"

He shook his head. He'd never spoken of this to a soul. He had said general things, but had never explained what had actually happened. Not once. Not this.

"I came off as they beat me. I couldn't control it. They were disgusted by me, the lot of them. At some point I lost consciousness from the severity of it all, and I never saw my brothers again. But that wasn't the last time I saw my father.

"He locked me in the attics here. He sent prostitutes to try to repair my damaged, malfunctioning body. I can only assume they reported back to him that they could do nothing of the sort, as I was…unwilling. Which surprises me, considering the amount of pain I was in at the time.

"I don't remember much beyond the women, the beatings, and my mother's screams as she tried to get to me." It felt an age before he thought he could continue, but he needed to see her. He lifted his head and met her gaze.

"I do not know how I lived, or why my father allowed it," he said. "I do not know who the man was who picked me up from the house. I do not know how I came to be in the service of Her Majesty in India. I only know that I did. I assumed my father bought the commission and shipped me off as soon as I was able to walk again, but that didn't happen in his house… in this house, where he and my brothers nearly killed me, and I came off because of it." He felt her hand still, and he closed his eyes tightly, unable to meet any censure that might show there. Her fingers slipped into the hair at his nape and pulled his head back.

"Open your eyes," she said.

He did, but he remained focused on his hands in her lap. She tugged, held his head tight in her grasp, and he looked up to her.

"If you are an aberration, so am I. If you are a child of the devil, then I am your sister. You may well be of your father's flesh, but you are not of his making, and you are not alone. You are your own man, and I am absolutely taken by you." Oh god but how this woman affected him. His skin warmed as she leaned forward, and her lips met his. He couldn't make himself move, so he simply allowed her to kiss him. "I'm sorry this happened to you. I'm so sorry," she said against him.

When she pulled back, she was finally looking into his eyes and seeing him. He had given her the absolute worst of him, and she didn't shy away. She kept on, steady.

"I know what it is to lose everything. I know. This is something I'm familiar with," he said, and he saw in her gaze when she made the connection. He hadn't told her this simply for his own sake.

"Yes. And your need for pain is something I'm familiar with. I don't find it abhorrent in the terms in which you were given. I find it one of the most beautiful things I've ever seen. I—" Her eyes faded, but she didn't look away, and he tensed his hands on her thighs.

"Lulu, I want you. More than that, I need you. I am loath to let you go, but I made a promise, and I'm only now understanding how difficult these promises are to keep when we don't even truly know each other yet. But I made a promise, and I will let you go. I don't want to. I cannot even begin to imagine the strength of mind and body required of me to release you, but I will. Just know this. I will wait for you, even if you leave and never return, I will be here waiting. I will give you all the time you need, and I will be here should you ever choose to come back," he said, he swallowed past a lump in his throat, tried to steady his voice as he heard it waver. "Now that I know… now that you've shown me my greatest shame in your eyes…I can never live without the possibility of you in my life. Even if that's the only thing I ever have. The possibility." He lessened his grip on her thighs when he realized how tight he held her, waited for her to speak, begged her to understand with only his eyes.

She released his hair and took his face in hers, her palms cooling his warm cheeks. She shook her head. "I just—"

He wasn't sure what she was going to say next, but he knew he couldn't hear it without first making her understand how certain he was of her in this moment. He pushed her knees apart and wrapped his arms around her waist, tucking his head to her chest and holding her. Her breath stilled and his rushed from him as if to make up for it.

Her hands came to his shoulders, skimmed the length of his back, and came back up, wrapping around his neck. Tilting him up to her, she looked in his eyes, and he pushed his mouth against hers. He moved slowly, determined.

His muscles juddered beneath his skin with the tension of restraint. He released her and reached up to skate a fingertip across her forehead, then he tucked her hair behind one ear and skimmed her jaw as he gently tipped her face to him for his kiss.

As much as he wanted her to give him pain, he wanted to give her pleasure more. His hands slid across her gently, her skin flushing at his perusal. He moved over her slowly, reverently, and when he got to her waist, he released the sash of her dressing gown and pushed it aside.

The world would be so disapproving of her, just as they were of him, if it knew how incredible she actually was.

He wished to worship her in the one way he knew he had not yet, with his mouth. So he put his hands under her knees and pulled, and she slipped against the fabric underneath her, sliding lower in the chair as she opened to him.

He slid his hands up her thighs then her abdomen, chasing the blush that rose there. He was afraid to look up at her, afraid he would see something in her eyes that would force him to stop. So he didn't look. He followed his hands with his gaze and then his mouth. He skimmed the sweet soft underside of one breast, then he licked her there, his thumbs teasing her nipples as he kissed her, and she fisted her hands on his lapels.

He worshipped at the altar of Lulu, with his hands, with his tongue, with his breath, licking then blowing across her skin to feel her shudder against him. He pushed her hands away when they tensed. He held her legs open to him when they attempted to close. He pushed his hips between her knees to keep her there, the wood of the chair biting into his abdomen in sharp contrast to the sweet wet heat of her quim just above it.

He kissed his way once again down the center of her body, until he came to her mons, and he lifted her knees, putting them over his shoulders as he tucked between her legs and licked her, her flavor exploding in his mouth in the sweet heat of passion.

He heard her scream, then her hands came back, shoving him away as her feet lifted to his shoulders and pushed.

He fell back to the floor as the chair slid back, and she hit the floor in front of him, then rolled to her side, trying to pull the robe around her.

Again.

He had no idea what to do. He was going to lose her to his ignorance because he simply didn't understand what was wrong. She didn't want him to touch her like that. She didn't want him to taste her, and he feared that she never would.

But he would wait. As he promised her he would. He pulled her into his arms and stood, carrying her to the bed. He laid her down and covered her up. "I'm sorry," he said as he smoothed her hair from her face. "I am nothing if not a patient man."

Then he turned silently and left the room.

Lulu let the guilt fall across her like the weight of a lead shirt for an X-ray. She lay still and let it sink upon her until she felt like she would never be able to rise from the bed.

He had opened himself up to her and given her everything he was. He laid himself out and expected judgment from her but received none, for she had none to give. He wasn't to be judged for this, but his family was.

She now knew everything about him, everything she needed to know, and what had she done in response? She had pushed him from her, knocked him to the floor, and sent him away. And actions spoke louder than words, particularly in her world.

She had behaved horribly toward him, and she paid her penance now. If she'd had a flogger, she would probably have taken it upon herself, if only to feel the physical manifestation of this pain. She had to make sure he knew that it wasn't him.

It was her. It was all her. That sounded so incredibly trite—but it was true and she didn't understand why, with everything she'd done in her life, why this one thing, the one step crossed such a line that she couldn't control the need to run from it.

She lay in the bed for a while, wondering when he might come back. Rakshan had come to her and brought tea, once again, and let her know that Gray was working in his office.

She was here to stay. No more of this dream business. This was it, and she was, now, okay with it. It had taken her by surprise earlier, that realization, but she no longer wanted for anything from her former life as it was now. All she wanted was Gray. All she wanted was to be able to open herself up to him the same way he had opened up to her.

He had dropped all his defenses and told her…horrific things. Tragic things. She wanted to reach through time and pull that young man to her and care for him, tell him he wasn't abhorrent, he wasn't a beast or the child of the devil.

He was blessed with a very special way to feel. Most of the world feared pain, but he embraced it, loved it—required it, even. Gray, unlike the majority of the world, could see pain for what it was, something that made passion that much stronger. Something that made you believe in life. Something that grounded you fully to living and not merely surviving but to feeling every possible thing that you could.

Because that was the beauty of a true masochist. They wrapped themselves around the world and took whatever she had to give, and they said thank you for it. Lulu didn't have words for how beautiful she thought him. So 'beautiful' was all she ever said, because he was, but he was also so much more than that. She hoped, truly, that he would embrace who he was.

That was something she wanted to see.

She should tell him, but she wasn't sure anything she had to say would be welcome at the moment. She couldn't lie here all day though, she had to do something so she decided to get up and work on her rooms on the third floor. No, fourth floor. Something else to get used to here, which floor she was on. It was ground floor, then first and second and so forth, not first, second, third, etc. This house had five floors, which meant here, in England, it actually had three floors, a ground floor, and attics. So much detail.

She rolled over and rose from the bed, letting the robe slide to the floor. She would pick it up later.

TWENTY-SIX

Successful war follows the path of destruction.

—Sun Tzu
The Art of War

When Grayson finally sat at his desk, he had to stare at the calendar for a full ten minutes before figuring out what day it was. It had been the longest four days of his life—the worst and the best.

He leaned back, feeling the stiff leather creak around him. His nature had been a revelation, but one that needed to be protected for both their sakes.

Certainly he was a duke, and that meant certain proclivities and eccentric behaviors would be overlooked by society as Calder had said, but at the same time, it would make him a target for a certain powerful few who wielded knowledge as a weapon. Of course, if she left him…there would be no actions to judge. Perhaps that would be best.

Rakshan entered the room carrying a tray.

"Your Grace," he said, then placed the tray on the table at the settee. "Her Grace asked that I prepare this for you."

Had she forgiven him? He had acted abominably. He should have known better than to push her again, but he had used his vulnerability as an excuse to try to push her through hers.

Grayson watched the steam rise from the teapot, then took a deep breath as the scents of cardamom, cinnamon, and cloves rushed to greet him. Before he knew it, he was sinking into the settee as Rakshan prepared a cup.

"Where is she?" he asked.

"She is directing the cleaning of the grand room on the upper floor."

He glanced at the window, but looked back when Rakshan lifted the cup to him. "Should we prepare a supper tonight?" Rakshan asked when Grayson took the cup.

"Yes, small, don't trouble much," he said.

Rakshan nodded. "Yes, Your Grace."

"Is there something else?" Grayson asked.

"My sister. She wishes to stay in London."

"Whatever you need from me is yours, as always."

"She will need a room for a small amount of time."

He didn't even need to consider. "She is family. She will stay here—"

"She will work."

"If that's her choice, then so be it, but Rakshan, she is not a servant. Just like you."

"And she will not behave as a servant. Just like me," he said, then he bowed and left him with his tea.

Grayson needed to figure out a way to get Rakshan to live his own life. He wanted him to be a friend, an equal, not a man in his house. He appreciated him greatly and wasn't sure how he would manage without him, but he would figure it out.

Grayson dipped his nose to the edge of the cup and inhaled, the warmth and strength of the spices sinking into his nerves and waking his mind. Thank god, Rakshan was staying with him, for now. He could almost see the colors of India, smell the saffron and curry spices in the bazaar, feel the heat of the sun pulsing down on him as he walked slowly through the marketplace buying fresh fruit, spice, vegetables, and rice.

It was the last time he had been so free with his person in public. He'd worn a loose shirt, a light jacket. No corset, no waistcoat, no buttons, no ties, no binding.

He never did anything like that here, but the thought of going out into a fog-filled, rancid London to buy something you eat raw simply turned his stomach. It wasn't that India was stunningly clean by comparison, but that the people there held their beliefs, and the way they did things, so very differently.

They were a thankful, and praiseful, and beautiful people. He missed the sounds most of all, the tiny silver bells that draped over the women's bodies, the sounds of the sitar and the lute.

He sat back in the chair and enjoyed the tea as he thought of Lulu and the night before. His left hand traveled up his thigh, and he ran it along the joint where she had pressed into him. She'd taken his virginity and turned his entire world upside down, then given him the most simple, and heartfelt, gift of tea.

Grayson still wasn't sure how he felt about the pain with the pleasure, but she was determined that it not be something to be ashamed of. She was determined that it was beautiful, and more common than he thought, and perfectly acceptable, and barring all that—that it was nobody's business but theirs.

This last happened to be his favorite, since he'd never had much care for society and what the *ton* at large considered to be proper. Which was exactly why he had liked her so much to begin with.

Could he embrace this way of life? Possibly, if she was his partner. He wasn't sure what was happening. He'd been determined to keep the marriage civil, but it was anything but that. They were like animals at each other, and he'd loved nearly every second of it. She was most absolutely a treasure.

And this morning…he wasn't sure what to think about what had happened this morning, but he wasn't going to obsess about it. One thing he had learned during the course of the last few days was that obsessing would come to no good. He had pushed her and pushed her, and pushed her again, even though he'd known she was frightened.

A knock came at the door, and it opened with Rakshan bearing a salver with a card. Grayson picked it up: *Calder*. He nodded, and a few moments later Calder came in and sat down across from him as Rakshan prepared another cup of chai.

Calder took it gratefully, his smile for Rakshan genuine—a smile Rakshan returned before leaving. "I haven't had this since…well—" he said.

They sat for a while in companionable silence, simply enjoying the chai.

"Like two damned old women," Grayson said suddenly.

Calder laughed. "I suppose we are right now, aren't we? Sipping our chai. Though there's no gossip. We need to add gossip for the illusion to be complete."

"Yes, of course, gossip," Grayson said.

"Oh, here's a brilliant one. The wayward duke takes a bride and isn't heard from again," Calder said with a grin.

Grayson groaned. "I take it Miss Witwick's is out to press?" he asked.

"Ah, yes. The wedding coverage was spectacular, including a few strange things overheard. Oh, and the detail of you picking up your wife and carrying her out of Buckingham like a sack of potatoes as the queen looked on. I believe that particular description to be one of the best."

Grayson looked up to him then. Obviously, there was someone in his circle giving out information they should not be. "I would probably sling a sack of potatoes over my shoulder should I ever find myself carrying one...which I won't." He finished his tea and looked into the pot to discern whether he could have more. Calder handed his over, and Grayson raised a brow in question.

"Go ahead," he said. "Has Rakshan been withholding?"

Grayson smiled and took the second cup. "Yes, though I'm not entirely sure why. I assumed a lack of the proper spices, or some such. But obviously not. Rakshan could prepare something else for you," he said.

"No, thank you. Don't trouble him. I was only stopping for a moment to see how you were...considering."

"Considering?" Grayson kept a steady gaze on him.

"Considering," he repeated.

Grayson nodded. "I'm well, and that's the second time I've said that today."

"Why on earth should your Rakshan be concerned for your well-being?"

"It wasn't Rakshan,"

"Well then, why would Lulu? Are you not staying in the same rooms?"

"We are. But she's...concerned."

"As she should be. Because you're"—Grayson watched Calder as he chose his words—"concerning," he said with a grin. "Did you two manage—

no, never mind, don't tell me any sordid details. I can see by your face much has happened since I saw you last. Have you told her?"

"Told her what?" Grayson asked, his shoulders tensing.

"Anything at all," Calder said cryptically.

"It seems that some things I didn't have to say, while others…I should not have, perhaps. Or perhaps I simply should have waited. I'm as yet unsure."

Another scratch came at the door, and Grayson stood, taking the card from Rakshan. He nodded, then turned to Calder. "It's Exeter," he said stiffly.

"Fuck's sake, what does he want?"

"Good question." Grayson walked to his desk and sat down as Calder followed him, standing to the side as if they had been discussing something of great import.

Rakshan opened the door and motioned to the man, not leading him in, just allowing the man to pass before shutting the door behind him. Grayson stood and waited for his now father-by-law to come across the room.

"Warrick," he said stiffly across the desk.

"Exeter," Warrick motioned to the chair across from him then sat down.

"I won't be a moment, I only wished to make myself known before seeing to my daughter."

"My wife? What need have you that you must see to her?"

"I have requested her presence at Exeter House several times."

Grayson didn't like where this was going. "Several times? We've been wed less than a sennight, and yet you've requested her presence several times?" Grayson asked.

"She is my daughter," he replied.

"She is my wife," Grayson reminded him, astounded at the man's tone. "We have only just been wed. Why in god's name would you assume to send for her the week of our wedding? Why would you request her come to you so soon?"

"I wished to know she is well."

"She is," Grayson said simply.

"That's not for you to say," Cecilia's father said, obviously becoming agitated.

Did he believe Grayson had hurt her somehow? Well, he had only this morning done things he shouldn't have, but they were things between a man and wife, not a man and his daughter. "As her husband, it is very much for me to say."

"As her father—"

Grayson stood. "You no longer have any claim on her."

"I do if you—"

"If I what?!" Grayson boomed and placed his fists on the desk between them. Grayson had done nothing so offensive that his wife needed some sort of protection from him. The very idea had him angered. "I am The Warrick. She is my wife. She is at my beck and call and does as I please in all things, because she belongs to me and me alone. What need, have you, of her?"

Exeter shrank against the strength of his voice and instantly shifted tack. "She sent for me," he replied, and Grayson inspected the man carefully.

"She did no such thing."

"How would you know?" His voice rose in concern. "Would you keep her from me? My only child?"

"If it was my wish, yes, but as it happens, it is not…currently. I only happen to know I have kept her much too busy to keep up with any correspondence at the moment."

"You would be so crass with me. The father of your wife."

"*My wife*," Grayson said solidly. "You would do good to remember that fact. You would also do good to remember that you, sir, refused to cancel the contract. This is your doing. What is it you want with her?"

"That is none of your concern," Exeter said.

"Again, sir, she is my wife, everything that conerns her, concerns me."

"I would see her now. I have nothing more to say to you."

"She isn't of a mood for visitors."

"Your Grace, I demand an audience with—"

Grayson moved forward, but Calder stepped up first. "Making demands in The Warrick's own study. That's quite brazen of you," Calder said easily.

Exeter just looked from one man to the other.

Grayson folded his arms across his chest as he considered Exeter. "Calder, entertain the man in my parlor, won't you? I'll go make the request of my duchess myself," he said.

"Why would you do such? You mean to prepare her, to warn her off of me."

"Necessary as all of that is, no. Furthermore, what reasons I may have for any actions I take are my own and none of your concern."

Grayson walked around his desk, noting that Exeter backed away from him a step in the process. Grayson paused to make sure Exeter knew he was aware of it, then he walked from the study.

He found Lulu in her rooms on the third floor, just where Rakshan had said she would be. She turned to him, and his palms went clammy, he hadn't seen her at all since this morning. He rubbed his hands together to dissipate her nervousness.

"What is it?" she asked as she walked to him.

He didn't want her to hide again, so he came right out with his purpose. "Cecilia's father is here. He wishes to see you."

She paused as she considered. Finally, she spoke. "He's nothing to me, I don't wish to see him. You said—"

"I know what I said, and I stand by it, but I won't send him away arbitrarily. I'll present you the opportunity until you tell me not to."

She was watching him a bit more closely than he liked.

"Do you want me to see him?" she asked.

He paused. Part of him wanted to know why Exeter was here. Had the man tried to set up his daughter as a spy in his household or for some other nefarious purpose that neither he nor Lulu would know about? There had to be a reason the man had refused to cancel the wedding contract, and it had to be for more than the behest of the queen.

"You do," she said.

"Only as far as I want to know what he's up to. *If* you think you can get him to divulge his reasons for being here, and only if you feel safe doing so."

Lulu nodded, then turned toward the windows. "I can command one simple man," she said.

"Only if you wish to. Not because I wish for you to," he said.

Lulu nodded. "Okay, I'll speak with him." She looked down to her filthy, dust-covered clothing. "This must be terribly inappropriate for a duchess, no?"

"Terribly," he said.

"Perfect then."

"Quite."

"What do I call him?" she asked.

Grayson wasn't sure about that. He had no idea how formal the man's family was in private. "Call him Your Grace until he corrects you," he said.

"So be it."

He followed her from the room.

Lulu wasn't sure what information Grayson wanted her to ferret out, but she was a master at getting to the bottom of things. She did have to tread lightly, however, since this man believed himself to be her father. She knew Gray would protect her, but…she didn't even know this man.

Part of her hoped he was a nice old man, and they would become friends, though she doubted that, considering the way Gray acted around him. Her husband didn't trust Cecilia's father. She would meet him with that fact foremost in her mind.

That, the truth of Gray's childhood, and that this man was an acquaintance of Gray's father.

Rakshan opened the door to the parlor, and she walked in. A man of similar age and bearing to Gray stood and walked to her. This man had been at her wedding. He'd stood with her husband and was at Buckingham with them. He must be a relation of his, though she'd met so many people that day she didn't remember much else. She held her hand out, and he took it, bowing over it with a kiss to the back.

"Your Grace, you are stunning even in such teasing dishabille," he said, only for her.

"You have me at a disadvantage, sir, even as you bend your lips to my filthy hand."

His eyebrows shot up in approval. Oh, she liked him already.

"I'm Calder. We met at Buckingham, but no doubt you've forgotten me. I would have forgotten me as well, should I be getting to know The Warrick as you are." He made a face at her, then chomped his teeth like a wolf.

Lulu laughed. She couldn't help it. "Well, I absolutely won't be forgetting you now, that much is certain, Calder," she said.

He stood tall and gave her a wink. "Glad I could make an impression. I'll just go keep your husband company while you speak with Daddy, shall I?"

"Oh, yes, please, won't you just?" She couldn't help but appreciate the broad smile he forced upon her and hoped he would visit them often. If Gray was dark, this man was light, and she needed a little balance right about now. "Please do come again," she said.

Calder bowed and walked from the room, leaving the door open behind him, and she had the sudden thought that she shouldn't have been quite so forward with him, but he'd just seemed to demand it by his demeanor.

Cecilia's father, Exeter, walked to the door and shut it soundly as he inspected her, top to bottom, a disapproving look in his gaze.

She gave him a slight curtsy, which didn't work quite so well, seeing as how she was dressed in pants. "Your Grace, my husband informed me you'd come for a visit and, though I'm quite obviously not in any shape for company, I came quickly to see you."

"What in the hell does that man have you doing? My daughter should never be treated so low," he spat.

"You misunderstand, Father. I wear this by my choice. I'm cleaning out some rooms to transform into my own personal—"

"Enough. I don't need the details of what he's forcing you to do. He is putting me in my place by casting you low in his own home, as a servant."

"He does no such thing. He's shown me nothing but the highest regard," she replied. It was true.

His voice dropped as he leaned toward her, and she tried to keep from shying from him. "You know what this marriage was to begin with. What have you discovered? Is he still as twisted and disgusting as his father said? What can we use against him?"

Lulu's breath stilled, and she turned for the window to keep from letting him see her shock. "I've discovered no such thing, Your Grace," she said.

"Nothing? Then what's come over you? Why are you acting in this manner? You should have been back home by now," he said.

"Back home, what for?"

"Don't be so dense."

"Sorry," she said with a shrug, "Female."

His eyes narrowed on her and she knew she needed to control herself better.

"Discredit the man somehow, Cecelia, then you can return home and marry someone worthy of my name."

Lulu looked back at him. Cecelia had been meant to marry Gray and then turn on him to the benefit of her father. "There's nothing to discredit. He's honorable," she said.

Her father's face wrinkled up. "Have you relinquished your maidenhead to him?"

"Excuse me?" she said as she turned.

"You're still here, following his orders, flirting with his cousin, behaving not at all like the daughter I raised you to be. You were to call him out for his inability to complete the task and leave him ruined."

"But the fact is he did complete the task—in stunning fashion. So perhaps we've come to an impasse, Your Grace. Perhaps we can no longer work in concert."

"What?" he yelled.

"Your Grace, I've found nothing to support what you speak of. I have no reason to believe Warrick is anything but a gentleman and worthy of all he has." Lulu wanted to say a whole lot more than this, but she held her tongue, afraid of saying something that he could use against Gray somehow.

"You're a foolish chit who has given away her only bargaining point as easily as a mouse takes cheese. I thought more of you."

"What more would you have me do? To what end should I be attempting to ruin my husband?" she asked.

"The end is none of your concern, only the means. You're but a woman."

"No, Father, you came here determined to ferret out some truth about Warrick. Tell me what it is you would have me do."

"You obviously don't have the intelligence to do more."

"I suppose I forgot what it was you needed me to do."

"What will it matter now?"

"Maybe I misunderstood, maybe I could still do what you need."

"You were supposed to discredit him as a man to the archbishop, you cannot do that if you've been compromised."

"Oh I'm compromised all right, is that all?"

"Is that—if you'd done your duty he would be ruined already. You failed." He just stared at her as the door opened and Gray entered the parlor.

She was shocked. He had wanted her to tell the world that Gray couldn't perform as a man should with his wife. Cecilia meant to shame him before the world. Lulu couldn't even speak. Whatever guilt she'd carried for taking over this woman's body vanished. It didn't matter if she

was merely following the orders of her father or acting on her own wishes, all that mattered was Lulu being here had saved Gray.

He walked to her, and one hand held her shoulder as he inspected her, then dropped to his side as he awaited her wishes.

She turned away from Exeter, looking out the window. "Gray, please, show His Grace to the door. I have no more use of him," she said.

Gray's eyebrows drew together for a moment, before he turned on Exeter. "It seems you've outstayed your welcome, Exeter."

"I will not be treated—"

"Exeter, I've asked you to leave as politely as I'm able. If my duchess chooses to entertain your company again, that's a choice that's entirely up to her. For now, she's asked that you leave."

"Of course you're easily led by a woman," Exeter spat as he turned for the door.

"Your Grace, the final contracts have cleared. Our business has concluded. Do not honor me with your presence again," Gray said.

He turned to her as she listened to the other man's footsteps fade. Then the front door opened and closed politely, certainly at the hand of Rakshan.

"He knows," she said as she looked up to him.

Calder walked in at that moment. "He doesn't have any idea what he knows. Don't let him fool you."

"He is much too close to the truth for me to be comfortable thinking he's just fishing for information," she said.

Gray tensed against her side and turned to his cousin. "Why would you say that?" he asked.

"I knew your father much too well for my own liking. He would never have detailed a secret about one of his family, no matter how estranged. He may have alluded to something with Exeter, but no more than that."

"It makes me uncomfortable that you knew my father better than I did," he said.

Calder stopped in front of them with a wicked half grin that faded slowly. "Believe me, Gray, it makes me uncomfortable as well. You have no idea how much. Your father was an arse, but he was too intelligent for the usual games. Exeter is fishing, and using your lovely duchess as bait."

TWENTY-SEVEN

When you are able to act, feign incapacity; when deploying, feign inactivity;
when you are close, appear to be far off; when you are distant, appear close.

—Sun Tzu
The Art of War

Grayson considered this. He might not have known his father, and Calder just might have, but Grayson knew Calder, and that was all he needed.

Calder nodded as he considered him, then his entire demeanor changed. "At any rate, I just wished to stop by, say hello, see if you were both still alive and see if there was anything I could bring you, or have sent in…seeing as how the two of you are so enamored of each other, you haven't made any of the requisite first-week of marriage appearances that society deems so necessary." Calder said these things as if to brush the prior discomfort away completely.

Grayson narrowed his eyes on him. "Is that so?"

Calder laughed. "For me? Not at all. For Miss Witwick's? I'm afraid it is. Remember, keeping a low profile is not doing what's expected of you. Nobody wants to believe your marriage to be a fairy tale. So what if it has ended up that way?"

"Are you attempting to give me lessons in stealth?" Grayson asked.

"Let's just call them gentle reminders, shall we? If they don't see you together often enough, they will start haranguing you. Then you won't be rid of them—ever. I would hate to have you fall to such a fate," Calder said.

"Only looking out for my best interests then, I see. Thank you, sir, I am in your debt." Calder turned for the entry, and Grayson followed.

"As ever," Calder replied with a wink.

Grayson shook his hand, then patted his shoulder.

"Goodness me," Calder said. "Next you'll be trying to embrace me. I'm not so sure I like the married Warrick. I much preferred the old, mean, crotchety—"

Grayson cut him off with a deep groan.

"Oh, there he is. Right, I'll be off. If you need ideas for appropriate outings with your ever lovely duchess"—he looked over Grayson's shoulder and winked at Lulu—"simply let me know. I could be tempted to accompany you, and your duchess, to the opera or a ball, should you need."

A shiver traveled Grayson's spine at the way Calder said duchess, then it settled in his skull, buzzing like a stuck bee.

Duchess. *His duchess.* He was suddenly terrified at how badly he wanted her again.

Lulu waved to Calder with a smile, and his cousin turned and left.

The parlor door closed behind him, and Grayson turned to Lulu. "I should get back to the paperwork. I wasn't nearly caught up." He needed to get away from her before he tried to force her, yet again, to let him in. It was overwhelming to him, this need for her to allow him the things he had allowed her.

She walked up to him and kissed his cheek. "Okay," she said, but he was stiff, and she stepped back and looked in his eyes. "Back to work." She opened the door, and he followed her as far as the grand staircase, pausing to look when she ran the stairs. Such an improper duchess. So incredibly lovely, entirely his, and completely unattainable at the moment.

Grayson returned to the study and walked to the settee. He picked up the teapot, removing the lid to peer inside, but what was left was cold and uninviting.

He wondered when Lulu would be amenable to his presence—though, it was he who had sent her off with a cold demeanor.

He moved back to the desk to finish settling the accounts so he could have the papers and drafts delivered to the bank. He pulled his thumb along the crease at his thigh once more as he tried his best to concentrate on all the numbers staring up at him.

Perhaps they could simply disappear, go on a grand tour and not come back. Then he would have his bride to himself whenever he wanted, and however he wanted. She would be forced by proximity to talk to him, and society could hang.

Lulu stood outside his study, staring at the door. He'd watched her go upstairs, but she'd stopped outside his view and waited for him to return to his study before walking back down.

He hadn't completely abandoned her yet, even though she fully expected him to after how she'd behaved. She'd pushed him away as he'd touched her—she wasn't even sure whether to call it that. It was so much more.

And then he shared his secret, and she'd pushed him away again.

She heard footsteps coming at her, and she panicked, running to the front of the house. The door to the study opened, and she slipped outside, sitting on the stoop, and trying to calm her heart before she was discovered. But he never came out.

She waved at a few people passing by who stared at her as if her pants were on fire. Pants... She sat on the top step like a—well, like a normal twenty-first-century woman in pants on the front steps of her house. She should probably get back inside before someone was so appalled they snitched on her to her husband. Or worse, to society at large.

She stood and went back inside, once again approaching the study. The door was open this time, and she heard Rakshan asking Grayson if he needed anything else before supper, to which Grayson declined.

Then the door opened further, and he exited with the tray.

She indicated the teapot. "Did he like it?" she asked.

"Yes, Your Grace," he said.

"Thank you," she said. "For doing that."

Rakshan smiled.

"Are you going out this afternoon?" she asked.

"Does madam require something?" he asked perfunctorily.

"No, no, not at all. I just heard you ask Gray if he needed anything and...I—" She shrugged. "Sorry, I'm just stalling."

Rakshan smiled. "Perhaps use your mouth in other ways." He leaned toward her. "You should try talking to him."

She was a bit shocked to hear something like that from him, considering everyone else around here was careful, and respectful, and actively practiced avoidance of confrontation. He was right, though. Gray had done plenty of talking. She hadn't done much at all, simply ordering him around, showing him possibilities.

"I think I like you," she said.

Rakshan winked at her. "If you have no further need, I will be leaving for the afternoon."

"Of course, have fun," she said.

His smile fell, and she thought maybe she'd gotten a bit too comfortable with him.

"Your Grace," he said, then nodded and took the tray and disappeared across the entry.

She watched him go. Stalling, really. She heard a crash come from the kitchen and moved to go check on him, but stopped when she sensed Gray behind her.

"Lulu," he said. She turned. "Did you forget something?" he asked.

"I—yes," she said.

He stared at her a moment, then asked, "What can I do for you?"

"I—um…do you have plans to be on the exchange?" she asked, remembering the phone thing. It was so odd how she felt so cut off from the world simply because of a lack of telephone. Not the change in time or physical being, but access to a telephone. Perhaps if she managed to gain some of these small pieces of freedom, she would be able to breathe again.

"I hadn't yet considered it, but if you wish it we can make that arrangement."

We can make that arrangement. So formal.

She nodded. Okay, good. She'd said something, and he'd answered, and he wasn't looking at her like she was going to fall apart, which is exactly what she'd done the last time they were in company, alone. But, oh, she felt like she was going to fall apart, because just this morning they'd been so close, so naked, so warm. He had been so open with her, so gentle, so sweet and tender as he explored her body, and it had felt like being burned alive.

The conflagration of her psyche when he'd reached beyond the physical—when he'd dared to be truly intimate with her—had stopped her cold. She was terrified of being that close to someone, of allowing so much, of letting them feel her when she fell apart and was pulled back together again. She was terrified of relinquishing control and now she just felt incredibly awkward around him.

"I thought you were returning to your rooms?" he asked.

She looked into his eyes, tried to read what was going on in there, and couldn't seem to catch anything. "I—" She shook her head, once again feeling as though she were on the edge of complete despair. This wasn't working.

Gray took one step toward her, but she shied away, because if he touched her, she would disintegrate. "I'm going to go…work on the room. If that's okay with you," she said.

"You don't need permission to do what you wish to, Lulu."

She nodded. He said that, but when it really came down to it, would that be true? He'd gotten over his caveman-esque break with reality, but that didn't mean that possessive part of him wasn't still there, even as skilled as he was at repressing. He slid his hands in his pockets, probably to keep them from reaching out to her. She wanted them to reach for her again, though. She wanted him to keep trying…didn't she?

She didn't know what she wanted, and she hadn't done what Rakshan had suggested. Instead, she turned and fled.

TWENTY-EIGHT

The spot where we intend to fight must not be made known; for then the enemy will
have to prepare against a possible attack at several different points.

—Sun Tzu
The Art of War

Grayson waited until she was gone, then turned back to his study, stopping when the bell on the door announced yet another arrival. He waited a moment for Rakshan to come, but realized he'd told him he could leave for the afternoon, so he walked to the door. He wasn't of a mood for any more company. He could simply ignore it.

The visitor thumped on the door, and Grayson opened it swiftly to force them back. "Yes?" he asked, then was immediately repentant when he saw the visitor was a mere boy.

"Sir, I beg pardon, there was no answer at the servants' entrance. My master said to make sure this were delivered today. He said not to return till it were." He held up a heavy package wrapped in paper, and Grayson took it.

"Thank you." He reached into his pocket to pull out a coin and hand it to the boy, then sent him on. He stood on the stoop and turned the plain, paper-wrapped package over in his hands. Something heavy and unbalanced shifted inside, and Grayson smiled as he turned back to the house perhaps he had a way to get Lulu to open up.

He stopped halfway across the entry, realizing nobody else was going to shut his front door, so he turned back and did it himself.

He heard the sturdy click of the catch, then felt the silence descend like a silk sheet. He looked up and thought of Lulu, who would be three floors above him, arranging the room she wanted to use for her photography. This house was much too big, because she could get much too far away from him, and he didn't like it.

He liked her underfoot. He wanted her underfoot, a constant reminder.

Grayson took a deep breath and forced his feet toward the ballroom instead of up the stairs. He needed to let her be. She'd made it perfectly clear that she wanted to be alone, and he would do his very best to respect that, because the next time he got close to her, he intended to get very close to her indeed.

At some point he wasn't merely going to break down her walls, but he was going to smash them to bits and force her to open up, just like she'd done him.

It seemed only fair.

He walked into the ballroom to find some of the other things she'd requested had arrived but had not yet been arranged. He set aside the package, took off his jacket and waistcoat, and got to work. By the time his stomach made its wishes known, Grayson was covered in sweat, his shirt plastered to his body, his trousers rolled at the ankles, and his shoes abandoned.

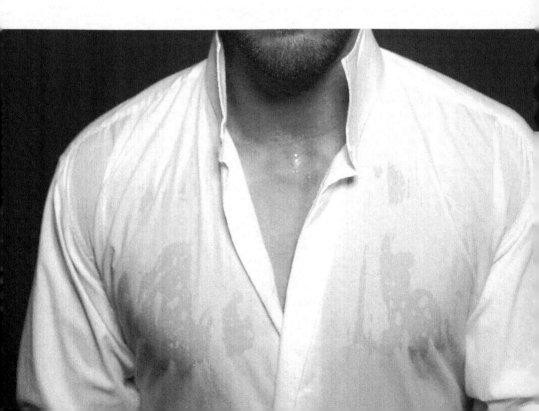

He paused and surveyed the room. He'd set up quadrants with a sparring lane, a bo staff and sword training circle, a weight area, and the fourth area with the mats she'd asked for, and the barre, which had yet to be installed. It looked good.

He would, at some point, need to have some additional lights installed, since the current lights were set up specifically for a ball atmosphere, heavily centered for the dance floor, bright on one end for the orchestra, dim at the edges for nefarious purpose.

He looked to the far edge of the room, where he and his brothers had always sparred. Then he shook his head. They meant nothing now. None of them. They were all dead and buried. There was nothing they could do to him now.

He wasn't sure how long he stood there staring up at the main chandelier or how long she watched him. But he did know he was aware of her presence by the sparking of his nerves along the ridge of his shoulders. He didn't move. He'd told her he could be patient, and he intended to prove it. He would allow her to come to him.

He knew when she approached, more from the shift in the air than any sound she made. She knew how to move silently, and that in itself was erotic to him. The ability to be stealthy, to stalk prey like a predator…and he wanted a predator. He wanted her to overpower him, to stalk him and take him. He wanted to allow her to do whatever she wished with the bones and flesh of his body when she captured him.

He shuddered through the thought and cast his gaze to the floor so she wouldn't see the passion he knew was burning in his eyes. He dropped his hands from his waist, hoping she would reach out and touch one of them, hoping that if they were farther from his person, she would feel safe enough to come into contact with him without too much intimacy.

He was rewarded by one cool fingertip skimming down his right palm before her fingers wove into his. He still didn't move other than to let his fingers wrap around hers.

"Good afternoon, husband," she said.

"Good afternoon, wife." He looked over to her. She was as much a wreck as he was, her hair a tangle of curls and cobwebs, her shirt streaked with filth. "I could have some men come clean the room for you," he said, turning to her.

She dropped his hand, and he instantly regretted moving. "No, I like the work. I need to move, and the space is mine. Cleaning it is taking a sort of ownership over it. I don't want strangers in there."

"I could help you... If you need it, simply ask," he said, then he left it. "Would you mind explaining a few things to me in more detail?" he said when she seemed to pull back from him.

"If I'm able, yes."

"Bondage and discipline, domination and submission, sadism and masochism."

"Yes," she said on a mere breath, and he saw the pulse in her neck pick up.

"I understand the terms, now, but...I want to know more." She nodded. "I understand bondage, tying someone up, but it seems to be in direct contradiction to submission. If you submit, you shouldn't move of your own volition. So why bondage?"

"There are as many combinations and levels and extremes within these words as there are stars in the sky, Gray. There isn't a manual."

"So, you don't have to feel a need for bondage *and* for submission?"

"No, you could want bondage, but to not submit willfully. As long as you consent to what happens, your partner could tie you up without you submitting to them."

"But that would be...wouldn't that be against their will somehow?"

"No, not if that's what they want. If someone wants to fight you, if that's their kink, then as long as both partners are consenting and know the limits, there's nothing wrong with it."

"Safe words," he said, and she nodded. "Tell me more. You said you help people...how?"

"Just...generally? Or specifically?"

"Either one. Tell me of a client."

"I can't—"

"Tell me generally then."

She smiled. "Let's say someone is unable to face a fear alone, and they want, more than anything, to face that fear. I could design a scene in which I make that person believe that I was going to do exactly what they feared.

I would bring them to the edge and then back away only to bring them to the edge again, until they faced their fear, then either embraced it or walked away from it."

"So, a tangible fear of something? Something physical?"

"Yes."

"Like…pigs?" he asked.

"Pigs?"

"A fear of pigs."

"Do you have a fear of pigs?" she asked.

"No, not me. I'm just thinking hypothetically. A fear of…pigs, or something."

"A hypothetical fear of pigs."

"Yes, or whatever," he said and paused. He could see in her eyes that she wasn't falling for his jest. Of course she wasn't going to allow him to make light of it. "What if my fear was pain?" he asked as he waited for her reaction.

"Hypothetically?" she asked.

"No." The word hung in the air between them like stilled dust in the sun. "You…helped me to face my fear. My fear was to submit. My fear was to admit that I…that I get off on pain."

She nodded.

"You're very good," he said. "But…what is it you're afraid of, Lulu?"

Her eyes flared, and she looked away quickly.

"There's a package for you," he said then. "I left it by the entry."

She turned and walked away from him, and he stayed and watched her sway, breathing slowly to control himself. He felt out of control and desperately needed to rein some of his hard-learned patience.

It just felt as though she'd done this thing to him, opened him up to this new experience. and now… How was he to walk away from that? How was he expected to not want that every second of every day moving forward? He breathed and kept his gaze on the floor, replacing his hands on his hips.

She had treated him like a client, even though it wasn't intended. He understood that on some level. It's just who she was. Could he turn that on her? Could he help her to face her fear of intimacy? And how?

The sonic boom of a whip cracked near the center of the room, startling him, and he turned to find Lulu, the wickedest, most incredible gleam in her eyes as her gaze narrowed in on him.

His instinct was to run, but he held still.

Crack!

The retorts sounded nearly in tandem as she wielded both whips, and he could not, for the life of him, take his eyes from her.

She grinned, and from across the room he could see the white of her teeth as she raised the whips slowly, her arms stretched out wide, then crack! Again, the sound doubled with the action of her movements, the small flick of her wrist, that commanded the long, braided leather of the bullwhips.

Oh god, he was in love. She was his everything. His cock thickened against the fall of his trousers, and he shifted uncomfortably. She hadn't even touched him, had not come close to him, and still, the very idea of those whips licking at his skin had him aroused.

Crack!

He fell for her hard.

Lulu felt like her face would cleave in two, she was grinning so hard. The muscles of her upper arms and shoulders already burned, and she'd lifted the whips only three, maybe four, times and held them steady.

She kept her gaze on Gray as she walked slowly across the ballroom toward him, her arms raised. She wouldn't go anywhere near him, not knowing exactly how her body would respond to the weight and feel of the whips yet. It wasn't safe. But there were things she could do. There were things she could show him without strikes and danger.

She cracked the whips again, this time a sidearm crack, bringing the tails almost together in front of her. She felt good. Better than good. She felt amazing. This was exactly what she needed to play again. She finished with four alternating overhead forward cracks before she came too close to him. To his credit, he did not shy, but held his ground. She could see the ridge of him pressed against the fall of his trousers and knew he wanted more than just to fuck her.

Her body responded in kind, and she let the whips trail the floor behind her until she was only a few feet from him. She twitched her right wrist, and the whip shot out and wrapped around his left wrist, and his eyes went black as she pulled him into her space.

"On your knees," she said.

He hit the floor, his knees spread slightly, his toes anchoring his feet behind him. He looked down and rested his hands on his thighs as she crowded him. His breathing slowed in pace but intensified in power, his shoulders rising and falling.

"Look at me."

His chin came up first, his gaze last, resting first on her mouth, then flaring as his eyes met hers. Oh, she was hot for him. Her skin tightened, her muscles vibrated, her heart beat against her lungs.

"Is this where it happened?" she asked.

His gaze snapped like a tightly leashed dragon, and she knew it was.

"This room, this large, irrelevant room, is where your life was changed forever?" she asked.

"I'm not a client."

"I'm not looking for one." She pulled his shirt aside and ran a hand down the scar. "I just want to know what you feel for your father now, being in this room again."

"Nothing. I feel nothing." His breath was steady, and she believed him.

"Why?" she asked.

"Because there's nothing left for him. Everything I feel…is for you," he said.

Her breath stopped at that, and she considered what to do next. This, she could do this, and he would let her. She flicked the bullwhip, releasing his wrist, then dragging the whip across the floor to rest behind her. His mouth dropped open as if to take in more oxygen, and his tongue came out to wet his lower lip.

She leaned over and met it, then straddled his thighs and sank down onto his lap as his arms came around her.

"Oh god, Lulu," he groaned. The words dragged the depths of his cavernous chest, nearly unintelligible. Their teeth clashed angrily, lips

bumping and bruising as his arms came around her rib cage, and she wrapped hers around his neck.

She dropped the bullwhips, and he lifted, pushing her over onto her back with his entire body, her back hitting the floor but her head carefully cradled in his hand as his full weight pressed down on top of her.

Then he stopped.

She gazed up at him, their panting breaths mingling between them. His head jerked to one side quickly as if to say, No…no.

Please, she thought. *Please. I can do this. This. THIS I can do.*

His hands came next to her sides and pushed, his body moving away from hers, and she shuddered from the loss of heat. She closed her eyes as he looked down on her, and she wanted to know what he was thinking… but she was too afraid to ask.

They stayed that way for a time, the wood starting to bite into her shoulders uncomfortably, her legs splayed about him irreverently, her hands fidgeting restlessly. "Gray…"

"Shhh…" was all he said as he continued to watch her.

Not again. She closed her eyes.

"Look at me," he said quietly, and Lulu turned her head to the side, the cool wood of the floor meeting her cheek like a slap. "Lulu."

She felt the muscles of her face tense, then she lifted her cheek from the wood and slowly opened her eyes. As soon as their gazes met, she snapped her eyes shut again and tried to push him off, but his hips came down and pinned her, and her useless hands fisted the fabric of his shirt. "Please," she said again, but this time it was for something completely different.

One of his arms bent, and he came down on his elbow, then his hand found hers, loosened the knot of her fingers, and took the emerald on her hand and turned it until it faced outward. He closed her fist to keep her from spinning it back round again and said, "Lulu."

She took a deep breath. She knew exactly what he was doing. She knew exactly what he wanted from her. But she couldn't do it. She felt her breath hitch, felt the muscles of her cheeks twist her face into a horrible mask of sadness, felt the heat of her tears streak her cheeks and pool in her ears.

"Please," she begged. "Please, I'm not ready."

She felt him make a decision without speaking, then he lifted away from her and stood. He reached down and wrapped his arms around her, lifting her to his chest without a word. He left the ballroom, went up the stairs and through their room, through the bathing room and into the shower room.

He carefully placed her on her feet, stripped her bare and then himself. The entire time, he stayed in contact with her, even if just the lightest touch of a finger, and that small touch kept her from running from the room.

He held her gently, reaching behind her to turn on the shower. She felt the spray of the cold water, felt the temperature heat until the steam began to rise, then he crowded her slowly until she backed into the secure steel ribs of the shower.

He let the water course both of them, washing the grime from the upper floor, the grime from the ballroom, the dirt from the day, and all that was between them seemed to wash away with it and down the drain. His hands skated up her sides, then he tilted her chin, and he kissed her.

His body swayed against her as though it sang her a lullaby, and she wrapped her arms around his narrow hips, her thumbs caressing the edges of his spine as they danced to the music of his body. His kiss was slow, languid, and searching. He asked for nothing from her. He simply gave.

The water rushed over them, fingers of water everywhere on her, soothing and cleansing, hiding her tears, allowing her to feel the myriad things she was afraid of. It felt like he'd created an entire world within this small cage, within the lee of his body, protected by the steel of the shower, wherein she could release that fear and allow for something she had always been afraid to reach for.

His hands searched her so gently she felt like the water was tears from her body, from her soul. Still, he didn't press her. Didn't ask for more. He just gave and gave until she felt her body relax so far into him she wasn't sure where his skin ended and hers began. They were simply one.

The next she knew, she was dry and warm in the curve of his form, his heavy breathing against her back, his arm weighing her down into the feather tick of the mattress, and she knew one thing for certain.

This man was going to destroy her.

TWENTY-NINE

But a kingdom that has once been destroyed can never come again into
being,
nor can the dead be brought back to life.

—Sun Tzu
The Art of War

ll the practice, meditation, and abstinence in the world could not
have prepared Grayson for the trial that was falling in love with
this woman.

He pulled her in tight, pushing his face into her hair at the nape of her
neck and breathing deeply of her scent. His fingertips strayed across her
skin, relearning the dips and valleys, memorizing the terrain of her body.

He felt her come awake in the quick tensing of muscles, and he calmed
her with kisses and a warm breath that sounded like her name.

Lulu…

Grayson carefully rolled her to her belly and loosened the knots of
her shoulders with his hands, smoothing down her back. She flinched and
groaned under his ministration. "You'll be sore after all the work you put
in today," he said.

She nodded into her pillow. "People don't know how much goes into
wielding those bullwhips, the amount of muscle mastery and control. It
looks fun, and it is, but it certainly isn't easy."

"You were magnificent," he said gently as he considered her. There had
to be something else that was keeping her from him. He worked her sore
muscles for a while before continuing. "Tell me more about Oliver."

Lulu rolled on the bed, and he lay down next to her until they were face-to-face. He took one of her hands and began to massage it, leading the tension out through her fingertips.

"What more do you want to know?" she asked.

"You were with him when you were injured and came here. Was he your lover?" he asked, attempting to keep any notes of censure from his voice.

"Oliver was… He was a client," she answered.

"And what services did he pay for?" Grayson asked.

Her gaze went over his shoulder to the windows, and he knew she was considering whether or not she would trust him. He took her other hand and worked on her fingers until her eyes softened.

"Ollie…I've already told you everything there is to know of him. There is no more. He was a client. He was my work of art, nothing more." She pulled her hand away and sat up on the bed, tucking her toes under her knees and pulling the blanket around her. Grayson did the same thing, facing her, his knees touching hers, his hands in his lap.

"Tell me of other ways you've helped your clients," he said.

"Well, sometimes it's just kink. Sometimes it's as simple as what someone needs in order to get off. But sometimes it's deeper than that, the facing of fears and that sort of thing."

"So what sorts of things help you with this?" he asked.

She thought for a moment. "Sensory deprivation can help. I think bondage has a lot to do with sensory deprivation. If I tie you up, you aren't able to touch me. You have to feel only what I give you, only what I allow you to feel."

"That sounds…difficult," he replied.

"It can be, but it can also be incredibly rewarding."

"I think I can understand that," he said. He felt his heartbeat pick up pace just thinking about being tied up.

"That's part of the my training," she said. "You have to be restrained. I would put you on your knees at the end of this bed, lift your arms high, and bind them to the posts."

Grayson nearly choked at her words, slow and honeyed. He knew she was trying to sway him, but he would fight her, for now. "What other sorts of sensory deprivation do you practice?" he asked. "That's touch, so there's what? Sight, sound, taste, smell?"

She nodded. "Some of those are better used as the opposite, though. To deprive one's sight is a very useful tool. I love to blindfold my subs. It strips them of the ability to perceive my actions through sight, leaving them to discern through other means, like sound."

He made some sort of sound of acknowledgment, but he wasn't sure it could be categorized as a word. She was good at this. He was fairly certain he had succeeded only in setting a trap for himself.

"As for the opposite, smell can be very useful when dealing with memories. If someone has a reaction to a specific scent, like a certain flower or perfume or…cinnamon rolls, whatever. I can use that to conjure memories, to repair the past or allow for a different future."

"I imagine taste would be similar to smell in that respect then."

"Yes," she said.

They sat for a while, legs folded, knees touching. He waited her out once again. He realized this was one way in which he was always able to force her hand. Patience, and quiet. She always responded to silence because she didn't like it.

"I still fear that you truly don't want to know me," she said.

"But I already do," he responded. He skimmed his fingertips over her knee through the linen of the bed sheet. "I know you feel very passionately for those lucky enough to be in your life. I know you have a deep-seated need to help those around you, no matter how peripheral. I know you to be thoughtful, passionate, and contagious in a way I only thought possible to horrible diseases, but for you…it matches perfectly, and there is no other way to describe it."

Lulu looked horrified, and he grinned, continuing on. "Hear me out," he said. "I was trepidatious and fearful when we met, determined to keep you from me, insistent that you not be a true part of my life, but I managed to catch you nonetheless. Somehow you managed to find a way in, and you contaminated my very soul, and if that sounds horrible and awful, so be it, because I would never be done with this illness. I will never pursue a cure or seek out remedy. I wish to languish in the evidence of your manifestation on my body, in my soul, and upon my heart. I am yours…and from here on out forever will be."

Lulu's gaze grew wide upon him, her lips dropping open in unabashed astonishment at his words.

"I am your humbled servant, my lady. I am yours. However you wish to hear these words, I will say them. I lay my life at your feet and will spend my days worshipping you."

"Grayson, I—" She turned her gaze on the light of the window, tears welling in the corner of her eye. "I never expected so much of you. But I'm still afraid that this is merely an infatuation born from the discovery of who you truly are and my place in revealing that."

"I realize you've done similar things for other people. I realize that you may believe what we have is merely another man bowing to his…to the woman who helped to change his life. But it isn't. What we have is different, and you know it, and that's why you're so frightened. You said it yourself—you'd never met someone who brought all the pieces of you together, The domination, the submission, the sex, the passion… the intimacy."

She started to shift away, and he tapped her knee, stilling her and bringing her attention back to him.

"I realize we have yet to pass any sort of time together, but I wish to pass that time wondering at the depths of you. Every morning I wake… Every night I fall asleep… I wish for it to be in your presence. I like you," he said. "Very much."

"So many words for such a silent man."

"Only because of you. Only because you willed them from me, brought forth like the sweet notes from a piano. You are the maestro of my life."

"I am overwhelmed," she said simply.

"I only wanted to be perfectly clear. I have made my decision, and I will await yours." At those words, Grayson stood from the bed and moved to the dressing room.

"But, Gray…"

He stopped and turned to her.

"I made my decision the day I met you. I haven't changed my mind," she said.

Grayson held his breath as he looked on her. The sun came through the window in a rare moment of strength, flushing her hair until it shone like a living thing as it haloed her.

"What you've said is true—you do already know me, so what of my past? Why is it still necessary to explain myself further to you, to define who I used to be, someone I can no longer be in this life? You just said you know me, so why do we keep going back to who I was?"

"Because I want to help you find the path to your future, and the possibilities are endless, but to have a map of the things that made you happy then…the people who filled your life with meaning—it would help me to action, to finding ways for you to be content."

"But I don't want to be content. There is no adventure in that. I just want to walk alongside you and be…happy."

Grayson nodded. "As much as that should make me happy, it doesn't for the simple fact that you should not be made an accessory to my life. You are much too important to me for that.

"Please understand, there are also selfish reasons for my wanting to know your past that go beyond my well-honed desire for control. I want to know everything about you, but I also want to know for certain that this— what we have—is different from anything you've had in the past. I want to know that you're experiencing the same thing that I am—that I believe you were brought to this life, a gift, for me. That you were born for me and no one else. It is no longer a concern for any improprietous behavior and such. It's a need to know that what I believe to be true, in this, is true." He waited patiently for her response, allowing the time for her to consider.

"I haven't ever…I realize in all things physical I am much more experienced, but that isn't the same as what we've shared between us. You have…you've touched me in ways that I've yet to comprehend, and perhaps that's why I continue to run from you. These are feelings I've never had and never expected to have, because I knew who I was in my previous life, and Gray…I was content! I was content."

He walked back toward the bed slowly, but she raised one hand to stay his advance. "Please, I need you to understand. You are so very overwhelming to me, to all of my senses. Your physical presence is overpowering, and your emotional depth is so intense, I'm afraid of what I've brought forth in you. But I'm not going anywhere. I'm not. I just need…I need some time to adjust. You are just *so very much*, and I need time to adjust to your muchliness," she said.

What she said struck a chord with him, and he filed it away to consider more later. Right now he wanted only to hear what she had to say. He took one more step so he could sit at the end of their bed, leaning back against the bedpost, waiting for her to continue.

"I'm going to tell you something, then give you time to consider it. I have gone into detail in my prior life, and the reasons for that…may not have been earnest. I now fear that my want to tell you everything may actually be my defense mechanism kicking in and attempting to push you away with the truth of who I am."

Grayson nodded, then steeled himself in the hopes she'd share just a little bit more.

Lulu took a deep breath, then looked at her fingers as they twisted together in her lap. "People paid me to make them bleed…or not. People similar to you, who like pain and submission and myriad variations thereof, paid me to design scenes wherein I hurt them."

Grayson nodded. "You mentioned that. You also said it never involved sex."

"No, no sex. At least, I didn't. Some do, but that's not what I did. I might have made someone come in other ways, but I didn't have sex with any of my clients. I specialized in a few things and had some very exclusive clients. I was well known in my circle, and Oliver…" She took a deep breath, and Grayson froze, waiting.

"Oliver paid very handsomely for me to paint wings on his back with my bullwhips."

Grayson tried to visualize what she described but couldn't, so he pressed her on, again, simply by waiting.

"Ollie trained for months to learn the proper muscle control. It's important to tense and release at just the right moments, to protect the flesh, the muscle, and the underlying tissues and organs. If I strike, and a muscle shifts revealing a bone, the strike could flay the skin, causing great damage. If I strike the wrong area, the damage could be irreparable. It's important to be precise," she said.

"I use the whips in tandem. That's why I trained so much. I would paint…I would paint their backs—I painted Ollie's back with angel wings created by welts from my whips. Then I would photograph them, as they were bound there, creating a piece of art to remind us both of the beauty of the moment."

"It sounds… You said you failed."

"I did. I never made the image for Ollie. I was brought here instead. Those images were beautiful… They were my treasures, and I'll never see them again," she sounded desperately saddened by that and Gray wanted to fix it with every fiber of his being.

"Did you love him?"

"As much as any artist loves their work," she said.

Grayson breathed through a relief he had wanted to feel ever since he first heard the man's name. "You mentioned the wings before. Would you be willing to show me?" His voice seemed so small to him.

Lulu was watching him carefully, and he only hoped that getting to know everything about her, that accepting everything about who she was, would help her trust him and let him in.

"I can't. I mean, first of all, I need months of practice with my whips before I'm even strong enough. I feel like my symmetry is not terribly off, but I haven't struck anything and won't strike a man until I know for certain that I'm able to do so safely. That's rule number one, remember? Safe, sane, consensual. Safe is rule number one in kink."

"Whatever I can do to help you, I will do. Just let me know what you need."

"You mean to say you'll allow me to continue this? You'll allow me to paint someone with… You'll allow me to top someone?" she asked.

Grayson had considered this when she'd told him about being a professional Dominant. He'd also come to a decision. "Not someone, no. Is this what you've been afraid of? That I would make you walk away from this part of yourself? Is this why you're scared? Because you want to continue doing these things, and you believe I won't allow for it?"

She looked away, then dropped her gaze and nodded.

He knew, though, that it wasn't the only thing holding her back. "I'm fairly certain I don't have the will to allow you to…top someone else. But you can do whatever you wish to—with me."

She froze. From the top of her head to her toes, every muscle locked into place. "I don't—" She took several very measured breaths, and he wasn't sure it was because she was frightened, or turned on, or terrified. "Gray, this is quite different from what we did. This isn't nerves and bruises. These are honest-to-god welts and possibly cuts. This isn't a decision to make lightly."

"Yet I told you I would do whatever you need of me to find yourself and to feel at home—and I meant that. If this is something that you need, specifically, then I am at your service. It is my duty, and I feel it could also be my pleasure.

"Beyond that, I don't think *allow* is the correct word, as I also remember quite clearly that you weren't to be asking permission for things, but that we were supposed to be equal partners in all of this. This is something between two people, and we are two people. What you do…this isn't something that will go beyond our marriage. I feel as though I should ask your permission to make that statement, but I hope that in this you will understand and allow my possessive mien."

Lulu loved the way he emphasized certain words for her, like allow and possessive, but she couldn't believe what he was saying. Beyond the fact that he was going to allow her to practice her whip play, he was volunteering as her submissive for wings.

Lulu turned and stood from the bed, pulling the sheet with her. "Is dinner soon? I'm suddenly rather hungry and perhaps we could…continue this discussion then."

"Would you prefer to dress or to eat here?" he asked.

"I think I would prefer to dress," she said.

He nodded and went to the pull, the drawers he'd worn in bed sliding low on his hips. She watched him as he crossed the room, inspecting his broad back and seeing the natural musculature that was all his and how she would be able to enhance that with wings. His wings would be wide across his shoulders, with dramatic curves toward his spine at his narrow hips. And they would be beautiful.

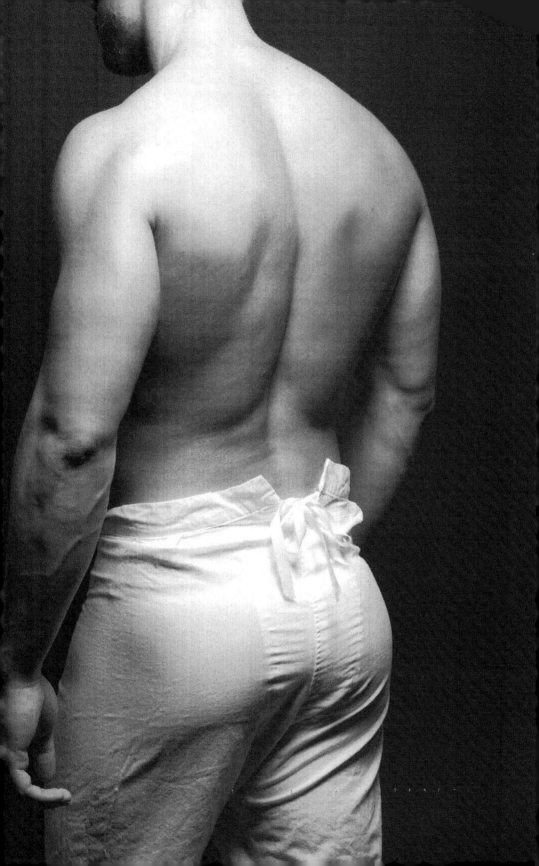

She shook the thoughts from her head. She needed to do something mindless and methodical, and dressing for dinner…that was about as close as she could get without a darkroom. She really needed somewhere to hide.

She walked toward the bathing room and closed the door behind her, sitting against the edge of the bathtub. She waited awhile before returning to their room to find it sadly empty.

Lulu wasn't sure how long it would take her to acclimate to this new life, but saying what she had to Gray had solidified for her some thoughts that had been jumbled since she arrived.

It had been an adventure, it had been a bit arduous, and he was certainly keeping her on her toes—but she had enjoyed the ride so far. Without doubt.

She hadn't realized that contentment, though something so many people strive for, wasn't something she was particularly interested in. She hadn't realized, until she'd come here and was tossed upside down, that she'd been content and hadn't even known.

She pulled her clothes from the wardrobe and laid them on the bed, then dropped her towel as she considered further. It wasn't that contentment was such a bad thing, not at all, really. But she was a woman of motion, and contentment assumed the distinct lack of such. Contentment was a stillness of body and mind, a deep happiness with what was happening and how you felt. So perhaps of a fashion it wasn't so bad to wish for contentment, but she was fairly certain she would become bored in it.

She heard the door open and close as she pulled the corset around her over the chemise and secured the busk, then she felt his hands on her shoulders and the corset tightening as she wiggled and adjusted herself in it. "Thank you," she said.

"Rakshan has already seen to supper. It should be ready within the hour if you would like to accompany me to the parlor for a small cordial before our meal. Perhaps we could speak?" he said.

"So terribly formal once again," she said with a smile. She turned and leaned into his broad chest, her fingers smoothing the fabric of his shirt at the edge of his waistcoat. He smiled and cupped her elbows as he leaned down and kissed her nose.

"Sometimes, formality forcefully removes a level of discomfort one may feel in certain situations. Formality, as in many tactics, is a valuable tool, one you will learn to wield just as masterfully as your whips."

"I see. Well, then"—she stood away from him and took up her dress— "if you don't mind, sir, I would ask you await me in the parlor while I finish readying for supper."

Gray's face tilted up, and he looked down at her from beneath those long, dark lashes of his. "As you wish, my lady." He turned and walked from the room, pulling the door closed behind him.

Lulu hoped, she hoped. That was all she could do, really, was hope— and so she did. She hoped her mind would catch up with her body and let him in. She hoped her body, in turn, would catch up with her mind

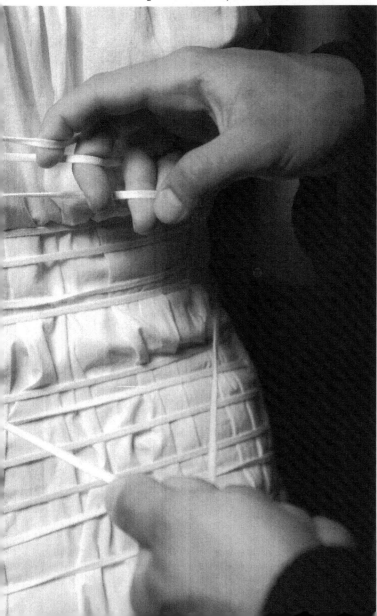

and allow her to do the things she loved to do. She whimpered a bit at the very thought of painting her husband with welts.

Then she finished readying for supper.

THIRTY

Success in warfare is gained by carefully accommodating ourselves to the enemy's purpose.

—Sun Tzu
The Art of War

"amn you, woman!" Grayson yelled as he parried, and she backed him into the corner. This was the most action he had seen from her this week.

"Don't you take me for granted, you jackass. Fight me!" Lulu yelled.

He twisted from the hole she pinned him in and advanced on her, but she pushed back, swinging the training sword over her head like some sort of wild thing.

"You want some of this?" she said breathlessly, and he knew her stamina was wearing thin and he would soon take the upper hand whether he wanted it or not.

He grunted and dived when the sword swept right through where his head had only just been. He came out of the somersault behind her, sweeping his sword at her feet and bringing her to the mat.

Lulu squealed and rolled, coming up to crouch before him, her sword high over her head, pointed in his general direction like the tail on a scorpion. Jesus, she was amazing.

They crouched there, facing each other, both breathing hard and calculating different offensive tactics while considering their defense against the opposite.

"I want to taste you," she said.

"Low blow, Lulu. No playing dirty," he replied.

"I want to take your cock in my mouth and suck you off until there's nothing left in your body but the air you breathe."

Grayson's jaw dropped at the shock of it. "Fuck's sake, Lulu, that's… that's perfectly lurid!"

She grinned. He dropped his sword. She laid hers aside. He launched at her and took her down to the mat, pinning her arms against her head.

"Now. Since I have the upper hand…"

"Do you?" she asked. Her leg came up, and she twisted, and before he knew what happened, the breath was knocked from him, and he lay on his belly, panting, as she sat across his back, screaming like a banshee.

"Lulu, the neighbors," he coughed out.

She stopped and leaned down to his ear. "Fuck the neighbors," she said, and he laughed. It was whole and full, and it felt so good coming from his chest. It felt like every time he laughed, more scar tissue broke up and evaporated with it.

He shifted to his back, keeping her straddled across his waist, and looked up to her. "We should be getting ready for the supper tonight."

She pushed away from him and stood. "Way to kill the mood, Gray."

"It wasn't my idea," he replied, shaking a finger at her.

It hadn't been her idea either. It had only been a threat on her part, but he'd turned it on her. Not very sportsmanlike, he admitted.

She reached out with a hand and yanked him off the floor. "I need a shower. It takes forever to get dressed properly, so I suppose you should go first," she said.

"Unless you wish to join me?" he said.

"Will it get me anywhere?" she countered stiffly.

"That's entirely up to you," he responded quietly.

"I miss being with you." She turned away, and he frowned because he knew she was still holding back.

He walked up behind her. "Soon enough," he whispered across her ear, then he went up to shower and dress for the evening.

It had been nearly a week since he'd started to refuse her because she was so adamant in refusing to open up to him in that way. Perhaps it was badly done of him, but he couldn't help it, he wanted all of her, and trying

to make love to a woman who imposed unwanted restrictions or held him at arm's length was uncomfortable for him, particularly when he was now completely open to her.

He went to his study and waited for their guests to arrive, and for the first time he could remember, he was looking forward to having his family, in his house.

The carriage pulled up to Warrick House, and Lulu steeled herself as she read the crest. It was Francine and Gideon. *Thank god*, they were first to arrive.

When she'd mentioned arranging a supper for his family, she hadn't exactly meant so soon. They'd scarcely spoken in the past week. He was avoiding her, and she knew it. He refused to give her anything until she let down her guard. He was frustrating the daylights out of her, so she'd threatened him with a supper party, and he'd called her bluff by sending out the invitations.

And here came the guests. Another carriage pulled up, and she tensed. It had the Warrick crest on the door. Gray's mother and sister.

Lulu turned from the window as the door to the parlor opened, and she rushed over to Francine. "I can't breathe. Oh my god, I don't think I can handle this."

Francine leaned back and looked at her. "It's only family," she said with a smile. "It will be much easier than you think."

"I know, I mean, I think I know. I'm just…so not proper."

Gideon laughed, and Lulu looked at him over Francine's shoulder.

He nodded and straightened. "My apologies, Your Grace, but might I introduce you to my wife? The Duchess of Improper?" he said.

Francine curtsied, and Lulu stood back and put her hands on her hips, ready to admonish him. But then she glanced between him and Francine and dropped her hands. "Point taken."

Roxleigh bowed slightly. "Is Gray in his study? I have something for him." He lifted a light, thin package and smiled at her.

"Yes, feel free to go harass him. I've no use for you," Lulu said.

Gideon bussed Francine's cheek, then kissed the back of her hand, then the bare inside of her wrist, before leaving the room. The action stole Lulu's breath. She looked up finally to see Francine staring after him. "Wow," Lulu said.

Francine turned. "I'll say," she replied with a sigh. She took Lulu's hand and pulled her to the settee. "So how are you? I haven't seen much of you."

"I've been busy, clearing the studio, training in the ballroom, you know, the usual duchess stuff," she said.

Francine laughed. "Oh, yeah, sure. Usual."

Lulu fidgeted. "He's still cockblocking me," she whispered.

Francine's hands flew to her mouth, then she laughed.

"With his own damned cock!" Lulu said. "It's just…so infuriating."

"I imagine it would be frustrating, but he has good reason for it, right? Doesn't he?"

"Oh, yeah, sure, good reasons. Doesn't mean I like it. I just don't know why…I just can't…"

"Hey, Lulu, come on, you've been here only a couple of weeks. Give yourself some time to get used to him, to your new self, the new world you're in."

"I'm trying, but…sometimes I just want to get laid, you know?"

Francine nodded and grinned.

"We fight a lot. Spar…you know, swords and such. It's good, but it's not the same thing."

"How is the studio coming?"

"Almost there. I can't wait to show you. You'll sit for me, right?"

"Of course I will. Oh, hey, I wanted to talk to you about something. I'm deciding what to write on the back of my portrait, the one my father found. I know the portrait survived, so I want to send a message to Madeleine, who, if I'm correct is now living in my body. I wondered if perhaps we should steer her to Cecilia?"

"That's a good question. It's difficult considering I'm not entirely fond of Cecilia. We'll have to really think about what to put on there, such limited space. It's fairly small, right?"

"Yes," Francine replied. "It's a miniature."

"Well, we have plenty of time to decide. We have to be sure to use the right kind of ink, or it will fade," Lulu said, and Francine nodded. "I think maybe we should get Madeleine and Cecelia together. I know I'm glad to have you to talk to. I don't know what I would do without that small connection."

"It wasn't so bad. I was used to being alone, and with Gideon, well, I suddenly wasn't alone…but I'm thankful for you."

The door opened, and they both stood quickly. Francine took Lulu's hand and gave it a squeeze. "You'll be fine," she whispered.

Lulu knew the family didn't know that she and Francine were from another time. They just knew they were…different, and they accepted them. But Lulu had the feeling, as unguarded as the family seemed to be within ranks, that they had some idea. She wouldn't be the one to break rank.

Lulu closed her eyes and took a deep breath, and when she opened them, Grayson's mother and sister walked in. They were both dark, like Gray, but his mothers hair was pulled tight in a knot and Poppy had a thick mane of curls that was barely contained, it shaded her face, but her bright green eyes caught the light. They were entirely familiar, those eyes. Francine reached for them. "Georgia, Poppy," she said. "I'm so glad you could join us." They hugged, and Francine pulled them both over to Lulu.

"I know you were probably all properly introduced at the wedding, but this is just family now so we'll start over. Lulu, this is Grayson's mom, Georgia, and his sister, Poppy."

Lulu reached out to take his mother's hand and was swiftly pulled into an embrace. "Thank you," the woman whispered. "Thank you for bringing my son home." She held her so tight Lulu couldn't get a full breath, and emotion clogged her throat.

"You're welcome," she said finally. Lulu thought she might cry. "I—I care very much for him."

The woman leaned back and looked at her. "So I hear." She glanced over Lulu's shoulder and smiled at Francine. Poppy cut in, wrapping Lulu up in a strong but quick hug.

"It's good to be here." Poppy grinned. "So, thank you. I've never really known Grayson, but thank you for inviting us."

"Please sit," Lulu said, pulling them toward the settees, but the door opened once again, and Lulu jumped.

Poppy squealed, "Lilly!"

She ran over and hugged her, and they came back in, arm in arm, as everyone said hello.

Before they were finished, five other women joined them. Calder's mother, Auberry, Duchess of St. Cyr, with her daughter, Izzy; and Fallon, Countess of Bradmore, and her daughters, Saoirse and Maebh.

It was a full house, but Lulu didn't have time to feel overwhelmed. Francine was a godsend, helping her keep up with hostessing activities while, in truth, nobody expected the formality.

Before long, it was time for supper, and the new butler Rakshan had just hired came in to retrieve them. The women all stood, walking out to the entry to meet the gentlemen, who'd been with Gray in his study.

The ladies took available proffered arms, and she and Gray led the group into the dining room. Gray was at the head of the table, and she sat to his right, instead of at the opposite end, because he'd insisted she do so. She was glad, now, that he had. The family crowded the table and took their places.

The lot of them insisted on first names, which was great, because if she heard another my lady or His or Her Grace, she was going to get dizzy. She was having enough trouble just keeping first names straight.

Lulu relaxed a bit as everyone chatted, all so familiar, so close to each other. It made her happy to see such a warm family, to see how easy they were with each other.

She turned to smile at Gray to find him watching, just as she was. He wasn't involved in the conversations, just like her, but for her, it was because she was new to the family. And that's when she realized they were both outsiders here.

She turned back to the rest of the table and slowly noticed how they would cut glances at Gray. They all looked at him as if he were an interloper they just weren't sure about. It struck her then how difficult it would have been to come back to a family that was so closely knit that there was little room to squeeze in. She wondered what his father had told the family when he left.

She wondered how much damage Gray had to reverse just by being exiled from this family.

Perry, Rox, and Calder, though, they treated him as an equal. They pulled him into conversation more than the others, but they didn't push him too far, and she was thankful for that. It was as though everyone knew there was something about him…but they didn't know what, and they weren't sure they wanted to.

She looked at Georgia and saw the tears then. She'd catch them above her smile before they fell, and they weren't overly noticeable. But they were there. She looked at her son with nothing but adoration, unlike his sister, who glanced at him as though he was a stranger, and Lulu supposed he was. She would have been quite young when Gray was sent away.

Lulu could see this was going to be a long road for this family, and she understood why he hadn't yet made any true overtures to reconciling with his people. She decided then that she would do what she could to support Gray with his family. She was thankful he'd called her bluff and invited his family to dinner.

When the women went to the parlor afterward, she invited Georgia and Poppy to return for lunch the next day, hopeful that she could bring Gray, his mother, and his sister closer together. She wanted to share his plans with them, that Gray had started to refurbish the guest suites of the house, not for guests, but for his family, for them.

He couldn't manage the thought of them being in the same wing as he and Lulu, but he did want them to return to what had once been their home, if they chose to. He had no cause, nor want, to keep them away anymore.

She thought about the people who'd been strangers to her at the wedding and how quickly they welcomed her into the fold. She could only hope that they would see Grayson was worth welcoming as well.

THIRTY-ONE

Rouse him and learn the principle of his activity or inactivity.
Force him to reveal himself so as to find out his vulnerable spots.

—Sun Tzu
The Art of War

Grayson watched the men in his study, drinking port and puffing cigars like old friends. He smiled to himself. He'd never thought he would have a moment like this.

He remembered seeing his father's friends retire to this very study after suppers, the men following this ancient ritual, gathering by the fire to discuss what men discussed.

He sat and let the moment wash over him, a moment that never would have happened if not for Lulu. If his wife had been Cecilia, the entire feel of tonight would have been different. It would have been formality to the rafters, not like this. Of course that was also dependent on whether she had carried out her father's wishes.

Cecilia would have made him a different man. She would have allowed him to remain aloof and hidden from his family and society. As long as they were above reproach on the outside, what happened in their home wouldn't have mattered, if they even made it that far.

Lulu was the exact opposite. She didn't care what the rest thought of her. Her only concern was him, how he was at home. All she wanted was for him to live, and to live well.

"Gray…"

He looked up, finally hearing his name. "Apologies, my mind was… somewhere else."

Bridger stood. "Let's be on, men. Gray is yet a newly married man, and we are encroaching on their private hours." He waved all the others from their seats. Grayson just smiled. He didn't mind them being here, but he was ready for them to leave. He also wanted them to return.

Grayson shook his hand when offered. Then Bridger pulled him closer. "I wasn't too keen when my sister married Warrick. I'm not sorry to say I'm happy to be rid of him, and to have my sister back to rights. That came with your return, even though you haven't seen it. Her world truly fell apart when you left."

"That wasn't by choice," Grayson said before he could stay the words.

"No…I realize, now, that it wasn't. Your family should have fought him—we—we should have fought him, but that man…"

Grayson shook his head. He didn't want to discuss his father. "Thank you," he said simply.

Bridger nodded, then pulled Grayson into a hug, hitting his back soundly. "Welcome home," he said.

Then he turned so nobody could see his face and walked from the study. Grayson just let him go. He had no words for the man who had been a good uncle to him as a child.

Rox, Perry, and Wilder nodded to Grayson and followed him, but Calder waited, then came closer to him once they were alone.

"You know we all now feel that way," he said.

"I am uncomfortable with the thought that you have all spoken of me outside my company," Grayson said.

"I'm aware, just as certainly as you're aware there's no stopping it. Everyone is talking about you, and your new bride. Her father in particular," Calder said.

"He hasn't left it?"

Calder shook his head. "Did you expect him to?"

"Once he had no willing audience."

"There's always a willing audience in the ton, and you have yet to disprove his accusations in public," Calder said.

"Make arrangements then. Speak with Lulu. I don't care what it is. I'll be there."

Calder nodded. "There's more."

"Is there?"

"Yes, I may need to return to India for a time."

"I haven't heard anything from—"

"You think the old bird would activate you now? So close to your wedding? She knows you're no longer someone who can easily hide. Everyone knows you, your bride, and your ugly face."

"Is that why?"

"From what I can see."

"Why are you returning to India?" Grayson asked.

"She needed someone to follow up on the leads we've procured."

"How did she—"

Calder cut him off with a glare. "Honestly, Gray, do you think anything gets past her?"

No. Nothing got past her. The fact that others often underestimated her was the reason she'd come so far, and she used it against them as often as she could.

"When do you leave?" Grayson asked him.

"Not sure. You'll know."

Grayson nodded.

"Another thing," Calder said. "Exeter may be pushing the wrong agenda, but if he continues to push, he may accidentally happen on the right one."

"What do we do?" Grayson asked.

"You do nothing. I'll handle him. I want you away from him. You now have too much to lose."

"Calder, I won't abandon you to take the fall for me."

"I'm not taking a fall. I'm doing what's right. If I need anything from you, I'll let you know. I won't cut you off from this entirely. I know your value." He winked.

Grayson laughed.

"I'll never get used to that sound." Calder said, "But I'm going to be happy to try."

"Fuck's sake. Get on then," Grayson said, pushing him to the door of his study.

Calder laughed heartily as they met the rest of the family, milling in the entryway as the carriages were pulled up. This house sounded good full of happy people, something he'd never heard.

Lulu walked up and wrapped one arm around his. "You have a wonderful family," she said.

"I know I do. Thank you for..." He didn't know what to say. "Thank you," he said faintly, "for saving me."

She looked up at him and was about to say something, but his mother and Poppy walked up. "We're off, Gray, but Lulu has graciously invited us to luncheon tomorrow, if you are amenable?" she said.

"Absolutely. I would love to have you both here. We have things to discuss," he said, and he was suddenly grateful that Lulu had come into his life and done everything she'd done.

His mother placed her hands on his shoulders, went up on her toes, and bussed his cheek, before turning and walking quickly from the house.

Poppy looked after her for a moment, then turned and threw herself at Grayson. He caught her as she wrapped her arms around his neck and kissed his cheek. "Thank you for making her happy again," she said. Then she turned, picked up her skirts, and ran from the house behind her mother.

His other cousins came and kissed Lulu's cheeks and shook his hand, exchanging small talk, making plans, and leaving the house until the echo of laughter faded and all that was left was an empty space he felt he wanted to fill.

"The quiet here is different now," he said to Lulu. "I don't think I like it anymore." Just like having Lulu underfoot, he now wanted the distraction of noise.

Lulu took his arm and pulled him toward the stairs. "Bedtime," she said.

Gray turned and swept her up into his arms, and she laughed. "Don't get any ideas. I'm exhausted, and so are you. I'm taking you to bed...to sleep."

"So be it," she replied as she played with his lapels, loosening his cravat and buttons to get a head start on him being naked and next to her. "What was in the package from Roxleigh?" she asked.

"Oh, merely a shirt. I'd left it behind at his house, and he returned it. Which reminds me there's something else needing returned and I—am not sure how to manage it."

"What's that?" Lulu asked.

"A corset," he said quietly.

"The pink one? I wondered about that."

He nodded then seemed to shake it off and Lulu left it alone. She leaned into Gray, smiling against his warm neck and absorbing his warmth as they ascended the steps and faded into the dark.

When they got to their room, they undressed silently and slipped beneath the clean white sheets of the bed. He wrapped his arms around her like a heavy vise, ratcheting her toward him and not letting go. "Thank you," he said. "Thank you for everything."

Lulu breathed slowly through the emotion, wondering why she couldn't let go of her fears and be closer to her husband. She wanted to let go for him, with him. She wanted to be free with him. He had taken everything she'd told him and accepted it, and even so wanted every bit of her.

But she still held back, and he didn't push. She couldn't understand how she had gotten so lucky. He believed she'd been brought to his life to save him, but Lulu didn't. Lulu believed something different. She believed she had been brought here so he could save her. She just had to allow him to do it.

She wanted to share her art with him, not just the domination aspect, but the photography. It was so much a part of her, and she needed him to understand that. She was almost finished with the renovations in the studio, and she thought, perhaps, once it was finished, she would be able to show him her world, all of it. Not pieces of it, but the whole of it.

THIRTY-TWO

Attack him where he is unprepared,
appear where you are not expected.

—Sun Tzu
The Art of War

Grayson had given Lulu much to consider, and he knew he needed to give her more time to consider it, but it was difficult. Of all things he had to do, waiting patiently for this was absolutely the most difficult thing he'd ever done where she was concerned, and nearly two weeks later, he felt like a madman.

He pulled the shirt Roxleigh brought him from the bottom drawer of his desk and unwrapped it, running his fingers over the soft linen of his wedding shirt, skimming his fingers softly over the crumple marks at the placket to keep from straightening and flattening them. Those crumple marks were the representation of the beginning. They were precious to him.

Grayson spent his days in here being available, but getting as much work done as possible. For when the time came that she needed something of him, anything of him, he would drop everything and run to her. His only distraction had been this shirt, and it only made him want for her even more. He tucked it away and tried to concentrate once again.

He hadn't seen her much except for meals, as she spent most of her days in her rooms on the third floor, or in the wine cellar they were modifying for a darkroom. She would train in the late afternoon before dinner, and sometimes he would join her. He'd show her some blade work, or he'd watch her train with her whips as he worked with his bō staff or training sword.

She was good, incredibly good. She'd asked Rakshan to bring her various fruits, and she used them as targets when training her strikes, perfecting the impact from a nearly gentle sweep to a sweet slice of flesh. Well…as gentle as a bullwhip could possibly be, at any rate.

At night they did very little speaking—and very little sleeping. He'd given in to her demands and that dirty mouth of hers after that second week. He just hadn't been able to take it anymore. So now he found himself napping in the afternoons on the settee in his study, his feet propped up on a side table since his legs were too long for the seat.

Not that he was terribly put out by her attempts to…get in his pants, as she put it. A man who survives the desert doesn't refuse water when offered, but he may take only sips. Otherwise, his stomach may turn on him.

What truly fascinated him about their current shared existence was how methodically normal it felt. They moved through their days from moment to moment, and Grayson did his best to savor each one.

As for all that normalcy, he couldn't wait to be done with it. He wanted the fire back in her. They were content and needed to be shaken up.

He wanted to see her true self, not the confused woman who'd come here and married him, not the one who'd thrown up defensive strategies by deflecting back at him, and not the frightened woman who was terrified of his judgment.

Grayson had a feeling the true woman he'd come to know as Lulu was a force to be reckoned with, and he *would* wait her out, because that's what he was good at. He'd laid all the traps and set about waiting for them to snap. Though *traps* wasn't perhaps the best word for it… He was giving her everything he could possibly give to make her feel this was her home and she had control of her new life, as it was. Because control was the issue.

He felt she was still much too afraid to open up to him, to trust that he'd meant what he said when he told her that he would allow her to do whatever she wished with his body. She was holding out for proof, but he wouldn't be able to give her that until she trained, and it seemed her training went on and on. He'd seen the fruit, he'd seen the patterns, the gentle strikes. He knew she could do this, and he already trusted her absolutely, so she was stalling him for other reasons. He intended to do something about that.

He had plenty of time to consider everything they talked about, specifically the sensory deprivation and how it could be used to help someone face their fears.

He also thought about how she always talked about his muchliness, whatever that meant, and how he overwhelmed her with it.

He thought that, possibly, the one could help with the other.

A scratch came at the door. "Come," he said as he stood from the settee and straightened his waistcoat. He looked up to find Lulu coming toward him with a brilliant smile on her face—a very welcome surprise.

"I have something to show you," she said.

He inspected her, top to toe. She looked freshly showered and perfectly dressed, prepared to keep him from her with all of her trappings. One of these days he hoped she would stop doing that and come to him filthy and dirty from cleaning and ready to be ruined. He felt like he wouldn't have to be so careful with her then.

Grayson took a deep breath to clear his mind and nodded, holding his hand out then motioning for her to lead the way. She took that hand in hers, and he followed her from the room. He watched her hips sway as she pulled him with her up the stairs, her hand tensing in his the farther up in the house they went.

When they got to the door that led to her studio, she stopped and turned, placing her hand on his chest, then looking down.

"I'm nervous…" She dropped her hand and twisted her fingers in front of her. "I want to thank you for everything you've done for me, particularly for giving me free rein to create this space. I would very much appreciate it if you would be my first subject. If you would sit…for a portrait?"

"I should dress—"

She shook her head and looked up to him, catching his gaze. "No, I want you as you are. These images, they aren't for your family's portrait gallery. They're solely for me." Her voice was quiet and nervous, something that seemed quite foreign to her, but she didn't look away from him.

They're solely for me…

Grayson flinched because it seemed one of the traps he'd set had just snapped—on him. Always a danger for the hunter to become the hunted… particularly when the prey was as cunning as she.

Her hand reached for his as the words echoed in his head—*solely for me*—then followed when she pulled him into her space. And it was her space, entirely. It looked nothing like what it had, or ever had, in his memories. The room was open and bright, the windows clean and unshuttered. Truthfully, it looked like nothing he'd ever seen. The design, the layout, it wasn't familiar at all.

She had giant swaths of fabric hung from the ceiling, staggered at varying depths in the room, and they were mounted on wires, with pulleys so they could be moved easily. The lighter-weight fabrics swayed with the breeze coming in through the windows, and a heavier fabric was pulled aside, allowing what was left of the afternoon's light to come in unimpeded— save the usual smog it fought outside the house.

She led him toward the windows, to a large moss-green velvet chaise longue, then she released his hand and turned to him. She said nothing, merely set to work undoing his cravat, unbuttoning his waistcoat, pushing his jacket to the floor at his feet.

For me...

He suddenly understood what she'd meant by that, but when he stood before her in his trousers and boots, she stopped, and he released the breath that had yet to escape his sudden panic.

She walked back past him, and he tracked her, turning his back to the chaise as she made adjustments to her camera. She dipped below the black cloth at the back of the camera, only her pale hand emerging to fiddle with dials and switches before she reappeared.

He stood there, one hand on his hip, fully unsure what exactly he should do next.

"Did I ever tell you about my camera?" she asked. He shook his head. "I purchased it from an estate sale in London. The name of the family was Danforth."

This camera? he thought, as he narrowed his eyes at her in confusion. She beamed back as her fingers squeezed a small metal plunger, and he heard the lightest snick come from the camera.

He looked behind himself, then back to her. "What was that?" he asked.

"That was it. That was your portrait. That's exactly what I wanted… that look on your face, your amazing stance, your beautiful structure. I can't wait to develop it. Would you like to help me?"

He almost didn't hear that last, because she spoke so softly. "I don't know anything about photography," he said.

"You don't have to. I can teach you," she said as she clicked and moved pieces of her camera, then pulled a large, thin box from the back of it and reached out for him.

He looked back at his clothes on the chaise, quite aware of his lack of dress.

"You don't need a shirt for the darkroom," she said. "Come."

And he did, because when she smiled at him like that, he was likely to do anything she wanted.

"Darkroom," he said. "Is that a proper name for a physical description?"

"Yes, not like a parlor, certainly, for how does one parl? A darkroom is merely that, a dark room."

"I hadn't considered that until you said it. However, parl could be the conjugation of the verb *parler*, the French for to speak. *Je parle, tu parles, il parle, nous parlons, vous parlez, ils parlent…*"

She stopped and turned back to look at him. "Good lord, you should speak French more often. Please." She seemed to consider his thoughts before continuing on as she spoke. "*Parler, je parle, nous parlons, of course!*"

"Do you speak French?" he asked.

"*Un petit peu; ménage à trois, le petit mort, soixante-neuf...etcetera.*" she said coyly without looking back at him.

He grinned to himself as he followed her. A dark room, he thought. He could work with this situation, and perhaps the tables would once again turn.

Lulu reached around Gray to push the door shut tight, pulling a dark cloth across the entry to bar any offending light. She turned and placed the negative holder with its precious first exposure on her new workbench as she waited for Gray to follow.

It didn't take long, considering it had been a small room to begin with, but with the added workbench and the equipment, he definitely crowded into her space. It was then she realized just how small it was, his big body looming over her as she shifted around him, moving and adjusting the workspace to make it more comfortable for the both of them.

It didn't help that he was only half-clothed, all that lovely skin of his on display for her, wanting to be touched. She couldn't wait to shut out the light and at least remove the visual impact of him on her senses. She felt her heart pace faster, and she hurried to put the last few crates away underneath the workbench.

"Come here," she said, and she knew it was much more breathless than it should have been. But he was here in her world, and it felt so much more intimate than anything she'd ever done with him to this point, because this was so very much more than mere proximity. This was opening up her mind and her soul to him. This was sharing something so much more than simple pleasure or pain with him.

She tightened her hands on the edge of her workbench when he came up behind her, and she knew he'd done it purposefully. She reached back and took his forearm in her grasp and pulled him next to her.

"Don't move from this spot, and don't touch anything without permission. This is a very delicate procedure. One wrong move, one shaft of light, and everything will be ruined," she said as she turned to look at him. "I'll have three trays with open chemicals in them, and the room will be full dark. So you must be careful."

"I am at your command," he responded simply.

She turned back to the table and checked her layout, then she laid the negative carrier on the bench first, with three large trays next to it and the wash sink at the end of the bench ready.

She pulled the first bottle down from the cupboard and filled the tray about an inch deep to give the glass room to sink in the developer, and when she did the same with the second tray and the stop bath, she felt his body tense next to her.

"What is that ungodly smell?" he asked.

"Glacial acetic acid, also known as stop," she answered. "Don't breathe too deeply over the tray. The acid stops the developer from developing, which is why we call it stop." Lulu let the stop sting her nose as she poured it, then put the container away and pulled down the bottle of fix.

"That one doesn't smell nearly as bad, but it's hard to smell anything over the…stop? Is that correct?"

"Yes, stop."

"Are you sure it's safe?" he asked.

"It's safe. We have ventilation just here." She pointed at the wall in front of them on the other side of her workbench where a shuttered opening led outside. "Rakshan has made a rather ingenious fan system that pulls the air outside. Put your hand up just here. You can feel the air moving." She lifted his hand in hers and felt his muscles relax a bit.

"Now," she said, "this is all going to happen in complete darkness. That's why you must be careful." She turned and looked up to him. "Are you ready?"

"Complete darkness? I thought you could allow a small amount of light."

"Not for film or negatives. They must be developed in total darkness."

He nodded, looking around the room as if to memorize his surroundings and get his bearings. He moved his hands over the surface of the workbench, measuring the space to the wall before them, the space in front of him, and over to the trays, visually measuring the distance to the door at his back.

"All right, I think I'm ready. How will you know how long it takes if we're in complete darkness?" he asked.

"Until I can think of something better, we have to listen to a clock ticking and count it off. I used to have a recording. The music was the exact time needed for each stage, about four minutes for developing, thirty seconds for stop, and at least two minutes for the fix. But I'll need to play with the timing until I get it perfected again." She turned toward him, and he moved infinitely closer to her, the heat of him radiating off his naked skin.

"How precise is this operation?" he asked.

"Very precise," she replied. "Timing is of utmost importance to re-creating results. No second goes unnoticed."

"Sounds like this requires a great deal of concentration," he said.

"Yes, concentration and timing."

"So you need a precise countdown. I can count down seconds with military precision," he said as he shifted until he had her hips pressed back against the edge of the workbench. He crowded her between his arms on the edges of the workbench, then brought one hand up to her arm and started ticking, his finger moving in a very precise arc away from her skin then back down as he started to count. "One…two…three…" His finger bounced three beats after the first strike, then paused a beat as it withdrew to strike again.

Her breath came faster as he pushed closer to her, his mouth coming down to whisper the numbers as he continued to pace the time for her. "Six…seven…eight… Is this sufficient?"

She coughed. "Good. Yes. Sufficient," she said. "That will be incredibly… helpful." She twisted away from him and steadied herself as he stopped counting and moved back by her side.

Perhaps bringing him in here hadn't been the best idea. She really wanted this image to come out, even as she knew the chances were slim with so many unknown factors—the glass plate itself, the chemistry, the exposure, the lens… But she wanted to see the exposure. There was nothing like that first image from a new camera or process. She was entirely too impatient to stop this now.

"Okay, shall we? I'm going to shut out the light, then take the raw negative from this case"—she tapped it—"the moment it comes out, there's

no turning back. I'll put it in the developer, and when I say, 'Go,' you start counting. Sound good?" she asked.

"Four minutes?"

She nodded.

"That's two hundred and forty seconds."

"Yes," she answered.

"Brilliant," he said.

She reached above her head as she watched him. His gaze settled into hers, his strong arms leaning on the workbench as he awaited her command. She nearly lost her breath just watching him as her hand hunted for the string attached to the overhead light, then paused when her fingers finally found it. She could stop this now. She could tell him to leave the room. She didn't. She tugged the string quickly, shutting it off and inhaling deeply.

She half-expected him to grab her about the waist and ravage her on the darkroom floor so she paused, because she didn't want to ruin the negative if that was his intent. Priorities. But he didn't and after a few breathless moments she knew he wouldn't, and she let out a deep breath. She needed to start moving before imaginary men started dancing across her blind field of vision.

She reached for the negative case and flipped the lock open, then slid the cover away. She could see nothing, not even the ghosts of anything. There was a complete void of light, but she sensed him move by the hairs on the back of her neck standing up like little dowsing sticks searching for him.

She must already be imagining things, as you do in full dark. The things under the bed, or in the closet…but even the darkest of bedrooms weren't devoid of light like this room was. She pulled the glass plate from the holder and reached for the first tray.

"Ready?" she asked.

"Absolutely," he replied and she squeaked. His voice came from just behind her shoulder, and she shuddered into it, knowing that she could not replace the plate in the holder without chancing damage from scratches. She took a deep breath and slipped the glass plate into the tray, submerging it fully as quickly as she could.

"Go," she said as she lifted one corner of the tray just off the surface of the workbench to send a wave of developer careening across the negative.

"One…" She felt his fingertip start its tattoo against the skin of her shoulder and his breath as he counted the beats at her ear.

"Two…" She shrugged her shoulder against his finger and concentrated on the tray, on a steady rocking of the liquid across the plate as he set about to unnerve her.

"Gray."

She felt him shake his head once, as if to admonish her for attempting to stop him, then she felt his tongue dart out and swirl against the shell of her ear, his numbers momentarily stunted but still audible.

"Thirty-two…thirty-three…" His finger on her shoulder moved closer and closer to her spine, and her hand slipped on the tray. She held on to the edge of the workbench to steady herself.

"This is important… Consider your work and nothing else," he said.

How was she supposed to concentrate with him doing what he was doing? At least he seemed to be keeping time well.

"Forty-seven…forty-eight…"

Which begged the question, how was he able to concentrate while doing what he was doing? She lifted the corner of the tray once more and continued the steady agitation across the surface of the negative.

"Fifty…fifty-one…fifty-two…fifty-three…"

She felt her skirts lifting, the thin ruffle of her single petticoat dragging up her calves as she tried and failed to scoot the other direction, but his hand and the tapping finger moved to her opposite arm, steadying her where she was.

"Gray," she said.

He shook his head again, his tongue darting out to lick, then kiss each small bump of the vertebra in her neck between numbers sending shivers up and down her spine. "Sixty-four"—kiss—"sixty-five"—kiss—"sixty-six"—kiss.

"Please, Gray—"

"*Soixante-neuf…*" he said in a heavy, threadbare voice, and a spark like electricity shot through her from the top of her head to the tips of her toes.

The tapping finger left her shoulder, and she could hear the slightest whisper as he tapped two of his fingers together… Then she felt it again,

right at the dimples of her backside, tapping her bared skin where the two halves of her drawers didn't quite meet in the middle.

"Can you trust me with your secrets in full dark? Can you open yourself to me?" he asked as his breath warmed her lower back.

She arched her back toward him, unable to help herself as he moved. "I don't…I can't…"

"Eighty-one…eighty-two…eighty-three…"

His count was steady and incessant, like nothing she'd ever heard in her life. Though had he been off at this point, she would hardly have even known.

"Ninety-one…" One hand slid down her backside, one finger gently pushing at the crease of her buttocks and she pulled at her shirt, trying to get some cooling air to her chest. "Ninety-seven…" His fingers skimmed the lines just below the globes of her buttocks, all the while tapping her skin. "One hundred four…" His thumbs came back to the center and she hoped they would sweep back out again, her skin ached for it. Instead, "One hundred nine…" He ground out the number as his thumbs spread her cheeks and his long pointing fingers kept tapping the count, and he pushed his hips against hers, her pelvic bone meeting the hard edge of the workbench in front of her as he pressed himself to her and she flung her hand out to catch herself on the wall at the other edge of the bench. Her heart raced his fingers and she was certain he was picking up speed, though she had no proof. She rubbed her mons against the edge of the bench through her skirts wishing for a modicum of relief from his pervasive tactics.

"One hundred and twelve…" His hands skimmed around to the front of her hips, pulling her back against him, and she was sure he clucked his tongue to admonish her as his fingers continued tapping the code into her skin.

"One hundred twenty…" His tongue coasted down her spine, then disappeared at the edge of her dress, and she felt his legs drag down the outsides of hers as his knees bent and hit the floor next to her feet. "One hundred fifty-six…" He licked one of the dimples on her backside and kissed the other as he passed by. Her belly clenched, sending a wave of fluid to her pussy and she widened her stance without even thinking about it. "One hundred fifty-nine…" He tilted her hips, opening her up to him. She felt the heat of his breath cooling her pussy as the wetness he'd called forth slid to her thighs.

"One hundred sixty-seven…one hundred sixty-eight…cent soixante-neuf…" She felt his smile spread across her backside against her skin, and the heat of his mouth against her vulva pushed her forward, her hands coming down to the surface of the workbench to steady herself.

"Oh god, Gray, please," she breathed. She listened to the sound of the water in the tray, concerned that it must be kept agitated—until he pushed against her, bumping her hips against the table and sending waves of developer across the glass negative.

"Gray!"

"You've no reason to fear me. One hundred eighty-three…"

Lulu shook at the want of him, her nipples sharp points of arousal against the inside of her corset as she silently begged him to take her with his fingers if his cock couldn't manage it. "Gray, Gray, please."

"Two hundred." She felt his thumbs slipping through her folds, his tongue playing. One long finger slipped inside her, and she fell forward on her elbows, her hips pushing back against him. She needed him in side her. She needed him to fill the emptiness, to scratch the itch only he could reach. She couldn't drag in a full breath against the corset and the edge of the bench and she did see stars as her whole body started to shake from holding off.

"One…two…three… Let me inside you, Lulu."

"Gray, I can't. I—"

"Ten…eleven…Lulu…"

He terrified her, in this moment, in her darkroom, no defenses and the want of him in every vein. He blew across her clitoris and she broke.

"Yes," she said breathlessly as his fingers continued to count. He pushed her legs wider with one hand, running up the inside of her leg, then her inner thigh past the drawers, then his fingers against her clitoris.

"Twenty-one…twenty-two…"

She felt the cool of his nose skim the round of her ass, then the crease where her thigh met her buttocks.

"Thirty… You have ten seconds to come for me," he said, then reached out with his tongue and swept it the length of her folds.

She screamed and came with only the barest introduction of his tongue to her clitoris.

He never lost a beat.

She had nearly lost her wits entirely, but the countdown was twofold, the incessant counting driving her body in ways she'd never expected, but it also kept part of her grounded. The part of her that insisted she get this negative developed properly. The extreme disconnect of the two processes elevated her fervency immeasurably.

A mere two seconds past time, she knew, because—

"One…two…" his voice warned, and she pulled the negative from the soup and slipped it into the stop, disturbing the surface tension and sending notes of the acid burning through the dark.

"How precise is this next bit?" Gray asked, his fingers tapping her legs where he held her.

"Thirty seconds…give or take…not nearly as precise." She was breathless.

He stopped tapping.

THIRTY-THREE

Let your plans be dark and impenetrable as night and when you move…
fall like a thunderbolt.

—Sun Tzu
The Art of War

e felt her straighten as she shifted and transferred the precious negative to the next bath. He remained kneeling behind her, resting his cheek against the back of her exposed thigh, his hands skimming up and down the lengths of her calves.

He wondered how far into herself she would recede once the lights came on, and how much damage control he could manage before they did. He had just over two minutes to do whatever it was he needed to do.

He heard the water dripping as she held the glass above the tray, then the slosh as it slid into the next. He now had a mere two minutes. He stood and turned her, his hands on her hips now, his legs still bracketing hers.

The smell of the chemicals poisoned his nose and kept him from enjoying the proximity of her in that way. It frustrated him, because he knew she would smell heavily sweet, as she always did after she came off for him, an intoxicating bouquet of woman.

He leaned closer and tucked his nose into her neck, breathing of her as close as he was able. She mewled a complaint, and her arm twitched, so he reached out, finding the third tray and lifting one corner to send the waves across the glass. Her hand came to the back of his head, fisted in his hair, and pulled his head back.

He waited patiently, trying to breathe lightly to avoid the smell of the chemicals. He opened his mouth to breathe easier, and her tongue slipped in, skimming the roof of his mouth, the backs of his teeth, his lower lip. He pulled against her hold, but she didn't let him move. If the kiss was to be deepened, she would be doing it.

"Again?" he whispered against her.

"My turn," she replied.

"Not yet," he said and shook off her grip.

His arms went around her, and he picked her up, placing her on the workbench at the left end, pushing aside the empty negative holder.

"Please," she begged.

"Just let me..." he said as he pressed her shoulders toward the wall behind her. He wrapped one hand around her throat, his fingers on her pulse as he nuzzled her cleavage, pressing sweet kisses to her chest.

"Grayson." She begged with his name. "Grayson."

He felt a tear spill over his hand, hot and wet, and he lifted up and kissed her. "I love you, Lulu."

"If you're to say that, please, Grayson, call me by my name." Her voice was so low he almost didn't hear her, but he straightened as his brain deciphered the words.

"Your name? I thought... Tell me," he said, running his thumb across her chin.

"My name...my name is Talulah Loraine," she said.

He knew she was searching the dark for him, because he could feel her gaze looking for him. He could feel all of her concentration on him, as his was on her, boring through the darkness.

He stepped away for one second, tipped the third tray with one finger to slosh the fix, then stepped back. He judged her proximity by the warmth of her breath and the heat of her body, and without second-guessing, he reached into the abyss and took her face, pulling her toward him. "Talulah, Talulah Loraine, I love you," he said. "You, Talulah. I love you." And he kissed her.

Her hands came up and wrapped around his wrists, and he buried his fingers in her hair, holding her to him. "Talulah."

It had never occurred to him that Lulu was merely a nickname. She'd given it to him, and he'd accepted it. He only just realized that he'd taken

her at face value from the start after all, and after all she'd done for him, he'd never questioned it.

He'd harangued her about who she was, and he hadn't even known her name. He hadn't even considered it. He needed to pay more attention. He would pay more attention.

"Talulah. You are brilliant and amazing. Let me know you. I want to know you, and I promise to do better. I should have done better."

"Just remember I'm not a war to be won," she said.

He pulled back, again searching the dark that hung between them like a thick blanket.

"Oh god, Tallulah, no, I—" He stopped to consider, but it took only a moment for him to concede even to himself. He was an idiot. "I'm sorry. It's all I know. I'm—" He felt her nod, then he skimmed his hands over her face as if to feel her, to determine her emotions. She closed her eyes and allowed his perusal.

He skimmed her eyebrows and down her cheeks, cradling her face as if it were the most delicate rose on the verge of losing its petals. Then there were no more words.

He didn't want to release her again, so he bumped his hips against the workbench, sending the trays and their contents to sway as he softly worked his way down her body, and she opened to him. Her hard exterior fell away until there was nothing before him but the softness of her body under his hands, the sound of her name on his lips, and taste of her flesh on his tongue.

Gray had broken her heart and held the pieces so very delicately in his hands, but her heart was in better care now, with him, than it ever had been in her own chest. She was so easily swayed, so easily lost, but now…she had no choice. Everything was up to him. She was his, and she gave herself up and relaxed into him.

He had worn her down using his precious war tactics, and they did work. She was worn down. More than that, though, much more than that, she was filled and fulfilled. Something she'd never felt. He hadn't berated her into submission. He'd given her everything, including time, in abundance. Something nobody had ever given her.

Space.

Not just physical space, not just the room upstairs and the cellar down here. It was another kind of space. One that came from inside, one that allowed her to process and to think.

He moved down her body, and she allowed it. She opened for him. She shifted beneath him. She helped him progress instead of hindering him. He took her into his mouth, tasting of her, drinking of her, savoring her. He would know her now as no one ever had. He knew her name. He knew her passion. He would now know her flavor. What more was there to know of a woman?

She leaned against the wall behind her, holding on to one of his hands with both of hers.

He pushed her skirts away, then held them up with the arm she clasped to her breast.

His hands were delicate on her skin, his breathing heavy.

"Tallulah, you are lovely…so very lovely."

"You can't see me," she said.

"No, but I can feel you. I can breathe of you, and…" He licked her folds, dipped his tongue into her, then leaned away just slightly so that his words sent tremors through her wet skin. "I can taste you…and you are lovely," he said.

Her heart raced in her chest, and she tangled her fingers with his as he played, and she felt, and he breathed, and she shuddered.

EPILOGUE

The general must be possessed of wisdom, honesty, benevolence, courage, and discipline.

—Sun Tzu
The Art of War

Gray watched as Lulu tinkered with the bellows extension. She was trying to modify the enlarger he'd purchased for her, so she could use it to make larger negatives for giant cyanotype contact prints.

At least...that's what she'd said, and that's what he believed she would accomplish, even though he had no idea what it all actually meant. Bigger pictures, she'd said when he asked for clarification. He couldn't argue with that. He couldn't really argue with anything she told him, wanted from him, asked of him.

A few months had passed and they'd settled into a life that was, by no means, contented. By day they were two people, doing the separate things that people did. She with her photography, he with the business of his title. But at night, when they went to their rooms, they were no longer two independent people. They were two halves of one whole.

He'd even taken some pleasure, albeit superficial, in ordering her around during the day. He liked to see how his command affected her, how her gaze flared and her legs shifted and tightened beneath her skirts. He also liked her style of revenge for how he teased her. And for this he was merciless in his teasing.

He turned back to the desk to take his mind from the night and sorted out the correspondence he'd received for the week, hoping to find something from Calder or Rakshan, but knowing it was too soon. Even if they could send something, which they couldn't, Calder had been gone for only a sennight, which meant he hadn't sent anything from Marseilles, and Gray wouldn't hear anything from him until Alexandria.

He missed his cousin a great deal, but he missed his friend more. Rakshan had been at his side through the worst, and though he wasn't needed in the same way any longer, it didn't make the separation any easier. Rakshan and Gray were free to merely be friends, and Gray wanted that friendship and very much looked forward to it when Rakshan returned.

Rakshan had plans to buy his own home as soon as he was back, and live there with his sister, Hemakshi, who was currently residing in the guest suite at Warrick House as well as cooking up a storm to combat whatever frustration was working on her.

To be honest, however, Gray was also extremely jealous of their travel. He still loved India because it was his first true home. He'd liked the adventures he had there as well, regardless of the safety or purpose. Now they were someone else's adventures, and he was…on to something completely different…and yet, it seemed no less adventurous.

He looked up from his correspondence again to see Lulu concentrating, her tongue sweeping across her lower lip as she did so. He would survive this bit of jealousy. He could no longer do that sort of work for the queen, but he worried for Calder nonetheless. He worried less since Rakshan was with him. As for Rakshan, he wasn't concerned for his safety in India—he was the safest of all men there because he was naught but a ghost.

Grayson stood and walked over to the workbench that had been brought into the study so he and Lulu could spend their days together, one of the best decisions he'd made, because she was constantly underfoot, exactly where he'd always wanted her.

"Do you—"

She shushed him, trying to concentrate.

Gray grinned and pulled the bell, then walked to the main entry where the new butler, Gavin, met him halfway. "Has supper been prepared?" Gray asked.

"Your Grace, it has. Hemakshi has finished everything as requested, and it will be ready for you in the kitchens, as will tomorrow's breakfast and luncheon. The staff will be leaving within the hour and will return tomorrow evening, no earlier than six o'clock.

"Your man Bourke will remain to ensure security. He has taken up in the park across the street."

Grayson smiled at the thought of his man wandering the park all night keeping watch over his house. He wished there wasn't a need for security, but with all the unknowns still surrounding Exeter and his ilk, there most certainly was cause. Particularly with the letters Calder had found before he left.

Grayson would not, however, give up his privacy. Not tonight of all nights.

"Good. Thank you. Give my thanks to Hemakshi and the others." Grayson shook his hand, then felt the awareness of Lulu in the prickle of his skin on the ridge of his shoulders. He smiled to himself and let her approach.

"Is the house ours?"

"Soon," he said without turning. He knew it was already beginning… the dance of give and take, domination and submission, pain and pleasure. He knew the next twenty-four hours would be added to some of the most powerful moments of his life.

"I want you to take a hot shower."

"I want you to join me," he replied.

"I will."

He turned and picked her up, carrying her up to their room. He did this at least once a day, carried her up these stairs. There was no reason for it beyond his need to hold her close, to carry her and all that she carried with her. Her fears and wishes, her needs and wants. He liked to feel as though everything that was a piece of her, he carried in his arms. Supporting her.

They entered their bedroom, and he placed her on her feet, then dropped his hands to his sides. She took one of his hands and kissed it, then pulled the ring from her finger and handed it to him. She couldn't wear the ring while wielding the bullwhips because it unbalanced her grip.

He took the ring and placed it in the tray next to their bed, then turned again as she walked to him. She pushed his jacket off, then his waistcoat. She took them and hung them on his cherrywood jacket butler. Grayson wrapped his hand around one of the posts at the end of his bed, and she knelt at his feet, pulling his shoes and socks off.

She ran her hands up his legs as she stood, then unbuttoned his trousers—pants—and he smiled, and she pushed them down, leaving his drawers.

"Would you like another memento?" she asked quietly as she removed his cuff links and cravat, unbuttoning the neck of his shirt.

"Always," he replied. He had an entire drawer of shirts and other accessories she'd ruined by fisting and tearing or tying the fabric in knots. Her hands fisted in the placket of this shirt and tore it down the front, letting it slide from his shoulders before she folded it neatly and placed it on the settee by the fire.

When she came back to him, all that was left on his body were his long drawers. She ran a finger up his chest, then tipped his head back, tucking her face into his neck.

"I miss your corset," she whispered against the softer underside of his chin.

"I do, too," he replied honestly. But he knew why he couldn't wear it. He needed to be in perfect form for what came next. His muscles needed to be heavy with blood, and his ribs needed to be unconstricted and protective.

He swallowed, and the action brought his neck in contact with her wet mouth. So he swallowed again on a groan, then again on a breath. He knew he was shaking. He could feel the tension running his muscles as he attempted to steady them. She took the small bit of skin over his Adam's apple between her teeth and gave it a gentle pinch.

"Undress me," she said.

"With pleasure, Duchess," he replied. His hands came up and began to unbutton, unlace, and undress his wife. His wife. Only a few months ago, they'd done something he'd had absolutely no interest in, and now he couldn't fathom living without her.

When Lulu was naked, her clothing strewn across the chairs, she took his hand and pulled him toward the shower. When she tied her hair up in a knot on top of her head, he reached for his drawers to remove them. "Stop," she said. "Leave them on."

He straightened, not entirely sure what she had in mind, and waited patiently as she walked back into their bedroom, then returned with her camera, already set on the tripod.

"We have to move quickly, because the light is fading and the steam will begin to rise too heavily, and it will affect the images. I want you in the cage. Look up at me," she said.

Gray walked into the shower with his drawers on, immediately soaking them. The fabric plastered itself to the lines of his thigh muscles, the waistband sliding against his hips. He turned, looked at her, and heard the shutter, then saw the blur of her arms as she switched out the negative carrier.

"Grab the two ribs by your shoulders," she said.

He did, and he leaned forward and looked at her as though there were nothing between her and his soul.

"Jesus," she whispered as the shutter clicked. He let the water course down his form, the ropes of water adding dimension and shine to his body as he looked down and awaited further instruction while she switched another plate. He heard the heavy slide of metal on wood, the click as it seated in the back of the camera, then she spoke.

"Turn around. Same thing. Hurry," she said.

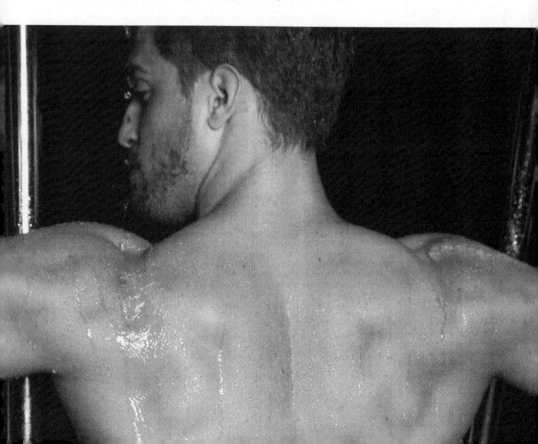

He did as instructed, relaxing then flexing the muscles across his back. He dipped his chin to the side, opening his mouth to take in air around the streams of water cascading from the top of the cage as he looked at her over his shoulder.

"Oh, my fucking hell, Gray. You'll be the death of me." He heard her murmur as she moved and shifted the camera. "Arms down, face up into the water," she said then.

He did. He heard the quiet snick of the shutter one more time, and when he opened his eyes again, he could see nothing but steam.

Gray had looked forward to this night since the day she picked up the bullwhips in his ballroom. He thought about the first crack of those whips, how it tensed his muscles and sent blood to his cock. They'd used many different kinds of pain since then, his favorite being the pain she bestowed directly with her hands. He also liked the floggers and canes, because they were altogether different experiences, and he savored her care of those injuries in the days that followed while he healed, and her touch would bring him to rise so easily.

That was one of the most powerful gifts of this pain, that it gave him some control over his arousal, allowing a more simple and easy way to take his wife whenever he felt the need, which was often and intensely. He'd taken her in every way a man could take a woman once she finished giving him pain. Using his mouth, his hands, his cock—and his pain during the recovery was so close to the surface, so fresh and new. It made him think he knew what it would be like to be normal. In some fashion anyway.

He heard her shuffling around in the rooms beyond the shower and closed his eyes, letting the water run his skin and loosen his muscles as she wanted. A moment later her hands came around his sides, her arms wrapping around him securely as he tangled his fingers with hers.

"I love you," he said, letting the steam carry the words, buffer them, hold them aloft between them.

Lulu shuddered as the words came to her, his breath clearing a path in the steam between them. Lulu had lost her people, her world, her photography, her talent, even her body, and Grayson had helped to systematically replace it all. Now the final piece was shifting into place as he allowed her to do something she'd thought she'd never do again. She had resigned herself to the loss of it, grieved for it, felt the loss like a tangible thing, and then let it go, and now she felt so full her heart would burst. Good thing her heart was in his safe keeping.

The images they'd just made would be absolutely beautiful. Instead of taking the negatives straight to the darkroom, like she would have wanted to in the past, with other men, Lulu had no trouble returning to the mostly naked man in the shower now. When she did return, she melted into him and knew the glass plates could wait.

It was the first time she'd ever felt this peace and quiet after exposing plates. The excitement and heady rush of seeing the exposed silver was far outweighed by the need to be in this moment, right now, with him, and she realized that in this with him, she didn't need the remembrance of something so fleeting, because what they had together…it wasn't fleeting, it was forever.

"I love you," she whispered against his back. He released one of her hands and turned in the shower, wrapping her up in him.

"Are you ready for this?" he asked quietly.

"Physically? Yes, absolutely."

"Are you nervous?" he asked.

"Yes, absolutely. Perhaps we should wait," she said.

He shook his head. "Lulu, we've been training for months. You've flayed those melons with a singularly perfect technique for weeks now. You're ready," he said, "and I trust you."

"Tell me your safe word?" she asked, just as she did at the beginning of any scene with him.

"I've decided to change it," he answered as he twirled a loose lock of her hair around his finger.

"Why—" Her breath caught before she could finish the sentence. She steeled herself. They'd talked a lot about safe words, about every aspect of domination and submission, about pain. He was a sponge, learning everything he could about this life. "Tell me," she said finally.

"Talulah," he replied.

She shook her head, not understanding at first, then his strong hands framed her face, and he bent to kiss her, the water washing down both of them, taking the past and everything that kept them apart away with it. And she just knew.

"You are my safe place, Talulah Loraine. You will always be my safe word." He sealed his words in a kiss without breath, the only oxygen they had what they shared between them.

She smiled against him. and he broke the kiss.

"Tell me again. What is your safe word?"

"Talulah," he said, and she felt his hands roaming over her body, massaging her muscles, and she sighed into him.

"I'm ready," she said then, and she looked up to him.

His fingers coasted over her cheeks, then wrapped around her head, his thumbs tipping her face to him before he explored her mouth yet again, softly, sweetly. She couldn't believe this was actually happening.

She'd been topping Gray for months now, and it had been the most incredible time of her life. They'd become so close she could read his mind even while he slept. His hands moving across her skin, as if to make sure she was still there. His body wrapping around her, telling her he feared losing her. His hands grabbing and possessive when he wanted for something more.

Some of her favorite moments were those where she used only her hands on his body, because of the intimacy of it, hand to flesh, so direct, so personal and emotional. But the sex they had when she practiced or used implements on him? She knew he loved that as well, because whenever he watched her practice with her bullwhips, his eyes flared so hotly he made her wet, and the sex they had after her practice sessions was the most passionate they ever had. Dirty, sweaty, hard, wet sex.

"It's time," she said on a breath, and he immediately dropped his hands and his gaze, stepping back from her. "Shut it off and turn around."

He did as she bade him, then her hands came up to his back, holding his sides tight for a moment before they slipped against his skin at the edge of his wet drawers and came together at the middle of his back. She dug her knuckles sharply into the flesh between his spine and those gorgeous dimples as she fisted the waist of his drawers, then split them down the back, letting the legs fall to the floor around his ankles. He kicked them away.

Lulu took his wrists and put them on the metal ribs above his head. "Hold on." She stepped out of the shower and went to the bedroom. She slipped on a pair of drawers and a corset before returning. She took a towel and pressed the soft, heavy weight to his back, sweeping the wetness from his body.

He really was beautiful, this man. She'd once thought Ollie was her masterpiece, but she'd been mistaken. This man before her, this man with his perfect submission and his absolute dedication and his passionate will, this man would be her masterpiece.

Every time she'd photographed him, every image they made together, he'd allowed her to see just a bit more of his soul. This, tonight, this was the culmination of months of practice on her part, and training and trust on his.

She tossed the towel out, then reached up and took his hand, turning him gently and bidding him follow her. When they reached the bedroom, she stopped and turned to him.

"Kiss me," she said, and he did. Like a man possessed, he took her mouth and her body and her soul in a searing kiss that reached beyond who she used to be, surpassed who she had become, and reached for who she was to be.

"You would wear this corset," he said against her.

"I thought it only fitting, I think of that day as our true beginning," she said. "and it's pink."

"I suppose you'll be keeping it now?"

"I never intended to return it. Francine can do with a little mystery. The minute you tightened the laces of this corset on your body, it became mine."

His hand pressed into her shoulder blade, grabbing the edge of the corset, as his other hand slid through the opening of the drawers and grabbed her hip. He held her to him like no one ever had before, and she allowed it, because it was everything she'd ever wanted. She wanted his marks on her tomorrow, just as hers would be on him.

When he softened upon her, began to withdraw, she leaned her forehead against his neck, kissed his chest, and just breathed of him.

She felt his heart beating steady and slow, and she knew it was time. "On your knees at the bed."

He released her and walked to the end of their bed, falling to his knees on the silk pillows she'd laid down for him. Then he reached high above his head, grasped the bedposts and flexed hard, his muscles vibrating, the solid wood posts flexing toward his body. Then he relaxed his muscles methodically, from his shoulders to his waist, like heavy ripples in a pond.

She took each wrist and secured it with leather to a post to help steady him, then placed another, wider leather thong between his teeth to protect him from the shock of the first strikes. She stepped back and picked up her whips. Lulu glanced over his head at the image of Gray above the headboard. The first one they'd made together in the darkroom, and she smiled. Lulu dropped her gaze to the broad expanse of his beautiful back, she lifted the bullwhips high above her head and began to make them dance.

from the author:

Grayson Locke Danforth, the Duke of Warrick, is a trained military strategist, to put it…mildly. He would have studied those who came before him, Sun Tzu in particular. Sun Tzu, a Chinese general who was a master strategist and philosopher, is believed to have originally written The Art of War. I studied several different translations of The Art of War and reference the translated text throughout this book with quotes at chapter headers.

While Warrick would most likely have studied the original French translation by French Jesuit Jean Joseph Maire Amiot in 1772, that translation wouldn't have lent itself to use here, as I have no intention of translating it from French for you.

The first known English translation was done by Everard Ferguson Calthrop, a British officer, in 1905, but it's incomplete. The first complete English translation I could find any reference to was the Giles translation of 1910.

This book takes place in 1885…so you see my dilemma.

Since Sun Tzu is believed to have lived somewhere in the neighborhood of 544 to 496 BC, it is logical to believe Warrick would have found and used the text in one of its various forms and translations. I decided on the French, because it was complete long before he was born, and was well known.

I will say my favorite of the translations is the most recent, done by James Trapp, even though I didn't use his in the final manuscript simply because it's so recent and I wanted to use something that was as timely as possible, as well as in English.

However, I purchased the hard-bound edition of James Trapp's translation from Powell's in Portland, Oregon. If you would like a copy of the text, get that one. It's a lovely book, with a traditional Chinese book binding and beautiful printing.

Sun Tzu
The Art of War
Translation used completed by:
Lionel Giles, 1910

Find me:

If you loved this book you can also join my newsletter to be notified of releases before they come out, and to participate in fun giveaways.

Come find me and join the conversation!

Twitter: @JennLeBlanc
Instagram: @JennLeBlanc
Facebook: Facebook.com/IllustratedRomance
Email: JennLeBlanc.com/contact

Made in the USA
Charleston, SC
15 September 2016